point
of
dreams

Also by Melissa Scott and Lisa A. Barnett

The Armor of Light
Point of Hopes

point
of
dreams

Melissa Scott
and
Lisa A. Barnett

TOR®

A Tom Doherty Associates Book / New York

POINT OF DREAMS

Copyright © 2001 by Melissa Scott and Lisa A. Barnett

Edited by David G. Hartwell

A Tor Book
Published by Tom Doherty Associates, LLC
175 Fifth Avenue
New York, NY 10010

www.tor.com

Tor® is a registered trademark of Tom Doherty Associates, LLC.

Library of Congress Cataloging-in-Publication Data

Scott, Melissa.
    Point of dreams / Melissa Scott and Lisa A. Barnett.—1st ed.
        p.   cm.
    "A Tom Doherty Associates book."
    ISBN 0-312-86782-4 (alk. paper)
    1. Theater—Fiction. I. Barnett, Lisa A. II. Title.

    PS3569.C672 P6 2001
    813'.54—dc21
                                                            00-048805

First Edition: February 2001

Printed in the United States of America

0 9 8 7 6 5 4 3 2 1

Acknowledgment

Thanks to Frank Mohler of Appalachian State University, whose presentation on the development of scenic spectacle at the 1999 Southeastern Theatre Conference in Greensboro, North Carolina, gave us entirely too many ideas.

point
of
dreams

1

hilip Eslingen settled himself more comfortably on the padded stool, watching as the woman seated opposite made the final adjustments to her orrery. It was a standing orrery, tiny bronze planets moving on bronze orbits against a silver washed zodiac, and in spite of himself he shivered at the memory of another similar machine. But that one had been gold, the peculiarly vivid gold of aurichalcum, not solid, reputable bronze, and in any case, it was long gone, consumed by the power it had contained. This was just another astrologer's tool, though no one would be foolish enough to call Sibilla Meening just another astrologer. She had a name in Point of Dreams, was revered by those actors rich enough to consult her, and feared by the ones who were poor enough to believe that she advised sharers on casting. Caiazzo's household knew of her, too, and spoke well of her, even Denizard, which was what had finally induced him to part with five seillings—half a week's wages—when he was about to lose his place and should be saving every demming. At second glance, he was less sure he'd been wise—the consulting room was a little too lavish, too much like a stage set of an astrologer's room, lined with books and leather cylinders that could only hold scrolls, preferably rotting and mysterious, and Meening herself was portentous in the most formal of university robes, the enormous sleeves held back with gold pins in the shape of a scallop shell, a pearl poised carefully in each fan. Not the symbol Eslingen would have expected—the Starsmith was the usual patron of astrologers, not Oriane—but probably reassuring for the players and musicians and occasional slumming nobles who were her patrons.

"So, Lieutenant Eslingen," Meening said, and Eslingen jerked himself back to the present.

"Magist." He had no idea if she was actually a magist as well as an astrologer, but from the look of the room, it would do him no harm to assume the higher rank.

Meening smiled, and shook her head. "I'm only an astrologer, Lieutenant."

"'Only'?" Eslingen repeated. "I've never heard that word applied to you, madame."

Meening blinked once, and then, unexpectedly, grinned. "Gavi warned me about you."

Eslingen blinked in his turn, and allowed himself a rueful smile. "Of course you know Gavi."

"And, forgive me," Meening said, "but there's not an astrologer in the city who doesn't remember the names of the men who rescued the children not six months past. There's no need to flatter me like some stumbling bit player who wants a lower fee."

"My apologies."

Meening nodded. "Now, are you familiar with astrological terms?"

"I read the broadsheets," Eslingen said. Beneath the paint and the elaborate gown, he saw, too late, that she was sharply amused. "I've even read some of yours."

Deliberately, he added nothing more, and Meening dipped her head, acknowledging the hit. "Then you're aware of the current circumstances."

"It's ghost-tide," Eslingen said, and suppressed a shudder that he was sure she recognized. No soldier liked to think of his ghosts coming back to haunt him, no matter how benign.

"That certainly. The sun is in the Mother, and the moon is in opposition. That is the ghost-tide." She paused. "Anything more?"

Eslingen spread his hands. "Madame, I've come to you for guidance."

"And you say you read my broadsheets." The mockery was back in her voice, but only briefly. "Very well. In general, then, and then particulars." She reached out, tapped the orrery gently, making the planets shiver in their courses. "In general, Lieutenant, there are only two planets in a day house, the moon and Seidos, both in the Maiden—the planet of the private person and the planet of tradition both in the house of finance, liberty, and the individual household. That's good so far as it goes, but all the other planets are in the night houses, the interior world, impulse and intuition, largely unbridled, and their aspects drown this good influence. The sun is largely unaspected, and the aspects that do exist, a triple conjunction and a powerful opposition, tend to cancel each other out. The individual is without direction, particularly in regard to public, everyday affairs. And there is a four way conjunction"—she reached across the narrow table to turn the orrery on its carved stone base, so that the tangle of planets was obvious—"here, with the Winter-Sun, Tyrseis, Sofia, and Oriane, that overbalances everything. That places the Winter-Sun, planet of transitions and changes, together with the heedless fortune and fertility of Oriane, Tyrseis the trickster, and a retrograde Sofia—justice unblinded, seeing all too clearly—in the Sea-bull, one of its exaltations, the sign of fertile chaos: this is an overwhelming desire to take chances, to gamble, to find a cause to back, a passion to pursue to the point of obsession. It's also in sextile with Heira— the planet of contracts in the house of secrets and hidden treasures— which just encourages this folly. More, it's in quincunx with Metenere, which suggests that these gambles and passions will be fruitless, but that's the only negative aspect to the Winter-Sun. It's not usually this unaspected."

She paused, considering, then turned the orrery again. "This also. The Homestar is in the Dolphin, the house of divine discontent, and it squares Oriane, which is in its exaltation. Again, the individual is without direction. Areton squares the moon: action will be difficult. In general, Lieutenant, Astreiant is primed for folly."

"What sort of folly?" Eslingen asked.

"Ah." Meening gave her thin smile again. "I thought you wanted a personal reading."

"I should think it would have some bearing on my personal follies," Eslingen answered, and Meening laughed.

"True enough. Have you seen *The Drowned Island*?"

Eslingen blinked, thinking for a second that it was a change of subject—that play had held the interest of almost everyone in Astreiant, from apprentice to merchants resident to the nobles in the Western Reach for almost two months now, unprecedented time, and he had not been able to understand the cause—then tipped his head to one side, considering. "You're a critic, madame."

"I've lived in Point of Dreams all my life, Lieutenant. The stars would have to be in a unique configuration before that piece of tripe could catch the imagination of the city. No offense to Gavi, of course."

"Of course," Eslingen echoed. Gavi Jhirassi played the lead, and was making a tidy profit from it, by all accounts. *I'll have to tell Nico*, he thought. Maybe it would make him feel better about the play.

"And that's only the beginning," Meening said. "I'll tell you that for free. There's a folly coming that will make *The Drowned Island* and its followers look like the wisest of women."

I've read that broadsheet, Eslingen thought, suddenly. He'd bought it only a few days ago, and, yes, it had borne Meening's name, though he'd been told often enough that mere names meant nothing to the printers, that it was common practice to attach a more popular name to an unknown work. The writer—Meening in truth, it seemed—had predicted foolishness to end all foolishness, and warned the wise to lock up their purses and their hearts until the storm had passed. In retrospect, it didn't seem to be a good omen.

"And now the personal," Meening said. She reached for a flat orrery, already set to mimic the stars of Eslingen's birth. "It's a pity you don't know your time more closely."

"Yes." Eslingen felt the stab of a familiar pain. His mother had had too many children by the time she'd borne him, and been too poor to pay a real midwife; she'd given birth with the help of a neighbor and her own oldest daughter, and no one had thought to check the nearest clock until the baby had been cleaned and swaddled.

Meening went on as though it hardly mattered. "Still, there's enough for me to work with. In short, Lieutenant, you think you've been through some changes lately, personal and professional, but the greatest of them is yet to come. Your world is about to be turned sideways, and with Seidos still in the Maiden, you'll be without your usual armor until it returns to the Horse. You're not immune to the urge to gamble, but you'll have less to lose than usual, so you would be well advised to be very wary."

Eslingen drew a shaken breath—there were very few astrologers who'd give so blunt a reading—and Meening smiled as though she'd guessed his thought.

"I don't see disaster, though there is always the potential for it, but a mistake now will waste time you will someday regret."

"Is this my private life or my profession, madame?" Eslingen asked.

Meening glanced up, then bent her head to the orrery again. "Are you in love?"

What a very good question, particularly since I'm about to lose my job over it. "Honestly, madame, I—"

"You'd better decide then," Meening said. She straightened in her chair, her eyes suddenly hard, and Eslingen knew then why the actors worshiped her. "Great changes are coming for you, Lieutenant. And great chances, too."

Wonderful, Eslingen thought, but couldn't muster his usual distance. "I have reason to believe that I'm about to lose my position," he began, and Meening smiled.

"You will."

"And then?"

"I told you. Your life will be turned sideways. I also see the threat of delays. So you will find another position, probably of comparable worth. I do warn you, you have less to lose right now, so I wouldn't take any unnecessary chances. And don't gamble. You will lose there."

Eslingen hesitated, knowing he shouldn't ask, but couldn't stop himself. "This position that I'm going to find—"

"You expect much for five seillings," Meening said.

"Madame—"

Meening held up her hand. "My apologies, Lieutenant, truly. I simply don't know more than I've told you. Without better times, there's nothing more I can do."

Eslingen bowed his head in acknowledgment, swallowing an older anger, less at Meening than at his own careless mother. "Then I thank you for what you have done, madame."

Meening lifted a hand in casual, infuriating dismissal, and Eslingen was reminded again of the actors who were her most avid patrons. "The best I could, Lieutenant. And remember, beware of folly."

It was a long walk back to Customs Point, where Caiazzo kept his house, and the wind off the Sier carried a definite edge. Eslingen drew his coat tighter around his shoulders, glanced at the nearest clock tower, its face bright against the dull pewter clouds. Plenty of time, he thought, he wasn't due until the evening meal, or it would be if he didn't dawdle, but in spite of himself, in spite of knowing better, he found his steps slowing. He didn't really want to go back to Caiazzo's house, where everyone knew he was on sufferance, Caiazzo only waiting for the right moment to be rid of him. The streets in their own way were warmer, particularly in the pocket markets where candy-sellers vied with the hot-nuts women outside the doors of the more settled stores. Shop-girls and respectable matrons stood in line for both, and the air was heavy with wood smoke and the sharp smell of the roasting nuts. There would be hot cider in the taverns, better than warmed beer on an autumn evening, and he wished, suddenly, that Rathe was there to share a glass with him. It would have been nice to talk over Meening's reading with the pointsman, let him turn his southriver common sense loose on it, and hopefully talk him out of the mood that was settling into his bones. Not a bad mood, Eslingen thought, and not a bad feeling, just a melancholy as tart as the smoke-tinged air, and he hesitated for an instant, almost ready to turn on his heel and walk back to Point of Dreams. Then his own common sense reasserted itself—it was too far, too impractical, and besides, it was still wise to be discreet, to give Caiazzo time to bring about whatever it was he was planning—and he joined the line in front of the nearest sweet-seller instead. They sold soft sugar candies this time of year, molded in the shapes of castles and horses and—this year—*The Drowned Island*; he bought four running horses, honoring his birth sign, and paused to nibble one in the doorway of the nearest tavern. The sugar melted on his tongue, sweet with the faintest undertone of bitterness, the taste of autumn itself, and he glanced sideways to see the tavern suddenly crammed with figures. He blinked, startled—he would have sworn there had been only a pair of old men, drinking by the fire—and then recognized at least some few of the faces. Dead men, all of them, old friends and one or two old enemies, and even the winter lover he hadn't thought of in at least ten years, lounging long-legged against the mantelpiece, laughing with Contemine Laduri, handsome as he'd ever been before a ball smashed his face in some nameless town ten leagues from Altheim. Eslingen caught his breath, turning fully to the door, and the shades vanished again. It was just the ghost-tide, he told himself, nothing more, but in spite of himself he stepped into the cool shadows, and was disappointed when they didn't reappear.

He made his way to the bar anyway, feeling the ghosts gathering again behind him, and the barmaid came to meet him with the faint lines of a frown between her brows. She was no maid, more likely a grandmother, and Eslingen forced a smile.

"Is there hot whiskey, dame?"

She nodded, slowly, her eyes fixed on the room behind him, and it was all Eslingen could do to keep from turning. "Ay, soldier. Three demmings."

Eslingen produced the coins, laid them carefully on the knife-scarred counter. "How'd you know I'd been a soldier?"

The old woman laughed, a cackle that stirred the old men at the fire to look curiously at them. "You brought your company with you."

And so I did. Eslingen nodded, seeing them again at the edges of his sight—companionable, really, a company on the verge of going into winter quarters—and slowly felt himself relax a little. It was the ghost-tide, that was all, the ghosts and his melancholy and maybe even his fears, just the stars turning, opening a brief door, letting the ghosts of the timely dead walk where usually only the untimely could, or did. And the violence of the deaths around him had nothing to do with untimeliness. They had accepted the possibility when they signed on. None of these shades meant ill.

He watched the old woman pour a thrifty dram from the stone bottle warming in its simmering pot, wrapped his long fingers around the thick clay as it warmed to his touch. The liquor smelled of cloves and allspice, and he lifted the glass to the empty room before he drained it. The old woman nodded, grim approval, and he set the glass back on the bar, feeling oddly better. He'd been dreading seeing his ghosts, he realized; at least these weren't the ones he feared.

Nicolas Rathe hesitated at the top of the stair that led down to the main room of the station at Point of Dreams, ready to offer a hand to the tiny woman at his side. She smiled abstractedly, recognizing the thought, but made her own way down without hesitation, her heeled shoes tapping on the wood. Even with them, her head barely reached his shoulder, and he was merely of middling height himself. In the room below, he could see the duty points watching them side-long, with barely concealed amusement, and he frowned down at them, willing them to keep silent. Every ghost-tide—when the shades of the timely as well as the untimely dead made their presence felt, from the greatest to the least—brought people to the points, afraid that their mothers or rich aunts or neighbors had been murdered after all, and most of those could be dismissed as either honest error or hopeful greed. But this one. . . . He suppressed the desire to shake his head, schooled his face to careful neutrality. Sohier, the duty point, had warned him when she escorted the woman up to his workroom: *Every ghost-tide,* she said, *every ghost-tide Mistress Evaly comes to say she fears her sister who died last spring might have been murdered after all, and every year for all the four years I've been here, it's been last spring the sister died.* They had had the same thing in Point of Hopes, a seamstress whose daughter died in childbed still convinced the girl's lover had murdered her and the baby, and all any pointsman could do was listen to the tale and send her home again as kindly as possible. He frowned at Leenderts, who seemed inclined to say something, and the younger man swallowed the words unspoken. At least that had been the policy in Point of Hopes; he would make sure it was followed in Point of Dreams as well.

He opened the station door, miming surprise at finding it fully dark outside. "Mistress, do you need company home?"

As he spoke, he let his eyes roam across the waiting points. He was still getting used to Point of Dreams, a lateral promotion if ever there was one, but he'd already learned whom he couldn't trust with such a delicate task. Leenderts, for one, the man had the sensitivity of a cargo barge; but Sohier was clever, could handle it, and Amireau as well. Voillemin, the other adjunct point, would probably make a decent job of it, had learned his manners from a merchant-resident mother, but the door to his workroom was closed.

Evaly looked startled by the offer, and pleased, but then flushed faintly, and shook her head. "Bless you, Adjunct Point, no, I know these streets well. I was born here, just three streets over, my sister and I, and grew up here. But it was a kind offer."

Rathe nodded, stepped out into the darkness with her, intending at least to see her to the station gate, and she made no protest, her shoes loud on the cobbles. At the gate, she put her hand on his arm and looked up into his face, and Rathe could see that she must have been something like beautiful when she was younger, not breathtaking, but what his mother would call heart-lovely. "My sister. She wasn't murdered, was she, Adjunct Point?"

Rathe took a careful breath, not knowing quite what to make of the suddenly lucid question. "I don't believe so, mistress, no. But I will look into it for you."

"After all this time." Evaly shook her head, not a hair out of place under her neat cap. "Six years, come spring. It's just lovely to have her back, but I can't talk to her. I need to talk to someone."

"I understand."

Her hand tightened briefly, and then she was gone. Rathe watched her to the corner, a grey shadow quickly lost in the growing dark, then shook his head, and went back into the main room. The air was warmer than it had been: someone, Sohier probably, had built up the fire in the third stove, and he was grateful for it.

"That was kind, Nico," Sohier said with a glance at Leenderts, and Rathe shrugged.

"It wasn't much. Not if it brings her comfort."

From the skeptical look on Leenderts's face, the younger man didn't accept the lesson—didn't see the point, probably, didn't think it was the points' job to bring comfort, only law, if that—and Rathe sighed. No man, no leman, no child, just the ghost of a beloved sister: no one should be left so utterly alone. And she probably wasn't totally alone, probably had staff and servants, but he couldn't shake the chill of it completely. The clock whirred and struck the quarter hour, and he turned to collect his coat from its hook between the stoves. Sohier held the daybook open for him, and he glanced quickly over the entries before initialing them.

"Oh, Adjunct Point." Voillemin's door had opened, and the other adjunct made his way to the worktable, turning the daybook so that he could read the entries.

Rathe bit back a frown—that was really the duty point's job, not Voillemin's, particularly when Voillemin had been so quick to hide himself when Mistress Evaly appeared—but swallowed his automatic reproof. He and Voillemin were technically equal in rank, and it was no secret that Voillemin thought he should have had Rathe's job when the former Chief Point DeChaix retired. It behooved them both to tread warily until the station had gotten used to the change of regime. "What's up?"

"Well, sir." Voillemin's tone was stiff, and Rathe sighed. Voillemin was young, that was all, he told himself, young to be even a junior adjunct—his mother's properties in Dreams had earned him quick promotion under DeChaix—and both his youth and his connections meant he should have been stationed elsewhere. It wasn't that he was a bad pointsman, or even merely, ordinarily, corrupt, it was just that he hadn't ever had the chance to find his own feet, instead behaved as though points' service was some great game, the rules of which he hadn't quite learned yet. And he was equally uncertain about Rathe himself: he knew the story of the stolen children, knew that Rathe had been one of the heroes of the summer, but also knew that the man was commoner than most, southriver born and bred and a leveller like most of that sort, and the two did not sit well together in Voillemin's eyes. Or at least not until *The Drowned Island* had opened, Rathe amended, and admitted to himself that this was one of his greatest grievances against the miserable play. He didn't know which was worse, watching Voillemin deplore his background, or seeing him look at him wide-eyed, like the apprentices clogging the Tyrseia's pit.

"There are people to see you. They came while you were with Mistress Evaly. I had them wait in my workroom."

From the tone, he was on the verge of making a grievance of it, too. Rathe waited, but nothing more seemed to be forthcoming. "And?"

Voillemin shifted. "It's the necromancer, b'Estorr. With another man."

"His proper title is magist," Rathe said. "Or master. As in fellow of the university."

Voillemin ignored the rebuke. "He said he needed to see you, even if it was the end of your day. So I said he could wait. I know you're close."

Not the way you mean it. Rathe bit back the words, said, "You may have need of his services someday yourself, Voillemin."

The younger man's eyes widened in something almost like horror, and Rathe wondered if the boy's father was Chadroni or a Leaguer, that he was so nervous about necromancers. More likely his nurse filled him with tales, he thought, and managed to smile as he initialed the daybook. "Send the boy to fetch some tea," he said aloud, and moved toward the door of Voillemin's workroom.

Istre b'Estorr was waiting as promised, together with a slim, plain man in an advocat's scarlet robe that hung open over a plain brown suit. He looked vaguely familiar, and Rathe hid a frown, trying to place the stranger. Nothing came, and he nodded to the magist.

"Evening, Istre. Hope you weren't waiting long."

b'Estorr gave him a preoccupied smile. "Not too long. I'm sorry we're here so late. I hate to catch you just at the end of your day."

"It's not a problem," Rathe answered. In spite of himself, he glanced at the stranger, and b'Estorr picked up smoothly on the cue.

"Nico, you know Advocat Holles?"

Of course. Rathe nodded, gave a bow. "By reputation, and

through the intendant, of course." Kurin Holles was an advocat in the court of Point of Hearts, and a good one, by rumor, but he was also the leman of the late intendant Bourtrou Leussi, one of the better judges that Rathe appeared before—and one of the chamberlains, too, though he had died before the masque could be chosen, and Rathe didn't envy the intendant who inherited the task. He sighed, remembering the last time he had seen Leussi—after hours, at the intendant's comfortable, unlavish house, discussing the proper response to a case of forged licenses. Holles had been there, too, he remembered, a shadow in warm amber, formal robes discarded for a dressing gown, glancing through a door to find his leman busy, and withdrawing as quietly as he'd appeared. Rathe doubted Leussi had known he'd been there, so intent had the other man been on the problem at hand.

"I was very sorry to hear about the intendant," he said aloud. "I had the pleasure of working with him a number of times—one of the fairest I've ever known. I'll miss him."

Holles inclined his head, the gesture not hiding the pain in his eyes, and Rathe wondered if it would have been better not to mention the man. But it was ghost-tide, and Leussi must be all too present to his grieving friend.

"Thank you, Adjunct Point—and my compliments on the promotion. Bourtrou was pleased to hear of it, he always felt you would advance . . ." Holles paused, took a breath. "Which is why I presumed on Magist b'Estorr for the introduction."

Rathe looked at b'Estorr, a chill settling in the pit of his stomach, not helped by the crackling stove. "Let's go upstairs," he said, and the necromancer nodded.

Rathe led the way back up the stairs to his narrow workroom. The stove was banked for the night, but the runner who had refilled the teapot was already stirring the coals to new life. Rathe nodded his thanks, and waved the others to a seat as the runner shut the door again behind him. "I take it there's a problem?"

"Yes." b'Estorr glanced at Holles as though seeking permission, and the older man nodded.

"Better he hear it from you, Istre. You know the—ramifications— even better than I."

b'Estorr nodded, his arms folded across his chest as though the cold had reached him, too, and Rathe didn't bother to hide his frown.

Chadron was a cold place; winter never seemed to bother b'Estorr, so this was something more.

"Nico, I know you get a lot of people coming to you during ghost-tide, telling tales of murder where there's no such thing."

Rathe nodded, warily. "We just had such a one."

"Whereas the presence of a ghost during ghost-tide is a likelier confirmation of timely death, rather than untimely. Though it has been known." b'Estorr's voice was momentarily tutorial, but then he shook the story away. "What would you say the absence of a ghost would mean?"

"During ghost-tide?"

"During ghost-tide," b'Estorr agreed.

Rathe shook his head in turn. "Advocat—you've not touched Leussi's ghost?"

Holles shook his head once, his eyes closing briefly over some sorrow too private to share. "And the ghost-tide is more than a week old, Adjunct Point. And we had been lemen for almost twenty years."

"Dis Aidones." Rathe paused, imagining the other's pain—gods, if he were to lose Eslingen, without even that much comfort—then forced himself to think rationally. There were a few other explanations than the obvious, and he took a breath. "Forgive me, Advocat, but there are a few questions—"

"I understand." Holles managed a brief smile. "But I can tell you that we had not quarreled, nor was he expecting or looking forward to his death. It was—very sudden."

And I will find out the details, Rathe thought, *but not from you.* The alchemists would have the records he needed, no need to cause the man further pain. "Those were my questions," he said aloud, and didn't add what they all knew. There were no reasons for Leussi's ghost not to return. "Istre. You said the ghosts of the untimely dead walk at ghost-tide, too, that it's been known. Then why . . . ?"

"Because his ghost has been bound," b'Estorr said flatly.

Rathe shuddered. He had seen b'Estorr bind a ghost once, tying it to the spot where the man had fallen—the magist who had orchestrated the theft of the children, mad and powerful—and it had not been a pleasant sight. Or, not sight, but feeling, like the sour smell of a house fire, a reminder of loss. The landame's successor had had to build a stone cairn over the spot, to keep the horses from shying at it.

b'Estorr went on, "I can't find it, whispers only. The only ghost that doesn't make its presence felt during the ghost-tide is an untimely ghost that has been bound—yes, I know, the points have to ask about either desire for death or some quarrel that would keep the ghost away, but that's really not what's happening. In those cases, the ghosts are there, but withholding themselves, and if that were the case, I'd have touched him. There is no other explanation. Especially not in a case like this, where the ties of lemanry were so strong."

"All right," Rathe said, "I'll accept that. Was he bound at death, or could it have been malice after death, instead of murder?"

It was the first time the word had been spoken, even though they had all known it was lurking, and he saw Holles wince. b'Estorr shook his head. "Timing wouldn't work. You'd have to be by pretty much at the moment of death in order to bind the ghost."

"He was still warm when I found him that night," Holles said, raw-voiced.

Rathe scoured his face with his hands, as though he could wipe away the image Holles created for him. "I'm sorry," he said again. "What do you want of me?"

The words came out as more of a challenge than he'd meant, but Holles seemed not to hear anything but the offer of help. "I want you to go to the regents with me. The death has already been signed as natural, he's in the ground, and the matter's closed. But I want it investigated. I want his murderer found and punished. So I need the regents' warrant to reopen the matter and refer it back to the points. I thought if I brought a pointsman, particularly one of your reputation, plus a necromancer and anyone else who'd support me—well, I thought it could only help."

"Am I your best choice?" Rathe asked, exchanging a quick look with b'Estorr. "Don't mistake me, I consider—my professional opinion is—that you have grave cause for concern." He used the judicial phrase deliberately, and was pleased to surprise a faint smile from the advocat. "And I want to help however I can, but . . ." He paused, wondering how to explain the situation, settled for, "I'm not best regarded by the regents."

Holles frowned, and b'Estorr gave a thin smile. "The metropolitan took the points' side against the regents last summer, largely on Nico's say-so."

"And was proved right," Holles said. He shook his head, suddenly obstinate. "I don't care. Bourtrou held you in high regard, and you're not afraid of necromancers and alchemists, not like some of your fellows—not like the one we were dealing with just now, to name names. I would take it as a great favor if you would stand with me in this. But I will go to the metropolitan herself if necessary."

And use my name, which would just about seal my reputation with the regents, Rathe thought. "Of course I'll do it, I just wanted you to be aware that my presence may—make things more difficult for you than it has to be."

"I'll take my chances," Holles said, and smiled again, the expression briefly erasing the lines shadowing his thin face. "I would prefer you to handle the investigation, in any case."

"Thank you," Rathe said, and swallowed a sigh. If the folly stars were in the ascendant, there would be little he could do until their time was past. "Do you have any idea who might have wanted to kill him?"

Holles's hands clenched, then consciously relaxed. "He had enemies, no one is without them, especially a man in his position. But I can't think of anyone who held him in such disrespect that they would—do this to him. Kill him, yes, but not bind him."

"Or fear?" b'Estorr asked. "That's a strong reason to bind a ghost, Kurin, stronger than hate. Who feared him?"

The advocat shook his head, almost helplessly. "No one. Rathe knows, you know, he was one of the fairest, and kindest, of the intendants, people would go to him for advice, and he was always willing to give it."

And that was loss speaking, Rathe knew. It was never that simple, there was always someone who feared or hated the victim, or both, and Leussi would be no different—unless of course it was madness, and that was its own kind of fear. But there was no point in grieving the man further, not until they had the necessary warrant. "When do you go before the regents?"

"The day after tomorrow, in the morning. At ten o'clock." Holles took a breath. "Rathe—"

"I'll be there," Rathe said. How Chief Point Trijn would react, he could not begin to guess.

Holles dipped his head again, almost a bow. "Thank you, Adjunct Point. "I am more grateful than I can begin to express."

b'Estorr touched his arm gently, and Holles managed a smile.

"I don't speak of fees, I know your reputation. But I'm grateful."

"We'll leave you to your—more ordinary—business," b'Estorr said, and led the other man away.

Trijn was working late herself, until second sunrise, according to her runner, and Rathe, bracing himself, presented himself at her door with more than an hour of her day to spare. She listened impassively, staring past him at the shuttered window. When he had finished, she sat silent for a few moments, then reached for her silver-banded pipe. "They'll never allow it," she said.

"Allow which?" Rathe asked. "The reexamination of the death, the investigation—Leussi was important enough, they'd be fools to try to deny Holles."

Trijn made a face, tamping the shards of tobacco into the bowl. "They might allow the reexamination, even the investigation, but as I understand it you've not endeared yourself to the grand bourgeoise, have you?"

"I told the advocat that, Chief, but he insists on having me there."

"Do you really think they'll give it to you?" Trijn's eyebrows shot up, even as she gestured to the stove.

Rathe lit a twig from the bundle that hung ready, handed it to her. "That's not the issue, Chief, though I won't deny I'd like to have the chance to handle it. But the main thing right now is to get the death recognized as murder."

Trijn gave him a humorless smile, and her black eyes were very dark indeed, little flames dancing in them as she pulled on her pipe. She spoke around its stem. "You know precious little of the magistracy, Rathe, if you think Holles will let it go at that." Rathe opened his mouth to protest, but Trijn overrode him. "I know you liked the intendant, but Holles is going to want someone he can trust on this." The pipe was lit, and she leaned back, releasing a cloud of smoke.

Rathe said, "Holles knows I'm not fee'able, I won't find what's not there, it's not like he wants to own me."

"No," Trijn agreed, "and he's one of the few who wouldn't, I imagine. That's exactly why he'll want you, Nico. Almost anybody else is going to trip all over herself to find something, anything, but you won't. You'll go at your own pace, and probably by your own rules, until you find something like the truth."

"And what's wrong with that, Chief?"

"Rathe. An intendant is apparently murdered. An intendant who has lived happily with his leman for, what, seventeen years? So we can probably rule out a crime of passion. And that puts it squarely in the realm of the political. Someone there is likely to be who will not want the truth. Maybe not among the regents, maybe even not at the Tour, but somewhere. And that someone will make sure that an honest pointsman—worse, someone that all the broadsheets in Astreiant proclaim to be an honest pointsman—will not be assigned to this matter. And there's damn little I can do about it. And even if by some miracle the regents were to agree, the surintendant won't, because there's no way you can win this one. Let me tell you that from the start."

Rathe stared at her, disbelief turning to anger. "With all respect, Chief, I think you're reaching."

"Do you? Knowing the regents as we both do?"

She was right about that, if nothing else. Rathe knew the regents, and their temper, very well indeed. "But you can't really think they'd be willing to let murder go, the murder of one of their own. . . ."

Trijn smiled again through a cloud of smoke. "Have you read the astrologers' sheets lately? The city's primed for just such stupidity, and the regents have been primed for it for years." She frowned at the window again. "If you make this plea, the regents are going to try to stall, just to spite you—and, I suspect, the metropolitan."

"What's she got to do with this?" Rathe demanded.

"She stood patronne to you over the children," Trijn answered. "Don't be dense, Rathe."

"The important thing is the investigation," Rathe said stubbornly. "Not who conducts it."

"No." Trijn released another cloud of smoke. "All right. I'm coming with you."

"Chief?"

"I'm not going to let the regents eat my senior adjunct for breakfast simply because the metropolitan took his part against them once. The grande bourgeoise has a long memory."

From the tone of her voice, Rathe wondered if she had some other motive as well, but put the thought aside. Her support could only help, he hoped, and pushed himself to his feet.

"With your permission, Chief, I thought I'd send to the alchemists first thing tomorrow, get the death signings." He raised a hand. "Not as part of any investigation, of course, but there might be something there that would support our case."

Trijn grinned. "Of course. Give Fanier my regards."

❁   ❁   ❁

Eslingen made his way back to Customs Point in good time, pushed his way through the garden gate just as the clock on the old Factors' Hall was striking the quarter hour. He'd made better time than he'd expected, would have time to change before dinner if he chose, and he picked his way through the last drifts of leaves with some satisfaction. The garden was bare in the falling night, the tender plants already bundled against the coming cold, the last beds of vegetables piled with hay to keep the frosts at bay, and the light from the windows haloed the last spare sticks. Caiazzo was in his workroom, Eslingen saw without surprise—the merchant-venturer tended to work late in any event, and with the winter-sun rising later every day, after nine now, Caiazzo's more discreet visitors tended to arrive in the hours of true dark between sunset and winter-sunrise. No one had been expected, though—otherwise, he himself would not have been allowed the afternoon to himself—and Eslingen guessed the older man was just working on his books, allotting the capital for next year's caravans. The loss of the de Mailhac gold mines had hurt, meant that Caiazzo had to be more careful than he had been, but recently the merchant-venturer had expressed himself cautiously satisfied. *Which would make me happier,* Eslingen thought, *if I were staying the winter.*

The kitchen door was half open, one of the cooks leaning out to catch her breath; Eslingen lifted a hand in greeting, but kept on toward the side door, remembering a line from the last play he and Rathe had seen together. *Magists by the front door, undertakers by the back, and the knife goes in at the side door.* He thought it had been good, but they had had a box to themselves, and he hadn't followed much of the story. Still, it captured his position well enough, somewhere between servant and colleague, and in any case, he liked the sound of it. He was smiling as he pushed open the heavy door, nodding to the runner who was sitting on the tabouret at the end of the short hall. To his surprise, the boy caught his sleeve as he passed.

"Lieutenant. Master Caiazzo wants to see you right away."

"Right away?" Eslingen repeated, a thrill of apprehension shooting through him. An unexpected visitor, maybe, one of Caiazzo's less reputable agents from the Court of the Thirty-two Knives, and him not here to offer backup. . . . But Denizard was here, and she was effective protection in her own right, and Caiazzo would have no compunction about refusing to see someone, if he had the slightest suspicion of trouble.

"As soon as you came in," the boy said, and Eslingen nodded.
"Show me up."

Caiazzo's workroom was warm and warmly lit, the polished stove
in the corner showing bright tongues of flame to match the enormous
candelabra. The candles were wax, too, all two dozen of them, and
there were more candles in the sconces above the long counter. That
surface was relatively clear, for once, the ledgers stacked, tallyboards
turned face to the wall, papers tucked into folios, and Eslingen looked
curiously at the stranger. There was no missing him, a big man, dark
as Caiazzo, but older, his black hair streaked with silver under the
candles' light. The same brilliance reflected from a satin coat, bottle-
green striped with gold, and glinted from shoe buckles set with
stones. The ivory lace at the thick wrists and neck seemed to glow as
well. But there was no mistaking who was master here, Eslingen
thought as he made his bow. Caiazzo might be plainly dressed, as
plainly dressed as ever, but it was clear the big man deferred to him,
and to the magist seated demurely in the corner.

"I'm glad you're back, Philip," Caiazzo said, and the big man
lifted heavy eyebrows. There was something familiar about the gesture, gone so quickly that Eslingen couldn't place it.

"This is the man you meant?"

"It is." There was a warning in Caiazzo's voice, and the big man
lifted both hands in surrender, the lace flashing. "Lieutenant Philip Eslingen, currently of my household, formerly of Coindarel's Dragons."

"And the man who helped rescue the children," the big man said.
"No one will have forgotten that, Hanse."

"Which hardly seems a problem, surely." Caiazzo waved vaguely
in the direction of the sideboard. "Pour me a drink, please, Philip,
and yourself one, too."

Eslingen moved to obey, swallowing unworthy annoyance—it was
one thing to introduce him as a lieutenant, a gentleman in name at
least, and another to treat him like a servant—and turned toward the
stranger. "And for Master—?"

"Master Duca's been served," Caiazzo said.

There was a glass on the end of the worktable, barely touched.
Eslingen gave an inward shrug, and poured two glasses of the sweet,
light wine. He handed one to Caiazzo, who took it smiling, and himself retreated, his eyes on both men.

"Prettily done," Duca said, and sounded as though he grudged
the admission.

"Done like a gentleman," Caiazzo corrected. "Down to offering some to you."

Duca scowled, and for a moment it was as though he were looking into a distorting mirror, the expression so perfectly mimicked Caiazzo's own. Then the moment was gone, and the big man turned away, shaking his head. "He's a soldier. I don't need a soldier."

"Forgive me, Gerrat," Caiazzo said, "but I'd've thought that was exactly what you did need."

Eslingen's eyebrows rose in spite of himself. Whoever this Duca was, whatever he was, he, Eslingen, didn't appreciate being talked about as though he were cattle in the marketplace. If this was the place Caiazzo had found for him, he'd have none of it.

Caiazzo's eyes flicked his way, and too late, Eslingen smoothed his expression. The merchant-venturer grinned, and set his own glass carefully on the edge of the long counter. "Forgive me, Philip, you must be wondering what's going on."

Eslingen considered several responses, contented himself finally with a short bow. "Yes."

"We've had word today," Caiazzo said, "as principal financier, that *The Alphabet of Desire* has been chosen as the midwinter masque. The official announcement will be made tomorrow or the next day, but in the meantime, it seems to me that this may offer a—resolution—of our current dilemma. This is Gerrat Duca, senior master of the Guild of the Masters of Defense, who will be responsible for all the chorus displays—"

"For the fight displays," Duca said.

Caiazzo sighed. "For the chorus's fight displays. That's the drills, the procession set pieces, and any duels, though those will probably be handled by actors."

What does this have to do with me? Eslingen thought, and bowed again. "Congratulations."

This time, both Duca and Caiazzo lifted an eyebrow at him, and he wondered if Duca was copying the younger man's gesture. Duca was the first to look away.

"All right, that was good. But can he act?"

"Who knows?" Caiazzo answered. "Does it matter?"

Enough of this, Eslingen thought. "Excuse me, Master Caiazzo, but what—exactly—do you want me to do?"

To his annoyance, it was Duca who answered. "I need someone who knows how to run a drill, who can teach complete novices to handle weapons without hurting themselves or anyone else. It would help if that someone also knew the rudiments of military technique, more than what he's learned out of a book."

"I would have thought that the Masters of Defense had plenty of members with those qualifications," Eslingen said. Even he had heard of the Masters of Defense, had even seen a couple of their fencing exhibitions—the only time he'd been to the Tyrseia before he saw *The Drowned Island,* in fact. They taught swordplay, and general use of weapons, and some of the masters had even published chapbooks on the subject. He'd read a few of them himself, when he was with Coindarel, hoping to learn enough to pass for a gentleman.

"They're not, generally speaking, soldiers," Caiazzo said. "And that's not the only problem."

"The chorus is noble," Duca said. "Landames and vidames and even a castellan or palatine or two, for all I know, but all well born and used to having their own way. They'll take orders better from one of their own kind than they would from any of us."

Eslingen blinked, absurdly flattered—to be mistaken for gentry by an Astreianter of Duca's rank and experience was novelty indeed— and Caiazzo sighed again.

"As you've pointed out before now, Philip, your rank makes you a gentleman. And you know how to run a drill."

That I do. Eslingen blinked again, considering his options. He could do the job, that much he was certain of—it wasn't that different from what he'd done as one of Coindarel's sergeants, never mind as a lieutenant, taking new recruits and teaching them to handle arms and leading them through the basics of maneuvers. But whether he'd want to . . . Not that he was likely to have much say in the matter; he had known he was being kept on through sufferance since he had taken up with Rathe. Publicly, Caiazzo shrugged off the insinuations of his colleagues, maintained that the household of an honest businessman could consort where and with whom they wished. Privately, though . . .

"I can't keep you," Caiazzo said, suddenly silken-voiced. "You're becoming a liability."

"The pay is decent," Duca said. "We'll each take home a share—no less than a couple of pillars, maybe as much as a petty-crown if all goes well. Are you interested, Lieutenant?"

And to be fair, Caiazzo was under no obligation to have done this much, but it still rankled. "It seems like an—intriguing—position," Eslingen said.

"Good," Duca said. "We can arrange the trials."

" 'Trials'?" Eslingen repeated, knowing he'd made a mistake, and Duca smiled, the expression a mirror of Caiazzo's.

"Even under these circumstances, the formalities have to be observed. We can't just let anybody in."

"Just a moment," Caiazzo said, and Duca spread his hands.

"It can't be done, Hanse. I can make it as easy as possible, but that's all."

"What," Eslingen asked, "are these trials?" He had a feeling he already knew, that he'd seen a stage fight that was supposed to prove the fitness of one of the contenders either to join the Masters, or to move up in rank, and he schooled himself to show no surprise when Duca answered.

"Everyone who's admitted as a master has to prove her worth— his worth, in your case. Usually, it's in a public subscription match, three bouts against three proving masters with three different sets of weapons, their choice, not yours, with at least one win and no killing touches in a lost bout. As I said, I can set it up, but I can't eliminate the trial entirely."

Wonderful, Eslingen thought. *And is it worth it, to become drillmaster to a pack of half-disciplined nobles?* But of course that wasn't the real question: the real question was whether Caiazzo would allow him any alternative.

"Mind you," Duca went on, as though he'd sensed the other man's unease, "you've got the manners for it, and the looks, too. In fact—have you ever considered changing your name?"

"What?"

"Lieutenant d'Esling, no, vaan Esling, since you're a Leaguer." Duca smiled. "It would look better on the broadsheets."

Eslingen bit back a sudden peal of laughter. Folly, Meening had predicted, and here was a grand folly just waiting for him. Lieutenant vaan Esling, indeed, and him a whore's son from Esling. The other men were looking at him expectantly, knowing what his answer had to be, and this time Eslingen did laugh. "Very well, masters, it sounds like—interesting—work, and I've no desire to make Master Caiazzo's position difficult any longer. But what if I don't pass these trials?"

"Oh, you'll pass," Caiazzo said, and his smile matched Duca's. "Don't worry about that."

2

I t was cold already in All-Guilds, where the regents met. The heavy stones of wall and floor seemed to suck all warmth out of the air—pleasant enough in summer, Rathe thought, but hard to bear at this end of the year. The young women who bustled importantly about the lobby had buttoned their guild-robes to the chin, and more than one had thickened her ankles with an extra pair of stockings. At least the guild mothers had allowed the ancient guard to light a brazier at his post, and when they were finally ushered into the long room where the regents sat, he was glad to see another pair of stoves, as well as the massive fireplace. All were lit, and he edged gratefully toward the nearest of the stoves, letting it warm him at least from the knees up. Holles spoke first, impressive in the black-banded scarlet that contrasted so sharply with the regents' sober black, relieved only by spotless lace and the silver and gold of guild badges at neck and sleeves. The grande bourgeoise was the plainest of all, every stitch proclaiming that her family had held its shop in the Mercandry for a hundred years, and had no need of additional finery. Rathe glanced along the row, was not surprised to see the gold-edged lace and the frippery of black-on-black striping, satin on plain weave, only on the youngest woman. New-rich herself, or a new-rich merchant's daughter, she seemed to have no qualms about setting herself apart from the others, and he hoped that was a good sign.

Holles spoke well—speaking on his own behalf must be strange to him, Rathe thought, and had to admire if not the cold eloquence then the simple emotional justice of his plea. He showed good sense in not trying to make this a court-speech, downplaying the legal aspects in favor of the personal, and Rathe saw one or two of the regents nod in agreement as he worked his way toward his conclusion. Then, in spite of himself, he glanced toward the frieze that wound its way around the room, the carved figures centered above the grand bourgeoise's chair. In any of the courts, high or low, that frieze would show the Pillars of Justice, the four deities who guarded court matters. Here in All-Guilds, the theme was Heira's Banquet, Heira herself presiding over the great gathering of the goddesses, from the solid, familiar figures pressing toward her for her gifts, to the lesser known, less loved, clustering behind them. And somewhere, Rathe knew, probably opposite Heira herself for the balance of the composition, Bonfortune, the god of the Merchants-Venturer, would be at his tricks, persuading innocent Didion to give up her share in the spoils of the settled life. And that meant that Bonfortune stood above all petitioners, he realized, warning the regents against inevitable deceit. *Unfair,* he thought, but then, the regents were responsible for more than just the guilds now, and had good reason to be careful.

"Adjunct Point Rathe and Magist b'Estorr both worked with the intendant," Holles said, and Rathe jerked himself back to attention at the mention of his name. "And Chief Point Trijn is an impartial witness. They have all viewed the evidence I've laid before you, and have agreed to stand with me today, in support of my plea before you."

There was a moment of silence, and then the regents leaned toward each other, conferring in lower voice. The lines of their bodies mimicked the lines of the frieze above them, and Rathe wondered if they were aware of the effect. Finally the grand bourgeoise straightened, glancing to either side until the other women subsided. "It seems to me, with all due respect to the advocat, that there is no clear evidence of murder. Suggestions, yes, but nothing more."

Someone gasped—not Holles, Rathe thought, the advocat had himself too well in hand for that, but perhaps one of the regents. He glanced sideways to see b'Estorr looking dangerously demure, studying a crack in the stone floor with the same intensity he would focus on a particularly interesting set of bones. Holles started to speak again, but Trijn spoke first.

"It seems to me, with all due respect to the regents, that the

evidence in hand combined with the sanction—the agreement—of
the points should be enough to satisfy the regents that murder, in
fact, has been done, as well as violence after death. Even if the evidence were inconclusive, the matter must be resolved. The intendant
Leussi was one of the brighter ornaments of the judiciary. His murder
must not be allowed to go unpunished."

The regents were staring at Trijn, Gausaron with particular dis-
dain, and Rathe knew he was staring with them. It wasn't like Trijn
to make speeches, even less like her to antagonize the powers that
be—even in the short time Rathe had served with her, he had
learned that she was more likely to get her way by bowing and ca-
tering to people's pretensions. But this . . . There was a particular ring
in the chief point's voice, triumph almost, or sharp attack, that made
him suspect there was more here than he knew. *Which might explain
why she volunteered herself for this,* he thought, *but it doesn't mean
it's going to help us.*

A woman with a softly lined face under a starched cap said, "Forgive me, Advocat, but isn't it possible that there was some—quarrel,
some anger between you, perhaps even something petty of which you
weren't even aware, that's holding his ghost from you?"

"If I may, madame," b'Estorr said, and Gausaron waved her hand
in permission. "A ghost may withdraw itself from the people and
things she was most concerned with in her lifetime, but at the ghost-
tide she will still be present, if unfelt, until those people and things
have no more presence in this world. If that had been the case, I
would have felt the intendant's presence, and indeed, that was what
I expected to find. But there was nothing."

"The lack of a ghost is hardly decisive evidence," Gausaron said.

"In any other time of year," b'Estorr said, "the lack of a ghost
would hardly be evidence, indeed. There are many who die untimely
who don't feel they're—worthy—of the attention their ghost would
draw. Who feel, for one reason or another, that it was, however violently, their time to die. However. We are well into the ghost-tide.
The only time of year when the timely dead are felt. The city—this
very room—teems with them. And Intendant Leussi and Advocat
Holles were lemen for close to twenty years. The only possible reason
that neither the advocat nor I have touched the ghost is that his ghost
has been bound. And by the person who murdered him." He tilted
his head to one side, and smiled, a singularly sweet smile that Rathe

had learned to mistrust. "I hope that's sufficiently clear to the regents."

Gausaron glared at him, and leaned back in her chair.

"With respect," Rathe said, "the alchemist's report also suggests that there were—anomalies—involved with the death." He had received the report the previous afternoon, hastily copied but legible, and he'd worked with the chief alchemist Fanier often enough to recognize when the man was hedging his bets. Fanier had noted changes consonant with "external influences," though no internal evidence of that influence: not enough on its own, but coupled with the absence of a ghost, enough to raise questions in the mind of any pointsman. He only hoped it would be enough for the regents.

"And there have been similar cases in the court records," Holles said, "both precedents for reopening an investigation such as this, and for ghosts bound at death. I have taken the liberty of compiling a summary list of those cases, and my court clerks will be happy to bring any related documents the regents would like to see."

"A generous offer, Advocat," one of the regents murmured, and Gausaron's frown deepened.

"And one I see no need of."

"Madame," Holles said, "Do you deny me?"

Gausaron hesitated. "I do not see evidence—"

"I will have this murder investigated," Holles said. "I would prefer with your blessing, madame, and the blessing of the regents, but I will act without it if I must. The points bear the queen's authority, the regents oversee their activities only in that the points operate within the walls of the city. I am the queen's advocat, the points serve the queen's law. And the queen's law has been violated, and that takes precedence over the city's dignities."

Gausaron shook her head, but Rathe thought he saw defeat in her eyes. "You are determined to proceed in this course? Despite the scandal, the notoriety, that will inevitably ensue?"

Trijn made a noise in her throat, but her face was impassive. Holles's head lifted. "Being murdered is not a scandal, it is a tragedy. It is certainly not a disgrace. I'm not afraid of scandal, because there will be none. There will be truth."

"Even if you have to pay for it?" Gausaron snapped. "Be very wary, Advocat, that what you get is truth. You are at least entitled to value for money."

Her eyes were on Rathe as she spoke, and in spite of himself, his fists tightened. "As Madame has doubtless heard, I don't take fees."

Gausaron smiled thinly. "No. Nor will you in this case. Because it will not fall to you, pointsman."

"He's my senior adjunct," Trijn said tonelessly. "Address him by his proper rank."

An angry flush rose in Gausaron's cheeks, but she inclined her head. "My apologies, Adjunct Point. But this is a matter that needs to be handled with a certain amount of delicacy, of diplomacy, since the advocat insists that it be pursued. And such are almost unknown southriver. Point of Hopes, that is where you were last stationed, is it not, points—Adjunct Point?"

As you damn well know. Rathe controlled his temper. "Yes."

Gausaron smiled at the Regent on her right. "And southriver is so recently popular, at least on the common stages. However, the unfortunate events of last summer—an honest guildsman shot dead, near riots in the streets—we cannot have a repeat of that, not with the midwinter ceremonies almost upon us." She paused, glancing along the line of women, gathering nods of agreement. "This, then, is our official word. The regents will not tolerate such misrule as went on in Point of Hopes last summer. If this is to be a points matter, then it will be handled with the respect due to the persons of birth involved in it." She looked at Trijn, and this time there was triumph in her eyes. "I believe you have at your station an adjunct point named Voillemin, a man of respectable parentage. It shall be his responsibility to investigate this—murder, and bring it to a satisfactory conclusion."

"Satisfactory to whom?" Holles demanded, and Rathe saw him bite his lip as though he'd betrayed himself.

"It is not your place to tell me how to run my station," Trijn said.

"This or nothing," Gausaron answered. "Our responsibility is to the well-being of this city and its people, and that will not be served by another rout like last summer. That is our decision."

The dismissal was palpable. Holles hesitated for an instant, as though he wanted to say more, but then swept a bow that was a hair too deep for sincerity. Straightening, he turned on his heel and strode from the room, the scarlet robe billowing around him. The others followed, less gracefully, but no one spoke until they were outside All-Guilds. Rathe glanced up at the massive doorway, carved with yet another version of Heira's Banquet, and couldn't suppress a wry smile. Heira was one of the Pillars of Justice, but in this place, that incarnation was far from honored.

"So, Advocat," Trijn said, "what in hell has the advocacy done to earn the enmity of the regents?"

Holles rubbed his eyes as though they pained him. "I thought that was done with years ago—Gausaron wasn't even on the Council then." He shook himself. "It's not the advocacy, it was Bourtrou. The queen determined that the chamberlains should be chosen from among the judiciary, not just among the regents, since the position has a direct effect on the health of the entire realm, not just the city. Bourtrou wrote the brief in support, and the regents blamed him for it, instead of the queen."

Rathe grinned. "So we can maybe look for suspects among the regents?"

Trijn held up a hand. "No, Voillemin can look for suspects among the regents, and by Sofia, I am inclined to set that particular dog to hunt."

"This Voillemin," Holles said. "Is he any good at all?"

"He wouldn't be one of my adjuncts if he weren't," Trijn snapped, "I don't care who he's related to."

Holles's eyes sought Rathe, who shrugged infinitesimally. It was the kind of case that could make a pointsman's career, or destroy it, and from what he'd seen of Voillemin, he wasn't suited to that kind of pressure. If anything, he felt sorry for the man—and sorrier still for Holles, whose leman's murder was being used to punish the points.

"I just don't want it made—convenient," Holles said, almost helplessly, and Rathe wished he could reassure him. But anything he could think of, any words of comfort, sounded sour, almost hypocritical in the face of the regents' evident reluctance, and he could see the same thought in both Trijn's and b'Estorr's faces.

"No," Rathe said quietly, when no one else spoke. "I'll do what I can to keep an eye on Voillemin, Advocat, that's my proper duty, and I can at least promise that to you." It wasn't much, but it would have to be enough—*at least for now, at least until he makes a mistake*—and from the look on the advocat's face, relieved and grateful, it might be. Rathe sighed. So long as he was able to make good on the promise.

❖   ❖   ❖

The Masters of Defense had their own hall, a long, low building that might once have been a rope walk or a sailmakers' loft, hard by the river at the western end of Point of Dreams. The ground floor was broken up into a warren of rooms—classrooms on the river side, where the light was best, but also what looked like a students' commons and even a small library, where a lace-capped woman frowned over a stack of foolscap. She glared at them as they passed, and rose, skirts rustling, to close the door against intrusion. Caiazzo ignored her, as he ignored the crowd of students chattering outside one of the practice rooms, and Eslingen copied the merchant's carriage, bowing gracefully to a young man who seemed to want to take offense. That was one complaint the broadsheets made against the Masters, that their students, once half trained, spent too much time looking for an excuse to test their skills, and it was, Eslingen thought, probably true enough. The same thing happened in every regiment he'd ever served with—he'd probably done it himself, if he wanted to think about it; the only difference was that your fellow soldiers were quicker to beat those pretensions out of you, if only to save their own necks.

At the end of the long hall a stairway rose to a second floor, framed in a window that must have cost a young fortune. Caiazzo slowed his pace, and a scrawny, grey-haired woman—no, Eslingen realized, with some shock, a man in skirts and a woman's square-necked bodice, carrying a bated sword—appeared in the doorway of the nearer classroom.

"Master Caiazzo." He bowed, magnificently unconscious of his strange dress. "Master Duca says you should go on up."

"Thank you," Caiazzo answered. Eslingen blinked, schooling himself to show no reaction, but the merchant-venturer's gaze flicked toward him anyway, and the dark man smiled.

"Don't worry, Philip, I'm sure they won't waste you in dame's parts."

So presumably the man was rehearsing for, being trained for, one of the midwinter farces, short, silly plays for the short, cold days, Rathe had called them, where the players played against type and women dressed as men—and vice versa, apparently. Eslingen had been looking forward to seeing one, but it had never crossed his mind that he might be expected to participate.

The stairway opened onto a massive open space, a room that ran the full length of the building under the ceiling's arched beams. Light streamed in through another wall that was almost entirely windows, not good glass, green and bubbled, but glass all the same, and Eslingen was reminded instantly of a billet he'd once had south of Ivre. The town—it was a newly freed mercantile center—had offered them the use of the former landame's hall, and they'd discovered too late that the townspeople had already removed everything that was portable, including the wooden partition walls. The company had spent most of the summer sleeping in the single long room without even shutters to close the emptied window frames. It had been surprisingly comfortable—the weather had been ideal, the ventilation superb even in Ivre's heat—but the lack of privacy had become tiresome in the end.

This hall wasn't as big, but it was almost as empty, except for the rank of weapons that filled the far wall. There was a wild mix of blades, heavy cavalry swords and daggers long and short and lighter dueling weapons, as well as spontoons and a set of halberds and a handful of oddities like old-fashioned bucklers and mailed gloves, all seemingly in perfect condition, and Eslingen wondered just how much it had cost the Masters in fees to keep them all here, and not locked away at the Aretoncia. Outside the window, sunlight glittered on the river, the water cold and grey as steel, and the roofs of Point of Hearts on the far bank glowed red and blue in its light, but from the look of the sky, already filling with clouds, the light wouldn't last much longer. The air smelled of a cold stove and the river, tar and damp, and Eslingen flexed his shoulders under his coat. It was almost too cool now, but not once the fights began.

The admitting masters were already there, talking quietly at the far end of the hall, and there was a drummer, too, tuning her paniers in the farthest corner. The soft, dull notes filled the damp air like a live creature calling. Duca saw them coming, and moved to meet them, the other masters hanging back a little. There were three men and a woman, each one dressed as though for a different play, and Eslingen wondered again what he was letting himself in for. There was still time to refuse, to apologize politely and say that a mistake had been made, that he wasn't the man they were looking for. He could stand the embarrassment—except that Caiazzo would lose face, and that, Eslingen thought, was a responsibility he could not afford.

"Lieutenant," Duca said, and Eslingen sketched a bow, knowing he was committed. Caiazzo fell back a step, leaving him to his fate, and Eslingen glanced back to see him smiling faintly, as though the situation amused him.

"Master Duca."

"Welcome to our hall." Duca gestured widely, bringing the other masters forward. "My colleagues, proving master Sergeant Peyo Rieux, challenging masters Janne de Vicheau, Verre Siredy, and Urvan Soumet. My masters, the candidate Lieutenant Philip vaan Esling, formerly of Coindarel's Dragons."

The woman—Rieux—blinked once at that, but there was no other response. She and Duca would be the arbiters of the match, and Eslingen eyed the three men, wishing he knew more about the guild's rules and regulations. Soumet was short, but built like a young ox, with an ox's flat, expressionless face and liquid eyes, hair tied back under a sailor's kerchief that went oddly with his good linen. Of all of them, he was dressed for a match, coatless and barefoot; the other two were slim and elegant in well-cut coats and careful paint, but there the resemblance ended. One—de Vicheau?—was two fingers' breadth the taller, lean and severe, pale hair pulled back with a black ribbon that matched his breeches and the trim on his dark grey coat. He looked like a young landseur, and Eslingen wondered fleetingly if he was one of the Vidame of Vicheau's numerous progeny. She had at least half a dozen sons by as many fathers, all dropped as lightly as a dog whelps; she took ferocious care of her only daughter, and reportedly had settled a farm on the man who had sired her. But that was probably what he wanted people to think, Eslingen added silently. More likely he came from the town of Vicheau, and added the article to match his looks—*or Duca added it for him, the way he did for me.* The third man was dressed like a fop, his long hands painted with tiny golden suns to match the embroidered ones scattered across the wide skirts of his coat, but there were corded muscles beneath the paint, and Eslingen was not deceived. None of them were going to be easy opponents; about the best he could hope for was that they would choose styles that he could handle.

"Any objections?" Duca's tone made it clear the question was mere formality. "Then let's begin. Lieutenant, you understand the rules?"

Eslingen schooled his face to neutrality. "I've had them explained to me."

Duca smiled slightly, and Eslingen blinked. The trick of gesture really was very like Caiazzo himself. "Then you'll excuse me if I explain again." He gestured to the woman at his side. "Sergeant Rieux and I will be the judges of the match. It's our business to call the points, but we're also assessing style and performance. You'll fight each of the challengers—they're all full masters of the guild, in good standing—with their choice of weapon. If they choose a weapon you don't know, you may refuse, and another will be chosen, but two refusals will disqualify you. Do you understand?"

Eslingen nodded, newly aware of the stillness in the hall. Even the drummer had brought her pans to absolute silence, both palms flat against the drumheads. Duca might have agreed to Caiazzo's plan, but not all the masters were happy with it.

"Normally this is more of an event," Rieux said. "A public event. But, under the circumstances . . ."

"There are precedents," Siredy said easily, and the ox-faced man scowled.

"Performance is the test."

"Which is something that we, us here today, are more than capable of judging," Rieux said. It sounded like an old argument, and Soumet dipped his head.

"I'm not denying that, Sergeant. What I'm saying is we're not testing how the man will fight with a crowd looking on—no offense to anyone, Sergeant, to the lieutenant or to Master Duca, but we all know how different it is onstage."

De Vicheau sighed. "May we remember the reason for this test? He may never go onstage."

"But he'd be one of us," Soumet said.

"The point is that Gaifier's dead," Rieux said.

"He was hardly well last year," Siredy murmured. "And look how that went."

"But he'd won his place fairly in public battle," Soumet said. "Not like this."

"I can't do it alone," Rieux said. "And you, Urvan, are hardly the man to help me."

"I know my skills," Soumet said. "No one's ever complained of me."

He looked more than ever like an ox, and Duca lifted his hand. "Enough."

Instantly, Soumet fell silent, but Duca gave him a long look before he finally spoke. "The match continues. Have you decided your order?"

"Siredy won the toss," de Vicheau said.

"Very well. What weapon?"

"Dueling sword and dagger."

That was a relief, Eslingen thought—those were weapons he knew, even if he was hardly a duelist—and he risked a glance at Caiazzo. The merchant-venturer stood with his arms folded, visibly withdrawn from the occasion. *I brought you this far,* the stance seemed to say. *Now make the most of it.*

"Is that acceptable to you, Lieutenant?"

"Yes." Eslingen nodded.

"Then choose your weapons." Duca waved a hand at the racks against the wall, and Siredy moved smoothly toward them, already scanning the available blades. Eslingen took a quick breath, wondering when—or if—he could discard his coat, and moved to join him. The master gave him a soft smile from behind the mask of his paint, barely politeness, and gestured for him to choose first.

The very ordinariness of the movement did much to dispel the haze of ritual. This was something he knew, weapons and their use, and Eslingen scanned the racked blades with growing confidence. "May I try them?"

"Go ahead." It was Duca who answered, no surprise there, and Eslingen drew the first sword that looked suitable. It was good in the hand, heavy but well balanced and a little longer than he liked, and he slid it back in the rack to see if he could find a better. Its neighbor, a slightly lighter blade with the traces of silver inlay in the guard, was almost as good, but after a moment's hesitation, Eslingen went back to the heavier blade. Siredy looked like a finesse fighter; the weight could be an advantage. He chose a dagger as well, and then Siredy stepped up to the rack, pulling sword and dagger from among the ranked blades. De Vicheau came forward to take both sets of weapons, and Siredy quickly stripped off his coat, hanging it carefully over the shoulders of a target dummy. He removed his long bronze wig as well, placing it on the dummy's head, and in spite of everything Eslingen had to suppress a smile. For all his paint and vanity, Siredy's own hair was hopeless, far too red to hope that lemon-water would bleach it gold.

"Plastrons," Rieux said, and Eslingen stripped off his own coat to accept the padded jacket, let the woman fasten the straps at waist and shoulder. Duca did the same for Siredy, then motioned the two men into the center of the floor. Eslingen obeyed, swinging his arms to get the feel of the plastron and the weight of the weapons. The sun had vanished, but enough light streamed through the enormous windows that they would have no fear of shadows. Across the hall, Siredy stretched easily, and met his eye with a quick, almost conspiratorial smile.

"The bout is to three," Duca said, "unless the sergeant or I see a killing blow."

Behind him, Soumet made a face, but said nothing.

"Are you ready?"

"Ready," Siredy said, and Eslingen echoed him.

"Commence."

Siredy lifted his sword in a salute that swept instantly into a running attack. Eslingen had seen the move before, and swayed easily out of the slighter man's way. He parried the return stroke, and let himself wait to find the rhythm of the match. As he'd expected, Siredy fought with finesse, all quick strokes and clever bladework, but he lacked the raw strength that would allow him to bull his way through Eslingen's defenses. Eslingen let that guide him, let his own style shift to match the other's, meeting delicacy with strength, abandoning all his own favored moves for sheer brute force. Siredy won the first touch, and the second, but Eslingen took the next one with the return stroke, and took the next two in quick succession.

"Halt!"

Eslingen instantly grounded his blade, but Siredy flourished a salute. He wasn't really breathing hard, Eslingen realized, and felt the sweat running under his own plastron. So much for the cool air.

"Creditable," Rieux said, and Duca lifted a hand.

"Who's next?"

"I am." That was the ox, and Eslingen suppressed a groan, already guessing the other man's choice of weapon.

"What weapon?"

"Sword and roundshield." Soumet folded his arms across his chest.

"Lieutenant?"

Eslingen hesitated, then spread his hands. "I'm allowed a refusal?"

"One refusal," Duca said. He paused. "Do you refuse?"

I haven't fought with those weapons in—oh, it must be ten years, not since I was a common pikeman. One of us would get hurt, and that is certainly not the point today. Eslingen tried a polite smile, searching for the right words, and Soumet snorted.

"Even soldiers know sword and roundshield. Or don't you think you can win?"

I could take you. Eslingen swallowed the words, recognizing folly when he heard it, looked at Duca instead. "I haven't used sword and roundshield since I left the pike line. If this is a test and not a blood match, I must refuse. I can't promise your man's safety."

Rieux nodded, almost approvingly, but Duca's expression didn't change. "That is your one refusal, Lieutenant. Be certain."

Eslingen bowed, guessing the formality wouldn't hurt him. "I'm sure."

"Very well," Duca said. "Master Soumet, the candidate has refused your weapon. Choose another."

"Halberds," Soumet said, and behind him de Vicheau rolled his eyes. Duca frowned ponderously, and Soumet met his glare squarely. "It's a fair weapon—a listed weapon, and one we're actually going to use in this foolish play. I stand by my choice."

Duca's look did not bode well for the younger man's future career, but he turned to face Eslingen. "Lieutenant?"

"Halberds, then." Eslingen did his best to suppress a smirk. He'd been a sergeant far longer than he'd been a lieutenant, and the halberd was a line sergeant's weapon: this was a fight he knew he could handle. Apparently Soumet had been misled by the gentleman's name.

"Padding," Rieux said, and Siredy and de Vicheau brought out thickly quilted coats, the stuffing so thick from neck to groin that they looked liked oversized, swaddled infants. Eslingen let Siredy help him into the coat—the man had retrieved his wig, if not his coat, Eslingen saw with amusement—and secure the straps that would keep it in place. There were padded gauntlets as well, ungainly things like stiff mittens, and a padded hood, but all in all, Eslingen thought, one good blow from a regulation halberd could still break bones, even through the layers of felt and wadding. Then Siredy handed him the tasseled weapon, and Eslingen understood. It was only a stage copy of a halberd; the shaft was lighter, and the tiny ax-head at the peak—he tapped it to be sure—was only painted wood.

"Don't break it," Siredy said softly, and stepped away.

And that, Eslingen thought, might be harder than it looked. He was used to the real thing, a heavy oak shaft as thick as his wrist, with an iron sheathing running from the ax almost down to the grip. He swung it once, then again, trying to get the balance, and Duca said, "Ready?"

"Ready," Soumet answered promptly, and Eslingen nodded. "Ready."

Soumet came at him in a rush, using the halberd like a quarter-staff, feinting low and then high before landing a solid blow in Eslingen's ribs. Even through the padding, and even with the lighter weapon, it hurt, and Eslingen danced back, struggling to block the other man's blows while he caught his breath. He was looking bad, he knew, and failed to block a second painful strike. *One more*, he thought, *one more and I've lost*, but he couldn't seem to get the feel of the too-light weapon. He struck once, missed, landed a glancing blow off the block, and saw Rieux lift a hand, giving him the point. Soumet turned away, swearing under his breath, and Eslingen backed away, hardly able to blame the man. He needed a flashy way out, either by winning—not likely, not with Soumet outfighting him at every step—or by losing well. The halberd was light in his hands, too light, and he danced away from another rush, stumbling on the even floor. And then, suddenly, he knew, and shifted his grip on the shaft, sliding his hands apart as he lifted it to block another attack. Soumet's stick crashed between them, and the wood splintered under the blow. Eslingen dodged back, throwing away the pieces, and Soumet checked his follow-through barely in time.

"Halt!"

"A killing blow," Soumet cried, turning to Duca, but the big man shook his head.

"No. To the body only, if it had landed—"

"Which it didn't," Siredy said, to no one in particular, and Duca glared at him.

"The third hit, and the end of the bout. That's all."

"Sergeant—Master Rieux," Soumet said. "You can't stand by this."

"I can and I do," Rieux answered. Soumet looked as though he would have said more, but the woman drew herself up to her full height. "Enough! The match is ended. Be content with your victory. Though I for one will have words with you about weapons later."

Soumet subsided, scowling, and Eslingen submitted to having the padding pulled away from his body. He would be bruised, all right, he could feel half a dozen spots that would be agony in the morning—

but with luck, he told himself, he wouldn't stiffen until after this final bout. Siredy bundled the heavy coat away again, and Eslingen ran his fingers through his hair, loosening strands that clung to his forehead. Caiazzo was still in his corner, but sitting now, all at ease, and Eslingen wondered briefly who'd thought to fetch the stool.

"Water?" That was Siredy again, holding out a cup, and Eslingen took it gratefully. It had been on the stovetop—the masters clearly subscribed to the notion that cold water was dangerous to a fighting man—but he drank it down, glad of the relief.

"Master de Vicheau," Duca said. "You have the last bout."

De Vicheau bowed gracefully in answer. "I do, Master Duca."

"And your weapon?"

"Master Duca." De Vicheau bowed again. *They all know what's going to happen,* Eslingen thought suddenly. *They've got something planned, and I don't know what it is.*

"I cede choice of weapon, and replace it with a different challenge." De Vicheau waved a hand, and Rieux pulled open a cabinet that stood against the wall beside the drummer. There was something in it, a table on wheels, but a table covered with tiny, brightly painted figures that chimed softly as Rieux rolled it out into the light. Toy soldiers, Eslingen realized, a tiny—regiment? no, a company—all strung on wires in perfect rank and file, complete with flags and fife and drum, and in spite of himself, he glanced toward Caiazzo, to see the merchant-venturer frowning in what seemed to be honest confusion.

"Lieutenant Eslingen is called to our company to teach drill." De Vicheau smiled thinly. "I challenge him to put our little company through its paces."

Duca bowed in return, and looked at Eslingen. "Lieutenant?"

"I have a question first." Eslingen took a breath. He'd boasted once, years ago, that he could drill pigs if he had to; he'd been drunk, but it seemed that the words were coming back to haunt him. "I've never seen such a thing. How is it done?"

Soumet sneered at him, but Duca said, "No great trick to it, Lieutenant. The figures are set on wires and moved by gears and levers. Sergeant Rieux will work the mechanism, and move them as you call."

And she could destroy him if she wanted, Eslingen realized, but doubted somehow that she would cheat him. As if she guessed the thought, she smiled crookedly, and settled herself behind the table.

Eslingen looked back at Duca. "I accept, then. Will your drummer there give the cadence?"

"She will."

"Then set the figure." Eslingen looked at de Vicheau, whose fair head lifted in answer.

"To a hollow square, and then back to ranks."

Not the easiest figure, but not the hardest—and mercifully not one of the drillbook figures, stars and moons and octagons, that amateurs made up in winter quarters. Eslingen took a deep breath, marshaling old skills, and looked at the drummer. "Sound the march."

Instantly, the familiar beat filled the room, the heavy music almost palpable, and Eslingen said, "Forward march."

Instantly, the metal figures began to move, the mechanism clinking in time to the drum, and Eslingen realized there wouldn't be enough room if they kept going straight ahead. "About-face."

The figures turned, not quite as one—the machine was as real there as most regiments he'd served in—and he gave the next command. "Files to the right hand double."

There was a louder clank, and the lines lengthened and thinned. It was almost easier, seeing them from above like this, and he gave the next commands automatically, bringing the lines out still farther, hollowing out the column until he could turn them all outward, then brought them back again into column, finishing with a flourish as he turned them to face de Vicheau again.

"Silence, the drums."

The music stopped instantly, without the usual ruffle, and de Rieux straightened from the table. "Neatly done, Lieutenant."

"Indeed." Duca stepped forward, holding out his hand. "Master Lieutenant vaan Esling, allow me to be the first to welcome you as a Master of Defense."

So it was real, Eslingen thought, automatically accepting the other man's hand. It had really happened, and he was really one of them. In spite of everything, there was a part of him that felt like laughing, and he hoped this wasn't the folly he'd been warned against. Rieux nodded briskly, offering a calloused palm, and then de Vicheau and Siredy and, finally, Soumet. At least the ox had the grace to swallow his temper, Eslingen thought, and braced his fingers against the other's grasp. Caiazzo had risen to his feet, and came forward now, his smile matching Duca's.

"Congratulations, Philip. I can count you well bestowed, then."

"And I'm grateful, Master Caiazzo," Eslingen answered automatically, and then wondered how much time he'd have to get his belongings out of Caiazzo's house—and where he'd be living, for that matter.

"This is much more suitable for someone of your station," Caiazzo answered, and there was laughter in his black eyes. "So I'll leave you to it."

"Master Caiazzo—" Eslingen stopped, not quite knowing how to ask, and the merchant-venturer's smile became an open grin.

"Oh, you can send for your goods as soon as you're settled, Philip. There's no hurry, I'm sure."

"No, none," Eslingen repeated. Particularly since he didn't actually know where he would be sleeping. Oh, Rathe would give him house room until he found something else, but he didn't like to assume that he was that completely welcome. He shoved the thought aside, knowing Caiazzo had seen and was amused by the hesitation, and the merchant-venturer nodded to Duca.

"And I leave him to you. Good day, masters."

"And a good day to you," Duca answered, but Caiazzo was already starting down the stairs. The senior master sighed, and looked back at his people. "Under the circumstances, my masters, I trust none of you will object to starting at once to work."

Eslingen shook his head, recognizing an order when he heard it, and the others murmured their agreement. The panier rumbled as the drummer slacked the heads and covered them, and Duca put his hands on his hips.

"Right, then. The sides are ready, so we'd better take a look at them."

"I'll take the lieutenant," Rieux said, "and Siredy, if I may."

Duca nodded. "Janne, you'll work with me, and you, Urvan, can see what Mistress Gasquine wants for her people. And bring back something in writing, this time, if you have to draw it up yourself."

The flat-faced man scowled, but made no protest. Eslingen wondered briefly just how his manners were going to be received in the playhouse, and then Siredy tapped him on the shoulder.

"This way. And again, congratulations."

Eslingen followed the slighter man back down the stairs and into the library. The lace-capped woman was still there, still frowning over her stacks of papers, but as the others entered, she set aside her pen and tapped them into order.

"The sides are done, Master Duca, and one full copy."

She wore a Scriveners badge on her bodice, Eslingen saw, with some surprise—he would never have expected the Masters of Defense to employ a copyist—and Duca nodded absently. "Thank you, Auriol. We'll try not to disturb you too much."

"Not at all, master," the woman answered, demurely, and scooped up one of the stacks of paper. She retreated with it to a smaller table in the corner, and a moment later light flared as she lit a lamp and resumed her work, pen scratching over the paper.

"Now, my masters," Duca said. The papers were odd cuts, Eslingen saw, long and thin like the broadsheets that listed upcoming plays. Duca flipped through one, and then methodically handed a stack to each of the others. Eslingen took his curiously, skimming the half dozen pages. Each one held a few lines of dialogue, and then a description of an action—a battle and a dance, on the first page, and more of the same on each of the others. He looked up, confused, and Duca cleared his throat.

"Understand, my masters, I say this only because we have a newcomer among us, one who isn't familiar with our ways—and you, Lieutenant, understand I mean no disrespect, and don't touch on your honor at all. But the play is not yet published, will not be published until after the masque, and it is our bond to keep as much of the plot secret as we may. I hope we all understand that."

Eslingen murmured his agreement with the rest, wondering how much good it would do. The Masters might keep their mouths shut, but there were still the actors to consider, and the scenerymen, and, worst of all, the noble chorus. The playwright was going to be lucky if there was only one pirate copy circulating by midwinter.

"So." Duca paused, and Siredy lifted his head, shaking the strands of his wig back over his shoulders.

"So how bad is it, master?"

"Bad enough." Duca glanced down at his papers, though Eslingen doubted the man needed to refer to them. "There are five battle-pieces, and six drills, plus a sword-dance that may or may not become our responsibility, and, of course, the individual duels."

"How many of those are part of larger battles?" de Vicheau asked.

"About half." Duca rustled his papers again. "Including a climax that will have to stay in the piece, so it'll have to work with and without chorus."

Eslingen looked at the top sheet again. The familiar sloping letters ran across the narrow page, two lines of dialogue, then a call for trumpets, and then a battle in which one side had to seem to win, but be defeated at the last possible moment. Below that, the scrivener had drawn a neat line, and begun again with dialogue, an unnamed queen calling for entertainment. The script called for a company of Hasiri, the wild nomads who lived on the roof of the world, to show their skill with weapons. Eslingen blinked at that—from what he knew of the Hasiri, showing their skill meant hiding behind rocks to pick off stragglers from the caravans, not exactly the kind of drill that the script seemed to want—and he looked up to see Siredy grinning at him.

"Better you than me, Lieutenant."

"Right, then," Duca said. "Siredy, Janne, you break down the duels. Sergeant, you and the lieutenant and I will take a look at the drills. Just to see what we've got in hand."

Siredy nodded, rising easily to take a seat next to de Vicheau, and Rieux edged her chair closer.

"All right, Lieutenant, what do you think of when you think of Hasiri weapons?"

"Bow, slingshot, the occasional lock," Eslingen answered warily, and Duca chimed in heavily.

"And a taste for ambush. But we can work with bows, I think."

"If you can train the chorus not to use them," Rieux said.

"No bowstrings, maybe," Duca said. "But bows are a good start. And the first battle."

"Sashes for the chorus, to tell the sides?" Rieux asked, and Duca shrugged.

"Probably. Depends on how much they want to spend on it."

"And how big is the chorus this year?" Rieux frowned at the paper in front of her, then reached into her own wide sash for a set of wax tablets.

"Three dozen," Duca answered.

"Thank Seidos we have the Tyrseia, then," de Vicheau said, and earned a glare from the senior master.

"Fifteen to a side, then," Rieux said. "That leaves half a dozen for other work, and shouldn't crowd things too badly."

Eslingen rested his elbows on the table, wondering again what he'd gotten himself into. There was nothing he could contribute to this discussion, at least not so far, and at the moment he was inclined to think that Soumet was right, maybe he didn't belong in this company. He was a soldier, not a player, he had no idea what would look good onstage, only of what would be effective in an actual battle. . . . As if she'd read his thought, Rieux grinned at him.

"Oh, don't worry, Lieutenant, you'll earn your keep later. At the drills."

By the end of the day, Eslingen was exhausted, more from trying to absorb too many new ways of thinking than from the earlier fights, though the bruises he had earned earlier were making their presence felt. He paused outside the guildhall's main door to ease them, and stood for a moment, abruptly at a loss. It was strange, strange and a little unnerving, to be suddenly without a place again, perhaps even more at sea than he'd been when he'd first come to Astreiant. A shadow moved to his left, and he turned, not sure if it was a passerby, or a ghost, or even a late-working pickpocket. For an instant, he thought he saw something, recognized if not a face then the set of the shoulders, but then the door opened again behind him, spilling light into the street, and the foppish master, Siredy, paused, holding the door open for Rieux. He smiled, seeing the other man.

"Join us, why don't you, Philip? We're going to Anric's to drink and curse Chresta Aconin's name."

Eslingen laughed out loud. "That sounds very tempting, but I need to—regularize my living arrangements."

Both the other masters nodded in sympathy, and Siredy tipped his head to one side, the wig falling in precise curls across his chest. "If you need a place," he offered, but Eslingen shook his head. He was not precisely out of doors, if he would just admit it to himself.

"Thank you, but I think I'm settled. I just need to make arrangements to have my things brought there."

"Ah. Well, a good evening to you then, Philip," Rieux said, kindly enough. "I hope you get yourself sorted out." And then they were gone, arm in arm, Siredy bending gracefully to listen to the older master, heading up the street that led away from the river, into the closer environs of Point of Dreams. Eslingen watched them for a moment, not sure if he envied them, until the chill breeze from the river stirred his hair. The sun was down, and it would be cold. And he needed to let Rathe know that he had company.

Point of Dreams came alive at sunset, actors released from their day's labor or heading to small-shows joining early lovers on their way to Point of Hearts and pleasure-seekers from all over the city. Eslingen dodged the crowds, trying not to laugh at the way that fate seemed to be making the move neither he nor Rathe had been able to, at least to this point. Despite Meening's warning, he felt sure this was not folly. But neither was it the way he would have seen them living together, not as this chance throw, without warning, or even an offer made, and certainly no time to let Rathe know until he appeared on the man's doorstep. At that thought, he paused, scanning the stalls of the night market, mindful of his finances, but also remembering what Duca had said about their potential earnings from the masque. A share should be substantial, if he understood it correctly. And if he was going to move in with Rathe, and he fervently hoped that was the case, he was determined not to give folly a foothold, but come bearing gifts, or at least provisions. The stalls here were mostly broadsheets—and of *The Drowned Island*, at that, not the sort of gift he needed at all—and he looked in vain for a cookshop. Maybe wine would be better anyway, he thought, and wished for the first time that b'Estorr were around to advise him. The necromancer knew wine, give him that, was as much the gentleman as Duca had been looking for. . . . He smiled then. b'Estorr bought his wine from Wicked, and Wicked would know what Rathe liked. He would throw himself on her mercy, and she would see him safe.

The tavernkeeper was as good as he'd hoped, finding the right wine and throwing in a decent loaf for good measure, and he made his way back to the Dreams point station as the city clocks struck six, the chimes filling the air with discordant music. The station showed its military past more than most of the points stations, almost like an ancient castle, something out of the Leaguer hills, heavy-walled and short of windows, blocking the end of the street like a slumbering beast. It had been a garrison and an armory, he remembered Rathe mentioning, just as the other stations had been, and it was probably just the darkness that gave it an eldritch look.

There were half a dozen runners in the yard in spite of the cold, bundled in oversized coats and jerkins that looked as though they'd been handed down from mothers or older siblings, dodging from base to base in an intricate game of chase by the light of a half-dozen lanterns, and he half expected them to ask his business. The runners at Point of Hopes would have done so, he thought, or maybe that was just because they'd known him; one of the boys glanced at him, but a girl shouted, and he turned back to the game. Eslingen suppressed a wry smile. Dismissed, for the second time today.

The station's main room was much bigger than the room at Point of Hopes, and the air was warm and dry, smelling of herbs and smoke and tobacco instead of the points' reheated dinners. There was the familiar row of jerkins hanging on the far wall, ready to hand, and the low bench opposite where malefactors or those in trouble could sit and wait the points' pleasure, but the tall case-clock that stood beside the stairs was something unexpected, a beautiful piece that showed solar and lunar phases as well as the time. Tiny gilded hunt-resses and their dogs chased each other around the box where the block itself stood, and a forest of vines climbed the edges of the case, creatures peering out from among the leaves. Eslingen blinked, won-dering where that had come from—surely the points couldn't afford that fine clock on their own—and someone cleared her throat behind him.

"Can I help you, master?"

It was a young man, Eslingen saw, turning, a young man shaved to perfection, whose spotless linen and sober coat were badly at odds with his rough jerkin and pointsman's truncheon.

"Yes. I was wondering if Adjunct Point Rathe is available," he said, and saw the other man's eyes travel quickly over his own clothes, visibly assessing quality and cost. Whatever he saw made him come forward, waving for a less fashionable pointswoman to take his place behind the station's daybook.

"Yes, he is, master. Allow me to show him to you."

"I wouldn't want to interrupt," Eslingen offered, but the other shook his head.

"No interruption at all, sir."

"I meant to Rathe," Eslingen murmured, but softly enough that the young man could pretend he hadn't heard. Out of the corner of his eye, Eslingen thought he saw the woman hide a grin behind the tip of her quill, and schooled himself to follow the pointsman with due decorum. The man led him up the stairs and around the bulge of the massive central chimney, paused there to knock on a closed door. There was an indistinct mumble in response, which the points-man seemed to take for permission, and pushed open the door. "Someone to see you, Adjunct Point."

Rathe was sitting at a worktable set to catch the best light from the now-shuttered window, and looked up with a frown that faded as he saw who was with the pointsman. "All right, Voillemin, thanks. I'll see Lieutenant Eslingen."

Voillemin stepped back with a movement that was almost a bow, and Eslingen edged past him into the little room. It was warmer than he'd expected, given the expanse of window, and he realized that there was another little stove in the far corner. He held his hands out to it as the door closed behind him, wondering if Rathe would offer him some of the tea that stood steeping on the hob, and realized that his own smile was distinctly nervous.

Rathe leaned back in his chair. "And to what do I owe the pleasure, Lieutenant? Have a seat, you look tired."

"Thank you," Eslingen said sourly, but his muscles were stiffening again, and he was glad of the chair. Not for the first time that day, he wished he'd practiced harder while he was in Caiazzo's service. "Well, in one of those whirlwind changes of fate that seem to be my lot in life, I am officially no longer Caiazzo's knife."

"Not precisely unexpected," Rathe said. In the lamplit shadows, it was hard to read his expression, but his voice was dry.

"No, but sudden. Caiazzo finds his opportunities and takes them, let me tell you. Though you're probably the last person I need to tell that," Eslingen added, shaking his head. "Nor has he precisely cast me out into the streets . . ."

"You've got to stop going to the theatre," Rathe murmured. "Where'd he find you a place, then?"

Eslingen took a breath. "You are now looking at the newest member of the Masters of the Guild of Defense."

Rathe whistled soundlessly, the chair returning to the floor with a definite thump. "Gods, that's—well, it would be unbelievable, if it weren't Caiazzo."

"Because he seems able to get whatever he wants?" Eslingen asked. Rathe cocked his head, was looking amused.

"Because Gerrat Duca is his cousin, actually, as well as the other. Did you have to try for a place?"

Eslingen nodded. "Three bouts, at the guildhall today. Apparently I performed creditably enough."

"Which means," Rathe said slowly, "you'll be involved with the masque—Aconin's damned *Alphabet*."

"You know about that," Eslingen said, and didn't know why he was surprised.

"They told us two days ago, actually," Rathe said. "As soon as the chamberlains made their decision." He tipped his head to one side, slid a sheet of paper a little larger than a broadsheet across the tabletop. "What do you actually know about the masque, Philip?"

Eslingen reached for the announcement—it proclaimed Aconin's play the winner in two short lines, then went on to give a series of orders for the points stations, and Point of Dreams in particular—and set the sheet back on the table. "Mostly what I've heard from Caiazzo, which isn't much, and most of that was scathing. And what little I heard about the guild's work today. Hasiri, demonstrating their abilities with weapons, proving once again, I suppose, that Chresta Aconin has an outstanding imagination if he thinks rock throwing is a particularly difficult skill to master."

"Not his chosen weapon," Rathe muttered. Eslingen glanced curiously at him, wondering what had provoked the unmistakable bitterness of his tone, but the pointsman was already hurrying on, his voice consciously lighter. "It's supposed to be better for the masses than the usual run of play—"

"Like *The Drowned Island*?" Eslingen asked, and was pleased to see Rathe grin.

"It also reinforces the health of the country and the health of the queen. It's not so much the subject matter, but you'll see certain patterns appear in every single masque, esoteric ones—that's why there has to be a noble chorus, or so I'm told. That's in addition to the displays and drills you'll be working on, and that's why it takes all day, to get things done in more or less the right signs."

Eslingen sighed, trying to imagine fitting magistical workings into a show that already felt unwieldy. "Sounds like a very uneasy mating of Tyrseis and Seidos."

Rathe nodded. "Yeah, to my thought, but . . ." He shrugged. "It's a holiday at the darkest day of the year, and it reinforces the queen's rule. And every single point station in the city is expected to offer support to Point of Dreams."

"So it's no holiday for you, either," Eslingen said.

"Afraid not."

They sat silent for a moment, Eslingen wondering uneasily how he was going to raise the subject of his presence. Something scraped against the windowpane, and he jumped, knowing it had to be a tree branch. Rathe frowned, opened his mouth, and Eslingen spoke first, not wanting the other to have to ask what he'd come for.

"The thing of it is, Nico . . ." The last thing he wanted was to beg space from the other, when what he wanted was something more. He didn't want to phrase it like that, either; this was a bad time for

declarations, when it would sound like mere expedience. "Nico, I'm
out of doors, and this is not the way I would have wanted to handle
it, but would you be willing to have me—living with you?"

Rathe sat very still for a moment, his expression suddenly sober.
"I think I could tolerate that, Lieutenant," he said at last.

Eslingen hesitated, wary of the other man's tone, and did his best
to keep his own voice matter-of-fact. "It needn't be for long. Just
until I can find a place of my own."

Rathe looked up sharply, glass-green eyes widening in the lamplight. "That wasn't—" He shook his head. "I'm sorry, Philip, it's been
a trying day. We went before the regents first thing, and it hasn't
improved much since, with all the preparations for the masque."

"What did the regents want?" Eslingen asked, and Rathe grimaced.

"No, they didn't summon us, it was Holles who went before
them." He shook his head. "I'm not making sense, am I?"

Eslingen shook his head in answer. "Not really."

That raised the ghost of a smile. "Holles was the leman of an
intendant who died recently—Bourtrou Leussi, I don't know if I've
mentioned him, but I tell you, I missed him today. He was the senior
chamberlain, and no fool, not like the man they put in his place.
Tyrseis help the actors, with him in charge instead of Leussi!" Rathe
stopped, sighing. "But that's not to the point. The point is, Leussi's
dead, it's ghost-tide, and his leman hasn't felt his ghost."

Eslingen frowned. "I don't—had they quarreled?"

"Holles believes he was murdered," Rathe said flatly. "And the
ghost bound. Istre concurs, and the two of them—with me and Trijn
for support—spent this morning trying to persuade the regents that
the matter should be reopened."

"It sounds as though there's cause," Eslingen said cautiously. He
didn't like to think about the implications, about the pain of death
redoubled by the absent ghost, and was relieved when Rathe nodded.

"Oh, yes, I'd say so. Which is what I was there to say to the
regents, for all the good it did me or Holles." He grimaced. "You
didn't hear me say that."

"Hear what?" Eslingen paused. "You weren't—no, the matter
was given to someone else, wasn't it?"

"Just so." Rathe smiled again, without humor. "The man who
brought you up here, in actual fact."

Eslingen made a face in turn. "Not that I know anything against him, but—"

"You'd be guessing right just from the cut of his coat." Rathe sighed. "And there I'm being unfair. He's not a bad man, just not—proved, I suppose."

"Like a back-and-breast." Eslingen nodded, and Rathe reached for the scattered papers, tapping them into an untidy stack. He set a slate on top of them, letters imperfectly erased from its surface, and pushed himself to his feet, stretching.

"So, you can imagine, your arrival—your staying with me, since it's come to that—is the best thing that's happened all day."

Eslingen grinned, relieved in spite of himself, and Rathe nodded to the basket at the other man's feet.

"And if that's a bottle of wine, I'm at your service forever."

"And if it's a bottle of good wine?" Eslingen asked. Rathe, damping down the fire in the stove, grinned.

"Then we'll have to see, won't we?"

3

Rathe edged into the crowded room, trying to be as inconspicuous as possible until he tested the wind of the surintendant's temper. Oh, he was supposed to be there, along with the forty-some-odd senior points from all the districts, plus a few fellows of the university, but he was supposed to be there in company with his own chief point, and Trijn had flatly refused the summons. *You go,* she had said, handing him the much-sealed paper. *If I have to deal with Fourie this morning, I'll be kicking dogs by noontime.*

And I would hate very much to be the one who relays that message to our good Surintendant of Points, he thought, and found a place in a shadowed corner. Of course, that would probably be the first place Fourie would look for him, but maybe he could catch a brief nap, if the stars favored him.

He sighed softly, letting his eyes roam over the crowd. Not just senior points and the fellows mentioned in the summons, he saw, but a cluster of advocats resplendent in full scarlet robes and tall black caps, and he wondered what they were doing here. Probably to discuss prosecution of any points called, he decided, and wished he could afford a nap. The new play, based as it was on the so-called verifiable edition of spring-time rumor, was bidding fair to become a major headache for points and university alike—already, according to the summons, at least four printers had registered their intent to reprint just that edition of the Alphabet, and that meant that at least a dozen more were working on similar volumes without bothering to ask for license. Not to mention the flower merchants, who were happy to raise the price on every bulb or corm mentioned in play or book, and to force blooms out of season at equally exorbitant prices. . . . Someone, probably a lot of someones, was bound to cry fraud, and the surintendant wanted to discuss their options in detail. Personally, Rathe was inclined to let the buyers settle it among themselves, but he knew that was mostly exhaustion speaking. He had not quite adjusted to having Eslingen in his rooms on what seemed to be a semipermanent basis—and, frankly, this wasn't the way he would have chosen to acquire a new lover, not out of necessity and the sense that he owed the other man a place, since Eslingen had lost two positions because of him. *But I do want him living with me, it's just*—He shook his head, not quite able to articulate his disappointment. *I want him on my terms, not these. And that is damned foolish, and I'd do very well to get over that, stop mooning over romance like something out of a bad play.*

"So, Nico, how are you enjoying life at Dreams?"

Rathe looked up in honest pleasure, recognizing the voice of his former chief at Point of Hopes. "It's interesting, I'll say that for it. How are things in Hopes?"

Tersennes Monteia shrugged, her long horse-face wry. "That ass Ranaczy managed to fall down a ladder at the Maiden. Probably collecting his fee."

Rathe choked at the image—Ranaczy had never been a favorite of his—and struggled for a suitable comment. "Not dead, I hope."

Monteia snorted. "Not that one. But he'll be out of my hair for a while, at least. And everyone else's. It's just a pity he didn't land on something more vulnerable than his head. I've moved Salineis up, and with luck I can make it permanent."

A familiar voice called her name—Guillen Claes, the chief at Fair's Points—and she touched Rathe's shoulder in apology, moving to answer. Left to himself, Rathe looked around for further distraction, and to his mild surprise spotted Istre b'Estorr ducking through the heavy doors. The magist wasn't wearing university robes, and Rathe suspected the ghost-tide was beginning to wear on him already. Accustomed to ghosts the necromancer might be, but the sheer numbers during the tide could overwhelm even the best of them, and the strain was showing in b'Estorr's face. The dark grey robes would only accentuate his pallor, and the Chadroni was just vain enough to dislike the notion. Instead, he wore a dark red coat trimmed with embroidered wheat sheaves that matched his pale hair, and Rathe hid a smile, thinking that Eslingen would have snarled with envy. He lifted a hand, beckoning, and the other man moved to join him, his grim expression easing.

"The sur's in an ugly frame of mind," Rathe said, "if he's calling you lot in already."

b'Estorr glanced around. "And overreacting, surely."

"Fourie never does anything by halves," Rathe answered. He glanced sideways at the Chadroni, realizing he hadn't seen the man in weeks—*not since I started seeing Philip*—and winced inwardly at the dark circles under his eyes. "You all right?"

b'Estorr nodded, his eyes closing briefly, and Rathe realized that, in this room and at this time, there had to be a clamorous presence of ghosts. Bad enough outside the ghost-tide, the room was full of pointswomen and advocats, all of whom could be expected to have their own dead, but with the tide on the rise, there would be the timely dead to face, as well. He had felt his own Mud scurrying at his feet on the way into Dreams that morning. He was only vaguely aware of the presence of b'Estorr's own ghosts, usually an almost tangible presence, today damped down almost to nothing by the pressure of so many others.

"My students are, as usual, clamoring for me to cancel classes," b'Estorr said. "As are a few of the other masters. As if closing the shutters and going to bed with your head under a pillow for a week will help. It doesn't."

Rathe did his best to repress a grin—the thought of the elegant Chadroni cowering in his rooms was almost too good to bear. "It'll be over soon," he said. That was true enough; the lunar conjunctions were never long-lived, and the ghost-tide had only a few more days to run. Less than the current climate of foolishness, he thought, and b'Estorr nodded as though the other man had spoken aloud.

"This madness won't, though." The necromancer's voice was unwontedly grim.

Rathe nodded in commiseration, just as the door at the far end of the room opened abruptly, admitting two of the Tour's ushers, elegant in forest-green livery. One held the doors open while his senior slammed his heavy staff on the floor, drawing all eyes. He struck again, unnecessarily, and Rathe's eyes were drawn in spite of himself to the royal emblem that topped it. It was identical to the one that capped his own truncheon, his badge of office, and he ran his thumb over the worn metal. He was part of the royal household, in a sense, just as the ushers were.

"Masters all," the usher announced. "Rainart Fourie, Surintendant of Points."

Fourie swept in before the words were quite out of his mouth, lifting a hand in acknowledgment of courtesies already begun. He was dressed in his usual narrow black, unrelieved except for the flawless linen at neck and cuffs, and as usual he had forgone the wig that would look so foolish on his long and melancholy face. A clerk scuttled at his heels, tablets ready, and a young woman in a judicial gown followed him, eyes downcast, her hands folded in her sleeves. Behind her, another liveried usher held a brass orrery at the ready.

"Masters all," Fourie began, and the silence seemed to deepen as each one of them came to attention. "We're faced with an unusual situation. A midwinter masque that promises to become a popular hit."

That broke the silence, a ripple of laughter running around the room, but Fourie continued as though he hadn't heard. "Based on a work that seems to catch the popular imagination on a fairly regular basis. Combine the play with last year's rumor of an authentic *Alphabet*, and we have the possibility for massive fraud and more in the marketplaces. That is why I want the university to consult with us on this, and possibly in particular the college of necromancy. There are, by what is admittedly a rough count of a fluid situation, thirty-five licensed printers in the city. Licensed. There is an unofficial count of another forty or fifty unlicensed printers working at any one time. And all of them, my masters, will be printing copies of the Alphabet of Desire."

Rathe rolled his eyes to the painted ceiling, wondering why Fourie was telling them something they all already knew. A painted gargoyle peered back at him through a painted hole in the roof, its expression as disapproving as Fourie's, and he dragged his attention back to the lecture.

"They will be printing copies of the Alphabet because the people of this city will want, already want, to buy it, and this play will only feed that hunger." Fourie's long mouth drew down in a frown that rivaled the gargoyle's. "Many will want it as a curiosity, because it's the must-have of this particular season, and their copies will gather dust and be sent for kindling in a twelve-month. Some, however, will buy it because of what they believe it can do, the knowledge it can impart."

Rathe pulled himself up a little straighter at that. Of course, that was why Fourie wanted the university there, and the necromancers in particular. The Alphabet of Desire was just that, a book of formulae arranged in the order of the letters, formulae for flower arrangements designed to give the maker the desire of her heart, from true love to lust, to money, to power, to death. There was no way to tell, to certify, that the arrangements in any given edition would work at all, or work the way they were supposed to, without trying each one, and it would take a university-trained magist to make the assay without causing more harm, unless the necromancers could read the possibility of power the way they read the possibility of ghosts. But it was interesting to see that there were no university phytomancers present. He glanced sideways at b'Estorr, made a note to ask him about that.

"The timing," Fourie continued, "is unfortunate. May I remind you all that Her Majesty has promised to name her true successor after the turn of the year?"

As if we hadn't been hearing that for the last three years, Rathe thought, looking up at the gargoyle again. Although this time, it seemed to be true: with the Starchange approaching, the Starsmith moving from one sign to the next in its ponderously slow transit of its zodiac, the queen was finally running out of time to delay. The change of sign always signaled upheaval, or so the old text claimed; for the health of the kingdom, the queen would have to name her successor before that transit began.

"I am not one to doubt the wisdom of the regents," Fourie went on, and there was another ripple of suppressed laughter. The surintendant had a deserved reputation for quarreling with the regents, usually in defense of his own people. "But Her Majesty's decision has brought many of the potential candidates to Astreiant at a time when the madness for the Alphabet has sprung back to life, and we cannot ignore the conjunction." He paused, his eyes skimming over the audience. "On top of that, I'm concerned about keeping the peace in the marketplaces, especially those districts with large markets. There were some squabbles last spring over the corms—"

"Squabbles," a pointswoman standing in front of Rathe said, under her breath. She leaned close to a colleague, shoving up her faded sleeve to display a long white scar. "That's what one of those 'squabbles' got me, a knife in the arm."

"—but I'm afraid those will be as nothing compared to what we're likely to see now. We're in an unfortunate sign right now." Fourie paused, beckoned to the usher and the young woman in the judicial gown. "As you well know. The ghost-tide keeps us busy enough, but we also have to contend with a figure that seems to enhance the inherent foolishness of people."

"He's a loving soul," b'Estorr murmured, and Rathe stifled a laugh.

"Believes the best of people, Fourie does."

"And there's your explanation for *The Drowned Island*," the necromancer went on, closing his eyes as the younger astrologer made final, minute adjustments to the orrery.

"A question, Surintendant." The voice came from the front of the group, where the chief of Temple Point and the chancellor of the university sat side by side in matching chairs. That was a little daring of Fourie, Rathe thought. Under no other circumstances would even the most senior of the chiefs rank equal to the university's head. It was Temple Point who had spoken, her voice even and cultured, and for an instant Rathe wished Trijn had been forced to attend. Only the chiefs were expected to speak at these gatherings. "Do we have any chance of calling a point on the factors, if there's trouble, or are we left to deal with the petty dealers?"

Fourie's severe face relaxed into something like a smile. "The advocacy has been consulted on that, Chief Point. They hold that the factors are within their rights to take whatever the market will bear, and so the smaller dealers may—and will—do likewise."

"If they make claims outside the ordinary," Temple Point went on, "may we call it fraud?"

"If you think you and yours can make the point," Fourie said, "by all means."

Rathe laughed at that, knowing the sound was rueful, heard the same note echoing in the room. It was unlikely any of them could get such a point upheld, given the nature of the corms and the nature of the book, but at least the surintendant had given a qualified sort of approval.

"That does raise an interesting question, Surintendant." This was the chancellor, her voice deep and smoky, vivid contrast to the grey robes and pale lace. "An arrangement that turned out to be harmless—would the points call that a fraud, if it did no harm when it was designed in fact to kill?"

Fourie bowed slightly. "That, Madame Chancellor, would be a matter for the advocacy to decide. But the point could be called, I believe."

"Wonderful," Rathe said, and didn't realize he'd spoken aloud until b'Estorr jogged his elbow. But the surintendant's decision put all the burden on the points, on the individual pointswomen and -men, not on their chiefs—though to be fair, Rathe thought, he was probably right about the advocacy having the final say. And from the look of them, the row of women resplendent in scarlet and black, professionally inscrutable beneath their tall caps, they weren't prepared to give an opinion until they had an actual case before them.

There were more questions then, one from each of the chief points—restating Temple's questions, mostly, Rathe thought, with another glance at the ceiling—and then from several of the university officers, before Fourie finally nodded to the usher.

"I think that's all that needs to be said on the matter. For my people: be aware. Make sure all the printers in your districts are aware, as quickly as possible. And I want peace kept in the markets. I don't want trouble marring this masque."

"All rise," the usher called, and Temple Point and the chancellor rose gracefully to their feet. The second usher swung the doors open with a flourish, and Fourie swept out, the two women following him in a rush of satin. Rathe stretched surreptitiously, watching the other chiefs and adjuncts clustering around the orrery, a few of the advocats peering over their shoulders. It was early yet, and they were glad of the excuse to linger, like schoolchildren on holiday. Unfortunately, he needed to be back at Dreams, to give Trijn her report as soon as possible, and he turned toward the door, suddenly aware that b'Estorr was at his heels. The Chadroni smiled.

"Mind if I walk with you?"

"Of course not," Rathe answered, and felt lighter for the company.

They left the Tour by the side door that opened onto Clockmakers' Square, crossed the faded stones that had once sketched the face of a clock across the open marketplace. A lot of them were missing, or their colors had faded beyond recognition, but in the far corner a trio of laborers was working under the supervision of a clockmaker's journeyman, pulling up stones to replace them with another. A cold day for it, Rathe thought, and drew his own coat more closely around his shoulders. The wind was strong, from the north, not the river,

and the sky was the pale flat grey that meant snow was coming soon.
An early winter meant a long one; it seemed the almanacs were in
accord this year.

"How's Philip?" b'Estorr asked, and Rathe started.

"He's well—ah. I haven't had a chance to tell you. He's no longer
with Caiazzo." He could feel his face heating, hoped b'Estorr would
take it for the wind, but the Chadroni was minding his steps on the
uneven cobbles, and at least pretended not to notice.

"That must be a relief for both of you," he said. "Where has he
fetched up this time?"

"I think Hanse has done better by him than I did," Rathe answered. He remembered all too well b'Estorr's appalled reaction
when he'd first found Eslingen the position with Caiazzo. "He's got
a place with the Masters of the Guild of Defense."

"Really?" b'Estorr looked impressed. "I may see him there some
time, then; I exercise there. When I can." He smiled. "So he'll be
involved with the masque as well."

"Yes," Rathe said slowly, and b'Estorr shook his head.

"Never mind. I should be surprised by this, but I'm not." He
grinned suddenly, the movement transforming his rather sober face.
"In the midst of all this—folly—this feels like something else. Congratulations."

And in the midst of everything that was going on, he felt reas-
sured, trusting b'Estorr's knowledge the way Eslingen trusted the
better class of broadsheet astrologers. He matched the taller man's
stride with automatic ease, at once like and completely unlike the
ease he felt with Eslingen. There were no demands here, no complex
expectations on either side, just an unlikely friendship that had sprung
full-blown from the first moment he'd asked for a necromancer's help
to make a difficult point. *And, speaking of that. . . .*

"Do you think we're likely to see an increase in 'accidental' deaths
because of the Alphabet?" he asked.

"Alphabets," b'Estorr corrected, accepting the change of subject
without surprise. "It's hard to say. My own understanding is that the
Alphabet is at once extremely precise and rather vague. You would
have to read it carefully, and fully, to make anything in it work. I
don't know if it can—go off—like a badly charged gun. I do know
that I doubt the ability of the general populace to read anything that
carefully."

"Snob," Rathe said, without heat. "People might want to prove their version's the real one, make tests and so on."

"Which opens up a whole new line of business for actors not good enough to work in the theatres: faking tests for printers." b'Estorr grinned. "Like false necromancers, conjuring up ghosts that can be fully seen, and can speak, and accuse their murderers."

Rathe matched the grin, remembering the play that had dealt with ghosts in just that way. b'Estorr had liked it about as much as he himself had liked *The Drowned Island.*

"We're lucky in one thing, though," b'Estorr went on. "It's not going to be that easy to put arrangements together this time of year. Oh, the people who bought corms in the spring will be able to do some of it, but what you have right now is trouble in potential, I think. And not that many people are going to have the patience to buy a copy of the Alphabet now, and the corms, and then to wait the six to eight months for the corms to come into bloom. And they won't all want the same stars, or bloom at the same season."

"I think you underestimate some people's determination," Rathe said.

"I think it'll weed out the—casual villains," b'Estorr answered, and the pointsman nodded.

"What about flowers available from succession houses?"

b'Estorr shrugged. "Then it'll be people who can afford to buy the flowers themselves. Even odds whether they'll be more expensive than the corms, or less. I would wager on more."

"Yeah, but you remember last spring. Hell, you saw what people were buying around *The Drowned Island*, spending money they can't really afford to have a broadsheet copy of the ballads, or a working model of the stage machines. It won't just be the people with money, Istre. If they want it badly enough, they'll find a way—they'll find the money."

b'Estorr paused. They had reached the Hopes-point Bridge, Rathe realized, but the necromancer kept pace with him instead of turning back toward the university. As though he'd read the thought, b'Estorr shrugged. "I don't have a class for a while yet. And I think you're going to have your work cut out for you."

"Especially in Dreams," Rathe agreed, and in spite of himself quickened his pace. Plenty of work, that was certain, the morning's news to pass to Trijn, and then a few hours' thought as to how they could apply it, fairly and without favor, and then on to the rest of the day's labor, and whatever else the ghost-tide had brought them. He paused again at the edge of the market, put an impulsive hand on b'Estorr's arm. "I've been a rotten friend of late, haven't I?"

b'Estorr lifted an eyebrow, but his smile was gentle. "You've been busy."

"Like a love-struck apprentice," Rathe agreed.

"Well, it can't have been easy," b'Estorr said, reasonably.

"No . . ." Rathe would have argued more, but a movement in the crowd caught his eye. A new-looking painted banner snapped from a pole over one of the larger stalls, Bonfortune's stylized face offering fresh goods, and the market-goers were already six deep and still coming. A nearby food stall was owned by a big, raw-boned woman with a Leaguer voice and a soldier's past, a rumor that had served Graeten well in the past. She was scowling now behind her counter, more than the usual first-of-the-day ill temper on her face, and Rathe started toward her, b'Estorr trailing easily behind him.

"What's up, Graeten?"

"Just Bonfortune smiling on the corm sellers again," the woman answered. "A ship came in yesterday evening, and Wymar—that's his—managed to get his hands on some of the damned corms."

"Sweet Sofia, it's started already," Rathe said, and out of the corner of his eye saw b'Estorr's wry smile of agreement. "Silklands, I assume?"

Graeten nodded. "Just the ones. He's one of the worst, always has whatever the latest madness is. And I wouldn't mind, Nico, except he's stupid." She squinted against the sunlight, judging the crowd, and pulled the pot that held her morning's brew to a more stable central position on the counter. "He's going to have a riot on his hands one of these days, and sooner rather than later, the way he's selling them, and not bothered to hire a knife or anyone to keep order."

Rathe looked at b'Estorr, an unwilling smile on his face. "Fourie always calls it, doesn't he?"

"He seems to," the Chadroni answered. "What would this be, insufficient . . . ?"

"Inadequate attention to the queen's peace and public safety," Rathe quoted, and Graeten grinned openly. "Who's his factor, Graeten?"

The woman shook her head, still smiling. "No idea. There's a

dozen venturers and the same number of residents he could be buying from."

Maybe half that number, Rathe amended silently. If Wymar was
as much of a fool as Graeten said, there would be those who wouldn't
want to deal with him—a stallholder who failed to keep order was
dangerous for business. Still, it was a moot point. There was nothing
in law, as Fourie had pointed out, to prevent the merchants from
selling what was a common commodity at this time of year, and certainly no law would keep them from taking what the market would
bear. And it was Wymar who was the immediate problem. He swore
under his breath, seeing a woman's head and shoulders rise above
the crowd—stepped up onto a box, most likely—face flushed under
her neat linen coif.

"Come along, my ladies, there's plenty to buy, but don't damage
the goods, we've corms here worth a week's housekeeping, all for
your pleasure."

"No knife, and he hires a shill," Graeten said, with disgust, and
Rathe nodded, already taking a step toward the stall. Wymar's cli-
entele didn't look like the sort who could afford to spend a week's
house money on corms, not by the look of their clothes, but that was
a folly he couldn't mend. And then he saw it, the movement he'd
been dreading, bodies swirling aside from two potential combatants,
and this time he swore aloud.

"Excuse me, Istre," he said, and the magist leaned back against
Graeten's counter as the woman reached to sweep her better goods
out of sight and reach.

"You're not on watch," b'Estorr said.

"See any other pointsmen around?" Rathe called over his shoulder, but b'Estorr's words followed him.

"Never do, when you need one."

Rathe grimaced, drawing his truncheon, and flourished it to clear
a path through the crowd, the less-involved bystanders falling back
as they recognized a point's presence. Wymar himself was sprawled
across his front counter in an effort to protect his goods, and his head
from the two women, householders both, by the look of them, grap-
pling and sparring over a corm, their market baskets spilled and the
contents already half-trampled against the worn cobbles. The shill, of
course, was nowhere in sight, her stand empty, and Rathe caught the
eye of a thin woman who was starting to reach across the undefended
space. She ducked back out of sight, but another, bolder, grabbed

anyway, and he brought his truncheon down just short of her fingers, the blow loud against the wood. She shrieked as though he'd hit her, and Wymar turned, still flat on the counter, trying to drag the rest of his goods under his body. Rathe grabbed the nearer of the two combatants by the collar of her short coat and hauled her bodily back, wailing as her fingers finally left the corm. She was smaller than the other, but seemed to have a keener sense of how to succeed in a close-quarters fight: the other woman already had a split lip. Bloody mouth or not, she crowed in triumph, holding up the corm, and Rathe lifted his truncheon at her.

"Leave off, mistress." He released the other woman, careful to stay between them. "Brawling in the market, and without the excuse of drink?" He saw other, avid faces behind them, the thought that Wymar's goods were all but unguarded vivid in their eyes, and raised his truncheon again. "The rest of you, stand back unless you want me to call points on all of you for a mob."

"She cheated me," the taller woman said.

"No!" The other stiffened indignantly in his grip. "I had my hand on it first, had drawn out my money to pay Master Wymar—"

"Sweet Sofia, dames, it's one corm," Rathe said, and knew it was pointless even as he spoke.

"It is rather spectacular, pointsman," Wymar offered, almost apologetically, and Rathe saw to his relief that the merchant had managed to tidy most of his goods away out of reach. "It's in the rose style, but doubled, and yellow with the faintest of pink tracings—"

"That's the flower," Rathe said. "The corm—" He broke off, knowing it was pointless from the look in the women's eyes. The corm was only the flower in potential; each one had to be treated properly, allowed to winter over in its own time, or kept cold and then warm to force an early bloom, if the variety allowed it. His own mother was an herbalist, had taught him to keep his own small garden even though his stars had taken him a long way from her profession; she grew some of the corms as well, and he knew how tricky the showier varieties could be to coax to full majesty. But these—none of them were buying with that in mind, wanting only to have and to hold the source of the possible beauty. The thought was suddenly painful, a vision of wasted corms, misplanted, blooming blind, or left drying and neglected once the folly was past, sharpening his tongue.

"I can't tell you not to buy it, that's your own folly, and so be it. But brawling in the market, that is a points matter, and I'm inclined to call the point next time, Master Wymar." He took a breath. "I leave the judgment to you, master, as to which of these women is the rightful purchaser, and, frankly, I don't envy you. But give judgment now."

Wymar blinked, his face going even paler than before, flung out his arm to indicate the shorter woman. Her face split in a ferocious grin, and the other woman flung back her head.

"No! Gods above, he lies—"

"Shall I call the point?" Rathe demanded, and the woman faltered.

"You can't—it would be a disgrace. Unless you call it against this fool, this blind calf's-head, who only gives it to her because her son's in his guild—"

"Mistress," Rathe said, sharply, and the woman fell silent, controlling herself with an effort. "I didn't intend to call the point, I think you're both well paid for it, but if you insist, I will."

The smaller woman, he was pleased to see, had had the sense to get her money out smartly, and was already fading into the crowd, the corm clutched close beneath her skirt. The taller woman took another breath, shaking her head, but by her expression, she was far from appeased.

"If there's any more trouble," Rathe said, raising his voice to be sure he was heard, "if I or any other from the points sees another disturbance, I will call a point, and close this stall down. Is that understood?"

There was a murmur, ambiguous at best, but Wymar bobbed his head in rapid agreement. "Yes, pointsman—forgive me, Adjunct Point, anything you say."

I hope so. "And my warning to you is to keep order at your business," Rathe said. "That's one of the conditions of your bond, as you very well know, one of the terms of the license you hold for this spot. I'm sure I don't have to remind you of that, or check your license, do I?"

Wymar shook his head, paler than ever, and Rathe's eyes narrowed. Something wasn't right there, and he made a note to send Sohier around to check on the stallholder's papers. He thought he could guess what she would find.

"Then, Master Wymar, I wish you a—peaceful—day."

"Pointsman!" There was still no color in Wymar's face, but he made an attempt to smile, licking dry lips, and reached under the counter, came up with a small, heart-shaped corm half wrapped in a sheet of printed paper. "Might I not offer . . . In gratitude for your discretion . . . ?"

Rathe turned back, aware of the envious stares from the crowd around him. He had thought he recognized the corm, was sure of it when he saw the name on the smallsheet that wrapped it, and gave in to an unworthy impulse. "Thank you, no. I don't take fees, no matter how they're called. Those are pretty, though. My mother grows them in her garden."

And she'd probably smack him for taking such a mean pleasure in the fact, he thought, shouldering his way back through the crowd. b'Estorr had moved on from Graeten's stall, he saw, had found his way to a printer's, stood idly flipping through a folio. Rathe recognized the whispering gargoyle that adorned the banner as belonging to Bertrán Girodaia, and allowed himself a sigh of relief. Not only did Girodaia hire some of the better astrologers to provide her forecasts, she had the wit and the coin to keep all her licenses fully up-to-date. Girodaia herself was working the booth today, keeping an eye on two apprentices and a journeyman while chatting politely with a customer, a round-faced matron with the badge of the embroiderers' guild on one voluminous sleeve. She managed a nod and a half smile as Rathe approached, and Rathe's smile in return was honestly friendly. Girodaia might look all to sea, cuffs frayed, hem sagging, brilliant blue eyes wide set beneath grey hair cut short and ragged as a fever victim's, but she knew her business better than most, and kept a firm control of its every aspect. From the look of her eyes, Seidos was strong in her stars; maybe that, Rathe thought, had taught her the wisdom of keeping matters under close rule. He edged close to the counter, b'Estorr sliding sideways to give him room, and couldn't help glancing at the embroiderer's purchase. An edition of the Alphabet, he saw, without great surprise, according to the superscript newly revised and amended based on recent discoveries, and he wondered how many hours ago that had been completed. And b'Estorr was looking at one as well, and Rathe groaned aloud. *Damn Chresta Aconin.*

"I suppose," b'Estorr said, without looking up, "the university could demand to see each printer's master copy, and stamp it once we deemed it—harmless. But then, would we be liable for fraud if the formulae didn't work at all?"

Rathe looked at him. "Have you ever considered going into the advocacy?"

"Not ever," b'Estorr answered, and Rathe snorted.

"How does this one look?"

The necromancer shrugged. "I'm no expert, in printing or phytomancy."

He slid the volume across the counter, and Rathe took it, turning the pages carefully. If he remembered correctly, it looked much like the versions that had been circulating in the spring, when the verifiable Alphabet was first a rumor, a slim volume with crude plates accompanied by text that gave the desired effect and the formula for creating them. This one gave the stars under which the flowers should be gathered, something he didn't remember from the last editions, and on second glance the plates were less crude than old-fashioned. Probably taken from a much older edition that had been cannibalized for the plates in it, he guessed, and couldn't suppress a smile. First the printers had torn the old books apart, and now they were frantically trying to put them back together. He turned to say as much to b'Estorr, who was reading a broadsheet prophecy, and his eye was caught by a notice fluttering from one of the stall's supporting poles. *The Guild of the Masters of Defense announces a new master, prize played for and won. . . .* There was more, but it was the name that struck him silent, printed in enormous letters so that the words ran almost the width of the sheet: *Philip vaan Esling, lieutenant, late of Coindarel's Dragons.* He blinked, puzzled and then, slowly, annoyed—*what, you liked the play so much you had to cast yourself as the noble lover?*—and b'Estorr looked over his shoulder. He heard the necromancer's soft intake of breath, and then the sigh as it was released.

"He's working on the midwinter masque, Nico, with scores of nobles who have to be told what to do. I imagine it's rather easier for the guild to get them to cooperate if they can believe he might be something closer to their own class. It probably wasn't his decision. It looks more to me like the hand of Gerrat Duca. He's a master at keeping the nobles happy—he has to be."

"I'm sure you're right." Rathe shook his head, the annoyance fading to something like amusement—Eslingen was going to have his hands full keeping up the pretense in that company—and turned back to the stall.

"Hello, Nico, what can I do for you?" Girodaia had finished with her customer, waved away an apprentice to smile at Rathe herself.

"I see you're flogging a version of the Alphabet," he said.

"Not the play," Girodaia said hastily. By law and custom, the play could not be printed until after the masque had been performed, but in other years a few, favored printers had found themselves with copies some weeks earlier.

"No, I can see that," Rathe said. "And I know you're not on that good terms with Aconin."

Girodaia made a sour face, her big hands miming resignation. She had been on good terms with the playwright, Rathe knew, until she had refused to print something she considered too scurrilous about one of the playwright's former lovers. Aconin had taken his undoubted talent elsewhere, but it hadn't been too great a loss for Girodaia, as Aconin's first stage successes had followed closely. As he made a name for himself as a playwright, he'd eschewed the broadsheets altogether—or had he? Rathe wondered suddenly. Could Aconin, of all people, resist the temptation to let his wit run rampant under another name, while keeping his own pristine for the theatres? He shook the thought away—a speculation that might be useful at another time—and turned his attention to the matter at hand.

"I just wondered if you'd thought about the liabilities that might attach to you for selling it."

"Liabilities?" Girodaia frowned, her eyes going from Rathe to the man behind him, lingering on the Starsmith's badge at the knot of his stock.

"It's a practicum," Rathe said, "or at least anything that purports to be the Alphabet of Desire purports to be a practicum. You're putting recipes in unpracticed hands—like giving the procedures to making aurichalcum to people who don't have the wisdom to handle it."

"And we all know you'd know about that," Girodaia said, with a quick grin.

Rathe sighed. The affair of the children had turned out to involve the making of aurichalcum; he'd hoped to make her think he was serious, not angling for praise. "It's no joke, Bertran. Truly."

"It's a work of fiction, Nico." Her eyes slid again to the necromancer, visibly assessing the university's role in the matter. "Isn't it?"

"Probably," Rathe answered. "But suppose somewhere there was a copy that wasn't. And even ruling that out, because I admit it's unlikely, there could be something in here that would work. And without the imprimatur—the university's imprimatur—you could be liable."

It was thin, and they both knew it, an awkward point to call and even more difficult to prove, and Rathe silently damned Fourie. Without more solid authority, there was nothing he could do but go one by one to the printers and make these veiled threats that the brighter of them would know instantly were pointless.

Girodaia looked down at the book, ran a finger down the spine. "But you're not forbidding me to sell it?"

Rathe sighed. "You know I can't. Just consider it a friendly warning."

Girodaia frowned, shook her head. "I'll take my chances, I think, Nico. You understand."

"I understand," Rathe answered, and touched b'Estorr's arm. "Istre?"

The magist started slightly, turned to follow the other man with a sheepish smile. "Sorry."

"What is it?" Rathe asked.

"Verifiable is an interesting word," b'Estorr said. "Verifiable by whom, is what I've been wondering. Not by the university, we haven't seen anything of it."

"No copies in the great library?"

b'Estorr snorted. "Even if someone donated a copy at some point, I wouldn't know where to find it. The cataloging in the older sections leaves much to be desired. But my point is, it's not the word we would use."

"How about certifiable?" Rathe asked, and b'Estorr laughed.

"You're likely to become so, with all these flooding the market. But, no, the word the university would use is provenanced."

"So?"

"So," b'Estorr said slowly, "if it exists, it's unlikely to have ever been proved by the university. Which means that even this 'verifiable' edition may in fact be more dangerous than we thought."

"Everybody knows how to make gunpowder," Rathe said.

"Do you?" b'Estorr answered. "Do you really?"

Rathe blinked. "Charcoal, nitre, and saltpeter. . . ."

"In what proportions? And how do you mix it?"

"Very carefully," Rathe answered. "All right, point taken."

"And to use gunpowder once you've made it, generally speaking you also use a gun and ball or shot of some sort, and you stand there and take your chances, seen or unseen." b'Estorr shook his head. "This would be something very different."

Rathe blinked again, looked up at the taller man, seeing the breeze ruffle his straw-pale hair. "Istre, do you believe in the Alphabet of Desire?"

"I'm very much afraid that I'm afraid not to."

There was nothing to be said to that. Rathe looked away, kicked a stone from his path with more force than was needed, wishing the other hadn't put into words what he himself had already begun to fear. Fourie was right, as he so often was; the Alphabet was potentially very dangerous—if, he reminded himself, it actually existed. But b'Estorr was right, they couldn't afford to believe it didn't.

The market clock struck then, a fraction before the larger clock at the guildhall, and b'Estorr swore, more violently than Rathe could ever remember hearing him. The Chadroni shook his head, looking utterly disgusted. "Sorry, Nico, I lost complete track of the time. And I have a class in less than an hour."

Rathe couldn't repress the grin. "Let me guess in what subject."

"Don't bother. Look, if you learn anything more about this, let me know, all right?"

"If you do the same," Rathe answered. "You've got that look."

"What look?" b'Estorr paused, looked honestly curious.

"The look that says you're going to track down a puzzle and strangle it."

"Must be why it's like looking in a mirror," b'Estorr answered, and turned away.

Rathe made his way back to Point of Dreams, pausing twice more to check printers' shops for the Alphabet of Desire. There were at least two further editions, and a promise of a third, more elaborate volume keyed to the play itself, and all of them, Rathe thought, with disgust, equally likely to be harmless. But not guaranteed, and that was why Trijn, and every other chief point in the city, would be spending hard-earned favors or even the stations' close kept funds to make sure they had copies of everything.

Dreams was dark and chill in spite of the fires in three of the stoves, and he freed himself only reluctantly from the bulk of his jerkin, hanging it with the others beside the fireplace. The duty point cleared her throat uneasily, and Rathe controlled his annoyance with an effort. Yres Falasca had been passed over, at least in her view; she was doing her best to live with her disappointment.

"Yeah?"

Falasca pushed a package wrapped in brown paper across the desk toward him. "This came for you, this morning."

Rathe suppressed a sigh, recognized Gasquine's seal: the script, then, of *The Alphabet of Desire.* Just what he needed to finish a perfect morning, he thought, and tucked it under his arm. His own workroom was mercifully warmer—the duty runner had remembered to light his stove, and there was a fresh pot of tea on the hob—and he settled himself at his table with cautious relief. The package, unfortunately, was still there; he sighed, and broke the seal, peeling back the wrapping. The script was there, loosely bound with what looked like kitchen string, a copyist's tidy hand filling the pages, but he put it aside for the second item. This proved to be a list of the lottery winners, the nobles who would take part as members of the chorus. After the morning, he could hardly read the script with any equanimity; the nobles were far preferable. He read the list through once, then again, more slowly, and a third time, more closely still. He refolded the paper, and tipped his chair back so that his head could rest against the rough plaster wall. He could not, he told himself, couldn't possibly be seeing what he thought he was seeing. On the other hand, sheer luck could not possibly account for it, either. He took a deep breath, unfolded the paper again, and stared at the names, making the connections explicit in his own mind: yes, at least half of the dames and seurs were somehow related to a claimant to the throne.

"Sweet Sofia," he said, and started for Trijn's office at a pace just short of a run.

Trijn met him on the landing, anger turning to understanding as she saw what he held. "My workroom," she said. "You, Hina! Go to Laneten's, get two plates of whatever's going for lunch, and a jug of beer. A large one."

The runner bobbed a curtsy, eyes wide, and Trijn waved her away. "My workroom," she said again, and Rathe obeyed.

The chief point said nothing more until the door was closed firmly behind them, then shook her head. "All right," she said, "you first."

Thanks. Rathe took a breath. "Dumb chance couldn't possibly account for this," he said, and held out the paper. "More than half of the members of the masque chorus are directly related to one of the claimants to the throne."

Trijn waved for him to take a seat, and he obeyed automatically. Trijn's copy of the list lay facedown on her table, and she turned it over again before she spoke. "Half? I make it more like three-quarters, myself. Shit."

"What do you think it means?" Rathe asked cautiously. He was still wary of Trijn's temper. "It's not making a lot of sense to me. If the lottery was rigged, why? And by whom?"

"By whom is probably the easy part," Trijn said with a snarl. "There's only one person in Astreiant—hells, in Chenedolle—who could manage it, and that's Astreiant herself."

"The metropolitan?" Rathe shook his head. "Why?"

Trijn gave a humorless smile. "I know you like her, Rathe, but she's a consummate politician. At least, I would have thought so. This—" She lifted her copy of the list, and let it fall heavily to the tabletop. "I would suspect this was done at Her Majesty's behest. As to why . . . Rumor's a wonderful thing, Rathe. It runs on so many levels. There are rumors you hear that I probably never get wind of, even in this station, to say nothing of the rumors that run in your part of southriver, as opposed to my part of northriver. The rumors in Point of Knives will always be different from those running in Temple Point, or anywhere else in the city. And University Point rumors are like no other in Chenedolle. Neither are City Point rumors. And the most recent City Point rumors are extremely interesting."

"I'm not going to like this," Rathe said.

"The most recent City Point rumor is that the queen finally means to name her successor at midwinter. The time is finally propitious, they say."

"Fourie said that she might," Rathe said. "But I didn't believe it."

"They're betting on it in City Point," Trijn said, and Rathe nodded.

"Which means they're all hostages."

"For their families' good behavior." Trijn nodded in her turn.

Did Fourie actually know? Rathe wondered. And if he knew, why couldn't he say—did anyone know officially, or had the news simply been whispered in the right corners, the word trickling out through the familiar channels of gossip? And how wise was that? The worst of it was, if this was completely unofficial information . . . "What the hell are we supposed to do about it?" he said aloud.

Trijn gave a weary shrug, and Rathe wondered just when she had gotten in that morning. Dreams was new for both of them, they both had come from districts where the problems were more commonplace. "There's not a lot we can do," she said. "I'm thinking of calling Fourie on it, see if we can't get some kind of warrant for action, permission to keep an official eye on the Tyrseia, but until then, Rathe, I confess I'm relying on your connections in the theatre."

For a second, Rathe thought she meant Eslingen, but then realized she meant his friendship with Gavi Jhirassi. He had had connections within the theatre world long before he met Philip Eslingen. His eyes dropped to the cast list again, to the professionals, this time, and with a sick jolt he saw the name he had somehow avoided before. Guis Forveijl: yes, that was a connection he could well have lived without.

"Rathe?"

He shook himself. "Sorry."

Trijn nodded. "As you've nothing more pressing at the moment than these damned Alphabets, I'd take it kindly if you could manage to keep the Tyrseia under your eye. Unofficially, to be sure. Unless you can find an official reason—preferably one that's not too dire."

Rathe smiled faintly. "I might be able to concoct something. If nothing else, Chresta Aconin's responsible for this new craze for the Alphabets. I wonder if we mightn't score a point for inciting civic disquiet."

"Enjoy your dreams, Rathe," Trijn said. "Now, I want you to go over this chorus list again. If I'm right, they're all connected to claimants somehow or other, and I want to know exactly how—to what degree, and how many quarterings. You personally, not an apprentice."

"Yes, Chief," Rathe said with a sigh. He understood the need for secrecy, but he was duty point this afternoon; the assignment would mean several hours at the Sofian temple, or possibly the university, all in his supposedly free time. At this time of year, the libraries were particularly cold and dank, and he wished he could send an apprentice. The Sofians in particular never bothered to light fires until the first snow, a precaution against fire, they said, but, Rathe believed, more as an outward sign of their general perversity. He had spent more than enough time in both places, taking on assignments designed to prove that an apprentice could, in fact, read and write; it was hardly a job that suited his age and rank.

Trijn lifted an eyebrow, as though she'd guessed the thought. "Unless you'd like the task I've set myself, which is persuading Astreiant to at least make this information official to the points."

Rathe blinked, wondering how the chief point could be so free with the metropolitan's time, but shook his head. "I'm more than happy to leave that to you."

He made his way back to his workroom, stopping only to collect another pot of tea, and settled himself behind his table to frown at the list of chorus members again. He knew at least some of the connections, and he reached for a charcoal, began noting them down to save some time at the temples. Eslingen would know more, he thought, and wondered if he dared ask the other man. Trijn had made clear that she wanted it kept secret—*and wisely, too*—but Eslingen was hardly an apprentice pointsman. He grinned to himself at that: Trijn would agree, but hardly come to the same conclusion. And perhaps it would be less than wise to take the list out of the station.

A knock at the door interrupted his train of thought, and he flipped the list over automatically. "Come in."

"I'm sorry to disturb you, Adjunct Point." It was Kurin Holles, his formal robes discarded for a drab suit that did nothing to flatter his ivory coloring.

"Advocat, I'm sorry. Please, have a seat."

Holles hesitated for a moment, then shook himself and sat uneasily on the chair nearest the stove. He was carrying a paper-wrapped parcel, Rathe saw, and set it awkwardly on his knee, seemingly at a loss for words.

"Is there anything I can help you with?" Rathe prompted, and the other man managed a flinching smile.

"Not really. Reassurance, I suppose. It's been—days—and this pointsman, this Voillemin?"

Rathe nodded.

"Hasn't yet been to the house, or sought me at the courts. Will he really do his best to find Bourtrou's killer?"

Not spoken to the leman yet. Rathe suppressed his own anger—Voillemin might have been trying to spare Holles's feelings, pursue other leads before troubling a man bereaved, but somehow he doubted it—and fumbled for the right words. "Advocat, I—"

"I know," Holles said. "I'm sorry, the question wasn't fair. But, gods, Rathe! I expected better than this."

Rathe bit down anger again. "You heard the decree yourself. I can't intervene, or the regents will revoke their warrant." He lifted his hand to forestall Holles's answer. "And even if that weren't the case, I would have no right to interfere in another's case unless and until there were some concrete reason, some obvious failure, that had to be corrected."

"And not talking to me isn't an obvious failure?" Holles asked.

He had found the body, Rathe remembered, but tried for a conciliatory tone. "He may have been trying to spare your feelings, Advocat."

Holles took a deep breath and gave a jerky nod. "It isn't necessary. All I want—"

He broke off, and Rathe finished the sentence for him. "Is to know what happened, and why. And even that may not be enough, Advocat. You know that."

"I know." Holles's voice was almost a whisper. "Sofia's tits, I don't know where to set him looking, don't even know where I'd start if I were him, but I want justice. There's nothing else left for me." He shook his head, straightening. "I'm sorry. But I don't know who else I can come to with my concerns."

"It's a matter for the chief point," Rathe said, and Holles smiled again.

"Trijn has her own agenda in this, I think. I feel confident in you."

That matched Rathe's impression all too well, and in spite of himself Rathe nodded once. "He's not a bad pointsman, not corrupt, I give you my word on that. And I will pass him the word that he need not worry about your sensibilities. And if anything else happens to concern you, you can come to me, and I will speak to Voillemin about it. I'm the senior adjunct here, my job is not to undermine the points under me. Do you understand that?"

Holles nodded, a rueful smile on his face. "That's one of the many reasons I wish you were handling this investigation, Adjunct Point. I've said my piece, I won't trouble you further." He looked down at the parcel, and the smile twisted out of true. "Except one thing. A kind of jest, and probably in poor taste, but I thought you might appreciate it. Or an irony, at least. I found this at Bourtrou's office in the Tour, and thought you might want to add it to your collection."

Rathe took the package, frowning slightly, and unwrapped the paper to reveal a plainly bound octavo volume, the corners bent from hard use. There was no title stamped on spine or cover, and he opened it warily, only to laugh as he saw the title page. *Well, why not?* he thought, gazing down at it. It seemed a part of the way things were going these days.

It was a copy of the Alphabet of Desire.

Holles rose, bowing. "Thank you for your time, Adjunct Point. And for your help."

"Thank you for this," Rathe answered, but the other man was already gone. Rathe sighed, staring at the book he had been given. He should look at it, study it the same way he would study all the others that they'd collected, but his mind was on Holles's complaint. The man knew how the points worked, that was the trouble, saw it day to day in Hearts, and could be forgiven if he was suspicious of anyone he hadn't come to know personally. And in this case . . . Rathe sighed, and shoved himself away from his table, heading back to the main room to consult the daybook.

"Anything of interest?" he asked, flipping back through the day's notations, and the duty point shrugged.

"A couple more editions brought in."

And one more that I should log, Rathe thought, then stopped, frowning. He had reached the previous day, and one of the entries did not make sense. "Is Voillemin about?"

"He's got the bridge shift," the duty point answered, and Rathe's eyes went to the clock. Yes, the man should be here, was due to go off watch shortly.

"Has he done anything about this?" he asked, and pointed to the book. The duty point craned her neck to see, and shook her head.

"Not that I know. What me to check?"

"No." Rathe turned the book back toward her, moving carefully to hide his anger. "No. I'll ask him."

"Up to you. How were things at the Tour?"

"Fraught," Rathe answered, and the woman smirked.

"I can imagine. It's not a dull life, give us that."

Rathe murmured something in answer, turned away to stare at the station clock. The story was that it had been a gift from one of Dreams's greatest actresses, Herren Dornevil, in gratitude for the points' quelling the student riots and thus keeping the theatres open. Another story said that a former chief point had liberated it from one of the few pleasure houses operating in Dreams instead of Hearts— that Dornevil had, in fact, given it to the proprietor of that house, for services rendered. Whatever its origins, the movements were near perfect, and Rathe let himself watch for a few minutes, let the steady swing of the pendulum clear his head so that he could think. He hadn't thought that Voillemin was a fool, a coward, or lazy, but there was evidence of one of those in the daybook. One of the stallholders in Little Chain Market had sent a runner, claiming to have information about Leussi's death—and, yes, Little Chain was in Hearts, but it was merely a matter of making a courtesy call on the chief there, and Voillemin would be free to proceed. But he hadn't made any notation that he had, or planned to do so. In fact, there had been a line through the entry, indicating it had been considered and written off. And maybe there was cause, he told himself, damping down his anger, maybe there was something in the message that made it patently untrue, but if there was, he should have noted it. He took a breath, and started back up the stairs.

Voillemin shared a workroom with Leenderts, but the other half of the long table was empty, its surface swept clean of everything except a basket of slates weighting down a stack of papers. Rathe allowed himself a sigh of relief—he wanted no witnesses, if he had to interfere in this matter—and tapped on the door frame. Voillemin looked up with a fleeting expression of annoyance at the delay.

"Can I come in?" Rathe asked.

Voillemin nodded. "Yes, of course, Adjunct Point."

Rathe closed the door carefully behind him, reached for Leenderts's chair, and swung it to face the other man. "Tell me about the runner from Little Chain."

Voillemin shrugged. "Not much to tell, really. One of the market brats came and said her mistress wanted to speak with me about the intendant's death. She wouldn't say who the mistress was, just that she was a stall holder, and she wanted to know when the intendant died."

"And you did . . . ?"

Voillemin looked honestly startled. "I made a note of it, but frankly, I thought it was, well, just a prank. To get the death-time, cast a horoscope, something like that."

Possible, Rathe thought, striving for fairness, *but not likely*. "For what purpose?"

"You don't know this district very well yet, Adjunct Point." Voillemin's voice held a note of grievance. "There are printers in Little Chain, same as everywhere. I suspected this one wanted to get information his competitors didn't have, to bring out a scandal-sheet claiming Sofia knows what about the intendant's death. And we have a policy here—I think it's city-wide—of not feeding the broadsheets."

"I understand that you haven't yet spoken to Advocat Holles," Rathe said.

Voillemin blinked, caught off balance by the change of subject. "Well, no, I thought—" He stopped, tried again. "I didn't want to add to his burdens at such a time."

"He found the body," Rathe said gently, and a faint blush rose on Voillemin's cheeks.

"There was plenty of information in the alchemist's report. . . ."

His voice trailed off, and Rathe sighed. "You haven't questioned the first person to find the body. You didn't follow up on a potential source of information about Leussi's murder. You don't even use the word 'murder,' I notice. Very well, that's your prerogative, though prejudging a case is always dangerous, as you should well know. But you've been given this job, and it's your responsibility as a pointsman, your responsibility to this station, never mind to the advocat, to do it right. Valuable information has come from the unlikeliest sources, as you should know—as an apprentice learns in her first year." He took a breath, swallowing the rest of the lecture—Voillemin was an adjunct point, after all—and said carefully, "Advocat Holles sent word that he appreciates your scruples, but they're unnecessary. As for the other, you will look into it. Today."

"I'm about to go. . . ." Voillemin realized his mistake as soon as he started to speak, and closed his mouth tightly against the words. Rathe nodded.

"To Little Chain. Good."

The stage of the Tyrseia was set for a banquet, long tables placed in a square so that everyone could see and be seen, each one draped in spotless linen and set with dishes that gleamed in the doubled light from the mage-lights and the enormous candelabra that hung center stage. The newly chosen noble chorus glittered in their second-best— none of them would have put on best for this meeting, and none would wear less than that, to show themselves among their peers— and the black robes of the marshaling chamberlains, bustling back and forth among the various groups, set them off to perfection. It was like a scene in a play, Eslingen thought, except that the food and the wine was real, the smells savory enough to make his stomach growl. Presumably they would be free to eat at some point; for now, he would wait with the other Masters of Defense, and hope that no one took too much notice of the stranger among them.

He recognized a few of the actors, women and men he'd seen a dozen times onstage, the best of Astreiant's theatres, recognized, too, Rathe's upstairs neighbor, the object of a hundred glances, and looked away to spare him at least that stare. He felt distinctly out of place in this bright company, and knew he couldn't match the other masters' ease, fell back on the stance he'd practiced as a new-made lieutenant—after all, he told himself, they'd hired him as a soldier, and a soldier he'd be. Siredy quirked a smile at him, very fair today under a black wig, and Eslingen returned the smile unspeaking. Siredy seemed to take that as encouragement enough, and edged closer, tipping his head toward the cluster of the chorus.

"They look very fine, our noble amateurs. I wonder if any of them can act."

"What's the usual way of it?" Eslingen asked, genuinely curious, and the other man shrugged.

"Oh, maybe one in ten has some talent, or at least experience, most of that from the university. But the hard part is persuading them to do what they're told."

That was no surprise, Eslingen thought, watching the landames greet each other with kisses and cries shrill as a seabird's. Their skirts caught the light, the occasional silk overskirt hissing against fine linen and better wool, and their brothers and husbands, left behind, greeted each other more discreetly.

"At least you have the looks for it," Siredy said, without jealousy, and Eslingen glanced at him.

"Does that really make so much difference?"

"You'd be surprised," Siredy answered. "Though to be fair, it's less the looks than the manners." He smiled, this time with malice. "Soumet, now—he's never been able to persuade a single one of them to do what he wants, for all that he actually does know what he's doing."

No, Soumet wouldn't be to their taste, Eslingen thought, and shook himself. This was no different, or not much different, from serving with Coindarel. He'd drilled enough young nobles to know exactly how to handle them, how to flatter, when to drive, and how to make them proud to serve, even if it was a play this time, and not a regiment. He drew himself up, aware of a landame's smile, hidden instantly behind a flourished fan, and Siredy said softly, "See, now? You've already won them."

"Let's hope so," Eslingen answered, and Gasquine stepped out from among the actors. The movement was planned, drawing all eyes, and instantly the senior chamberlain moved to meet her, bowing with punctilious courtesy. She curtsied in answer, not deeply, and the chamberlain slammed his staff against the stage floor, calling in the same instant for silence. To Eslingen's surprise, he received it, and Gasquine turned slowly, one hand outstretched, welcoming them all. She had dressed for the occasion, not in finery—she must have known she couldn't compete with the chorus, Eslingen thought—but in a good, well-cut skirt and bodice, the sort of fine dark red wool that the city's best merchants wore. It was high-necked, the collar closed beneath her chin, and she wore a simple gold chain, ornamented with a single flower. With a real flower, Eslingen amended, one of the winter corms forced to early bloom, its long stem woven into the links so that its pale, pink-tipped bell lay along the curve of one breast. A perfect touch, Eslingen thought, and repressed the urge to applaud.

"My friends and colleagues," Gasquine said, "and the landames whom I hope will soon become our colleagues, welcome to the Tyrseia, and to our play. We are fortunate this year in our play, and in our noble sponsor, who has so generously pledged not only his name but his gift of flowers to make this piece the success it deserves to be. I ask you to begin by greeting him as he deserves: I present to you all the landseur Aubine, our patron and sponsor."

Eslingen clapped politely. The actors were more enthusiastic, the noble chorus distracted, still whispering among themselves, and he had to look twice before he could pick out the landseur. He was an older man—well, perhaps not as old as he looked, Eslingen amended, but certainly dressed like an old man, all in grey wool and white linen, without even a line of braid to trim his coat. Even his buttons were plain jet, expensive but undemonstrative—there were actors who were better dressed than he, and the chorus outshone him without effort. His brown hair was equally undistinguished, and it had to be his own, hanging loose without curl across his shoulders as he made his bow.

"The flowers are really nothing," he said. He had a good voice, Eslingen thought, surprised, low and resonant, and he knew how to project to be heard in the Tyrseia's cavernous space. "A small thing, from my succession houses. But I hope you will all take them as a tangible sign of my hope for our success."

"He has the most notable glass houses in the city," Siredy said softly.

So of course he'd sponsor *The Alphabet of Desire*, Eslingen thought. Why not? Though it did make a certain amount of sense, given how obsessed the city seemed to be with flowers. He said aloud, "He doesn't look like the sort to get involved in the theatre."

Siredy gave a knowing smile. "Oh, that's another story."

Gasquine stepped forward again, introducing the senior chancellor, who in turn would introduce the noble chorus, and Eslingen couldn't suppress a sigh. It was little to no surprise to him that Caiazzo was not present. He did not get involved with these things for the sake of either his name or reputation, he got involved with them because they were reasonable—and legal—investments. For a brief moment, he envied the merchant's absence, though his acerbic comments would have been amusing. Siredy touched his arm, took a careful step backward. Eslingen copied him, and realized that they had stepped into the shadow of one of the massive set pieces, out of sight of the majority of the chorus, and the few actors waiting on that side of the stage. It was a giant triangular column, painted on each side with a different part of *The Drowned Island*'s elaborate scenery—there were at least five of them on each side of the stage, and glancing up he thought he recognized part of the buildings lining the Sier. The columns must turn, he decided, presenting a new side to the audience with each new scene—and the gods forbid that the scenerymen get their signals crossed or, more likely, the mechanisms were somehow linked, to make sure the proper images came into view.

"Leussi would never have done this," Siredy said. "Introduced each of them, I mean. Sweet Tyrseis, we'll be here an hour."

"Leussi?" Eslingen repeated. The name was somehow familiar, but he couldn't place it.

"He used to be the senior chancellor," Siredy answered, "but he died, oh, not three weeks ago, poor man. He wasn't old, either— younger than this one, at any rate."

Rathe had mentioned the name, Eslingen remembered. That was the connection. And had seemed sorry at the loss himself, which was probably why it had stuck in his mind. He said, "Tell me about Aubine."

Siredy smiled, visibly gratified. "Ah, well—and I'm not sure I should tell you this, since I understand you're a friend of the points."

"Of at least one pointsman," Eslingen corrected. Siredy seemed to know entirely too much about everything—but then, it hardly mattered anymore. He wasn't likely to lose this place for sleeping with a pointsman.

"So one hears." Siredy glanced over his shoulder, lowered his voice until the other could just make out the words. "The landseur is the grandson of the Soueraine of Ledey, who was a lady of great pride in her lineage."

"Sixteen quarterings and not a demming in her pocket?" Eslingen asked.

"Thirty-two, actually, and the money to back them," Siredy answered. "And all the pride of the Ile'nord behind that. So the story is that, her daughter being sickly and unsuitable, she sent her grandchildren to court—the landseur and his sister, the present soueraine—to uphold the family name, and while they were there, young Aubine took a fancy for a life of learning. It being winter, and the roads into Ledey being blocked, the sister gave permission for him to enroll at the university—I understand he really is rather clever— and then to take lodgings in University Point. And of course while lodging with the common herd, he met another young man, a brewer's boy, I think, or at least so I've heard, and they fell to a liking and then to love. They swore lemanry by midwinter, the sister turning a blind eye to the matter, but with the spring thaw, the word went out to the Ile'nord, and the next thing anyone knew, the soueraine herself descended on Astreiant and snatched both grandchildren out of the city. And the brewer's boy was found beaten to death in an alley."

"At the grandmother's behest," Eslingen said.

Siredy shrugged. "The points—and here is where I don't wish to offend—the points said he died in the aftermath of a tavern quarrel. But, yes, that's the story."

"A sad one," Eslingen said, and craned his neck to find Aubine. He was standing well back, not quite part of either the noble chorus or the little knot of officials, a quiet, sober man to be the center of such gossip. And not really handsome enough, either, or even striking, utterly without the kind of physical presence that would go with such a story. "Like *The Drowned Island,* only—sideways."

Siredy suppressed a laugh, and earned a frown from Duca, standing to their left. "I suppose it is, at that. I wonder if Mistress Anonymous had the story in mind."

"Anonymous?" Eslingen asked. There had been no playwright's name on any of the copies he had seen, but all of them were pirated editions, would hardly be expected to credit the author when the printer could flaunt her cleverness at obtaining a copy.

"Oh, that's a scandal for another day," Siredy answered. "No, no one knows exactly who wrote it—though everybody has their suspicions—but it hardly matters. Tell me, what does your pointsman think of it?"

"Of *The Drowned Island?*" Eslingen stifled a laugh of his own. "We didn't see it together."

"What a pity." Siredy looked more amused than sympathetic, however, and Eslingen let his eyes wander back to the tangle of nobles, bowing one by one as the senior chamberlain called their names. He'd seen this many nobles gathered on one spot before, but only once, during the winter he served with Coindarel, and then they had been mostly younger sons, penniless landseurs and armigers and bannerets, striving to make their way, not daughters of good families. This—this was something different, impressive in spite of his willing it to be nothing more than another post. Rathe would laugh, he knew, but he remembered seeing Chenedolle's queen—only a few months before, but seemingly a lifetime—a bright shape stiff as a doll under a parasol, there to see them properly paid off. And now he would have a chance to see her again, closer than before, maybe even genuinely amused by the performance, which was more than he could say for her appreciation of the previous summer's muster. One of the boxes would be hers, if he understood the matter correctly—the masque was given in her honor, ostensibly for her entertainment and the health of her and her realm, even if the real purpose these days seemed to be to keep the city happy. Surely he would have a chance to see her more closely. He glanced at Siredy, wondering if the other master would think he was a fool if he asked which was the royal box, and a movement among the watching actors drew his eye.

He recognized the man instantly, to his own surprise, and took another soundless step back into the shadows, not yet ready to face this particular part of his past. Chresta Aconin had hardly changed in the intervening years, still boyishly slim, and still vain enough to increase his moderate height by a pair of red-heeled shoes. He leaned now on a tall walking stick, a cluster of embroidered ribbons frothing over hands that were probably painted to match, and there was a dark blue flower, another of the corms, tucked into the buttonhole of his rust-colored coat. The warm color flattered his sallow complexion, as did the bay-brown wig, rich as polished wood. He had always known how to dress, Eslingen thought, remotely, remembering a time when he had copied his then-friend's graces, and was suddenly aware of Siredy's eyes upon him.

"I see you've spotted our playwright."

"He's made a name for himself," Eslingen said. And that name was an ambivalent one at best: Aconin was counted one of the best male playwrights in the city, but he was also known as Aconite for his merciless pen. He had enemies to spare, and a dozen reluctant supporters among the theatre managers. Could he have written *The Drowned Island*? Eslingen wondered suddenly, and in spite of himself bit back a grin. If Aconin had written it, there would have been more irony—or perhaps there had been, and that was why the playwright wouldn't claim it.

"He hasn't made friends this autumn," Siredy said, "coming out of nowhere with this play. Even Mathiee had to think twice, but it was too good to turn down."

"Is it so unusual for a professional to write the winning masque?" Eslingen asked.

"Unusual for one to bother," Siredy said, frankly. "The masque—unless you're very good, which I have to say Aconite is, it plays once and is forgotten. Not that the money's that bad, for the playwright, at least, no one else gets anything out of it, but it's very hard to write something that can stand having all the set pieces added in, and still be worth performing later, and the fact that Aconin actually did it—well, it hasn't exactly endeared him to his peers. I heard Juliot Sedaien said that she'd cheerfully have knifed him, if she'd known he was at work on a play. She'd have won the masque, too, if it hadn't been for the Alphabet, and her with a new baby to keep."

"Not that Aconin would care," Eslingen said.

"You sound as though you know him," Siredy said, and Eslingen shrugged.

"Is there anyone in Astreiant who doesn't?"

Siredy gave him a speculative look, but the senior chamberlain finally called the last of the noble names, and anything else he would have said was drowned in relieved applause. Gasquine stepped forward again, hands raised, to announce the beginning of the dinner. The nobles were as quick to the table as the actors, Eslingen saw, with amusement, following at the deceptively swift pace he'd learned as a hungry sergeant, and wondered how many of them were as poor as he had been.

He accepted wine from a goggling servant, a boy all of twelve whom he suspected was usually a theatre runner, found a way to snag half a chicken pie from between two landames' sleeves, and stepped back again to enjoy his booty, trying to lose himself in the shadows between the turning columns. Siredy seemed to be enjoying himself, flirting cheerfully and impartially with a landseur and a landame in shades of peacock blue; beyond him, Aconin seemed lost in conversation with the noble patron. They made an odd pair, Aconin by far the showier, and yet more willing to defer than Eslingen remembered—but then, it was the landseur's name—and Caiazzo's coin—that made this particular triumph possible.

He stepped back again as a pair of actors slipped by him, laughing, and stumbled against a rope that stretched taut from a bolt in the floor. He caught himself instantly, not even spilling the wine, glanced up to see the rest of the cable vanish in the shadows of the stagehouse. The lights on the stage didn't reach to those heights, two stories, perhaps even three, above his head—easily the height of a town clock—and he wondered what the rope controlled. It was as thick as his wrist, and utterly without slack, like the ropes on a sailing ship. He swallowed the last of the pie and reached out to the cable, not quite testing it, and a voice from behind him said, "Don't touch that."

Eslingen controlled his start, and turned to see a stocky man frowning at him from the shadows. By the badge at his collar, a white, star-shaped flower on a blue ground, he belonged to Savatier's company, but unlike the other actors, he'd done nothing to dress for the occasion, was plainly workaday in a sailor's knit smock over drab breeches and mended hose.

"Don't you know anything? Never touch any of the stagehouse ropes, you don't know what they do. Leave it to us who made them."

A sceneryman, then, Eslingen thought. He said, "I'm sorry. I don't know all the rules yet."

"No. He's new to this game, grant him that."

Eslingen swore under his breath, recognizing the voice, turned again to greet Chresta Aconin with a sweeping bow. "Master Aconin."

"Lieutenant—vaan Esling?" Aconin lifted an eyebrow in delicate inquiry, and Eslingen suppressed another curse. Aconin had known him when they both carried their mother's names, knew better than almost anyone else in the world how little he deserved the noble prefix. He could see Siredy coming up behind him, followed by the landseur Aubine, and braced himself for the inevitable exposure. And the worst of it was, he couldn't blame Duca—even being true, it would sound petty, make thing even worse. . . .

"Late of Coindarel's Dragons," Aconin went on, and smiled. "Or so Siredy tells me. The prince-marshal always did have an eye for service."

Eslingen drew a careful breath, not quite believing in the reprieve, and thought Aubine blushed.

"You mustn't touch the ropes," the sceneryman said obstinately. "That's a first rule backstage, I don't care who you are. Don't touch anything. Especially not in this house."

"That's a rule I'll be careful to obey," Aubine said with a smile that included all of them. "But please, master—"

"Basa," Siredy said hastily. "Lial Basa, of Savatier's Women. My lord."

Aubine dipped his head. "Master Basa. Why in this theatre in particular?"

The sceneryman hesitated, eyes darting from Aubine to the playwright as though he'd just realized the company he was in. Aubine nodded again, his smile encouraging, unoffensive, and the sceneryman took a breath. "It's the engines, my lord. They're bigger than most, and they're new. For *The Drowned Island*."

"Really?"

All of Astreiant knew it, Eslingen thought, but Aubine's tone was honestly interested.

"What does this rope do, then?"

"Opens the trap, if we're particularly unlucky," Aconin murmured, almost in Eslingen's ear.

Basa heard, and slanted him a glare. "Not the traps, thank you. They're understage, so there can't be that error. This is for the clouds—it brings in the big bank of them, that comes in at the end of the play."

Eslingen frowned for an instant, then remembered. It had been a small effect, almost lost in the more elaborate sinking of the island itself. "When the island sinks," he said aloud, "and the waves come in. How is that done?"

Basa gave him a look that was balanced perfectly between approval and suspicion. "You must be new to the Masters, then."

"I am."

"And utterly changed," Aconin said, and laughed.

"Do you think so?" Eslingen asked. He was beginning to lose his patience with the playwright, dangerous though that might be.

"Changed enough," Aconin answered, still smiling. "The brave soldier, and now—a player, one of the Masters of Defense. Gods, it's been more years than I care to recall since I saw you last. Since before you left Esling, I think."

"I can recall how many," Eslingen said mildly, and the playwright lifted his hand. It was elaborately painted, Eslingen saw without surprise, a bouquet of black and gold flowers running up from his wrist to twine around each finger.

"Please don't. That literal habit of yours is one thing that hasn't changed."

"Master Basa," Aubine said, and Aconin's mouth closed over whatever else he had been going to say. The landseur smiled again, looking almost embarrassed. "The lieutenant asked a good question, and one I'm curious about. How is it done? Have you worked on it?"

Basa shook his head. "Not on the *Island*, no, I'm with Savatier, and that's Gasquine's piece. But I know how it's done."

"Tell us, please." Aubine folded his hands into the sleeves of his coat like a schoolboy, an unexpectedly charming gesture, and Eslingen felt himself warming to the man.

Basa glanced from one to the other. "I can show you, if you'd like. The machinery."

"Not me," Aconin said. "I know how it's done."

"No one asked you, Chresta," Aubine said. His tone was more indulgent than anything, but Aconin bowed.

"Then I'll leave you to it, my lord."

Aubine turned back to the sceneryman, still smiling, and Eslingen wondered for an instant just how well Aconin knew him. But then, Aconin had written the play that Aubine sponsored; that was enough of a connection.

"I would like to see," Aubine said, and glanced at the others. "If you wouldn't mind?"

"I'd like to see myself," Eslingen said with perfect truth, and Basa blinked as though the interest startled him.

"You'll miss the food."

Most of it was gone already, Eslingen saw, glancing over his shoulder to see a few actors still clustered around the last, least-favored dishes.

Aubine looked instantly contrite. "And I daresay you haven't had the chance to eat yourself, Master Basa. If you'd permit me to buy you dinner—"

"That's not necessary," Basa said gruffly, and Aubine held out his hand, something clasped in it.

"At least let me pay you for this treat."

"If you insist, my lord," Basa said, and over his shoulder Eslingen saw Siredy struggling to hide a grin. "If you'd like, then—this way."

"Will you come, Siredy?" Eslingen asked, and the other master nodded.

"Absolutely. I like to know what's under my feet."

"And very wise, too," Aubine murmured.

Basa sketched a kind of bow. "If you'll come with me?"

He led the way to a narrow stairhead, banded with iron, where a stairs so steep as to be little more than a ladder dropped into darkness. Eslingen eyed it warily, and the sceneryman slid down it like a sailor, his feet barely touching the side rails, to reappear a moment later with a mage fire lantern.

"As few lamps as possible backstage," Siredy said. "That's another rule of most houses."

Between the painted canvases and the stacked furniture that served to dress the sets, the risk of fire had to be enormous. "I'll bear that very much in mind," Eslingen said, and followed the others down the narrow ladder.

The space under the stage was dark and low, so that a tall man had to stoop beneath the cross beams. It smelled of oil, too, and tar, and polished metal, and Eslingen blinked hard, trying to force his eyes to adjust to the lantern light. Something bulked large behind Basa's shoulders, a dark shape that caught the light in places, and there were more ropes and strangely shaped pieces of wood and metal hanging between the beams. Basa lifted his lantern, did something to the aperture, and the light faded and spread in the same moment. The thing behind him resolved into a massive windlass, with six poles projecting from it like the spokes of a wheel, and for an instant Eslingen had a mad vision of tiny ponies, specially theatre-bred, brought down to turn them. But that would be the scenery-men's job, of course, and that windlass would drive the brass-toothed gears that rose from it, and those gears, it seemed, turned an enor-mous shaft that ran off into the darkness toward the back of the stage.

"This is the main engine," Basa said, and in the close space his voice was hushed, unresonant. But of course sound would be damped down here, Eslingen realized, to keep the noise of the machinery from spoiling the play. "It turns the versatiles—it'll do anything else you want, too, but that's what it's set for now." He pointed. "See there? Those are the cables that take the power off, and bring them around."

"There must be a stop," Aubine said, peering up into the dark-ness, and the sceneryman nodded.

"You have to release the lock first, of course, before you start to turn, and then it locks again at the next scene."

They were talking about the triangular columns, Eslingen real-ized, and filed the word in his memory. Versatiles . . . well, they were certainly that. "How many men does it take to move it?" he asked, and was startled again by the deadness of the sound.

"There's eight men working on *The Drowned Island*," Basa an-swered, "but you can work an ordinary play with three or four."

He lifted the lantern again, beckoning them with the light, and they followed him past the windlass into an area crowded with square shapes. Eslingen blinked, confused, then recognized the towers of the bannerdames' island. Up close, the colors were cruder than he remembered, the shapes overstated—but they were meant to be seen from the pit, from the balconies, not from close up. Beyond them, he could see more massive gears, ready to lift the island up, and drag it down again, and Basa glanced at him.

"Now that takes all eight on the windlass, bringing it down slow and safe—and putting it up at the start of the play, too."

Eslingen nodded, tracing the pattern of ropes and levers that was quickly lost in the shadows.

"How long does it take to switch machines?" Siredy asked, and Eslingen blinked, realizing what he was seeing. The windlass could drive either machine; it was the way the ropes were attached that decided where the power went.

"Less than ten minutes," Basa answered, and Eslingen could hear the pride in his voice—justifiable pride, too, if Siredy's expression was any indication. "Now, up here is the other engine."

He led the way past a cat's cradle of ropes, sliding down through slits in the stage overhead to wind around an array of cleats and pins. Everything was as neatly coiled as on a sailing ship, and Eslingen wondered if all the scenerymen had been sailors.

"That's for the midstage," Basa said, over his shoulder, and Siredy spoke at Eslingen's ear.

"That's where most effects are staged."

Eslingen jumped in spite of himself, glanced up again to see the pattern of light obscured as someone passed along the line of ropes. He'd been standing there himself, he realized, when he'd first tripped over the cable.

"This is where the waves are done," Basa said. The light from the lantern strengthened and focused again as he adjusted the shutters, and Eslingen found himself looking at a second, smaller windlass, with a second set of gears and thick leather bands to transfer the motion to another web of ropes. There seemed to be even more of them than he'd seen before, stretching to dozens of oddly shaped pieces of wood that hung from between the beams—the waves, Eslingen realized suddenly, strips of wood carved and painted to look like breaking waves, and the other strips were the white-painted boards of the breaking ice.

"We pull the stage floor up," Basa said. "You can see the channels, above there. The ice goes up for most of the play, and then, when the ice breaks, they turn down and the waves come up. Some of them are on rockers, and some of them are on spinners, and—well, it's a hell of an effect."

"Indeed it is," Aubine said. Eslingen nodded, but couldn't help looking up at the stage. Now that he knew what to look for, he could see the faint lines of light where the boards could be slipped aside, and he wondered just how strong the supports were. Basa laughed as if he'd read the thought.

"Oh, don't worry, Lieutenant, they'll hold you. You and your regiment, come to that, unless and until someone releases them."

It was, he supposed, reassuring. Siredy's suppressed grin didn't help, either. "The big waves at the end," he said aloud. "They're not here."

"They're in the wings, just back of the trap." Basa grinned. "Now if you want something to worry about, Lieutenant, that would be it.

They're counterweighted, with a rope release—so don't go pulling anything you don't recognize."

"I don't intend to," Eslingen said, more sharply than he'd meant, and Aubine frowned.

"I hope someone has made that announcement to the chorus."

"Tyrseis," Siredy said, not quite under his breath.

"We'd better see that someone does," Eslingen said, and the other master nodded.

"That would be all we need, to drop those on a handful of landames—begging your pardon, my lord."

"I take your point," Aubine agreed. "Master Basa, I thank you for this tour of your domain. I won't think of any play quite the same way again."

Basa ducked his head, looking at once embarrassed and pleased. "If you'll come with me, my lord, I'll show you another way back."

They came out from under the stage on the opposite side of the stagehouse, behind the wings where the noble chorus had stood. Most of them had moved on, were still clustering around the almost emptied tables, and Siredy touched Eslingen's shoulder.

"If you'll excuse me, I think I'll have a quick word with Mathiee."

Eslingen nodded, the image that Basa had raised all too clear in his mind, and Aubine smiled understandingly at him.

"A wise precaution, I think. Tell me, Lieutenant, what's your family?"

From one noble to another, it was an innocuous question, but from a noble to a commoner with pretensions, it was definitely to be avoided. "No one you'd know, I think, my lord. We're from Esling." Eslingen smiled, letting his eyes sweep beyond the older man. "And if you'll forgive me, I think Siredy needs me."

He made his bow without waiting for an answer and swept away into the crowd, not pausing until he'd put a knot of half a dozen landames between himself and Aubine, then looked around for Siredy. The other master waved to him, and Eslingen moved quickly to join him, newly aware of the boards beneath his feet.

"Mathiee says they've been warned, and she'll warn them again when the rehearsals start. We don't need that kind of accident."

"Gods, no," Eslingen agreed. There was enough that could go wrong without inviting that trouble.

❖   ❖   ❖

It was well past midnight by the time Eslingen, weary and yet still keenly awake, returned to Rathe's lodgings, but Rathe was up, sitting at the table, his hands fisted in his hair, staring at some papers and his tablets. He looked up sharply as the latch lifted, but relaxed and smiled when Eslingen entered, quickly shutting the door behind him against the cold.

"You're working late," Eslingen observed, holding his hands out over the stove, banked for the night, but still radiating a welcome heat. There were the remains of what looked to have been a home cooked dinner pushed to one side, and Eslingen restrained a sigh of regret. The evening had been far more fraught than he had expected it to be, and meeting Aconin had been a nasty surprise—or not a surprise, he corrected himself; he knew he would have to encounter him sometime, but balancing Aconin's malice and Aubine's curiosity had been exhausting.

"Yeah, well, the masque makes work for all of us," Rathe said, but pushed his tablets and some papers aside. "There's wine, and yes, I would welcome a cup right now. How did it go at the theatre?"

Eslingen groaned as he sat down on the edge of the bed to remove his boots. "Fascinating, as you can imagine," he drawled, drawing a quick grin from Rathe. "We were introduced to every blessed member of the chorus, I swear, by name and quarterings. . . ."

"Seriously?" Rathe asked quickly, and Eslingen stopped in the act of setting the boots neatly by the foot of the bed, looked at him, curious.

"Well, no, it wasn't that bad, but from what Siredy tells me, your friend Leussi would never have done it that way, Seidos's Horse, it must have taken close to an hour."

"And hungry actors waiting to get to the food," Rathe interjected.

"I was impressed by their ladyships' ability to secure as much food as possible without seeming to do so."

"You never went hungry?"

"I may be an officer and a gentleman, Nico, but I started in the ranks, and I can assure you, no landame or castellan can match me for seizing the main chance. I had half a pie, thank you, and what I imagine was some decent wine."

He brought the wine jug and two cups to the table, set them down before pulling out the chair opposite Rathe. "And some very interesting gossip," he added, and Rathe groaned.

"As if I don't get enough of that from Gavi, now you're going to be regaling me."

"Well, I thought it was interesting," Eslingen said mildly. "Seems our patron once contracted a mesalliance that was rather brutally put an end to by his grandmother, who sounds like something to frighten the children with. And the points wrote it off as a tavern brawl?"

Rathe bit back his annoyance, had to appreciate the way Eslingen delicately cast doubt on the story, but it rang faint bells in his mind. "When was this?" he asked, and Eslingen shrugged.

"Oh, before your time, I would imagine, from what Siredy says. Twenty years ago, almost."

"And the points' authority wasn't as recognized as it is these days. Astree knows, that's still little enough when a noble's involved." He was frowning, trying to recall the matter, which would have happened in the early days of his apprenticeship, but shook his head, gave it up. "Sad, though. One deserves at least that much consolation," he murmured, thinking of Holles. "And he's not at all nonplused by Aconin?"

"Doesn't seem to be, in fact, though he twitted me about my sudden accession of rank with the new name, Chresta seemed a lot more deferential than I'd ever seen him . . ." Eslingen trailed off as Rathe's head lifted sharply.

"You know Aconin?"

"Gods, I didn't mention it? No, I don't suppose I did, it's nothing really to brag about," Eslingen said uncomfortably, stopping in the act of unwinding his stock, wondering at the sudden harsh note in Rathe's voice. "My past comes back to haunt me. I knew him many years ago. We grew up on the same street in Esling, and from what I saw and heard tonight, he hasn't changed much. A quick wit and a nasty one, that was Chresta. Kept him in one piece when we were children, and the two of us motherless children. He found his way out, I found mine."

"You have my sympathies," Rathe murmured. There was something, some note in his voice that made Eslingen glance quickly at him, but Rathe was reaching for his tablets, closing them and neatly piling the papers, securing them with a lead weight. Was this just the general dislike many in the city seemed to have for Aconin, or something more? A deep yawn startled him, and he decided it could wait for another day to query Rathe about it.

4

◆ ⋯⋯⋯⋯⋯⋯⋯⋯⋯⋯⋯⋯⋯⋯⋯⋯⋯⋯⋯⋯⋯⋯⋯⋯⋯⋯⋯⋯ ◆

It was another cold morning, and cloudy, and Eslingen lay for a few minutes in the empty bed struggling to think just where he was before he remembered. He was still unused to being here, and he wasn't sure that either one of them liked this unexpected intimacy. Perverse, really, considering that he, at least, had been thinking in terms of lemanry—but not like this. Not because he'd lost his job and had no other place to stay.

He stretched, glad he'd been able to afford the baths the night before, assessing the protests from muscles he hadn't used in months. They'd gotten a thorough workout with the rest of the masters the day before, earning him the dour approval of Soumet. He stretched farther, experimentally. Not too bad, considering he hadn't had any reason to put in more than cursory practice, but he'd still have to warm up carefully before he went about leading any drills or teaching any lessons. And that meant getting an early start, or what passed for an early start among the actors. He suppressed a groan, and levered himself out of bed.

Rathe had left the teapot half full, still swaddled in a knitted cozy, and the end of a loaf of bread on the table beside it. That was welcoming enough, but the bags still standing in the corner of the main room were less so. Eslingen made a face as he carved himself a slice of the bread, but tidied them back into the corner once he'd found the day's clean linen. At least no one would expect him to wear a good shirt to a rehearsal—or at least he hoped they wouldn't expect it. Rathe had only a small shaving mirror, and Eslingen had to stoop and bend to fasten his stock by its reflection. He had had himself shaved at the baths, thank Seidos, and as he pulled his hair back into a loose queue he felt almost human. All things considered, though, it would probably be a good idea if he started looking for a place of his own. He and Rathe could sort things out between them once this latest crisis was over. He found the breadbox after a brief search, tidied the last of the loaf into it and poured the dregs of the tea into the slop bucket, and let himself out into the chill courtyard.

There had been frost the night before, and the morning light had done nothing yet to melt it except in the most exposed areas. The cobbles were still slick with it, and Eslingen picked his way carefully along the narrow street, grateful to finally reach the wider road that led toward the theatres. The doubled sunlight, the winter-sun setting, the day-sun well up, did little to dissipate the chill, and Eslingen hunched his shoulders under his coat, wishing he'd had the sense to bring his cloak. But the chill wouldn't last, he told himself, knowing it was fashion speaking rather than common sense, and quickened his pace as much as he dared.

Point of Dreams was just waking, though the nearest clock had already struck half-past nine, and the only people on the street were a few pairs of still-sleepy-looking apprentices, taking down shop shutters in preparation for the day's business. Not for the first time, Eslingen wondered how Rathe was adjusting to the change from Point of Hopes, where the day started before the first sunrise, but then put the thought aside. He had work to do, and mooning over Rathe wasn't going to put him in the right frame of mind to handle a full chorus of semitrained and bloody-minded nobles. At least the morning's work was just with the other Masters of Defense, trying to make sense of the script's set pieces. There were—he narrowed his eyes against the day-sun, counting—three staged battles, plus a victory drill, an armed wedding procession, and two separate sword dances, and, of course, the half-dozen duels. The last weren't his responsibility, but he'd be expected to contribute to the drill pieces, and it would be nice to show he was useful early on.

The Tyrseia loomed ahead, the dark slates of its half roof gleaming wetly in the doubled sunlight, and he slowed his pace, trying to remember where Duca had told him to enter the theatre. The main doors were closed and barred—it was not a day for *The Drowned*

Island, or they would never have had the use of the stagehouse—and the few low windows were heavily shuttered, and he hesitated for a second, debating whether to turn left or right around the building's solid curve.

"Philip!"

Eslingen turned, recognizing the voice with relief, and Verre Siredy lifted a hand in greeting.

"I'm glad I caught you up, I couldn't remember if Master Duca had told you where to go."

"Neither could I," Eslingen answered, with perfect truth, and Siredy grinned, showing good teeth. He was not, Eslingen thought again, a particularly handsome man, but there was something very engaging about him all the same. Eslingen had been aware, at the previous day's drills, of the other's interest. Amusing, flattering, certainly, but not a game he wanted to play at the moment.

"We go in by the players' door," Siredy said. "Below the middle stairs."

Eslingen let him lead the way, idly admiring the cut of the other man's coat, a dark red wool with huge jet buttons. It had to have been expensive, but then, in the queen's capital, it was possible to find good clothes barely worn once and then discarded. His own best linen had come from there, and he was seized by a sudden panicked thought: what if one of the noble landseurs recognized his discard? But that was foolish, no one who could afford to get rid of clothing barely worn knew their wardrobe that well—and in any case, his coat and vest were new, the fruits of his time with Caiazzo.

There was a watchman at the door, an older man, his mouth drawn down in permanent disapproval, and behind him the languid de Vicheau rolled his eyes in irritation.

"Is this the lot of you?" the watchman demanded, and de Vicheau shook his head, glancing over his shoulder into the shadows of the theatre.

"No—Master Duca and Sergeant Rieux aren't here."

"Then you'll have to wait here," the watchman said, and stood aside to let them into a narrow tunnel that ran under the lowest tier of galleries. "Hey, you, Mersine! You wait at the head of the ramp, and don't let any of them past you."

"All right." The voice was very young, and came from just below Eslingen's elbow. He repressed a start, and a skinny girl in a patched skirt and bodice pushed past him, to take up her place at the head of the ramp. He blinked, not quite able to repress a smile at the thought of that urchin holding in check the Masters of Defense, and de Vicheau rolled his eyes again.

"Master Watchman," he began, and the watchman held up both hands.

"Not my policy, master, there's nothing I can do. It's because of the machinery, nobody's supposed to be allowed onstage until there's a sceneryman to make sure all's well. And besides, Mistress Gasquine pays me well to make sure no strangers wander loose in her theatre."

"It's not her theatre," de Vicheau muttered, not quite under his breath.

"We're working with Mistress Gasquine on the masque," another man said with ponderous dignity. Eslingen jumped again—he hadn't seen the big man there in the shadows, or the round-faced girl beside him—and the master went on as though he hadn't noticed. "If that's her policy, I trust she's hired a sceneryman, then? Because we have the chorus here at half past noon, expecting to rehearse."

The watchman seemed to realize for the first time that he might be outside his authority, and his voice quavered. "It's the Tyrseia's policy, masters, but if you have to, I know someone you can send to—"

"That won't be necessary," Gerrat Duca said from the doorway, and at his side, Sergeant Rieux held out a slip of paper. "This is Gasquine's warrant, and the merchant-venturers', for us to use the stage."

"You understand, master," the watchman said, "I have to do as I'm told, it's not my right to say who can do what where, I just do what they tell me—"

He pushed past them all as he spoke, moving up the long passage, and the masters closed rank behind him. The girl Mersine bounced once, anticipating something, and then the mage-lights fired, filling the space with blue-toned light. Eslingen caught his breath, startled by the sheer size of the theatre. He had never been on the floor of the pit before, hadn't realized how the galleries loomed over it, three tiers high, each tier painted and gilded as brightly as the outside of the theatre, the colors gleaming in the mage-light that streamed from hundreds of fixed-fire globes. Compared to that, the stage itself seemed bare, pale wood only a few shades darker than the canvas that provided a temporary roof. The day-sun hadn't quite reached it, and the canvas hung slack and dark over the benches that filled the pit. More mage-lights glowed above the stage itself, casting unexpected shadows on the towering scenery—the riverside set for *The Drowned Island*—and Eslingen remembered that they had not been lit during the performance. There was something on the stage, though, a shape like a bundle of rags, and at his side de Vicheau gave a long sigh.

Eslingen echoed him, thinking of delay, looking for the weapons that weren't there, but then the true nature of the shape registered on him, long and low and dark, with one pale shape trailing away from it: not rags at all, but a man sprawled across the polished boards, one hand outstretched as though he was reaching for something.

"Sweet Tyrseis, has it started already?" That was Siredy, already striding forward, but Duca caught his shoulder.

"Wait." He looked at the watchman. "This isn't our sceneryman, I trust?"

The watchman shook his head, seemingly struck speechless, and it was Duca's turn to sigh.

"All right, let's get him sobered up and out of here, and then we can get to work. Siredy, you and Eslingen see to that, the rest of you, see if you can find where the damned carters left our gear."

"It was onstage when I left last night," Rieux protested, but let herself be drawn away with the others.

Eslingen looked at Siredy. "Does this happen often?"

Siredy made a face. "Only for the masque, really. A lot of the players don't take it all that seriously. And Tyrseis knows, they've cause not to. Ah, hells, let's get it over with."

Eslingen nodded, reluctantly, fearing what they'd find on the stage. But the new boy always got the nasty jobs, and at least he didn't smell anything yet. He followed Siredy down the long side aisle, and waited while the other dragged a set of steps from beneath the stage and set it into place, fitting hooks into brass fittings on the edge of the stage itself. It wasn't that tall, only about to a man's waist, but it would make it easier to move the drunk once they were in place.

"And that's something else that should have been done already," Siredy said. "I wonder if this is our sceneryman."

"If it is, I hope the theatre docks his pay." Eslingen followed the other man onto the stage, suddenly aware of the empty seats looming behind him. He had seen dozens of plays so far, but he'd never really imagined being onstage, at the center of that concentrated attention, and it took an effort of will to turn and look up into the galleries, across the empty pit. He tried to imagine those seats filled, a thousand faces and more staring down at him, at them, Siredy and the drunken sceneryman and himself, and felt a thrill that was at once fear and excitement. Someone had told him once that he was never happier than when he was at the center of attention. Well, this was that center with a vengeance, and he made himself turn away again, focusing on the sceneryman still sprawled unmoving in the center of the stage.

"Come along," Siredy said, moving toward him, and Eslingen froze. That was no sceneryman, there was lace at his cuff, shrouding the limp hand, and the hair that fell so heavily, hiding his face, was an expensive wig.

"Wait."

Siredy glanced over his shoulder, eyebrows raised, then drawn down into a frown as he read the other man's expression. "What is it?"

"I'm—not sure." Eslingen reached Siredy's side in two strides. A third brought him to the fallen man, and he knelt cautiously, aware of a nasty smell that wasn't vomit. "I think—" He reached for the man's shoulder as he spoke, felt the flesh hard as wood under his hand. He rolled it toward him, and the body moved all of a piece, stiff and ugly, unmistakably some hours' dead.

"Sweet Tyrseis," Siredy said, his thin face gone suddenly sallow, and Eslingen had to swallow hard himself. The man's face was vaguely familiar, someone he'd seen around the theatre, but the clothes were too good, too new, for this to be some player or fencer or sceneryman. "He's dead."

Eslingen nodded. "And stiff." There were no marks on the front of his body, linen unstained except where bladder and bowels had let go, and the strong high-boned face was curiously expressionless. Definitely someone he'd seen at the theatre, Eslingen thought again. "Siredy—"

"It's the landseur de Raçan," Siredy said, almost in the same moment, and Eslingen let his breath out sharply. One of the noble chorus, one of the names the chamberlain had called out during the interminable introductions.

"How?" Siredy dropped to his knees beside the body, and Eslingen let it fall back again. The wig fell away, revealing close-cut fair hair, and Siredy automatically reached for it, started to put it back, but Eslingen caught his hand.

"Wait." There were no marks on de Raçan's back, either, the well-cut coat undamaged, and stifling his revulsion, Eslingen ran his hand lightly over the dead man's skull. The bone seemed solid enough, no suspiciously soft spots, and he rocked back on his heels again. "I don't know, there's no mark on him—"

Siredy laid the wig carefully beside the dead man's head. "An apoplexy, maybe? He's young for that—"

"Or died of drink or sickness?" Eslingen shook his head. "He's a landseur, he could afford to die in his bed."

"Tyrseis," Siredy said again, and this time it sounded like a prayer.

Eslingen shook himself, stood up, shading his eyes against the mage-light, and thought he saw the girl Mersine moving at the top of one of the ramps. "You—Mersine, is it?"

"Yes, master." The girl came eagerly down the length of the aisle, and Eslingen waved for her to stop, moved by some obscure idea of protecting her.

"Go fetch Master Duca, tell him it's urgent. And then—" He hesitated, but made himself go on. "Then run to the station at Point of Dreams and bring back a pointsman—Adjunct Point Rathe, if he can be spared."

"The points?" Siredy said, rising, and scrubbed his hands on his breeches. "Are you sure about that? Master Duca—"

"Will surely see reason," Eslingen said. "Verre, there's no other choice. What else are we going to do, dump the body out the back door and hope someone else deals with him?"

From the look on Siredy's face, the thought had crossed his mind, and Eslingen was suddenly glad he'd taken matters into his own hands. "Go on," he said to the girl, and she darted back up the aisle, visibly delighted to be the bearer of such exciting news.

Rathe had left Eslingen still asleep, mildly bemused at the man's capacity for it, and spent the first hours of the morning at the Sofian temple, again working doggedly through the rolls. The stoves were empty still, and his hands and feet were like ice when he was done, despite the secretary's mitts and the extra stockings he'd brought to warm them. Still, he thought, huddling himself under his winter cloak as he walked toward Dreams, it had been a profitable morning's work. All the connections were there, only one a sibling, but the rest cousins and nieces and all the collateral kin. The most distant was a second cousin, and he had to admit it made sense even as he cursed the situation. These were the right degrees of kinship to create discreet hostages, the kind that might not ever be noticed—might, Seidos willing, never need to be noticed—and he had to admire the queen's, or Astreiant's, cleverness.

Aliez Sohier was the duty point, one of his private favorites, and he smiled in answer to her cheerful greeting, unwinding himself from cloak and jerkin.

"Any news in the markets?" she asked, and he looked up, startled, balancing on one foot as he started to strip off the extra stockings.

"About?"

She shrugged. "Scandals, mayhem. Earthquakes at the solstice?"

She was as fond of the broadsheets as Eslingen, and Rathe sighed. "Predictions of a harsher winter than normal, that's all I noticed."

"After last year?" Sohier made a face.

The previous year's almanacs had predicted a mild winter. In fact, the Sier had frozen, and there had been reports of wolves not far outside the city, but Astreiant had carried on as usual. It was winter, the old dames said, when the less hardy grumbled. Of course it was cold. *And that*, Rathe thought, scuffling his feet back into the heavy shoes, *was the typical Astreianter reaction. Not building towers on the ice*. He balled the stockings into his pocket along with the mitts, and crossed to the desk. Sohier pushed the daybook toward him, and he paged through the previous night's entries. Voillemin had gone to Little Chain, he saw with pleasure, but had made no note of what he'd found. And maybe it was nothing—probably was nothing—but it did no one any good to ignore the obvious.

The door slammed open, bouncing back against the wall, and Rathe spun to face it, hearing Sohier curse behind him. A skinny girl, no more than twelve, stood there, coatless, trying to catch her breath, her face and eyes alight with excitement. "Well?" Sohier demanded.

"Sorry, dame," the girl said, and bobbed a kind of a curtsy. "The masters sent me, for a pointsman. There's a body on the stage at the Tyrseia, and one of the masters insisted we send for the points, and the theatre was locked up last night, same as always—oh, and please, if he's here, it's someone named Rathe they're wanting."

Rathe looked at Sohier, knowing the shock on her face matched his own. "Get Falasca and Leenderts to take over, I want you with me."

She nodded, already shouting for a runner, and Falasca came scurrying, fastening her coat, to take the other woman's place at the table.

"Tell Trijn as soon as she arrives," Rathe said, and reached into his pocket, fingers closing on the folded sheets of paper that held his notes. *The Tyrseia*, he thought. *Sweet Astree*. All the chorus there— all the hostages there—and already a dead man, and—But it wouldn't be Eslingen, he told himself. A master who had insisted on sending for the points, who had asked for him by name, that could only be the Leaguer.

"Please, sir," the girl said, "they wanted a Master Rathe—"

"That's me," Rathe said, and shook himself back to the moment, managed what he hoped was a reassuring smile. He had to leave the papers, couldn't risk losing them, and he took the stairs two at a time, already groping in his pocket for the key to his seldom-used lockbox. It was, inevitably, buried under a stack of broadsheets and flimsy editions of the Alphabet, but he brushed them aside, slid the list into the otherwise empty container. He'd almost never had to use it before, except for holding found monies or other negotiables, and it seemed strange to use it now, for politics. He shook the thought away, locked the box again, and headed back to the main room.

Leenderts had arrived, was nodding as Sohier explained the situation. Someone had brought the girl to one of the stoves, Rathe saw with approval, and found a patched shawl to throw over her shoulders for the return journey.

"Do we know who it is?" Leenderts asked, and Rathe shook his head even as he glanced at the girl.

"They wouldn't let me see," she said, and sounded vaguely aggrieved. "And nobody said anything except fetch the points."

Rathe spread his hands in answer and reached for his own cloak. The extra stockings were still in his pocket, and he wished he had time to pull them on. "Keep things quiet," he said to Leenderts, and the other man nodded in perfect comprehension.

"I'll do that, Adjunct Point."

Not that there was much chance of it, Rathe thought as he and Sohier hurried through the drying streets, the girl bouncing between them. Even cloaked as they were, they were recognizably pointsmen, and he was all too aware of the eyes following them as they made their way toward the theatre. At least the open square in front of it was all but empty, the petty merchants who crowded the surrounding arcade on open days busy at the other theatres, too wise to waste their merchandise on starving actors. Only the tavern was unshuttered, and it was very quiet, its door dark and only the smell of wood smoke drifting from its chimney. That might help, Rathe thought, but then he saw the serving girl, skirts shortened to show bright red stockings, hovering just inside the doorway. She ducked back, seeing him looking, and in spite of himself, his mouth tightened. There was nothing to do about it, though, and he turned his head away, scanning the Tyrseia's imposing facade. All the doors were closed, the windows shuttered, but a cloaked figure was waiting beside one of the barred stairways, arms wrapped around his body to keep the heat in.

"Adjunct Point Rathe?" he asked, and Rathe nodded.

"That's me. And you are?"

"Verre Siredy, Adjunct Point. Of the Guild of Defense."

Eslingen had mentioned the name, and Rathe nodded. "The girl said there was a death."

"This way." Siredy pointed to the door beneath the stairway—the players' entrance, Rathe realized—and they ducked past the staring doorman into a tunnel that sloped up toward the floor of the pit. The masters were waiting there, huddled in groups among the benches, but the crumpled shape, stage center, drew every eye. At least they'd had the sense not to move it, Rathe thought, and guessed he could thank Eslingen for that. He looked around, searching for the person in charge, and Siredy cleared his throat.

"Master Duca."

A big man, florid faced and as brightly dressed, swung away from his low-voiced conversation with a stocky woman. "At last. So you're the pointsman."

"Adjunct Point," Siredy murmured, and the big man waved the words away. "And this is Master Duca, senior master of the Guild."

"Points—Adjunct Point, we have a rehearsal called for noon, and Gasquine's crew should be here before then, and what are we to do about this?" Duca waved to the stage, his voice scaling up before he had it under control.

Oh, that's all we need. Rathe swallowed the words, turned to Sohier. "Tell the doorman to keep them out—or, wait, ask Mathiee to step in to me, but keep the rest of them outside. I'll tell her myself she'll have to rehearse elsewhere today."

Sohier nodded and swung away, but Duca burst out, appalled, "You can't do that—" He broke off, as though he'd realized what he said, and Rathe managed a rueful smile.

"I have some idea of what I'm asking, master, believe me. And if there's any way I can give the house back to you, I will. But there's a man dead who needs his rights."

Duca nodded, jerkily. "You're right, of course. My apologies, Adjunct Point. It's just—Seidos's balls, why did it have to be one of them?"

" 'Them'?" Rathe repeated, the word curdling in his belly.

Duca swept off his hat to run his hand through his hair. "The chorus, damn them all."

And that's all we need to make this a perfect day. Rathe lifted his hand, forestalling anything else the big man would have said. "We'll get to that, master," he said in his most commanding voice, and glanced over his shoulder to see Sohier picking her way between the benches. "Sohier. Let's see what we've got."

There was a short staircase hooked to the side of the stage, and he climbed gingerly up onto the empty platform, weirdly aware of the empty seats as well as the staring masters. He glanced back once, saw Eslingen among them, then made himself concentrate on the body. It lay on its back, arms outspread, not a young man, but not old, tall, fair-haired beneath the disordered wig, and well built. The clothes were definitely too good to belong to any of the actors—not that the actors didn't dress as well as they could afford, but this was the kind of quality that didn't count the cost. For a moment, he regretted the list he'd left locked away at the station. Somewhere on it, he'd listed this man and his connections, had been studying him just this morning, most likely.

He shook the thought away, and knelt by the body, touched it gently. The skin was cold, and more than that, clammy, almost damp. In the mage-light, he could see that the skin had an odd tinge, almost a softness to it, and under the man's head was a small puddle of water. He'd expected to see blood, or worse, and ran his hands over the skull, probing for breaks in the arched bone. He found none, and nothing in the neck, either, or farther down the body, no wound, no sign of a blow, nothing to explain the death. Except for the puddle. Cautiously, he touched a finger to it, brought it to his nose, more carefully to his tongue. Nothing. He rocked back on his heels, looking up at Sohier, and saw the same puzzlement in her face. She saw him looking, and started to speak, but he held up a hand, silencing her.

"First things first," he said, and saw her confusion deepen, but he ignored it, looked past her into the pit. It was only the masters here, luckily; if the dead man was in fact a member of the chorus, they would only have known him for a day or two, if that, and so were not in a position to make the formal identification required by law. *And today may be the day I need that bit of formality*, Rathe thought, and hoped he was borrowing trouble.

He pushed himself to his feet. "All right. Do any of you recognize him?"

The masters exchanged glances, and then, reluctantly, Siredy stepped out from among the group.

"It's the landseur de Raçan, Adjunct Point."

"And who found the body?"

"We all saw it," Siredy answered, sounding faintly defensive, "but it was me and Lieutenant vaan Esling who saw he was dead."

In spite of himself, Rathe glanced at Eslingen, saw the Leaguer look faintly embarrassed at his new name. "And you know the landseur, Master Siredy?"

"Yes."

There was something in the single syllable, and Rathe's eyes narrowed, surprising a faint blush in the other man. There was something there, more than just the masque, but he couldn't afford to pursue it now, not if what he suspected was true. He looked down at the stage, at the tiny puddle, already shrinking. He needed the alchemists, needed their verdict on the death, and if he allowed the man to be named, formally and in law, he'd need the permission of the next of kin, whoever and wherever they might be. *And may the Good Counsellor pardon me*, he thought, *but I don't have time for that*. He looked around for the girl who'd come for them, found her peeping out from behind the broad-bodied woman's skirts. "You— what's your name, child?"

"Mersine."

She seemed remarkably unaffected by the presence of the dead, but then, Rathe thought, she'd grown up in Astreiant's theatres. "Are you the only runner here?"

"Not anymore." She shook her head for emphasis. "Tilly's here, too, with Master Cann."

"Good. I need you both to run two errands for me." He fished in his pocket for his purse, came up with a couple of seillings that he flipped to her. She caught them expertly, grinning now, and Rathe went on. "I need one of you to go to Point of Dreams and bring back the duty watch. I need the other to go to the deadhouse in University Point—take a low-flyer, they'll know the way—and tell them we have a body that needs transporting. And I need you both to hurry. Understand?"

Mersine nodded. "I'll go to the deadhouse," she said. "Tilly wouldn't dare." She darted away, skirts flying, and Duca stepped forward to close his hands on the edge of the stage.

"Adjunct Point." His voice was barely under control, and instinctively Rathe crouched beside him, hoping to defuse the anger. "Didn't you hear—don't you understand? Siredy knows him. That"—he pointed to the body—"is a landseur. You don't send their bodies off to the deadhouse, you send them to the priests of the Good Counsellor—"

"The law requires a formal identification, someone who knew him for more than your, what, two days, three days?" Rathe said, with as much patience as he could muster.

Duca waved his hand, brushing the words aside. "I'm not a fool, Adjunct Point, I've seen the formalities dispensed with before this."

"There's something very wrong with this death," Rathe said softly. "We need to know how he died."

Duca blinked at that, the words sinking home, and then he shook his head. "Sickness?" he asked, without much hope.

"Possibly," Rathe said. "But there's not a mark on him, Master Duca, not injury or illness, and before I call this an apoplexy, I want to be sure I know the truth."

"Tyrseis." Duca pushed himself away from the stage, his heavy face drained of color. "What will this do to the masque?"

That was a thought that hadn't occurred to Rathe, but it was a good question. If the masque and the realm's health were intimately bound, then there was all the more need to know everything possible about this death. "That's why I can't wait on his family's pleasure," he said aloud, and Duca nodded, jerkily.

"Of course, Adjunct Point. I don't mean to tell you your business."

"Thank you," Rathe said, and rose to his feet again, beckoning to Sohier. "Mathiee's people will be along any minute now, if I'm any judge, and I'll have to deal with her. I want you to walk the stage floor, see if you can spot any tubs, barrels, troughs, anything like that. You know what we're looking for."

She nodded, but her voice was a whisper of protest. "Nico, he can't have . . . drowned."

"What signs do you see?" Rathe asked, and her eyes fell.

"Yes, but—how can a man drown here?"

"Maybe not here," Rathe said, though from the sprawl of the body he doubted it had been moved far from where it lay. "That's the alchemists' business. But I want to rule out whatever we can. Now go."

"Right," Sohier said, pale but determined, and hurried away.

There was still no word from the door, and Rathe followed his own advice, moving along the opposite side of the stagehouse. The boards sounded hollow beneath his feet, and he stooped, to see the shallow troughs that held the carved waves of *The Drowned Island*'s effects. That looked promising, but when he levered up the nearest trap, he saw that the trough was pierced through with tiny holes. He let the trap fall again, frowning, and scanned the area around him. He was between two of the massive set towers, the versatiles, Eslingen had called them when he'd come home babbling of the machinery, but beyond them was a maze of more familiar gear, ropes and tables and a three-legged chair propped against the wall for mending. There was a large barrel, too, and he stepped over to it, lifting the lid. It was half full of ash, and he let the lid fall back with a thud that raised a puff of grey dust. There were half barrels, too, three of sawdust and one of sand, and a cracked leather bucket that looked as though it hadn't held water since the last queen's reign, but there was nothing, nothing in sight that held enough water to drown a man. Sohier will find something, he told himself, and didn't believe his own words. He looked back at the stage, hoping to see another answer from this different angle, saw only the sprawl of the body. The dead man's face rose in his mind. Drowning was a common death in Astreiant, the Sier took its share of the foolish and the unlucky every year; like most folk southriver born, he'd learned the signs of drowning even before he'd joined the points. And this was a drowned man, the slack, soft skin and, most of all, the telltale pool of water, all proclaimed him drowned, and it was up to Fanier, the best of the alchemists, to tell him how it had come about.

He looked up then, tracing the length of a versatile, saw above it the edge of the great carved wave that hung above the stage. In the soft mage-light, it was hard to tell, but he thought its shadow fell across the huddled body, and he looked away with a gasp, to see the second wave looming between the next pair of versatiles. Oh, there was water on the stage, carved and painted water in plenty, but surely, surely no mere effect could drown a man on dry land. The idea was mad, but he pulled his tablets from his pocket, began listing the scenery he saw around him, sketching it quickly and as best he could. He didn't look up as Sohier joined him, folding the wooden halves back over each other.

"Anything?"

"Nothing so far," she said stubbornly. "But there has to be—"

She broke off at the shout from the stage door, and Rathe turned to see Mathiee Gasquine pause for an instant at the top of the tunnel before sweeping down into the pit. The masters scattered before her, and behind her the watchman hovered helplessly, hands raised. Rathe took a breath, bracing himself, and she lifted her skirts to climb easily onto the stage.

"Adjunct Point—" She broke off, seeing the body perhaps for the first time, and Rathe came forward quickly, not to turn her away, she'd never submit to that, but to stand between her and the evidence.

"Mistress Gasquine." He gave her title for title.

"So it's true, then," she said, and Rathe blinked.

"Did you think I'd leave you that word for a joke?"

That surprised a quick grin from her, but she shook her head. "Hoped, maybe. Nico, I understand you need the theatre for a little while, need to search, do whatever you must, but this is the first day we've been able to work here, and I, my people, desperately need to work on the real stage, the one we're going to use. How soon can we have it back?"

Rathe shook his head in genuine apology. "Not today, Mathiee, I'm truly sorry."

"Not today?" Gasquine's voice rose, ringing effortlessly through the theatre, and behind her in the pit the masters drew together to watch. "Nico, *The Drowned Island* plays again tomorrow, I've no use of the place for two days more, and I don't have the time to waste. We need to work here."

"And so do I." Rathe knew better than to match her tone, let his own voice fall a little, become confidential. "There is—potentially— something very odd about this death—"

"Well, there would be," Gasquine snapped, "de Raçan dead on my stage."

Rathe winced. That killed any real pretense he had that the body hadn't been identified, but he went on as though she hadn't spoken. "And, there being something odd about it, it's my responsibility— given the place and the circumstances and the masque itself—to make very sure what happened before I turn the place back to you. For this or *The Drowned Island.*"

"You don't mean it." Gasquine's voice had lost its theatrical ring.

"Can and do," Rathe answered. "If we're not done, *The Drowned Island* won't play. Besides . . ." He paused. "You won't like this, either, Mathiee, but I'd say, if the death's not natural, the chamberlains may want to bring in a magist, perform, I don't know, some cleansing, to make sure it doesn't affect the masque."

"Oh, gods, they might," Gasquine said. "They would. Sweet Oriane, preserve me from the chamberlains." She took a breath. "All right. You've made your point, Nico, and I'll stand it. Master Duca, will you set one of your people to redirect mine, and I'll return to the Bells and roust out the rest of my people there."

"Thank you, mistress," Rathe said, bowing, and Duca came forward, offering his hand to the actress as she descended from the stage. She turned back, looking up at Rathe, her heart-shaped face set into an expression more regal than most queens'.

"But I will hold you to your promise, Adjunct Point. I want my stage again."

"As soon as may be, mistress," Rathe answered, and was grateful when she swept away.

The reinforcements from Point of Dreams arrived within the hour, and Rathe set them to a thorough search of the theatre, hoping they would find what he knew had to be there. The carters from the deadhouse were only a few minutes behind them, arriving with cart and boards just as Duca's men were turning away the first of the actors. The chorus would be along shortly, Rathe knew, and wondered how they would react to the news. Time enough for that after the body was dealt with, though, and he nodded to the strapping woman in a shabby blue coat who led the group.

She nodded back, already unfastening its buttons, tossed it to one of the men behind her. "Can we take something for you, Adjunct Point?"

He gestured to the body, and wondered if the actors were corrupting him. "I'd appreciate it if you'd confirm my suspicions."

The woman nodded briskly, rolling back her sleeves to reveal a stylized version of the Starsmith's badge tattooed into her forearm. She knelt by the body, automatically folding her short skirts well out of the way, ran her hands over it once, feeling for any signs of life. She sat back, reaching into her jerkin for a pair of brass-framed spectacles, and peered up at him over the top of the frame.

"You suspect he's dead?"

Among other things. "Something like that," he said aloud, and she nodded.

"He's dead. We'll take him along to Fanier for you."

"Wait." Rathe hesitated, then put aside his first question, not wanting to bias her with his own suspicions, said instead, "Can you tell if the body's been moved?"

Her eyebrows rose, but she turned back to the body willingly enough, hands moving over it again. This time, she tested limbs— loosening from the rigor, by the look of them, Rathe thought, and winced as she tugged the landseur's shirt free to examine his torso. "All things are possible," she said at last, "but by the look and feel of him, I'd say not. I'd say he dropped dead here."

And not a tub, barrel, or useful bucket anywhere in sight. Rathe glanced up at the overhanging wave, and saw the woman's eyes following his, suddenly widening as she realized what she'd seen. Then she shook herself with an exclamation of disgust and waved to her fellows. "All right, you lot, bring him along. You're welcome to ride with us, Adjunct Point."

That was not something he relished, a ride on the dead cart with apprentice alchemists and their very peculiar sense of right and wrong, but there was no help for it. "Thanks," he said. "Sohier!"

The pointswoman straightened from her examination of yet another trapdoor, and came to join him. "Sir?"

"I want your report as soon as you can get it. You know what you're looking for."

Sohier nodded, still pale, and Rathe sighed.

"Pray Sofia you find it."

The deadhouse lay in University Point, set discreetly away from the main quadrangle and the towering dome of the library in a tangled neighborhood of chairmakers and leatherworkers and the occasional chemist. By rights, of course, Rathe thought, trying to ignore the story the junior apprentice was recounting about someone sup-

posedly eaten by a giant fish, it should be in City Point, but that area
was far too grand for the homely business of examining the dead. It
was a long, low building, much like the petty manufactories surrounding it, except that its walls were stone rather than timber, and the
glassed-in windows glowed with mage-light instead of the warmer
lamplight. To his relief, the apprentices dropped him at the main
door instead of bringing him in with the body, and he took a breath,
bracing himself before pushing through into the narrow lobby. He
had been to the deadhouse dozens of times, but he still couldn't be
easy about it, no matter how often he'd been there. The place was
impeccably clean, floors and walls scrubbed, so scrupulously free of
odors that it was almost impossible not to think about what wasn't
there. Even the sharp stink of daybane would have been preferable.

A trio of apprentices were at work in the lobby, on their knees
with pails and scrubbing brushes, but at his entrance one rose, rubbing her hands on her skirts, and came to greet him.

"You're the pointsman with the body?"

There was no use in standing on rank at the deadhouse. Rathe
nodded.·

"Fanier said I should bring you straight back."

She was no more than thirteen, Rathe thought, bemused, as he
followed her down the long corridor that led to the workrooms, and
wondered what her stars were like that she'd been brought into this
profession. She paused at a cross-corridor, consulting a slate tacked
to the wall, then brought him to a closed door. She knocked, and it
swung open to her touch.

"Adjunct Point Rathe, master."

"Oh. Good." Fanier turned, blinking a little, and Rathe tried not
to look at the body that lay on the stone table behind him, an older
apprentice busy stripping away the last of the clothing. "Go on, then,
this isn't for you yet."

Rathe blinked, but he'd been talking to the girl. She made a face,
but turned away, closing the door a little too sharply behind her.

"Nice to get them eager," Fanier said, rubbing his hands together
as though to warm them for the work ahead, "but it's early days to
call her in. So this one's yours, eh? When did you transfer to
Dreams?"

He looked more than ever like a bear, Rathe thought, his already
bulky body thickened by a heavy fisherman's jersey and a leather
apron, his thick grey hair springing loose and untidy around his broad

face. Brass-framed glasses, like the first apprentice's, were perched awkwardly among the curls, as though he'd forgotten they were there. Beneath them, his expression was bearlike, too, and Rathe shook himself back to the question at hand. "I was advanced to senior adjunct there about a month ago."

"Liking it?" Fanier was still watching the apprentice straighten the body, and Rathe suppressed a shudder.

"It's interesting," he said. That was easily the safest answer. "Things like this don't happen much in Hopes."

"No. Straightforward place, Hopes," Fanier said, without a trace of a smile. "So. Dead on the Tyrseia stage, eh? And a man of quality, by his linen."

Rathe nodded. "Which is likely to make trouble, once the family finds out, so the sooner you can determine for me what killed him, the better I'll like it."

"Oh, yes," Fanier said, almost vaguely, and nodded to the apprentice. "All right, lad, I'll take him now."

Rathe looked away as the alchemist moved toward the body, focusing his attention instead on the empty courtyard he could see beyond the low windows. It had always seemed perverse to him to have windows in these workrooms or, rather, to have them set so low, where anyone walking past could see the alchemists at work. And where any local children could dare each other to steal glances, he thought, but then remembered Fanier saying that was how they found about a third of their apprentices. He could hear the others moving behind him, Fanier mumbling something that was answered with a clang of metal against stone, and Rathe winced, concentrating on the stones patterning the court. At least today there weren't any lurking children—no one in sight at all, not even the alchemists' own apprentices, and the stones looked dark with rain. Sleet soon, probably, Rathe thought, squinting at the slate-dark sky, and suppressed a shiver.

"Well, the cause of death's easy enough," Fanier announced, and Rathe glanced warily over his shoulder. The apprentice was just covering the body with a clean sheet, a last few flickers of mage-light dying from around it as he did so, and Rathe tried to hide his relief. "He drowned. Might have been unconscious before he went into the water, that's usually the way of it if it's murder. Hard to drown somebody otherwise, especially a man in as decent shape as this one." He tipped his head to one side, considering. "Thing is, that usually means a whacking great blow, usually on the head, and there's not a mark on him. Not in the water very long, either, just enough to die there. Does that help you?"

"Not much," Rathe said, and Fanier nodded.

"Didn't think so."

"Because so far, we haven't found anything that could hold enough water to drown a man," Rathe went on, and suppressed the memory of the looming waves, and the smaller ones lurking beneath the stage floor. "Could he have been moved? Drowned elsewhere, and his body left at the Tyrseia?"

"Ursine said she didn't think so," the apprentice said, and colored deeply as both men looked at him.

"Mmm." Fanier ran his hand through his hair, dislodging his glasses, but caught them before they could fall. He polished them absently, turning back to stare at the body, and Rathe saw another flicker of movement, almost as though a breeze had touched the concealing sheet. The air was utterly still. "No. Ursine's got a good eye for that, I must say. Died and left and found, all in the same place."

Rathe heard the distant note in his voice, as though he was listening to that same invisible wind, and Fanier shook himself. "Which is to say, the changes in the body have been steady and consistent since the moment of death. If he'd been moved, well, we'd feel it— you'd see it on him, most likely, how the blood pools."

"I take your word for it," Rathe said, a little faintly—there were times when he hated dealing with the deadhouse—and Fanier went on as though he hadn't spoken.

"Which would seem to indicate murder, if you can't find a bath to drown him in, but you're still missing that whacking great blow. It could be poison, I suppose, to keep him quiet. But that's going to take me a little longer to find out."

"We don't have a lot of time, Fan," Rathe answered. "The unofficial—highly unofficial—"

"And I daresay accurate," Fanier murmured.

"—identification is that this is the landseur de Raçan. And once his family is informed, the odds are we lose any chance of discovering anything more from that body."

Fanier made a sympathetic noise. "I'll do what I can, of course. And I sent for Istre, but I suspect he has a class."

"I gave it up as a bad bet."

Rathe turned, to see b'Estorr standing in the open door, the same apprentice who had escorted him from the door scowling at the magist.

"Magist b'Estorr," she said, with icy reproof, and Fanier nodded. "I can see that, and we still don't need you. Run along."

The girl's scowl deepened, but she closed the door gently enough behind her. b'Estorr wiped one hand over his mouth, and Rathe guessed he was hiding a smile.

"Students finally got to you, then?" Fanier asked. "Only took you, what, three years to cancel a class during ghost-tide?"

"It wasn't the students," b'Estorr answered, and this time the smile was rueful. "It was the other masters. What have you found, Nico?"

"A body in the Tyrseia," Rathe answered, and was meanly pleased to see the other man's eyes widen. "Drowned, and no obvious place to do it in, and Fanier says the body's not been moved. Can you tell if there's a ghost?"

With a sigh, b'Estorr crossed to the shrouded body, gently lifted the drapery away. He stared at the dead man for a long moment, then lightly placed a hand over the man's heart. His expression was calm, remote, eyes fixed on something the others couldn't see, and then Rathe sensed a shift in the vague—presence—that he recognized as b'Estorr's constant ghosts. Then b'Estorr's hand closed and lifted, and the magist turned away from the body, one eyebrow rising.

"Oh, yes. There's a ghost. Thought something of himself, did he?"

There was a strange note in b'Estorr's voice, the whisper of the upcountry Chadroni vowels that years at the university and the Chadroni court had beaten out of him, and Rathe blinked. "Why do you say that?"

b'Estorr shook himself. "I can't blame him for not taking kindly to being murdered, but I do dislike that kind of arrogance." He smiled wryly. "And that's arrogance of my own, I know. So he drowned, Fanier? Drugged?"

"If your lordship wouldn't mind waiting," Fanier said, and b'Estorr's grin became more genuine.

"Sorry."

Fanier nodded to the waiting apprentice, who had a tablet ready. "All right. There's no evidence of gross violence done to the body, either before or after death. That leaves poisons and other subtle violence, which it's now my duty to examine for."

The apprentice scribbled rapidly, charcoal moving across the sheet of rough paper, and Fanier glared at the body. "You know how much I hate trying to prove murder during the ghost-tide," he said. "And that's what you're after, Nico, isn't it?"

"I'd really rather it wasn't," Rathe answered. "But drowning on a bone-dry stage isn't likely to be accidental, is it?"

"No, no, I'll grant you that," Fanier said. "But it's going to take time."

"Fan—" Rathe stopped himself, tried again. "I'll wait. I want to know for certain before I send to the family."

b'Estorr's head lifted. "Do you mean we're sitting on a body whose family hasn't been notified yet?"

"Istre," Rathe began, and b'Estorr lifted both hands.

"I think I'll wait, too."

Fanier snorted, reaching beneath the table to clatter his tools together. "I thought you might."

"Do you know how many ordinances of the university are being broken by your acting without notifying the family?" b'Estorr demanded. Fanier ignored him, evidently taking the question as rhetorical, and the necromancer shook his head. "As a master of the university, it's my duty to remain and make sure you don't break any more—than you have to."

Fanier grinned at that, hands busy with something that was like but not quite an astrologer's flat orrery, and Rathe sighed. "Thanks," he said, and b'Estorr waved the word away, his face suddenly sober.

"If you're right, you'll have enough to worry about."

And that was all too true, Rathe thought. He made a face, watching out of the corner of his eye as Fanier stooped over the body, laying tiny brass figures over heart and lungs and viscera. The polished shapes seemed to catch the available light, concentrating it, and for a second, Rathe thought he saw the wet dark red shape of the man's liver, floating ghostlike above his unbroken skin. He looked away then, swallowing hard, saw the landseur's clothing discarded on a side table.

"Think there'll be a problem if I look through that?" he asked softly, and b'Estorr glanced at him, an expression almost of indulgence hovering on his face.

"It shouldn't bother them," he said aloud, and Rathe moved to the table, grateful for the distraction.

There wasn't much to find, and he hadn't expected much, but

he went methodically through pockets and purse, laid out his meager findings beside the man's stacked shoes. They were newly soled, Rathe saw, and a part of him winced, thinking of now-unnecessary expense. But the man could afford it, he told himself, at least by the look of the rest of his goods. There was a posy in a gilt-filigree holder, a simple spray of tiny bell-shaped blossoms poised against a single dark green leaf, a lace-edged handkerchief and a Silklands amber snuffbox, and a pair of bone dice. Rathe's attention sharpened at that—gamblers created their own personal hazards, more often than not—but a second look made him put that notion aside. The dice were carved with the signs of the solar zodiac, a child's toy, for idle fortune-telling, not the tool of a serious gambler. There were no small coins in the flat purse, just a couple of square pillars, and, folded very small, a recent letter of credit for an amount that raised Rathe's eyebrows. The man had not been kept on a short leash, that much was certain, but there was no way to tell if any or all of the draft had been used. There were no letters, threatening or demanding or even a scrawled invitation card, and the fashionable red-bound tablets were empty, the wax stiff from disuse. Little enough evidence of a life, he thought, saddened in spite of himself, and turned away again. Nothing to help him, certainly.

It was more than an hour before Fanier straightened at last, motioning for the apprentice to put away his tablets and recover the body, and b'Estorr met him with a faint smile. Fanier scowled.

"All right. What is it?"

b'Estorr looked down at his hands, but the movement didn't quite hide the smugness of his smile. "I don't think you'll find it's a traditional form of poison."

"You are not," Fanier said, "going to tell me it's some rare Chadroni poison, are you?"

b'Estorr shook his head. "I'm not even going to tell you it's a rare Silklands poison, which is what I was thinking—since the body does seem to be remarkably untouched." He paused. "Are you still cataloging Chadroni poisons?"

"Man has to have a hobby." Fanier pushed his glasses back to the top of his head. "Damn it all, there are changes consistent with poison, and for my best guess a vegetable poison, but I couldn't tell you which one, or how it was given him—not in food or drink, I suspect, but I can't swear. But the poison isn't what killed him, what killed him is the Dis-damned water in his lungs."

"So you'll swear it's murder, and not accident?" Rathe asked, and reached for his own folded tablets.

"I'm not happy," Fanier said. "Drowned he is, and probably poisoned, and on a dry stage, Nico."

"Fanier," Rathe said, and the alchemist cleared his throat.

"I'll swear to it. I just wish I had more to swear to."

Rathe nodded in sympathy, and looked to the clock that stood on the shelf that ran along the far wall. It was a pretty thing, painted with a wreath of flowers that went badly with the brass instruments surrounding it. Almost three o'clock, he saw, and made a note of it with a sigh. "All right, Fan."

"I have made a preliminary determination that the body brought to me a short time ago died by drowning at the hands of person or persons unknown, with other violence possibly perpetrated before death. This I do swear." Fanier lifted a hand to his forehead, an ancient gesture, and Rathe shivered again.

"And I state that the body is that of the landseur de Raçan," he said aloud, "identification being made by the examination of his belongings after the cause of death had been determined. So do I swear."

"And I bear witness to you both," b'Estorr said, "in the name of the university." He paused. "Now what are you going to do, Nico?"

Rathe lifted a shoulder wearily. "Now we send for the priests of the Good Counsellor and let them notify the family—their business, thank all the gods, not mine. And then—" He glanced at the clock again, trying to guess the actors' schedules. "Then I'm for Point of Dreams, and the Bells, and an evening talking to actors, if I'm lucky."

b'Estorr grimaced in sympathy, and Fanier said, "I'll have my report done up formally, Nico, and a copy for you by morning."

"Thank you," Rathe said with real gratitude, and let the apprentice lead him back out of the deadhouse.

His nose for weather was still good, he saw: the drizzle was changing to sleet as he made his way back across the river to Point of Dreams. The Bells was well lit, as he'd expected, and there were candy-sellers and a dozen other hangers-on clustered at the one unbarred entrance. At least some of the chorus was there, and a few of the actors, the latter gathered around a woman selling warm spiced beer. Happy to take a break from the day's work, Rathe guessed, but his eyes narrowed as he recognized one of the men on the fringes of the chattering crowd. Lyhin was a known gossipmonger, served at least a dozen printers, and Rathe took himself firmly in hand. There had been no hope of keeping this story out of the broadsheets; all he could do was try to minimize it. Even so, he was aware of the looks that followed him as he showed his truncheon to the doorman, and heard his name repeated behind him, rippling out through the crowd.

It was warmer in the theatre, and someone had spread sawdust to absorb the worst of the mud. It made Rathe think of the Tyrseia, the dry barrels of sand and wood chips, and he shook his head, hoping Sohier had found something more. He paused for a moment at the edge of the stagehouse, looking for Gasquine, and found her finally on the stage itself, talking urgently to a tall, well-built woman that Rathe recognized as Anjesine bes'Hallen. All the rivalries were suspended for the masque, he knew, but this was surprising: bes'Hallen was Savatier's leading player, had the right to refuse a play she didn't care for, so to see her here boded well for the quality of Aconin's play. The air smelled of sweat and too much perfume, and he glanced into the pit to see what seemed to be half the chorus gathered idle. It didn't take much imagination to guess what they were talking about, Rathe thought, and suppressed a sigh. One of them must have known de Raçan—no one could have so lackluster a life as the man's belongings suggested—but for the rest . . . Well, he was a nine-days' wonder, if that, and nothing more. He started toward the stage just as a burst of laughter came from the group sitting closest, center front, and Gasquine rounded on them.

"And if you've nothing to do, I suggest you take yourselves to the loft, and let the masters put you through your paces."

There was an appalled silence—their ladyships weren't used to being spoken to in that fashion, Rathe thought, amused—but then one of them rose, and the rest followed, sweeping past Rathe up the center aisle. Gasquine remained standing, hands on hips, glowered down at him as he approached.

"And what in the names of all the hells do you want now?"

Rathe took a breath, trying to remember that the woman's day had probably been as hard as his own. "A quarter hour of your time, for a start." He held up his hand, forestalling protest. "I'm sorry, Mathiee, but you'd better get it over now."

Gasquine took a breath in turn, visibly conquering her fury, and nodded abruptly. "At least I won't be paying a fortune in fees—or not to you." She pointed to the stairs that led up to the stage. "Come up, come up, and we'll talk. The rest of you—" She looked over her shoulder, her face grim. "Silla, put them through the scene again. At least they can take the time to learn their lines."

Rathe followed her into the relative quiet of the wings, was relieved when she waved him to a stool set in a sort of alcove, and seated herself in turn opposite him. "So what's the word?" she asked, without hope, and Rathe grimaced in sympathy.

"De Raçan was murdered," he answered. "That's the alchemist's and necromancer's finding, which means it falls to Point of Dreams to find out who killed him. And that, Mathiee, is the official word, so you can take it up with the chamberlains as need be."

"Tyrseis." She sighed. "I'll tell my people, too."

"And there's more." Rathe braced himself, seeing the woman's painted brows draw down into a deep frown. "I need to talk to your people, the ones who knew him today, the rest as soon as may be. I'll do my best not to interrupt you, but time is of the essence."

To his surprise, she nodded. "I understand. And if you take them one by one—well, maybe that won't be so bad." She glanced toward the stage. "And you might as well start with me, they'll do without me for a while."

"I'd fully intended to," Rathe answered, and managed a smile to take the sting out of the words. Gasquine smiled back, the expression wry, and Rathe reached for his tablets again. The wax was getting crowded; he planed over a few old notes, and settled himself to begin. "First, who among the chorus or cast knew him well?"

Gasquine paused, blinking. "Ah. A hard question. He was most in company with the vidame DuSorre, but I'm not sure she knew him well."

"Oh?"

"I saw her haul off and hit him once, hard, right across the face." Gasquine smiled. "It wasn't the action of an intimate."

"When was this?"

"A day or so ago," Gasquine answered.

"She hit him in public?" Rathe repeated, and Gasquine shrugged.

"Not quite public, Nico, but not in private, either. There must have been a dozen of us who saw. It's a funny thing, though, it seemed to—even things up between them. She looked pleased, and he looked, I suppose, resigned. I doubt she'd have need to resort to murder."

"And which one is DuSorre?" Rathe asked.

Gasquine looked around again. "Not here. Not a brayer, like the ones you saw before, a woman who works hard at whatever comes to hand. I was surprised she'd put in for the lottery, she doesn't seem theatre-mad like the ones we usually get, but then, it's nice to have some cooler heads around." Her eyes widened. "Nico, you can't think . . ."

"I'm going to have to talk to her," Rathe said. "Who else would you say knew the man?"

Gasquine swallowed whatever else she had been going to say. "Ah. That's harder. I saw him playing at star-dice with the landseur de Beleme, but I doubt that was more than passing time. And of course . . ." She hesitated, then shook her head. "But I don't know anything about that."

You know everything about everything within these walls, Rathe thought. *And that note means it's someone in the theatre.* He frowned then, remembering the master of defense who had found the body, the hesitation in his voice as he named it, and said, "Master Siredy?"

"You know, then," Gasquine said.

Rathe shook his head. "Not details. But he identified the body, and I thought he knew him."

Gasquine sighed. "I'm old for tricks like that. Very well, the gossip is, they were intimates, at least for a while. But it was over and done long ago, to my understanding."

She met his eyes guilelessly, and Rathe frowned. "You're sure about that?"

"As sure as one can be."

"No hints, no mentions, no one wanting to start it up again?"

Gasquine hesitated for a fraction of a second, then shook her head. "Not that I know of."

"I'll bear that in mind," Rathe said, and jotted that name down as well. He wasn't fully sure he believed her, but there was no reason yet to push her to an outright lie. "Anyone else?"

"I don't know—he was a quiet one himself, I didn't have to notice him."

"Tell me about him," Rathe said, and she gave him a look of surprise.

"Not much to tell, as I said."

"Come on, Mathiee, people are your lifework. How would you play him?"

Gasquine grinned at that. "A good question. He was young, but not as young as he liked to think he looked. He was quiet enough, but not shy, and not especially considerate, I would say. A—watching sort of man. I'd say he was enjoying himself, in some way or another, but he's another one I was surprised put in for the lottery." Her grin widened, took on a tinge of malice. "If I were to cast him, Nico, I'd probably use Guis Forveijl."

Rathe made a face—he'd have to meet his former lover some-time, though he was hoping, cowardly, to put it off as long as possi-ble—but the description was enough to give him some idea of the dead man's personality. Forveijl had had a careful streak in him, a holding-back, and a habit of storing incautious words for later re-proach. *Which might be a cause for murder,* he thought, *but Guis's death, not de Raçan's, unless Mathiee's speaking clearer than she knows.* He filed that thought for later, and looked down at his tablets.

"And your quarter hour's run," Gasquine said, echoing his own thought, and Rathe sighed.

"Two favors, then, before I let you go?"

Gasquine nodded, already on her feet.

"The use of a runner, I need to send word to Dreams, and then—would you ask the vidame to step down to me?"

Gasquine stared. "You're not—do you want me to—fetch her—for you?"

"If you would," Rathe answered, and kept his expression as bland as possible. Gasquine swore under her breath, and turned away.

She was better than her word, sending two runners, a tall skinny boy in a jacket already too short in the sleeves and a plump girl who looked to be close to formal apprenticeship. She had a flower pinned to her bodice—someone's castoff, Rathe guessed, seeing it wilted, but clearly she couldn't resist the flourish of style. She had brought paper and charcoal, and he scrawled a note to Trijn, warning her that they would need more people at the Bells tomorrow, to question the rest of the chorus and company. *And that'll make her happy,* he thought, dismissing the girl with a smile, looked up to see Gasquine approaching, a tall, well-dressed woman in tow. Rathe nodded to the boy.

"Take your stool over there, warn off any eavesdroppers."

The boy nodded, eyes wide, and scurried away. Rathe rose, hop-ing DuSorre wouldn't be one of the ones who was appalled at the idea of the queen's law being administered by commoners, and ap-plied to the better folk like herself. "Vidame."

"Adjunct Point." She was Silklands dark, her ochre wool skirt and bodice chosen to set off her coloring, and she'd taken the time to wipe away the sweat and set herself to rights. "Mistress Gasquine said you wanted to speak with me."

Rathe nodded, hoping her getting his title right was a good sign. "Yes. Thank you." He gestured to the stool, and she sat gracefully, her skirts pooling around her. The sleeves of her bodice and chemise were pinned back, showing bare skin, and a fine bracelet of filigree beads banded one wrist.

"About de Raçan?"

Rathe nodded again. "You knew him."

"Yes." DuSorre's voice was perfectly calm.

"And he gave you cause to strike him."

She gave a rueful smile, and her whole face lightened. "Yes to that, too. Bad as any actor, wasn't I, to do that?"

"Were you?" Rathe matched the smile, and she ducked her head—hiding laughter, he suspected, rather than embarrassment.

"He made a suggestion that annoyed me, and when he wouldn't stop making it, I decided to give him a taste of what he was letting himself in for if he didn't stop." She paused, considering, and this time he was sure he saw amusement in her eyes. "It just occurred to me, I should have waited for a time when we were drilling. Then I could have taught him a lesson he really wouldn't have forgotten." She did laugh, then, an easy, unforced music.

"And did you?" Rathe asked quietly, cutting across the laughter, and she stopped, frowning.

"Did I—do what?"

"Teach him a lesson."

DuSorre blinked. "You're asking me whether I killed him."

Rathe braced himself, expecting anger, defiance, accusations of disrespect, but instead, DuSorre slowly shook her head, the laughter dying from her face.

"And he is dead, isn't he, and I'm behaving very badly. I'm sorry, I just can't imagine . . ." She shook her head again. "No, Adjunct Point, I did not kill him. He wasn't worth it to me, I'm afraid, though obviously he was to somebody. I think we got on rather better once I put him in his place."

Which was obviously several ranks below DuSorre, Rathe thought, and couldn't help admiring her candor. *And besides, I think she would have done the same thing if she'd been left a motherless child in Point of Knives.* "You said you couldn't imagine—what?"

"Why anyone would bother killing him," DuSorre said. She spread her hands. "I'm sorry, Adjunct Point, he simply wasn't—a person of substance."

It was a bitter epitaph. "And yet you kept company with him," he said aloud, and she shrugged.

"He had an idle tongue, could be amusing. And our mothers are friends. I don't know many of the others, you understand. We only come to Astreiant for the winter-tide."

All good reasons, all equally unhelpful. He took her through more questions, all with the same answer—de Raçan was a nonentity, of no importance at all to her—and by the end was fairly sure she was telling the truth. There was simply not enough passion in her response to make her seem a likely murderer. He closed his tablets, sighing.

"Did you see *The Drowned Island*?" he asked, not knowing precisely why, and to his surprise she blushed.

"Yes. Yes, several times, since we took up residence in the city."

"And you enjoyed it?"

This time, the blush was more pronounced, though she met his gaze squarely. "Foolish, I know, but there was something about it— not just sad, though it was that. Perhaps it was that it believed in itself?" She smiled again. "Setting it next to Master Aconin's play, it is rather embarrassing to think how many times I went to see it. Why do you ask?"

Rathe smiled, not quite able to articulate it himself. "The land-seur's body was discovered on the Tyrseia stage," he answered. "Between two of the scenic machines—the waves."

DuSorre grimaced. "He wasn't killed by the machinery, surely?"

"No. It doesn't appear so." Rathe paused. "He may have been poisoned."

"Commonly thought to be a woman's weapon," DuSorre said, and he wondered from her voice if she'd finally taken offense. "What more do you need from me?"

"Your whereabouts between second sunrise and first dawn," Rathe answered.

"At home," DuSorre answered. "And it's not so big and busy a household that there won't be people who can vouch that I was there. My mother hosted a reception last night for the other members of the cast—the chorus," she corrected, and Rathe nodded at the distinction. "It was well past second sunrise when I went to bed. And my maid can swear that I didn't leave my bed until long past the second sunset." She smiled then. "The one similarity between us and the real actors, I imagine, is the hours we keep."

"Thank you," Rathe said, and had to suppress a yawn of his own at the reminder.

"Is there anything more?"

"No," Rathe said. "And I appreciate both your candor and your willingness to cooperate."

DuSorre's eyes met his. "Not at all. My mother has always told me to embrace new experiences." She swept him a mocking curtsy, and turned away.

And I could think she was flirting with me, if I didn't know better. Rathe shook himself, and looked around for a clock. There were none in sight, but from the sounds on the stage, the rehearsal was winding to an untidy end. He made a face, hoping he had time, and beckoned to the waiting runner.

"Fetch Verre Siredy—of the Masters of Defense," he said.

The boy nodded, as excited as the other runner had been, returned in record time with Siredy trailing behind him, his coat draped over one shoulder.

"Master Siredy, sir," the runner announced, and retired without being told to his stool.

Rathe took a step forward, motioned for the other man to join him in the alcove. "If I might speak with you for a few minutes?"

"Of course, Adjunct Point."

From Eslingen's brief comments, Rathe had been expecting a more handsome man, and wondered briefly if he should be jealous. Even under the paint, he could see the freckles scattering the man's nose and cheeks, and knew that the hair beneath the fashionably dark wig would be bright as scrubbed copper. "You named the landseur for me this morning. Thank you."

"You're welcome." Siredy looked, if anything, more wary, and Rathe's attention sharpened.

"And it was you and Lieutenant—vaan Esling—who found the body?"

"Yes." Siredy went through the story in a colorless voice, and Rathe made a note to get the same tale from Eslingen later. There was something about Siredy's attitude, the care with which he recounted the events, that made the pointsman wary. But of course

that could be the other story Gasquine had hinted at, and he leaned
back on his stool as Siredy finished his account.

"How well did you know him?"

"The landseur?"

Stalling for time, Rathe thought. He nodded. Siredy didn't look
like a comfortable liar, his easy air would make lies mostly unnecessary—*of course, I've been wrong about that before. But not, I think,
this time.*

"Oh, well, in the way of business," Siredy said. "As long as anyone
else in the masque."

"And out of the way of business?"

Siredy hesitated, and Rathe said gently, "I've spoken to one or
two here."

"You don't mince words, do you?"

"I'd prefer to hear the tale from you."

"No tale." Siredy sighed. "Ridiculous, I admit, but nothing you
haven't heard, I daresay. We were lovers, briefly—he took up fencing
for a bit, and took me up with it, I suppose, and when he gave up
swordplay, he gave me up, too."

There was a brittle note in the other man's voice that made
Rathe's eyes narrow. "And not gently, I gather," he said, and saw
Siredy flinch. "You did not part friends."

"I doubt we ever were that," Siredy flared. He stopped, went on
in a more controlled tone, "His lordship lacked sufficient grace, when
he called it off, to—" He stopped again, flushing, and Rathe sighed.

"Sufficiently express his regret and gratitude?"

"Oh, nicely put." Siredy seemed to have his voice under control
again, though there were two spots of color high on his cheeks, vivid
through the paint. "Please don't think me mercenary, it's more a
matter of—expectations."

Rathe nodded. He knew the rules for such affairs as well as
anyone southriver, knew, too, that they were more honored in the
broadsheets and onstage than in reality. But even actors could get
caught in their own fictions, he thought, and glanced at his tablets
again. "In your time with the landseur, did you ever hear him speak
of an enemy? Or anyone who'd have cause to injure him?"

Siredy shook his head. "No. He was—not that sort of man."

"What sort of man?"

"The kind who made enemies." Siredy shrugged. "You will have heard, the vidame DuSorre slapped his face the other day, and that's more thought than I ever saw anyone give to him."

Another bitter epitaph, Rathe thought. "And—you'll pardon my asking, I'm sure—did anyone step into your shoes?"

"Not that I know of," Siredy answered. "As far as I know, I'm the only person here to have committed that particular folly." He seemed to bite the words off, and Rathe frowned faintly down at his tablets, trying to quell his own sympathy, knowing what it felt like to feel yourself made a fool of, by your own devices. But there were Gasquine's words to consider, and he put stylus to wax.

"And now that you'd seen him again?" he asked quietly, lifting his eyes to meet Siredy's. The master stared at him for a moment, then sighed, leaning his arms on his knees, tangling his hands carelessly in his hair—wig, Rathe corrected himself, remembering Eslingen's description.

"Still the only one," he admitted. "But this time, I stopped it before it started. I think he wanted to have bragging rights. Whether as the first to bring one of us to bed, or as having a prior connection, I'm not sure, but I don't make mistakes twice, Adjunct Point. And there are some mistakes I don't make once. Killing him would have been more than he deserved."

Rathe nodded, accepting that at face value for the moment. "One thing more, then. Where did you spend your night, from second sunrise to first dawn?"

Siredy made a face. "Alas, I was alone, Adjunct Point. For most of the night, anyway. As soon as we finished here, I went to the baths—Philip, Lieutenant vaan Esling, can vouch for that, we had a drink there. But once we parted ways, well, there was no one. I lodge alone."

There was no real significance to it, Rathe knew—in his experience, it was the ones who had a dozen witnesses to their every movement who were the ones to watch—and he made a note in his tablets. The clock struck as he carved the last letter, and he heard one of Gasquine's assistants shouting the end of the day. Siredy looked over his shoulder.

"Are you done with me, Adjunct Point?"

"Yes."

Siredy nodded, rising easily to shrug on his coat, and Rathe beckoned to the runner. "Tell Mathiee I'm done for now, but I or mine will be back tomorrow as soon as you open. She'll know what I want."

"Yes, Adjunct Point," the boy answered, and hurried away.

Left to himself, Rathe joined the stream of actors and chorus members leaving the theatre, paused in the courtyard to scan the waiting crowd. It was bigger than ever, the nobles' private carriages jostling one another at the edge of the main street, while a new set of market-folk were clustered at the door, each fighting to call her wares louder than the rest. Rathe tucked his truncheon under his cloak, hoping to pass unnoticed, found himself a place at the edge of the throng. Eslingen would be out soon, he hoped, and even as he thought it, he saw the tall figure poised for an instant at the top of the stairs. He moved forward, smiling in spite of himself, and Eslingen came to join him, drawing his cloak tighter around his shoulders.

"Seidos's Horse, what miserable weather. But I'm glad to see you, Nico."

"Lieutenant vaan Esling," Rathe said. The other man winced, and Rathe grinned, relenting. "You might have warned me, before I saw it in the broadsheets." He beckoned to one of the marketwomen, her covered basket filled with hot spiced nuts, and accepted a paper cone in exchange for a demming. It was the first thing he'd eaten since before noon, and he was startled by his own hunger. "Still," he said, around the first mouthful, "you should be thrilled, getting your name in one of them."

Eslingen helped himself as well. "True gentlemen do everything in their power to keep their names out of the sheets."

"Only their names?"

Eslingen lifted an eyebrow. "Adjunct Point, that sounded remarkably like a double entendre."

"Was it?" Rathe asked. "I must be tired, then, I'd never consider going to bed with someone so far above my station."

"Idiot," Eslingen said, and helped himself to another nut. "You look tired."

"It's been a hell of a day," Rathe answered. "Yours?"

"After discovering the body?" Eslingen laughed. "Oh, distinctly improved, especially by the discovery that there seems to be a romance among three of our landames—only each member of the triangle is unaware that it is a triangle."

Rathe shook his head. "I don't envy you that one, Philip."

"Nor I you your murder," Eslingen answered, and cast a quick glance over his shoulder. "With everything you tell me about the symbolism of the masque, one has to look with a less than easy eye on the death of any noble taking part in it."

"Which is probably why the chamberlains will want to purify the whole theatre," Rathe said. *And I wonder what you know of the landseur,* he thought, *and what you can see for me.* He shoved the thought away, appalled, but it made too much sense. A murder in the theatre, and Eslingen working there, with the people likeliest to have been involved, it was too good an opportunity to squander. . . .

"Nico?" Eslingen asked, and Rathe shook his head.

"Let's go home. We can talk there."

By the time they reached Rathe's flat, the sleet had thickened, gathering on Eslingen's broad-brimmed hat so that it caught the passing light like a crust of diamonds. The courtyard with its shared garden was treacherous underfoot, despite the sand the weaver had scattered carelessly across her end of the walk, and Rathe was glad to reach the shelter of his own rooms. The stove was cold, and Eslingen stooped to fumble with flint and tinder, lighting first one candle and then the lamp, while Rathe ran his hand through his hair, wringing out the worst of the damp. He felt like the southriver rat more than one person had called him—a drowned rat, he amended, and loosened his cloak reluctantly, leaving his jerkin on as he moved to relight the stove. Eslingen murmured something, and lit a second candle, another pinpoint of heat. The stove caught quickly, and Rathe straightened, stripping off jerkin and coat and hanging them on the peg by the door. Eslingen tended his own coat more carefully, settling it so it would dry without unfortunate creases, and Rathe turned away to find bread and cheese. It wasn't the meal he would have chosen, if the weather had been better, but it would be enough.

Eslingen had freed himself from his waistcoat as well, wrapped himself in a dressing gown that was magnificent except for the frayed hem, and Rathe had to admit that there was a certain practicality in the ridiculous garment. Something like that, on a cold night . . . He shook himself, telling himself he'd look idiotic, and reached for the jug of wine. "The landseur," he said. "You probably didn't have any time to form an impression of him."

Eslingen shrugged, accepting the filled cup, and settled himself at the table, stockinged feet reaching out to the stove. "A bit of one. I think he was used to getting his own way."

"More than the rest of them?" The stove was blazing now, and Rathe sat down opposite the other man, feeling its warmth along his side. It was strange, this wasn't how he would have wanted to acquire a lover, certainly wasn't how he'd wanted to have Eslingen move into his life, but at the same time, there was an ease between them that he couldn't deny.

"Oh, yes," Eslingen answered. "Much more. But, as I'm sure you've heard, the vidame DuSorre put him in his place."

"I hate that phrase," Rathe said, and shook himself. "You didn't see it, did you?"

"Not I, but it was common gossip." Eslingen reached for the bread, tore off a healthy chunk. "I must have heard half a dozen versions of the story."

"Not well liked, then," Rathe said, and to his surprise Eslingen shook his head.

"No, it wasn't that, it was just a good story. Nobody really cared, I don't think. Seidos's Horse, he was, what, the youngest of five, with three older sisters and an older brother who got what was left of anything that was on offer."

"That's sad," Rathe said. It was also what the others had said, Gasquine and Siredy and even DuSorre all in perfect agreement, and he shook his head, wondering if the man had had any purpose to his life.

Eslingen nodded. "My impression is that he was the kind of person someone might trouble to slap, but never, ever, bother to kill."

"But someone did," Rathe said.

"What did happen to him?" Eslingen asked. "I didn't see any wounds—how did he die?"

Rathe made a face, as though saying it made it worse. "He was drowned."

Eslingen leaned back in his chair. "That's a revolting thought. Do you mean someone drowned him and left him at the Tyrseia?"

"No." Rathe rubbed his eyes, made himself take a piece of the sharp, creamy cheese. "I mean he was drowned at the Tyrseia. That's according to Fanier, the best alchemist I've ever worked with. And unless Sohier found something I didn't see, there wasn't any way it could have been done. No troughs, no tubs, no buckets, nothing except—"

He broke off, shaking his head, and Eslingen frowned. "Except what?"

"You were there. You tell me."

"I'm not a pointsman," Eslingen said. "I don't think I notice the same things you do."

"I'm sorry, Philip, I'm not trying to be coy, I'm just not sure what it means. If it means anything." *And I really hope it doesn't*, he added silently. "Think about where you found him."

"Onstage," Eslingen said. "Center stage."

Rathe nodded. "At the Tyrseia. Where the damned *Drowned Island* is still on. Philip, he was lying between two pieces of the machinery. The final flood effect."

There was a little silence, then Eslingen whistled softly through his teeth. "You can't be saying he was drowned by the scenery."

"Not yet, I'm not," Rathe answered. "And never, if I can help it. But Fanier says he was drowned where he lay; the body wasn't moved, period. He did allow as how there might be poison involved, but the cause of death was drowning. I just hope Sohier found something I missed."

"But you don't think she will," Eslingen said.

Rathe shook his head. The thought was suddenly utterly depressing, this—unnecessary—man, dead for no cause. Except he wasn't quite unnecessary, Rathe thought, and grimaced. If he was in the masque he was related to one of the potential claimants, and that made him necessary after all. He saw Eslingen watching him, mouth opening to ask a question—*and if I tell him, I know what the next step will be, exactly what I'll ask him to do next, and that's not fair, not after the last time.*

"What?" Eslingen said, and Rathe sighed.

"This is not for public consumption, I know I don't have to tell you."

Eslingen shook his head, waiting.

"What makes this death particularly interesting is that every single member of the chorus is directly related to one of the queen's possible successors—and Her Majesty plans to name her heir after the masque."

Eslingen's mouth dropped open for an instant. "Which makes them all hostages for their families' good behavior. Dis, that's—clever."

"Sound I wouldn't dare hazard," Rathe said, and Eslingen laughed.

"What have I gotten myself into?"

"You do seem to have a talent for finding yourself at the center of things," Rathe answered.

"It's a recent knack, I assure you," Eslingen answered. "Not one you want to cultivate in the army."

Rathe grinned, but sobered in an instant. "Philip, I need your help."

"You have it." Eslingen leaned forward, his hands wrapped around his wineglass, and Rathe sighed.

"I feel like ten kinds of bastard, especially after the last time. But. You're at the theatre, every day, with these people every day. I would take it kindly if . . ."

"I'd keep an eye on them for you?" Eslingen was smiling slightly, and Rathe hesitated, wondering what it meant.

"Yes. I'm just sorry to have to ask you again."

Eslingen reached out, laid a hand gently over Rathe's, the fingers still cold. "Why?"

"Why what?"

"Why not ask me? I'm pleased, I'm honored, and for the gods' sake, I'm there. I think we work well together." Eslingen's smile widened. "Hells, if you hadn't had the sense to ask, I'd probably have committed the ultimate folly and volunteered."

We do work well together, Rathe thought. *It's been proved, last summer under fire, and in the dull aftermath.* "At least I spared you that," he said, and Eslingen's hand tightened, a caress and a question. Rathe shook his head. "Philip, I'm going to be asleep as soon as my head hits the mattress."

One eyebrow quirked upward. "If I had suspected our living together would have a deleterious effect on the admittedly vulgar pursuit of pleasure . . ."

Rathe laughed out loud. "All right, Lieutenant. If only to allay your suspicions."

5

◆ ·· ◆

$\mathcal{T}$he performance banners were flying from the tower of the Tyrseia as Rathe made his way into Dreams station, and he hoped that meant that Sohier had found something after all. More likely, though, Trijn had been pressured into releasing the theatre as soon as possible, for fear that the unstable common folk wouldn't be able to stand being deprived of their favorite play for an extra day. He was being unfair, he knew, as he stopped to consult the notices fluttering from a broadsheet-seller's display board, and took a careful breath, trying to control his temper. If anything, he was angry because he suspected the chamberlains might be right.

At least only one of the broadsheets mentioned the murder, and it was a crude thing, with a woodcut of two men dueling that Rathe had last seen illustrating an announcement of a fencing match. The paragraph below, smudged from hasty printing, spoke of mysterious death at the Tyrseia, and hinted at breathless possibilities, but, all in all, said less that he'd expected. It wouldn't last, he knew, but at least they might have a day's breathing space before the details were spread around the city. And one good thing might come of the mystery, he thought, turning away: the fact of the death might help hide the significance of the chorus.

Voillemin was still on duty, finishing out the night shift, and Rathe had to suppress the desire to ask what was happening with Leussi's death. That was the other man's case, he reminded himself, scanning the daybook; he'd do no one any good by interfering. There was a note from Sohier, stating that she and four others had searched the Tyrseia stage and stagehouse, but no note of the results.

Voillemin cleared his throat. "The chief wants to see you. As soon as may be."

"No surprise there," Rathe answered, and slid the book back to the other man. "What did Sohier find?"

The younger man shrugged. "Officially, the report's still being copied. But unofficially—nothing. How in Astree's name can the man have drowned?"

"Your guess is as good as mine," Rathe said.

"Maybe—could the necromancer have made a mistake?" Voillemin asked, and Rathe sighed.

"We may be hoping that. But I've never seen Fanier make that kind of a mistake."

Voillemin shook his head—he looked tired, Rathe thought, and felt an unexpected pang of sympathy. "Go home," he said, and Voillemin smiled.

"As soon as Leenderts gets here. And the chief does want to see you."

"I bet she does," Rathe answered, and took the stairs two at a time.

The door to Trijn's workroom stood open, sunlight spilling across the room and out into the narrow hallway. The last of the previous night's ice was melting from the eaves, spangling the bubbled glass, and a kettle hissed on the roaring stove. Rathe tapped on the door frame, feeling the heat radiating from it even there, and Trijn looked up with a nod.

"Come in and shut the door. Fanier sent this for you."

Rathe did as he was told, accepting the still-sealed packet of papers addressed in Fanier's thick scrawl. A lot of chief points would have taken it as their right and privilege to read it before him, he thought as he broke the seal and skimmed through the neatly copied pages, but not Trijn.

"Of course you had no idea who it was when you sent the body to Fanier," Trijn said. She made it a statement, Rathe noted with relief. "This damned district. Everything has to be larger than life. It's a hothouse. Not enough that we have a murder, no, it has to be—" She lifted her hand, ticking the points off on her fingers. "At the Tyrseia, involve a landseur—a landseur who is the brother of the castellan of Raçan, not an insignificant holding, as well as being related to Her Majesty—and not a straightforward bludgeoning or knifing, either, but something utterly mysterious." She gestured to the report still in Rathe's hands. "And how did he die, by the way?"

"He drowned," Rathe said, and braced himself for the outburst.

It never came. Trijn rested her head in her hands. "Of course he did. What else? Did Fanier hazard a guess as to how he drowned? Nothing ordinary, I wager, like having drowned elsewhere and the body moved to the theatre?"

Rathe shook his head, sliding the three closely written sheets across the table toward her. "He died where he was found. There's evidence of poison—Fanier said some of the body changes were consistent with poison, but—"

"He drowned," Trijn finished for him. "Sofia's tits. Which is why you kept five of my people busy yesterday looking for barrels and tubs that they did not find."

"I had hoped we'd missed something," Rathe said, and Trijn shook her head.

"No."

So, Rathe thought. Drowned on a dry stage, among the machines that represent water. "I'll need them again today," he said. "I only had the chance to talk to a few of the cast, and it'll go faster with more of us."

"Understood," Trijn answered. "I've already warned Sohier, she has a good head on her. But I want you to deal with the family first."

"De Raçan's family?" Rathe hid a grimace. "I had a messenger from the Temple inform them, I thought—"

"We'll want his horoscope," Trijn said firmly, and Rathe sighed. Yes, it was a logical first step, particularly in a death as odd as this one—a good horoscope could often reveal people destined for uncanny ends—but he'd hoped he wouldn't have to be the one to collect it.

"I may need a writ from the surintendant, if the family doesn't choose to release it," he said aloud. "Because the university won't help me without one."

"I'll see you get it," Trijn answered. "But you may not need it. My understanding it, the castellan is a sensible soul."

"Let's hope so," Rathe said, and Trijn smiled.

"Serves the regents right, you bagging a landseur when they couldn't stomach the idea of you tampering with a mere intendant.

Still, it may be political—see what you can find out about the family's leanings while you're at it."

And how, Rathe thought, *am I supposed to do that? You're the one who brags of being intimate with Astreiant.* He put the thought aside—he had his contacts, they all did, but his might ask more than he cared to pay—and pushed himself to his feet as the clock chimed ten.

"She lodges in Point of Hearts," Trijn said, and Rathe's eyebrows rose. Trijn met his look blandly. "Apparently the de Raçans prefer to enjoy themselves over midwinter."

He had no trouble finding the house, a narrow-fronted, white-stone building with twisted iron gates that gave a glimpse of severely formal gardens. The stone troughs were mostly empty, the larger plants bound up for winter, but Rathe recognized at least one flowering cherry beyond the formal hedges. It was the sort of place one might rent for a new lover, Rathe thought, but not long-term, and wondered whether the castellan recognized or even cared about the distinction.

The gatekeeper belonged to the house, not the castellan, and made no difficulty admitting a pointsman. In fact, Rathe thought, he seemed more perturbed by the black-bound spray of ghostberry decorating the main door. It wasn't much of a sign of mourning, but it was more than he had generally seen in Point of Hearts. To his surprise, the stiff-legged footman did not try to send him to the tradesman's entrance, and Rathe waited in the entry as bidden, glancing quickly around. The footman had worn a mourning band, black ribbon over white, but there were few other signs of anything but formal grief. The incense bowl was cold, its sand drifted with only the faintest shadow of ash, and no one had bothered to cover the elegant long mirror that lengthened the narrow hall. The maid who appeared at last to escort him wore no black, and he wondered if she too, had been hired with the house.

The castellan was waiting in the receiving room, the curtains drawn full back to let in the most of the morning's sun. The room smelled of flowers, and Rathe looked around, startled, to see a dozen forcing-jars set on a side table where the light could catch them. All of them were in use, and greenery and flowers sprouted from them, the Silklands corms blooming in unseasonal profusion. He recognized a white type his mother called Mama Moon, and another golden trumpet, but the rest were strange, red and pink and green-tinged

yellow, vividly striped and ruffled, a landame's ransom set carelessly
to use.

"Adjunct Point Rathe," the maid said with a curtsy, and seated
herself at the far end of the room.

The castellan herself was seated on a chaise that looked as though
it might be silk, and the remains of a hearty breakfast lay on the table
at her elbow. Served on silver, too, Rathe thought, and made a careful
bow. She was a small, plump woman, and looked utterly unlike her
dead brother—if anything, she reminded him of a wren, though no
wren was ever so brightly colored. At least she wore a mourning
ribbon, fashionably stark against the poppy-red silk of her bodice, but
there was no reading her emotions in her painted face.

"Adjunct Point," she said. "You're welcome to the house."

"Thank you," Rathe answered. "Allow me to offer my condo-
lences."

The castellan smiled, and Rathe wondered how many other call-
ers she'd had already. "I hope you won't think me tactless, but I have
a hundred questions for you. How did Visteijn die?"

Rathe took a breath. "The alchemical reports say that he
drowned."

"The alchemical reports?" she repeated softly.

"Yes, maseigne."

"You had my brother's body brought to an alchemist."

"We needed to determine the cause of death, Castellan."

She was silent for a moment, the sunlight slanting through the
tall windows to glitter from the gold threads banding her skirt. "You
didn't seek permission. Permission that was mine to give."

"I didn't know who he was at the time," Rathe answered, and
from the look she gave him, guessed she recognized the lie.

The castellan sighed, and looked away from him, frowning at the
flowers on the table. "It has been suggested to me that a death like
this—of a relative, however close, who was more a nuisance than a
help—should be kept as unobtrusive as possible. I don't, however,
agree. How could he drown, if he was found at the Tyrseia?"

"That we don't yet know," Rathe said. "Though we hope to find
out. And to that end, Castellan, I would like to ask you a few questions."

She waved a hand in careless permission. "Ask away."

Rathe reached for his tablets, aware and mildly amused that she
wouldn't ask him to sit down—her tolerance of pointsmen extended

only so far—and ran through the same questions he had asked DuSorre and Siredy the night before. If anything, the castellan knew even less of her brother's activities—they each kept their own households, her brother's consisting of a valet and a groom, and had no cause to spend much time in company.

"And now that he was in the masque,"the castellan went on, "I saw even less of him than before. He put his name into the lottery as a joke, or so I understood; I think he was a little put out at actually having been selected—more work than he was used to, you understand. But I don't know of any enemies among his fellows."

"Debts?" Rathe asked, and the castellan smiled.

"He wasn't a careful man. He had debts, some of which I paid, some—" She glanced again at the flowers, frowning again. "Some of which I left him to handle on his own. That's a piece of his folly, to spend crowns on those corms, and then let them bloom. They don't come again that way, or so I'm told, you waste them, growing them in the jars. We quarreled over that, the last time I dined with him. But no one would kill a man for that."

"No," Rathe said, though, privately, he was not so sure. He could think of one or two avid cultivators who hated the idea of forcing the corms, who would rather wait half a year to see the flower just to be sure it would bloom again. But at least the landseur had gotten the pleasure of his purchases, instead of letting them rot for speculation. It was the most appealing thing he'd heard yet about the man. "There is one thing more, Castellan."

"Name it."

"Your brother's horoscope. I would appreciate it if I could get a copy of it."

The castellan's eyes widened, but then she nodded. "I will have my secretary copy it out for you, and send to Point of Dreams."

"Thank you," Rathe said.

"I don't want to see his murderer escape unpunished," the castellan said. "I thank you for everything you've done so far, and expect you to do everything in your power to see this to its conclusion." She smiled, a little ruefully. "You have only to name your fee."

Rathe returned the smile, but shook his head. "That's not necessary, Castellan. I will find out who killed your brother, or do my best at it, anyway, but—I don't take fees. From anyone."

"Are you a leveller, Adjunct Point?"

Rathe hesitated. "Philosophically, I suppose so, Castellan."

"I thought you might be." The castellan studied him for a long moment. Not so wrenlike now, Rathe thought, and tried to meet her stare without challenge. "So you do this out of conviction, or stubbornness?"

"I do enjoy my work, Castellan," Rathe answered.

"Then I trust you will take a certain satisfaction in finding out who killed my poor fool of a brother. If there is anything further you need, you must not hesitate to let me know, or any member of my household. It shall not be denied you, I promise you that."

It was dismissal, Rathe knew, and something more, a speculation in her glance that made him wonder if he'd been in Point of Hearts too long. Or perhaps she had: she might have to dance attendance at the court until midwinter was past, but from the look of the house, she was determined to enjoy herself. But still, he had what he needed from her, and with more grace than he'd had any right to expect. "Thank you, maseigne," he said aloud, and the maid rose at her gesture. "I'll send word as soon as I have any news for you."

He paused at the corner of the road to look back at the narrow house, so neat on its sculpted grounds, wondering if there were other questions he should have asked the castellan, questions about her own intentions in Astreiant. But if he wanted to know that . . . He sighed. If he truly wanted the answer to that question, there was only one source for it, and he looked up as the clock chimed the quarter hour. Almost eleven: Annechon would be receiving by now, he thought, and wished the mere thought didn't make him blush.

Her house was a fraction smaller than the castellan's, and older, but the walls and the gatehouse were bright with new paint, and from the look of it the narrow garden had been redug over the summer season. And Annechon herself held the freehold of it, Rathe knew, not for the first time shaking his head at her acumen. No gift, either, there was no one great lover to pay her way, but a dozen or more dear friends, and a sharp sense of business had kept her more than solvent. That and the charm of manner that made women and men grateful to see their gifts sold to pay a chandler's bills, he added silently, smiling in spite of himself. He had seen that charm at work more than once, and it frankly terrified him.

Her people knew him, and the Silklands maid brought him at once to her bedroom, shooing away a pair of half-bred pocket terriers and a slim young man with equally bouncing manners. The curtains were drawn well back here, too, letting the light stream in, and the

air smelled of rosemary. No common scents for Annechon, he
thought, and she rose to greet him, both hands outstretched. She was
easily as tall as he, perhaps a little taller; the strong light made no
secret of the lines that were beginning to show on her hard-boned
face, but her hair was still darkly lustrous, without the slightest touch
of silver. And she would be beautiful greying, Rathe thought helplessly, she had been beautiful when she was the baker's fourth and
skinny daughter, hired to keep an eye on a gardener's son in Point
of Knives. He'd adored her then, at the age of seven, and she'd never
let him forget that he'd once—misunderstanding matters—proposed
lemanry. She wasn't skinny now, but ripely beautiful, her dressing
gown, scarlet as an advocat's robe, flowing loose over corset and petticoats. He returned her embrace, feeling like a child again, and she
waved him to a seat on the tambour reserved for her favorites.

"What a pleasure!" she said, and her voice still held a hint of the
southriver accent. "But it must be business, you'd never come here
without that protection."

Rathe sighed, knowing she was right. "I'm really that ungracious?"

"You know you are," Annechon answered. "But I am flattered.
It's not every woman who can still fluster her first nurseling."

"Hardly that," Rathe protested. "You were the child-minder.
Never a nurse."

"Would you rather I said first suitor?"

"I'd take it more kindly if you'd forget that," Rathe said, and she
grinned.

"Even more ungracious. But probably wise, if the tale I hear is
true. Did you finally bring your black dog to heel?"

Rathe felt the color stain his cheeks. "Yes."

"And that's all I'm to hear of it?" Annechon said.

"I need your help," Rathe said, in something like desperation,
and she leaned back in her painted chair.

"And you'll have it—if I can, of course. Have you had breakfast?"

The remains of hers was on a side table, and Rathe couldn't help
a longing glance. "I've eaten," he said, and she waved toward it.

"Well, have some more, there's plenty. Ring for more tea if it's
cold."

The plate of pastries, barely touched, was too tempting, and
Rathe took one, biting into a pocket of dried fruits flavored with
Silklands spices. It dripped, of course, and he caught the blob of

filling awkwardly, feeling more than ever like a child again. Annechon laughed without malice, and after a moment, he smiled back.

"What do you want of me?" she asked.

"Do you know the castellan de Raçan?" Rathe asked around a second bite of pastry, and Annechon managed a theatrical sigh.

"Never the question I want from you, Nico. Yes, I know of her— we don't move in the same circles, mind you, or not much, but we have friends in common."

"I thought it was interesting she took a house in Point of Hearts," Rathe said.

Annechon nodded. "Interested in her pleasure, that one, and doesn't care a bit for her reputation. What I know of her, I like, there's no pretense there."

"And her ambitions?"

"She hasn't any that I know of," Annechon answered, and Rathe made a face.

"Aspirations, then."

"Purely of pleasure," Annechon said. "Raçan's a cold holding, so I hear, so she spends her winters rather warmer." She paused. "Is it true it was her brother who was killed at the Tyrseia?"

"Yeah." Rathe hesitated in turn. "Did you know him, Anne?"

"Not that one. He's—he was just as intent on his pleasure as his sister, but not as generous. It could be she kept him short of funds, but I think it was more a habit of his own."

Which went with what Siredy had said, Rathe thought. "Did he have political ambitions at all?"

"That one?" Annechon laughed. "Why in Oriane's name would you ask that?"

"Because they're somehow related to the crown," Rathe answered, "by blood, not stars, and he was in the masque that's designed to bring health to the state of Chenedolle. I have to ask it."

"Then you can consider yourself answered," Annechon said. "The de Raçans, Larivey or Visteijn both, don't give a gargoyle's kiss for affairs of state. Affairs of the heart only, except I believe that isn't the organ either prefers."

"Enemies, then?" Rathe asked, without hope, and wasn't surprised when she shook her head.

"I doubt anyone would bother." She paused, frowning slightly now. "Have I been any help at all?"

"In a negative way," Rathe answered frankly. "But I pretty much expected that."

"I hate meeting expectations," Annechon said. "And now you'll meet mine, and find some excuse to scurry away again."

"I have work to do," Rathe said, and knew the truth sounded like a lame excuse. Annechon laughed and waved him away, offering a last pastry just as she had when he was a boy, and Rathe accepted it, following her maidservant back down the unfashionable stairs past a trio of waiting gallants. It would do for lunch, he told himself, hearing the clock strike noon, and he was due at the Bells.

Sohier was there before him, as he'd expected, but the lurking runner was quick to fetch her, and they found another of the quiet alcoves in which to confer.

"You read my report?" she asked, and Rathe nodded.

"You're sure?"

"Sure as can be." Sohier shook her head. "There was nothing, Nico, nothing bigger than a barber's basin, and I'd hate to try to drown a man in that. Even stunned, or drugged." She paused. "There's already talk."

"No surprise," Rathe said again. "We'll keep it as quiet as we can, not that there's much we can do about it. What have you found today?"

"Not much," Sohier answered, and reached beneath her skirt for her own tablets. "Let's see, two people have said he'd spoken of a marriage with the Heugenins—with the vidame herself, according to one young miss, trying to recoup his debts—but the vidame herself says she was trifling. She'd have bedded him, maybe settled an allowance on him if they were successful—she's childless—but swears she had no intention of making a contract with him."

"That's the most promising thing we've heard so far," Rathe said, and Sohier shook her head.

"Not wanting to disappoint, Nico, but I believe her. Even the people who mentioned it in the first place said it was all de Raçan boasting, nothing they really believed."

Rathe sighed. Sohier's judgment was generally reliable, too; if she said de Heugenin was telling the truth, odds were she was. "What's left for the day?"

"We're just about done with the chorus," Sohier answered.

"Nobles taking precedence?" Rathe asked with a grin, and the younger woman shook her head.

"They've been easier to find. Gasquine's been working the actors hard." She glanced over her shoulder. "In fact, I should be getting back to them."

Rathe nodded. "Go ahead. I'll be along as soon as I can catch a word with Mathiee."

"Good luck to you," Sohier answered, and turned away.

The rehearsal was well under way, he saw, the chorus idle while two of the principals held the stage. It was the first time Rathe had heard more than a few lines of the play, the first full scene he'd heard, and in spite of himself he found himself standing silent between two of the massive set engines, caught in the story's moment. Anjesine bes'Hallen, a Silklands scarf standing in for the old-fashioned veil she would wear later, held center stage with the ease of long practice, commanding in her silence, while Caradai Hyver raged around her, reminding her leman of promises made and broken. Hyver belonged to Gasquine's company, bes'Hallen to Savatier's; the chance to see them onstage together, in the two leads, would bring Astreiant flocking to the masque, and to the play. Hyver paused—she played the Bannerdame Ramani, whose stars made her a great general—but bes'Hallen remained still a heartbeat longer, long hands posed against her skirt. Then, slowly, she shook her head, rejecting not her leman but the anger she carried, swallowing her pride again for the sake of the kingdom. And that much, at least, was legend, Rathe thought. The Soueraine de Galhac had held her hand as long as she could, swallowed insult after insult, until finally the Palatine of Artins refused the marriage, her daughter to de Galhac's son, that would have restored the fortune de Galhac had ruined in her service. On the stage, Hyver paused in her turn, then swept into a deep curtsy, skirts pooling on the stage around her. It was the obeisance one gave a queen, and from leman to leman it was disconcerting and strangely moving, and the pause before bes'Hallen moved to raise her friend was even more unsettling. But then, the play didn't deny the ambition on both sides, the need of the palatine to be free of de Galhac, and de Galhac's need to dominate in Artins.

The actors moved off, arm in arm, never quite leaving their characters even after they were well out of sight in the far wing, and Rathe drew a slow breath. Oh, they were good, both of them, bes'Hallen at the top of her career, Hyver only a little behind, but without Aconin's lines to speak, those gestures would have fallen flat, meaningless. Something moved then, in the shadows to his left, and he looked over, startled, to see Aconin watching from behind a painted pillar. The playwright's eyes fell, as though he was embarrassed—*something I never thought to see*—but then he straightened and came toward the other man.

"Well, Adjunct Point, how'd you like the scene?"

The tone was mocking, as was the punctilious insistence on the proper title—but the question, Rathe realized, was genuine. Aconin had been watching not the actors, but the man watching them, and he was good enough, the play was good enough, to deserve an honest answer. "You'll have Astreiant at your feet if there's any justice."

Aconin paused, but then his painted lips quirked up into a smile. "Have you seen *The Drowned Island*?"

In spite of himself, Rathe grinned. "Can I ask you a question?"

"Is it by way of business? Or about the play?"

"Both."

Aconin spread his hands, a graceful, easy movement that displayed the black and gold paint and his long fingers. "I'm at your service, Adjunct Point."

"Where'd you get the idea for the play?"

"And how does that have to do with your business?" Aconin asked. "If I'd stolen someone else's idea, they'd beat me to death, not complain to the points."

Rathe smiled again, recognizing the truth of the playwright's words. One thing he'd learned since coming to Point of Dreams, the players tended to settle their own affairs as much as possible. "I was thinking more about the way you use the Alphabet, actually. I don't remember that being part of the de Galhac tales."

"Ah." Aconin's eyes slid sideways, and Rathe followed his gaze, to see the landseur Aubine frankly listening, a self-deprecating smile on his plain face. "Not in Astreiant, as far as I know, but in the west, there are tales that make her to be a descendant of the Ancient Queens, and a magist herself."

The Ancient Queens were also known as the Southern Witches. Trust Aconin to find them appealing. Rathe nodded, not wanting to break the thread, but Aconin shrugged one shoulder, said nothing more.

"So why the Alphabet?" Rathe asked after a moment, and Aconin sighed.

"I don't—honestly, I couldn't say, it just seemed . . . suitable. I suppose because there was all the talk last spring about the verifiable copy, and it stuck in my head." He shrugged again. "It's an anachronism, of course, but I don't think anyone will care."

There was something not quite right about the playwright's answer, Rathe thought. Maybe he wasn't being fair, but somehow he was certain that Aconin always knew exactly why he'd made his choices. "Did you read it?" he said aloud, and could have sworn that Aconin jumped.

"What?"

"Did you read it—this verifiable copy?"

Aconin smiled, already turning away. "There's no such thing."

And you're lying, Rathe thought. *Either you've seen it or, more likely, you know it exists, but you are lying.* He took a step forward, intending to pursue the matter, and Aubine cleared his throat.

"I'm sorry to interrupt, Chresta, but Mathiee wants to talk to you."

Rathe swore under his breath, and Aconin spread his hands again. "I'm in demand. If you'll excuse me, Adjunct Point—"

"Of course," Rathe said, knowing the moment was lost, and the playwright disappeared between another set of scenery. Aubine gave him an apologetic smile, and Rathe returned it. It wasn't the land seur's fault that he'd been given a message—*but one of these days, Chresta, you and I will finish this conversation.*

"Do you believe in the Alphabet, Adjunct Point?" Aubine asked, and Rathe shook himself back to the present.

"I find it hard to believe there could be so many false editions of something that never existed."

Aubine's smile seemed genuine enough. "I'd never thought of it that way." He turned away, losing himself in the stack of hampers and cases that filled the backstage. Waiting to be carted to the Tyrseia, Rathe guessed, and realized he'd lost track of Gasquine.

The actors were rearranging themselves for the next scene under the watchful eye of one of Gasquine's assistants, and Rathe winced, hearing a once-familiar voice. He had managed to forget, or at least ignore, the fact that Guis Forveijl had been chosen for the masque, but there he was, tall and still good to look at, with hair of just the right shade of gold to be popular at any season. He seemed to be playing some sort of messenger—to be setting up one of the drills or dances, Rathe realized, and even as he thought it, he saw Eslingen coming down one of the backstage stairways. He looked as fine as any of the nobles, a new red coat warm in the mage-light, and he inclined his head gracefully to listen to something one of the land-seurs was saying to him. *Lieutenant vaan Esling is settling in all too well.* Rathe thought, and was ashamed of his jealousy. He had been jealous of Forveijl, too, jealous of the friendships and the parts that had seduced him away more than once before the final, showy role that Aconin had given him. They had been together for three years then, almost lemanry, though Rathe thanked Sofia he hadn't com-mitted at least that folly; to see it all vanish for the sake of a play, no matter how good, was almost enough to sour him on the theater. *Maybe Philip's finding a place here wasn't such good fortune after all,* he thought, and winced as Gasquine strode onto the stage, waving her hands to stop the action. Forveijl listened, head drooping, as she corrected something in the performance, and Rathe was grateful she kept her voice down.

"Nico," Eslingen said, and Rathe turned to greet him, forcing a smile. "I didn't expect to see you here."

"There's still plenty to be done," Rathe answered, and Eslingen sighed.

"I know that, I meant, when you weren't here this morning. I looked for you, you know."

Rathe felt his smile become more genuine. "I had business with the family. And how has your morning been?"

Eslingen rolled his eyes. "Like nothing in this world—" He broke off as a smiling woman touched his shoulder, murmuring something in his ear as she passed, and Rathe suppressed another stab of jeal-ousy. Eslingen smiled back, but the expression faded as he turned back to face the other man. "As you see. And there's a deal of gossip about the death, as you can well imagine. Some people are saying they'll have to call in the necromancers to clear the stagehouse."

"I doubt that," Rathe said. "Besides, a necromancer's already seen the body."

"b'Estorr, of course," Eslingen said, and a new voice spoke from behind them both.

"Of course. You must know about Nico's white dog, Lieutenant."

Forveijl, Rathe realized, and damned himself for not realizing the scene had ended. Eslingen gave him his most blandly cheerful smile.

"Keeps pocket terriers, does he?"

Forveijl blinked at the non sequitur, and Rathe took a breath, turning to face him. "Guis."

"Nicolas. We're keeping you busy these days."

"Among other things," Rathe answered. Forveijl opened his mouth to say something more, but someone—Gasquine's assistant, by the sound of it—called his name. Forveijl smiled, sweeping a too-deep bow, and moved away in answer. Eslingen lifted an eyebrow.

"That one . . . ?"

Rathe, to his own surprise, laughed softly. "Bad judgment, coming back to haunt me."

Eslingen shrugged. "Your life never started with me. But whatever did you see in him?"

"I'm not sure anymore," Rathe answered.

Eslingen's eyebrow rose even higher. "I hope he was at least—amusing?"

"Oh, yeah, that, certainly."

"I'd like to think you got something out of it," Eslingen said.

"It seemed enough at the time," Rathe answered. The stage was crowded now, chorus and actors and even a few scenerymen milling about in the open space, and he shook his head, thinking of the Tyrseia. "The whole thing's backwards," he said, and realized he'd spoken aloud only when Eslingen cocked his head at him.

"From the usual run of murdered landseurs?"

"From any other murder I've handled," Rathe said. He paused, but there was no one in earshot. "I'm talking about the pure mechanics of the thing. Usually, it's pretty straightforward how someone was killed, that's not the problem. The problem is who, and you look hard and deep, and one reason usually stands out, and that's the why that gives you the who. But you start from how." He shook his head. "I have a bad feeling that with this one, if I can just figure out how de Raçan was killed, I might have a chance at figuring out who."

Eslingen whistled softly, but anything more he would have said was cut off by a call from the stage itself. "That's us," he said, and quirked a smile. "I wouldn't stay."

"Not a pretty sight?" Rathe asked with a grin, and Eslingen rolled his eyes.

"If they were my company, I'd have the lot of them digging ditches."

He was gone then, and Rathe turned away. He'd find Sohier, he decided, and see if they could finish the interviews before the day's rehearsal ended.

✿   ✿   ✿

The rehearsal was going about as well as could be expected, considering that neither he nor the chorus really understood yet what was expected of them. Eslingen rested the butt of his half-pike against his shoe, grateful for the break while Gasquine argued with Hyver about some trick of gesture. At least it was real, the proper weight and heft, brought out of the weapons pawned and abandoned at the Aretoneia, unlike everything else onstage. He let his eyes skim past the arguing actors—not quarreling, they never quarreled, but discussed or at worst argued—looking for Rathe, but the pointsman was nowhere in sight, had already left, taking Eslingen's advice. He turned his attention back to the stage, trying to imagine his work seen from the pit. The chorus had broken out of their tidy lines, the banners drooping as they relaxed to murmured conversation, and Eslingen sighed, the moment's vision lost. This was one of the smaller set pieces, an entrance for the Bannerdame Ramani, but already they'd spent half the afternoon on it.

"And no closer to being finished," he muttered, and flushed, hearing a soft laugh behind him. He turned, frowning, and the landseur Aubine gave him a self-deprecating smile over an armload of flowers.

"I beg your pardon, Lieutenant, I shouldn't have laughed. But I think we're all thinking the same thing."

"All this for at most a quarter hour on the stage," Eslingen said. "My respect for the actors grows daily."

"Hourly," Aubine agreed, and set the flowers carefully into a tub that stood ready. A few drops of water splashed onto the stage, and the landseur drew a rag from his sleeve, stooped carefully to wipe them up.

And if that had been in the Tyrseia yesterday, Eslingen thought, his attention sharpening, *Nico might have found his "how."* But the tubs were new, delivered only this morning, and the runners had been busy hauling water ever since.

Aubine straightened, easing his back almost absently, and nodded to the half-pike. "That's an old weapon, isn't it, Lieutenant?"

Eslingen nodded, idly counting heads. There were at least three people missing from the chorus, and he hoped they'd merely seized the chance to use the privy. "From before the League Wars, I'd guess."

"A family heirloom?"

Eslingen blinked, aware of the trap he'd almost fallen into, gave his easiest smile. "Alas, no, my lord. I bought it out of pawn at the Aretoneia."

"Oh." Aubine looked disappointed, and Eslingen cast around for a topic that would distract him.

"May I ask a question, maseigneur? About the flowers?"

"Of course." For an instant, Aubine looked almost smug. "I can't promise an answer, though."

"Why bring them in now? Surely they'll wilt and die before the masque."

"Oh," Aubine said again, and the smug look was gone again, so quickly Eslingen could have believed he imagined it. "Oh, no, these aren't the flowers that will be used for the masque itself. I have others for that. No, these are—well, partly I've picked them already, and I don't want them to go to waste, even if we're not in the Tyrseia yet. I wanted to see how long they'll last, the air, the heat is different everywhere. And partly I've brought them in the hopes that they'll sweeten tempers, or at least ease the path for the actors, and the chorus, for that matter." He touched a bloom, pale pink, lush and multi-petaled, looked up with a smile that was at once rueful and self-aware. "But mostly, I suppose, I do it because I can."

"Which is our good fortune, maseigneur." That was Siredy, coming up behind them, and Eslingen turned to him with something like relief.

"Verre. We seem to be missing some of the chorus."

"Seidos—" Siredy bit off the rest of the curse with an apologetic glance toward Aubine. "I suppose we'd better go find them. If you'll excuse us, maseigneur?"

Aubine waved a hand, already focused on his flowers, and Eslingen followed his fellow master, glad to have forestalled any more questions about his family. "I imagine they're out back," he said aloud, and Siredy glared at him.

"I hope so. You should have kept an eye on them." He stopped, consciously relaxing his shoulders. "I'm sorry, Philip, I don't know what's gotten into me."

Eslingen stopped, really looking at the other man for the first time that day. Siredy was definitely out of curl, his skin pale, eyes shadowed, wig thrown back so carelessly that a few strands of red showed against his forehead. His shirt was crumpled, with a visible darn at one elbow, and his breeches had clearly seen better days. Not unreasonable clothes, for the workout they had ahead of them, but equally unlike anything he'd ever seen the other wear. Even for the challenge, he'd been better dressed. "Are you all right?"

Siredy forced a smile, and then a shrug. "I've had better days. Death's no way to begin a production."

"No." Eslingen took a careful breath, remembering something Rathe had said, something about Siredy and the dead man—pillow friends, nothing more, but a man might grieve regardless.

"And they couldn't care less," Siredy went on, glaring now at the chorus. "Except for the gossip value. De Raçan's more interesting dead than he ever was alive."

"You should try to get some sleep," Eslingen said. Worthless advice, he knew, but it was the best he could do.

Siredy shook himself, managed another smile. "Oh, believe me, I try—"

He broke off, interrupted by the hammering of Gasquine's tall staff on the stage's hollow floor, and swung to count heads. "Tyrseis, we're still missing two of them."

"Places," Gasquine called, and was instantly echoed by the book-holder, a tall woman in black. "Masters, if you're ready, let's begin—from the trumpet cue."

"Yes, mistress," Siredy answered, and Eslingen lifted his half-pike, the old signal to reassemble. The line straightened again, the flags rising with a ragged flourish—not fast enough, he thought, but they'd work on that—and the bored-looking woman in the musicians' guild badge lifted her trumpet for the salute. Out of the corner of his eye, he saw at least two of the stragglers hesitating at the edge of the stage, one about to hasten to join them before the other caught her back. *At least one of them is showing common sense,* he thought, and as the trumpet sounded lowered his pike to signal the beginning of the display. It was hardly complicated, the sort of thing any regiment accustomed to displays of arms could have done in its sleep, and would have disdained to perform in public, but the landames seemed to be having a hard time understanding the rhythm of the gestures. At least a third of the line missed the half-bow before the lines split, and one particularly graceless boy almost ended up in the wrong line, but then, just as Ramani made her entrance, the lines fell into unexpected alignment, the banners unfurling in almost perfect unison. Ramani strode between them, every fiber of her body singing with the victory just won, stopped just downstage of the last pair to begin her speech. Gasquine let her get through it—a complicated piece, not quite there, but with the bones of the emotion already showing—and lifted her hand only when the actor had finished.

"Very nice, Caradai."

Hyver curtsied, not quite out of character, and Gasquine went on easily. "As for the chorus—it needs work, you know that, but I think you can see how it goes. Masters, I thank you for your efforts. We'll rest a quarter hour, and move on to the next act."

Out of the corner of his eye, Eslingen saw Siredy sketch a bow, and hastily copied him. A clock struck, somewhere in the upper levels, a quarter-hour chime, and the closest of the landames looked up toward it, her long horse-face relaxing into a grin.

"Thank Seidos, my feet are dying."

In those shoes, I'm not surprised, Eslingen thought. The embroidered mules had a high foresole as well as a heel, gave her a few much-needed inches.

"My ladies," Siredy said hastily. "A moment, please—"

They looked inclined to ignore him, and Eslingen tapped the half-pike lightly on the stage, pleased when the chorus turned almost as one to stare.

"We'll begin the fight work when we return," Siredy said. "For those of you who were chosen."

"We'll need the stage, Verre," Gasquine said, not turning from her low-voiced conversation with Hyver, and Siredy sighed.

"Is it still fine out?" Eslingen asked, and a sweet-faced boy who looked barely old enough to qualify for the lottery gave him a blinding smile.

"It's very nice, Lieutenant, sunny and warm and the wind's died down."

"Then why don't we take it to the courtyard?" Eslingen said, and Siredy nodded.

"At the quarter hour, my ladies. In the courtyard, if you please."

There was a ripple of agreement, and the line broke apart, the majority vanishing into the backstage, a few, the stragglers among them, climbing down into the pit to find seats on the benches. The scenerymen who had been playing dice in the last row looked up curiously—more silks and satins than ever graced the pit on any other occasion—and the horse-faced girl winked at one of them, her shoes already discarded so that she could rub her stockinged toes.

"Maybe she'll think better of them," he said under his breath, and at his side Siredy gave a grunt of amusement.

"A seilling says she'll wear them through the masque itself."

Eslingen grinned. "No, I don't bet against a sure thing." He worked his shoulders, hearing muscles crack. "How do you think we're doing?"

"Not badly, actually," Siredy answered.

"If you say so." Eslingen frowned, startled by his own ill temper, and not appeased by Siredy's answering laugh.

"No, really, this is good. They just need time."

And he was right, Eslingen knew, forcing himself to remember the days he'd spent training soldiers. It always took time, he just had to remember that he was starting with raw recruits, not the half-trained men who'd been his more recent students. "So what do we do next?"

Siredy made a face. "We probably should have started this sooner, it's the hardest thing they'll have to learn. But we had the stage this morning."

"So what is it that we should have started sooner?" Eslingen asked, with waning patience.

"The small duels." Siredy shook himself, visibly collecting the rags of what was normally a cheerful disposition. "Oh, it shouldn't be too bad, they know the rudiments—"

"Enough to know what they don't know?" Eslingen asked, and Siredy managed a smile.

"I think so. We have four pairs, so we'll match them up for height and looks, and see what they can do."

"Do you know which ones they are?"

"I haven't matched the titles to the faces yet," Siredy said. "Or at least not above half of them. The pretty boy, the one who's making eyes at you—"

Eslingen rolled his own eyes at that, and Siredy went on placidly.

"Besselin, his name is, the vavaseur de Besselin. And the sallow landseur with the flowers."

Eslingen nodded. He didn't know that man's name either, but the posy tucked into his lapel had been meant to draw every eye. Even Aubine had been impressed, it seemed; he remembered seeing the older man draw the landseur aside for a quiet conversation.

"Then the girl with the shoes, all the gods help us," Siredy said, "she's the daughter of the castellan of Jarielle, and the rest—" He shrugged. "All I have is the names."

"Four women and four men?" Eslingen asked, and Siredy nodded.

"For balance. I thought we'd place them two and two, a pair of each to each side, the tallest toward the center."

The clock struck before Eslingen could answer, and Gasquine swept onto the stage, followed by the actors who were in the next scene. Most of the chorus settled themselves more comfortably on their benches, ready to enjoy someone else's labor; the group who had been chosen for the duels separated themselves out, some with backward glances, and made their way out into the narrow courtyard behind the stagehouse.

It wasn't an ideal spot for fencing, Eslingen thought as he made sure each of the duelists had plastrons and well-bated blades, was too long and narrow, but at least they would be able to make a start. Already he could see Siredy sizing up the group, the wig pushed even farther back, showing a line of red hair at his forehead, arranging them by height and coloring. It looked as though the group had been well chosen; it would be easy to make four pairs that would look like an even match, and the sweet-faced boy, de Besselin, cleared his throat.

"Lieutenant? May I have a word with you?"

He sounded at once shy and eager, usually a bad combination, and Eslingen braced himself. "Of course."

"You know about Maseigne de Txi and the landame de Vannevaux, don't you?"

"Should I?"

The boy blinked. "It might be relevant?"

"Well?"

"Txi and the Silvans of Damirai—that's de Vannevaux's family—they've been at odds for years. Generations."

"Which is de Vannevaux?" Eslingen asked, but suspected he already knew.

"Her." De Besselin tipped his head sideways, indicating a woman in blue, apparently deep in conversation with the landseur of the flowers. She was, of course, the same age and height as Txi, and her fair complexion would contrast perfectly with Txi's dark and lively face.

"Excuse me," Eslingen said, and crossed the yard in three strides to tap Siredy on the shoulder. "Verre . . ."

"I've heard," Siredy answered grimly. "What else am I to do with them? There's no other way to divide them up."

"Maybe they don't believe in the feud," Eslingen said, without much hope, and Siredy shook his head.

"Not a chance of that."

"Areton's—" Eslingen swallowed the rest of the curse. "All right. Let's pretend we think they can behave like—"

"Ladies?" Siredy asked sweetly, and Eslingen held up his hand, acknowledging the hit.

"Like—well, something other than what they are. This is the midwinter masque, the queen expects it. We expect it."

Siredy's look was frankly disbelieving, but Eslingen drew himself up to his full height, stilled his face to hauteur copied from a captain he'd once known, a man who could make you thank him for letting you loan him a silver pillar. It had worked before; it might work this time.

"Let's begin," he said, pitching his voice to carry, and the group of nobles turned to face him.

Siredy took a breath. "Right. The first order of business is to pair off." He held up his hand as de Besselin took a step toward the landseur with the flowers. "A moment, please. You're to be paired by height, to make a better show."

De Vannevaux was quicker than the others, glancing along the line. "No, Master Siredy, not if it means being paired with her." She flung out her hand in a gesture copied from one of the minor actors, pointing at Txi with a disdainful flourish.

"Oh," Txi said, much too sweetly, "I don't mind at all."

Right, let them get together with swords in their hands, Eslingen thought. *Seidos, why did I ever agree to this? Folly stars, indeed.* "What's this?" He lifted an eyebrow, fixed them both with a stare that he hoped would abash.

"The castellans of Txi stole our land," de Vannevaux said. "I will not be paired with her."

"Stole?" Txi's voice rose. "Damirai has claimed that for years, and never yet made good on the boast. The highlands are ours, they go with the city, not the forest—and I, for one, will be happy to meet her, under any circumstance."

"That's not your family's usual style," de Vannevaux said.

"Enough," Eslingen said, and they both looked at him, startled. "Would you prefer not to be part of the masque?"

Out of the corner of his eye, he saw a flash of pure horror cross Siredy's face, and hoped the landames hadn't seen it. There was an instant of silence, and then Txi said quickly, "No, Lieutenant, but—"

"We won our places fairly," de Vannevaux interrupted, looking mulish, and Eslingen lifted his hand again.

"Enough. Then you're in the queen's service here, and you can leave your petty family quarrels behind."

"Petty?" de Vannevaux said, on a note of outrage.

"I have seen sons of Havigot and Artimalec fighting side by side, guarding each other's backs," Eslingen said. That feud was ancient and proverbial, and he just hoped there were descendants left. "You are under discipline, no less than they were. I expect no less of you."

There was an instant of silence, Txi's eyes wide, de Vannevaux's delicately painted mouth slack with surprise, and then, to his relief, both women made quick curtsies. "Yes, Lieutenant," de Vannevaux said, and an instant later Txi echoed her.

"Very well," Eslingen said, and looked at Siredy, who quickly closed his own mouth. "Then let's begin."

The day dragged to an end at last, and Eslingen made his way out of the theatre with some relief. Not that they'd had any great successes, but at least the landames hadn't actually tried to kill each other. In fact, they'd been remarkably silent, speaking only when one or the other needed some point of the swordplay explained, and he supposed he would have to take it as a favorable sign. The sun was low, and the yard was in shadow, making him grateful for the cloak he'd thrown on that morning. Unfashionable it might be, but at least he would be warm for the walk back to Rathe's lodgings. And, now that he thought of it, it might be a notion to buy a loaf of bread, or even a hot pie, contribute something to their dinner. There were inns enough in Dreams where he could find something.

"Philip?"

Eslingen suppressed a groan. This was all he needed to complete a less than perfect day—but maybe he could get rid of the playwright quickly. He smoothed his expression as he turned. "Well, Chresta?"

"How unwelcoming," Aconin murmured. "So unlike the charming lieutenant."

"Let's not play that game," Eslingen said, and to his surprise, Aconin grinned.

"Fair enough. It's been a bear of a day, hasn't it? I'm even bored with myself."

"So you seek me out," Eslingen said.

"I wondered if we might talk."

Eslingen looked at the other man, wondering if he had heard the fleeting note of fear in Aconin's voice, and the theatre's side door opened behind him. Aubine emerged into the amber light, an empty trug over his arm—looking, Eslingen thought, for all the stars like Nico on a garden day. He dipped his head, not quite a bow, and Aconin turned with a start, the bright hazel eyes widening fractionally before he swept into an overdone courtier's bow. Aubine gave him an almost indulgent look, and nodded to Eslingen.

"A late-stayer also, Lieutenant? Can I offer you a lift?" Even as he spoke, Eslingen heard the clatter of harness and the soft chirp of a groom, looked around to see a comfortable-looking carriage pull into the theatre yard. It wasn't new, but it had been expensive, and Eslingen wondered again how he could ever hope to pull off this deception. But there were more poor landame's sons than rich ones, he reminded himself; just don't let him see that you're living off a pointsman, and you should be all right.

"Thank you, my lord, that's very kind. But I've promised Chresta my company."

"Ah." Aubine smiled again. "Be careful, Lieutenant, Master Aconin has a sharp—tongue."

"I'll bear that in mind, my lord," Eslingen said, and Aubine nodded, already moving away. Eslingen watched him into the carriage, the groom holding the step and handing in the trug, then closing the door to climb back to the box.

"Promised me your company," Aconin said, the mockery back in his voice.

"You said you wanted to talk," Eslingen answered. "I'll listen."

"I'd prefer somewhere less public than this," Aconin said, and Eslingen shook his head.

"Then we can talk as we go, Chresta. I want to get home."

"To your pointsman?"

"Home," Eslingen said, and hoped it was true. "This is not the way to get me to—is it help you want, Chresta?"

Aconin sighed, fell into step with the taller man. "I'm not sure, frankly. At this point, I think I just want to talk to someone."

"Why me?" Eslingen asked, and the words were almost a plea.

Aconin laughed softly. "Because I trust you."

"Oh, very likely. You haven't seen me in fifteen years."

"I trusted you to remember that, didn't I?" They turned a corner, and the harsh light caught them full on, deepening the sharp, discontented lines bracketing the playwright's mouth. "I—think I'm in trouble, Philip."

"Father it on someone else, it's not mine."

"Bastard," Aconin said, and Eslingen spread his hands.

"And all the world knows it."

He winced as he said it, remembering too late that he was no longer part of that world, that in fact this new world didn't know it at all, and Aconin smiled again. "Except here." He paused, shook his head. "I'll make a bargain with you, Philip. I won't say a word about your parentage if you'll give me a hand."

Eslingen caught the other man's shoulder, swung him so that they stood face to face in the empty street. The shops to either side were shuttered; they stood bathed in the red-gold light that swept up the street from the Sier, their shadows falling away behind them. "I don't make that kind of bargain," he said. "Not without knowing a good deal more about your troubles."

Aconin looked away. "It's complicated—"

"No, then."

Aconin took a breath. "All right. Wait. It's—there's something about this play, the whole damned folly of it—"

Eslingen caught the first flash out of the corner of his eye, shoved Aconin so that the snap of the lock caught the playwright already stumbling backward, arms flailing for balance. He cried out, hand flying to his upper arm, and Eslingen drew his knife, wishing he had a sword—wishing for pistol-proofed back-and-breast, and a lock of his own—spinning to put his body between the attacker and Aconin. The street was empty, and the doorways, even the dead-end alley where he thought he'd seen the flash of the priming powder, and he turned on his heel again, scanning windows. They were all closed, too, and he turned to Aconin.

"Quickly, into cover."

Aconin nodded, still clutching his arm, and Eslingen pushed him toward the nearest doorway, waiting for a second shot. It never came, and he leaned against the cold stone, trying to catch his breath. "Are you all right?"

Aconin nodded, but his face was pale beneath the paint. Eslingen frowned, and saw the first threads of blood on the playwright's fingers.

"Let me see," he said, and pried the other man's hand gently away.

Aconin hissed with pain, but did not resist, and Eslingen allowed himself a sigh of relief. Aconin's coat and shirt were ripped and bloody, but the wound was little more than a scratch, a shallow graze barely wider than his finger, painful enough, but hardly serious. "Not bad," he said, and folded Aconin's fingers back to stop the bleeding. "Come on, I think we can make it to Point of Dreams—"

"No." Aconin shook his head hard, almost dislodging his wig. "No, this is not a points matter."

"And if this isn't, what is?" Eslingen demanded. "Chresta, someone just took a shot at you."

"It's not a matter for the points," Aconin said again. "I'm serious, Philip."

"Then you know who did it, and you're going after him," Eslingen said. "The points don't take kindly to private revenge."

"You mean your Nico doesn't," Aconin answered, and shivered suddenly. "No, Philip, I don't know who did it. I swear to you. I just want to get home. . . ."

In one piece, Eslingen finished silently. "Not to the Court," he said aloud, and Aconin shook his head.

"No. Guis—Guis Forveijl. I'm still staying with him, on and off."

"You should go to Point of Dreams," Eslingen said again. "Come on, Chresta, you must have some idea what this is all about."

"I don't." There was the hint of a tremor in Aconin's voice. "I swear, I don't."

"Is it the play?"

Aconin shook his head again, again too hard, and Eslingen's eyes narrowed. "I've heard that some of the rejected playwrights aren't too fond of you these days."

Aconin managed a laugh, and this time there was real humor in it. "None of them would know how to load a lock, much less come this close to hitting me. Knives and clubs would be more their game—or more likely just a nasty piece for the printers."

That had the ring of truth to it, Eslingen admitted. "So who, then? You used to write a few broadsheets yourself, I hear."

"Not recently," Aconin answered. "I swear to you, Philip, on anything you want, I don't know."

"On your career?" Eslingen asked.

Aconin seemed to pause, then laughed softly, much more naturally this time. "You are a suspicious man."

"And you haven't answered me." Aconin was, Eslingen thought, a better actor than he'd believed.

"I swear to you, on my career, that I do not know who took a shot at me." In the shadowed doorway, Aconin's expression was unreadable. "Tyrseis, Philip, this hurts."

"You've been shot," Eslingen said. "Be glad the ball's not still in you." He leaned carefully around the edge of the doorway, trying to judge distances in the fading light. They should be on their way, and soon, before the twilight settled over the city and gave more cover to the assassin if she decided to return. "Where does Forveijl lodge?"

"Not far," Aconin said, and straightened with a visible wince. "Not too far from the Salle, in fact."

"Right." Eslingen sighed, scanning the street a final time. It surprised him that no one had called out, protested the shot or questioned what they were doing skulking in doorways, but then, this was a chancy district when the playhouses were not in session, a place where the locals kept to themselves as much or more than they had ever done in Point of Hopes or Customs Point. And, to be fair, some of the shops were too small to house the shopkeepers, probably were looked after by watchmen or perhaps a dog or two. "Let's go."

The sun was on the horizon now, the air thick with shadow. Aconin glanced nervously over his shoulder as he stepped into the street, as though he still expected an attack. Eslingen took a slow breath, wishing again that he had a lock of his own, and body armor to go with it.

"Which way?"

"Toward the river," Aconin said. He was still holding his arm, though the bleeding was sure to have slowed by now, and Eslingen flinched in sympathy. Flesh wounds were miserably painful, sometimes worse than something more serious; the playwright would be even more sore in the morning once the swelling set in. Something caught his eye then, more by its shadow, freakishly long just at sunset, a small patch of color just beyond the entrance to a narrow alley. He moved to pick it up, ignoring Aconin's soft cry of warning, and saw it was a posy, a knot of flowers wound with a strip of ribbon. There were perhaps three flowers, jewel-dark in the fading light, tight buds no bigger than his thumb, and he held it out to Aconin.

"Yours?" He didn't remember seeing it on the other man's coat, but the playwright shrugged it away.

"Hardly."

The sun was almost down, just a narrow sliver showing above the rooftops, and Eslingen shook himself, tucking the posy into a pocket. First to get Aconin home, or at least to Forveijl's lodgings, and then take himself home again before the second sunrise. He sighed to himself, knowing he'd be too late to buy bread or anything more than a pitcher of beer to contribute to his own dinner, and wished for an uncharitable moment that he could leave Aconin to his own devices. But the playwright was in trouble, and he could hardly leave him. . . .

"And that reminds me," he said as they started toward the river and Forveijl's lodgings. "What was it you wanted to talk to me about?"

Aconin paused, looked almost startled. "Do you know, it's gone completely out of my head."

Liar, Eslingen thought, but swallowed the word. "You're not my problem, Chresta," he said. "Go to the points, let them deal with you."

"I can't," Aconin said, almost too softly for the other man to hear, and shook his head. "Leave it, Philip, will you?"

And that's what I get for listening to you in the first place, Eslingen thought. *If I'd taken Aubine's offer, you'd've been killed—well, at least there's more of a chance that you would have—but do I get a word of gratitude? Not likely.* In spite of himself, he smiled. *And so typical of Aconin.*

They reached Forveijl's lodgings without further incident, and Eslingen left the playwright arguing with the landlady's man. As he'd expected, the shops were shut by the time he reached Rathe's neighborhood, and he climbed the steps empty-handed. Rathe opened the door almost before he could knock, an almost worried look dissolving into something like impatience.

"You're later than I expected."

"Yes. Sorry." Eslingen came into the sudden warmth and the smell of cooking—not Rathe's, probably, the smells were too rich, must have come from Wicked's—and stood for a second blinking in the lamplight before he started to unwind his cloak.

"Are you all right?"

"Sorry," Eslingen said again. "Yes, I'm fine."

"What happened?" Rathe turned back to the stove, shifting a pot from the hob to a hotter surface, but Eslingen could see the tension in his back.

"Somebody took a shot at Chresta Aconin," he said, and hung his cloak carefully on the hook by the door. Rathe's coat was tossed over the back of one of his chairs, and Eslingen adjusted it so that the shoulders hung straight before he removed his own.

"What?" Rathe turned quickly, and Eslingen spread his hands.

"Someone shot at him."

"Why didn't I know that?"

"Because it just happened, oh, less than an hour ago," Eslingen answered.

"I was at Dreams less than an hour ago," Rathe said.

"He didn't report it to the points." Eslingen took a breath. "And he's not going to report it."

Rathe slammed a wooden spoon down hard on the stove's iron lid. "Is he mad? Or is it just the stars?" He paused. "And by any chance were you there?"

"Yes," Eslingen said, and decided it could stand as an answer to all of them.

"Astree—" Rathe shook his head. "All right. What happened?"

I wish I knew. Eslingen sighed, reached for his dressing gown, pulled it close about his shoulders as the heat of his exertions faded. "I—it was not a good day, Nico, we had landames at feud who were assigned as partners, and, well, that's not important now."

In spite of everything, Rathe suppressed a smile as he came to sit at the table. "I will want to hear that story."

Eslingen nodded. "But later." He took a breath, composing his thoughts, and Rathe slid a glass of the harsh red wine across the table toward him. He sipped it, slightly warm from its place by the stove, said, "Aconin was leaving when I was, said he had something he wanted to talk to me about. And so I said I'd walk a way with him—I was going to pick up a loaf of bread, truly—but when we turned down one of the streets that runs straight to the river, someone took a shot at him. I saw the priming powder fire, pushed him, but I'm not sure it wouldn't have missed him anyway." He went through the rest of it, everything he could remember, lingering on Aconin's refusal to take the matter to the points, and leaned back in the chair when he'd finished, stretching legs that were stiff from the day's drill.

"You could make the complaint, I suppose," Rathe said, but without conviction, and Eslingen shook his head.

"What good would that do? All he'd have to do is deny it, and where would you be?"

"There's the wound," Rathe said, and shook his own head. "No, you're right, I'd never be able to prove it happened the way you said. Damn the man, anyway."

"Why do I suspect that none of this would be happening if someone else had written the masque?" Eslingen slid his hands into the pocket of his coat, found the posy he'd picked up. He tossed it onto the table, and Rathe took it curiously.

"What's this?"

"I found it in the street," Eslingen answered. "After the attack."

Rathe turned it over in his fingers, studying the flowers. They were very dark, Eslingen realized, that hadn't been a trick of the light, a purpled red that was almost black. Probably when the buds opened, they'd be brighter, but for now they looked almost ominous, furled tight against the cold. The only spot of color was the narrow ribbon that bound them together, a spot of brighter red against the dark green of the stems.

"A posy for a knife," he said, meaning a joke, and Rathe looked up sharply.

"Do you know the flowers?"

Eslingen shook his head. "You know I don't."

"Winter-roses, they're called, though they're not really roses." Rathe turned the posy over again, studying the ribbon now. "In Hearts, I'm told, you send them to end a relationship."

"Do you think they were meant for Aconin?" Eslingen asked, and the other man shrugged.

"It would be a bit of a coincidence if they weren't. But then, this never happened, right?"

Eslingen nodded, feeling unreasonably depressed.

Rathe shook himself, setting the flowers aside, and stood again, turning his attention to the stove. "Well, if Chresta Aconin doesn't want our help, I'm not going to foist it on him. With all that's going on, I've got problems enough to deal with without him."

6

The next few days were, mercifully, quiet, and Eslingen allowed himself, slowly, to relax a little. Aconin had been least in sight for the first day after the attack, and even after that, he'd kept to himself, consulting primarily with Gasquine and her assistants, and staying well clear of the chorus. So maybe it was a love affair gone wrong, Eslingen thought, making his way toward the Tyrseia once again, or maybe just Aconin's unruly tongue had finally made an enemy who could do something about his hatred. In any case, it had worked to his advantage: the day after the attack he had seen the playwright lurking in the shadows, watching the rehearsal. *How are you?* he'd asked, and Aconin had given him a single, angry look.

My silence for yours, Philip. Agreed?

Eslingen smiled to himself. Agreed, definitely, even though it infuriated Rathe: anything that would help him keep his balance in this strange new world was to be embraced, particularly with Aubine watching him, seeking a kindred spirit. The landseur didn't seem to have much in common with the rest of the chorus, seemed if anything older than his years, sober—still saddened, maybe, by the lost leman, if Siredy's story was true. *And I hope it isn't*, Eslingen added silently. *No one deserves that sorrow.*

He turned the last corner then, coming out into the plaza in front of the Tyrseia, and swore under his breath. At least half the other masters were there before him, clustered outside the actors' entrance, and a cart was drawn up behind them, a heavy canvas pulled over its contents. The first batch of flowers, Eslingen guessed, as Aubine came out from behind the cart, and was relieved to see Siredy waiting with the others.

"Now what?" he asked softly, and the other man rolled his eyes.

"Oh, a lovely beginning to the day. The thrice-damned doors are locked, and we can't raise the watchman."

"The plants won't stand it," Aubine said from the head of the wagon, and Duca threw up his hands in despair.

"I understand, maseigneur, but there's nothing I can do."

"I've wrapped them as best I can," Aubine went on, as though the other man hadn't spoken. "But they don't like the cold."

"Someone must have a key," Eslingen said to Siredy, and the other master sighed.

"Gasquine does—the Venturers, too, probably, but Mathiee's closer. Master Duca sent Peyo Rieux, but it'll be a good half hour before she gets back. More, if she has to wake Gasquine."

"Seidos's Horse." Eslingen took a step backward, looking up the long staircase that led to the narrow gallery door. It would be locked, of course, but there was a shuttered window on the tier above that might give access to the seats.

"And Master Duca's not best pleased," Siredy said, squinting up at the gallery. "You don't seriously think you could get through there?"

"Maybe," Eslingen answered. Actually, the hardest part would be getting to the window, clambering up over the staircase railing; after that, it would just be a matter of shouldering the shutters open— unless there was glass in the frame, he thought, and opened his mouth to ask the question.

Duca forestalled him. "Lieutenant vaan Esling. You're late."

The clock struck the hour as he spoke, giving him the lie, and Eslingen bit back an annoyed retort. "Sorry," he said, without pre- tense of sincerity, and looked back up at the facade. "Would it be too much if one of us climbed up there and opened the door from the inside?"

"As long as you don't strangle the damned watch while you're at it," Duca answered. "I'm reserving that for my particular privilege. Areton's sword and shield, what next?"

For all his bluster, Duca sounded genuinely worried, and Eslin- gen felt a thin finger of fear work its way down his spine. Surely there was nothing seriously wrong, he told himself, just a man asleep on duty—but the watchman had seemed reasonably conscientious. He frowned, and saw the same concern reflected in Siredy's eyes.

"Well, get on with it," Duca said, scowling, and Eslingen shrugged out of his coat. The stairs were guarded only by a low gate, easy enough to step over, but the window of the gallery was more difficult, a good half his body length above the door it lit. He took a careful breath, kicking off his heavy shoes, and stepped cautiously onto the gallery rail. It was wide and dry, worn smooth by thousands of clutching hands, and he wished he'd thought to remove his stockings as well. It was solid enough, though, and he reached cautiously for the carved rails that bordered the narrow window, tugging first gently and then harder to make sure they'd hold his weight. They were firmly set, and he pulled himself up, grunting as his shoulders took the strain, to crouch awkwardly on the narrow sill. *Bad as a gargoyle*, he thought, and glanced down once, to see the others looking up at him, Aubine with his hand to his mouth as though afraid. It was farther down than he wanted to think about; he looked quickly away, one hand still locked to the rail, and pushed gently at the shutters. They gave a little, by the feel of them secured only by a simple latch, and he braced himself to give them a blow with his shoulder. The latch groaned and held, but the second, harder shove knocked them open, and he teetered for a second on the sill before he regained his balance. The others were still watching, and he lifted his free hand in reassurance before sliding through the empty frame.

The window gave onto one of the side corridors, unlit except for the patch of light from the open window, and he stood for a moment in the dark, letting his eyes adjust.

"Hello? Anyone here?"

There was no answer, not even an echo, and he wished he could remember the watchman's name. A little more light seeped in between another pair of shutters farther along the building's curve, and he turned toward it, trying to orient himself in the musty dark. There were curtains to his left, that was the source of the dusty smell, and he fumbled with the nearest set until he found the gap.

There was more light in the main house, filtered through the canvas roof, but the mage-lights were dark. Nothing moved in the boxes, or in what he could see of the pit, and the stage itself lay bare and empty. That was a mercy, he thought, and leaned between the curtains to scan that section of the seats. Nothing there either, as much as he could see in the dim light, and he shouted again. The theatre swallowed the sound, and he shivered. *All right*, he told himself. *Get on with it.* He was on the upper tier, walking behind the cheapest good seats, which meant that he should soon find the stairs leading down to the boxes. Even as he thought that, the stairway yawned before him, and he climbed quickly down to the main floor, glancing from side to side as though he might stumble over the watchman at any moment. There was still no sign of him, and he crossed the pit, checking the stage again, to head up the sloping tunnel to the actors' door. The lock was old-fashioned, heavy iron, and he turned the fluted key with an effort. The tumblers fell into place, and he pulled back the doors to find Duca staring at him.

"Did you find the fool?"

Eslingen shook his head mutely, stepping back to let the bigger man inside. Siredy followed, holding out his shoes, and Eslingen balanced awkwardly on one leg, sliding them back on again. He was lucky not to have put a hole in his stockings, he thought—*and, damnation, I did tear my sleeve.* It was a small rip, on the seam, and he craned his neck to try to see how bad it was. Siredy offered his coat as well, and Eslingen took it, sighing. At least it would hide the worst of the damage.

"Artinou!" That was Duca's voice, well trained to carry through the theatre, and Siredy shook his head.

"He'll have the man's head for this."

"And well he might." Eslingen started back up the tunnel, ducked out of the way as Aubine turned back toward the open door.

"And where should I have the flowers brought, do you think? I don't want them underfoot, but I need to bring them in out of the cold."

"Into the pit, maybe?" Siredy said, and Eslingen nodded.

"If your man can wait until we find the watch, maseigneur, he can tell you where they'd best be placed."

"Ah. Yes. Very wise." Aubine brushed past them with a vague smile, and Eslingen looked at the other master.

"Where is he, do you think?"

"Asleep in the dressing rooms, I hope," Siredy answered, but even as he spoke, de Vicheau came down the narrow stairs shaking his head.

"All the rooms are empty, Master Duca."

Eslingen moved to join them, seeing his own frown reflected on the other men's faces. "Is anything else wrong?" he asked, and climbed carefully to the stage itself. The first baskets of props were where they had been left the day before, and the racked weapons looked untouched, their ribbons hanging limp in the still air.

"Isn't this enough?" Duca demanded.

"I was thinking of theft," Eslingen answered, and the man's expression eased fractionally.

"That's always a risk," he admitted, and looked quickly around the wings. "Our gear is all there."

"But—" Siredy stopped, shaking his head.

"What?" Duca put hands on hips, scowling.

"I thought. . . ." Siredy moved to the nearest rack, examining the row of half pikes. "I thought we left those in better order—separated out, not all in a bunch. Isn't that right, Philip?"

Eslingen nodded slowly. They had taken the half-pikes back from the chorus the evening before, set them back in the rack with all the red-ribboned pikes on the left and the white-ribboned ones on the right. Now—they weren't all mixed, but there were a few red ones in with the white, as though someone had knocked over half a dozen, and put them back without looking. "That's not how we left them."

Duca swore under his breath, and spun to examine the racks himself. "Nothing missing," he said after a moment, and de Vicheau nodded in agreement.

"But they're players' weapons," Siredy said. "Dulled and bated. Why would anyone bother with them?"

No one answered, and Eslingen looked past them into the darkness of the stagehouse. Something else was different, too, he thought, something teasing at the edge of memory—something not quite the way it had been the last time he'd seen it. The machinery loomed overhead, the versatiles locked in their first position, the ropes that held the traps and hanging scenery all taut and perfect—except one. One of the lines was out of place, missing altogether, and he reached out to grab Siredy's shoulder.

"The machines," he said, and the other master's eyes went wide. "Tyrseis, not that."

"Get the trap," Duca ordered, and de Vicheau bent to lift the narrow door. It was dark below, but a mage-fire lantern hung ready, and de Vicheau lit it with the touch of his hand, his face very pale.

"There are more below," he said, but made no move to descend the narrow ladder.

"We'll all go," Duca said grimly, and swung himself down into the pit.

Eslingen followed more cautiously, found another of the mage-lights hanging ready on the nearest pillar, and fumbled with the smoothly polished ring until it sprang to light. Siredy did the same, and the doubled sphere of light spread to fill the low-ceilinged space. It looked much the same as it had before, Eslingen thought, or at least as it had the one time he'd been shown the machines. The windlass stood immobile, and beyond it, the massive gears that lifted the bannerdame's towers were dark with new oil. Except there was something bright caught between the lower teeth, the merest rag of white, and Eslingen took a careful breath, fighting nausea. The rest of it was red-tinged brown, the thick rusty shade of drying blood, and the white thing was the watchman's stockinged leg.

"Master Duca," he said, dry-mouthed, and heard the big man swallow hard.

"I see it. The poor bastard."

"It must be an accident," Siredy said, his voice too high, and Eslingen made a face. This was worse than cannon fire, worse even than a sappers' accident because there was more left to see, the legs all but severed from the crushed torso, the head invisible on the far side of the gear, only the one arm and the stocky legs holding a semblance of human shape. He choked, glad he had eaten lightly, cleared his throat with an effort.

"It is the watch, isn't it?"

Duca nodded, though he made no move to look more closely. "Yes—at least, I'm almost certain. That's his coat."

"Mathiee told him to keep a better eye out these nights," de Vicheau said. "Poor Artinou."

"The rope must have given way," Siredy said. "Gods, if it had been a performance . . ."

He let his voice trail off, but there was no need to finish the sentence. If it had happened during a performance, not only might a sceneryman have been killed, caught like the watchman in the suddenly moving gears, but the actors on the tower would have been brought down abruptly, perhaps thrown off the set piece into the mechanism as well. Eslingen shook his head, trying to banish the picture, and Duca said hoarsely, "And was it an accident?"

The master was looking at him, Eslingen realized, and he took a careful breath. "I don't know," he began, knowing what the other wanted to hear, and then shook himself. He had been around Rathe long enough to know what questions the pointsman might ask, knew what questions he'd ask himself. "If it was an accident, master, why are there no lights in sight? He wouldn't come down here in the dark, surely. And the trap was closed, too."

"He might have done that himself," de Vicheau said, but the objection was halfhearted.

"But not without lights," Duca said, and made a face as though he wanted to spit. "Sweet Tyrseis. What a way to kill a man."

There aren't many good ways to die, Eslingen thought, *but this one is particularly ugly.* "Leave him for now," he said, and thought he saw Siredy give him a look of gratitude. "And send to Point of Dreams. It's in their hands now."

"The house was just purified," Duca began, and shook himself to silence. "Right. Back onstage with all of you, and make sure no one comes down here."

"And that the other trap isn't open," Siredy said.

Duca gave him a look. "Good thought. See to it, Verre. And you, Janne, send to Point of Dreams. I want Rathe, and don't take no for an answer."

They found the second trap closed as well, and Duca straightened from it, breathing heavily through his mouth. "This is hard on Mathiee," he said, and winced as the tower clock struck the half hour. "And she should be along any minute now, with her keys to let us in. Sofia, what a welcome."

"You found the man?" The voice came from the pit, and Eslingen stepped back out onto the stage to see Aubine looking up from the pit. He was surrounded by tubs of plants, at least half a dozen half barrels packed full of greenery and blooms, too bright after the darkness below the stage. From the look in Duca's eyes, the other master was thinking the same thing, and Siredy turned away with a muffled curse, leaning hard against the nearest versatile.

"I'm afraid so, my lord," Eslingen said.

"Dead, then?" Aubine sounded more surprised than anything. "Oh, surely not."

"Caught in the machinery," Duca said, and cleared his throat hard. "The biggest of the lifts."

Aubine said nothing for a long moment, his face very still, and then, slowly, he shook his head. "I've only seen the machines once,

Master Duca, but they struck me then as treacherous things. What a terrible accident."

"If it is an accident," Eslingen said, in spite of himself, and Aubine frowned.

"Surely you're not—oh, no, not again."

The landseur looked genuinely horrified, and Duca lifted both hands placatingly. "It may not be, my lord, but we have to be sure."

"What will it do to the masque?" Aubine asked. "A second death, so soon—practically on the heels of poor de Raçan—if it is untimely, and I pray it is not, Seidos, will they allow us to continue?"

There was no answer to that, the same question the other masters had to have been asking themselves, and Eslingen glanced over his shoulder at the sound of women's voices from the tunnel.

"So you got in all right without me, I see." Gasquine was wrapped in a serviceable-looking cloak of grey wool, her thick hair untidy beneath a linen cap. "What in the name of all the gods is going on? And where's Artinou?"

"Dead," Duca answered, and the actor stopped as though she had been struck.

"Dead?"

Duca nodded. "In the gears, below stage. It's not pretty."

Gasquine paused, her foot on the first step leading up to the stage. "Tyrseis. The Starsmith forge his soul anew."

Duca touched his forehead in respect, and Eslingen, belatedly, copied him.

"Did a rope break?" Gasquine began, and answered her own question. "No, the cordage is new—and what was he doing down there anyway?"

"We don't know," Duca said. "But it may not be an accident, Mathiee. We've sent for the points."

For a second, Gasquine looked old and tired, but then she straightened, pulling herself back together with an effort of will. "Good," she said, and sounded as though she was trying to convince herself.

Rathe arrived within the half hour, flanked by a pair Eslingen recognized from the Dreams station. He quickly commandeered Gasquine's replacement watchman, setting him to guard the single open door, then made his way onto the stage. He hardly looked as though he belonged there, Eslingen thought, a wiry, unexceptional man in a badly battered coat under the pointsman's leather jerkin, but then he nodded to Gasquine, the gesture drawing all eyes, and Eslingen couldn't repress a smile.

"Mathiee." Although he spoke directly to the actress, Rathe was careful to let his voice carry, taking in the other authority, Duca's and Aubine's, as well. "I'm sorry to see you again, at least like this."

Gasquine managed a wan smile. "As are we all, Nico. Gerrat says he doubts it was an accident, and I'm afraid so do I."

Rathe nodded. "Who found the body?"

"Master Duca and his people. They were to have the stage early this morning."

So much for that plan, Eslingen thought. *As things were, they'd be lucky to get any work done at all today—and I suppose I should feel guilty for thinking it, but Seidos knows, there's work enough to be done.* Rathe's eyes slid over him without acknowledgment, but then, as the pointsman turned back to face Gasquine, Eslingen thought he saw the hint of a smile.

"All right. Let's get it over with. I take it the body's below stage—and who found it, anyway?"

"We did," Siredy said. "All of us together. Philip saw that a rope was missing, so naturally we looked to the machinery, and—"

He stopped abruptly, grimacing, and Eslingen said, "The body's caught in the gears. It's not nice."

Rathe made a face as well, but nodded. "Show me."

Duca pointed to the trapdoor, and de Vicheau, still pale, lifted the heavy boards. Rathe slid down easily enough, stood for a moment in the dark before Eslingen followed with a lantern. Rathe took it with a nod and moved forward into the shadows. Eslingen hung back, not wanting to see again, heard Rathe swear as he found the mangled body. There was a little silence then, Eslingen careful not to see, and then a scuffling sound, and Rathe came back, bringing the light with him. His expression, in the mage-light, was unreadable, but he was rubbing one hand convulsively on the edge of his jerkin.

"Did someone identify the man?"

"Master Duca said he recognized him," Eslingen said. "From the clothes."

"Not from the face, by the look of him," Rathe answered. He took a deep breath. "Was it like this when you found him?"

Eslingen nodded. "We didn't touch anything, just came down to look, found him, and came away."

"No lights?" Rathe asked, and Eslingen felt a perverse thrill of pride at having guessed the right question.

"None. The lanterns were hanging by the ladder."

"And the trap was closed," Rathe said.

"Both of them," Eslingen answered.

Rathe sighed. "Are any of the scenerymen around?"

"I don't think so," Eslingen answered. "Unless Mathiee's sent for them already."

"She'd better," Rathe said, and motioned toward the ladder. "Come on, let's get back up. They'll need help to get him out of there."

Eslingen made a face at the all-too-vivid image, and heard one of the other pointsmen choke. He hadn't realized they'd come down behind him until then.

"And we'll want to know if the ropes gave way," Rathe went on, as though he hadn't heard, "or if anything else is wrong. Len, find something heavy and block off the other trap—these are the only two ways down, right, Philip?"

"As far as I know," Eslingen answered, and pulled himself up onto the stage again.

"And then watch this one yourself," Rathe went on. "Sohier, I want you to wait for the people from the deadhouse, see if you can slip them in discreetly—"

The pointswoman shook her head, the braided lovelock flying. "It's not going to happen, Nico, I'm sorry. There's already a crowd gathering, and the Five Rings is open for business."

Rathe swore again. "I've a mind to call a point on them for contributing to the disturbance. All right, do what you can. Let's hope they hurry."

Gasquine had sent for her sceneryman already, and he arrived with the deadhouse carters and a knot of actors, the group swirling down the tunnel into the pit in a confusion of voices. Rathe straightened from his examination of the loosened rope, and bit back an exclamation of disgust. The apprentice alchemist—the same woman who'd collected de Raçan's body, he saw without surprise—matched him stare for stare, but he ignored her, beckoned to Gasquine instead.

"Mathiee. Get your people under control, please—and now that they're here, they can stay until I've had a word with them. Keep them here in the pit, and I'll get to them as soon as I can."

Gasquine nodded, turned away to give her own orders, and Rathe went on without a pause. "Leenderts, you watch the door. Make sure no one else gets in without my or Mathiee's say-so—"

"Adjunct Point!" That was the new watchman, hesitating at the head of the tunnel, and Rathe bit back another curse. "Adjunct Point, the chorus is here, or some of them, and what am I to tell them?"

"Tell them—" Rathe stopped, looking at the meager man, and swallowed what he would have said. "Sohier, hold the alchemists here, and wait for me. There's a sceneryman to help with the machine."

The alchemist nodded, clambering up the stairs behind the sceneryman.

"Right, Nico," Sohier answered, and Rathe climbed back down to the pit. There were at least a dozen actors there, he saw, plus the masters and of course Aubine, standing among his flowers like a man bereft. *I'll deal with them later,* he thought, and started back up the tunnel, only to stop short, seeing Eslingen and the younger master, Siredy, already standing in the now-open door.

"My compliments to the vidame," Eslingen was saying, his voice so polite as to be almost a parody, "and the rehearsal plans have changed again. If she'd be so good as to continue on to the Bells, the rehearsal will take place there instead."

Someone—a woman in coachman's livery, Rathe saw, her whip tucked up over her shoulder—asked a question, and Eslingen drew himself up to his full height.

"I wouldn't know. I'm sure all your questions will be answered at the Bells."

He stepped back, swinging the door closed almost in the coachman's face, and looked back over his shoulder with a wry grin. "Sorry. The watch didn't seem able to cope."

Rathe nodded. "Thanks. Are they listening?"

"Reluctantly," Eslingen answered. "They all want to know what's going on."

Rathe stooped to peer through the scratched and bubbled window that ran parallel to the doorway. As Sohier had warned, the tavern across the plaza was already open for business—two hours before its regular time, Rathe thought, and grimaced, seeing another serving girl scurry in the kitchen door. Clearly, the theatre murders were starting to rival *The Drowned Island* in the popular imagination.

The long, low windows were crowded with staring faces, and there were still more people gathered along the edges of the square to stare and gossip. The alchemists' cart stood ready, a flat-faced man slouching on the tongue, shaking his head at a thin man in a torn coat. "So does everybody, it seems," he said aloud, and waved the watchman forward. "Can you keep the door, Master—"

"Pelegrim." The watchman touched his forehead again. "I'm doing my best, sir, honestly—"

"I'll stay with him," Eslingen offered. "Between us, we can keep things quiet."

Rathe shook his head. "Actually, I may need you. But if you'd be willing to help Leenderts, Master Siredy . . ."

"Of course," the other man said with a sweet smile, and the watchman ducked his head again.

"I'm doing my best, masters, all I can do."

"I'll keep an eye on him," Leenderts said, and Rathe nodded.

"I do my job," the watchman said again, and Leenderts's eyes met Rathe's over the man's shoulder.

Rathe nodded—*the man's been up to something, watch him*—but there was no time to pursue the question as another knock sounded at the door. Pelegrim moved to answer it, Siredy at his back, and he waved Eslingen back toward the main house. "I'm sorry to do this, Philip," he said aloud, "but there's still the body to deal with."

Eslingen grimaced, but nodded. "I'm at your disposal," he said, and the tone was warmer than the formal words.

Sohier had collected both the sceneryman and the alchemists at the unblocked trap, saw them return with undisguised relief. "Nico—"

"The sooner you let us at the body, the sooner you'll have your answers," the alchemist said, riding over anything the pointswoman would have said, and Rathe took a breath, controlling his annoyance with an effort.

"Take them down, Sohier," he said, and nodded to the sceneryman. "Master—?"

"Basa," the sceneryman answered. He was an older man, easily a grandfather, with big hands marked by heavy, swollen joints. Retired from the river, maybe? Rathe guessed, when the winters got too hard to bear. "Pointsman, they tell me the machinery gave way, but I don't see how. All the cordage, that's all new, not two weeks old, we change all the ropes once a fortnight."

"Expensive," Eslingen said, and the sceneryman scowled.

"Cheaper than new actors."

"Show me the rope that failed," Rathe said, and the sceneryman pointed into the shadows.

"There's not much to see, pointsman, that's where that cable should be."

"We noticed it was missing as soon as we looked," Eslingen said.

Rathe nodded. "Show me," he said again, and Basa hunched his shoulders.

"Over here."

Rathe followed him into the wings, stepping carefully over cleats that held other ropes stretched taut, stopped as Basa crouched beside an opening in the floor. There was no sign of a rope there, but looking up, Rathe thought he could see the end of one dangling somewhere in the gloom overhead.

"Now, then," the sceneryman said, and straightened, reaching for a pole that hung on the nearest pillar. It had a hook at one end, like a boathook, Rathe saw, and ducked as Basa reached up to catch a loop of leather that had been hanging, invisible, among the ropes. There was a rattle of metal, and then a length of rope dropped to the stage floor. Basa prodded at it, still scowling, then stooped again to hold it out like an accusation.

"Now, see there. That was in the brake."

Rathe took it gingerly, not quite knowing what he was looking for. It was new cable, all right, still bright and barely scarred, five finger-thick strands wound tight on each other. One end was bound with bright red cording, and the other hung loose, just starting to unwind from its tight twist.

"That's not frayed," Basa said. "And it's not been cut, either. I'd stake my reputation on that."

"So what then?" Rathe asked, and handed the length back to him. "A fault in the mechanism?"

Basa didn't answer immediately, reversing the hook to probe through the hole in the stage floor, came up at last with a second length of rope. This one was still attached somewhere below, but the sceneryman caught it before it could slither back out of sight, laying it flat on the boards and pinning it with his hook.

"And that's the other end." He glared at it. "Not the mechanism, pointsman, but the splice, or at least that's what someone wants you to think. But no line I mend gives way, not like this. There's been murder done, pointsman, and I want it solved."

Rathe stared at the new length of cable. It didn't look that different from the first one, the same bright new rope, one end a little more frayed than the first one had been, and he looked back at Basa. "You're saying that this was, what, unraveled?"

"See there?" Basa pointed with his toe, keeping the hook firmly on the length of line. Rathe squinted, thought he saw a length of thinner rope among the heavy strands. "The binding, there, see? The rope was spliced and the join bound off to make it stronger, that's the way we always do it here. But someone's unbound it, to make you think the rope failed."

Rathe nodded slowly. "And you're telling me—forgive me, Master Basa, but are you saying that the rope couldn't have failed? That this join couldn't have given way?"

Basa's eyes flickered, and he shrugged one shoulder. "All right, I'll never say never could happen. But I've never seen it done before."

"What if the brake gave way?" Rathe asked again, and Basa shook his head.

"If the brake had let go, you'd find the whole coil down below, not just a part of it."

Not that I expected anything different, not the way things have been going. Rathe took a deep breath, and Sohier appeared in the opening of the trap. Her face was very pale, but she had her voice well under control.

"Excuse me, Nico, but the alchemists would like a word with you. And with the sceneryman, if you please."

Rathe nodded, glanced at Basa. "I'm sorry to do this, but—I think they'll need your help getting the body free of the machinery."

Basa made a face. "Oh, yeah. But I'll need some backs to work the windlass, with the brake off."

"How many?" Rathe asked.

"Three, at least," Basa answered. "Four's better."

"Sohier and me," Rathe said, and Eslingen's head rose.

"And me, if you'd like."

"Thanks," Rathe said, and looked at Basa. "Enough?"

"It'll do."

They climbed back down into the understage, and Rathe was grateful for the overwhelming smell of the oil that coated the gears and the massive turnshaft. The alchemists were clustered around the body, mage-lights poised to cast as much light as possible, and Rathe looked away from the too-vivid picture. The woman apprentice— Ursine, Fanier had named her—looked over her shoulder at their approach, and came to join them, wiping her hands on her leather apron. There were new smears on it already, Rathe saw, and swallowed hard.

"You don't deal in the common run of deaths, do you?" Ursine shook her head. "Dis Aidones, what a mess."

And for an alchemist to say so. . . . Rathe killed the thought, said, "What can you tell me?"

"Well, he's dead for sure," Ursine said with a fleeting smile. "But I'm not happy about this one, Adjunct Point. He—well, Master Fanier can say for sure, but I'd lay money he didn't die where he's lying."

"Seidos's Horse," Eslingen said, and Rathe grimaced.

"You mean he died, or was killed, somewhere else, and then put into the machine?"

Ursine nodded, rubbing her hands on her apron again. "That would be my guess, Adjunct Point. But, as I say, Master Fanier can say for sure."

"That's an ugly thought," Eslingen said, and Rathe nodded. It wasn't hard to guess why someone would do it—the gears had crushed the man's torso, would hide even a stab wound or a bullet hole, and without the alchemists' testimony, there was a good chance that it would be taken for an accident—but it argued a colder heart than he'd thought they were dealing with. *And it's exactly the opposite of de Raçan's death,* he thought suddenly. *He was found dead without apparent cause, with no chance of it being an accident, while what killed the watchman is almost too obvious, and almost too obviously an accident.*

"I want to know as soon as possible," he said aloud, and Ursine nodded again.

"We've done as much as we can here," she said. "But I'm not sure of the best way to get him out of there."

"I can help." That was Basa, his voice cracking, and he cleared his throat. "Give me a minute, sir, dame, and I'll get the machines switched over."

He was as good as his word, pulling levers to move heavy bands of leather from one shaft to the next, careful to check each length of rope before he finally took his place at the main controls. "If you'll take the windlass, pointsman—no, the other way—and just take up the strain. . . ."

Rathe took his place at one of the long poles, saw Sohier and Eslingen do the same. He leaned his weight against the length of wood, felt the others doing the same, and then, slowly, the windlass moved, easily at first, and then more stiffly. The enormous shaft that ran the length of the understage turned with it, and there was a sigh of metal on metal as the great gears trembled behind them.

"Ready?" Basa called, and one of the alchemists lifted a hand.

"We're ready."

"Stay clear of the gears," Basa warned, and Rathe bit down on unhappy laughter. Not that anyone should need that warning, with that object lesson staring them in the face.

"Clear," the alchemist answered, and Basa dropped his hand.

"Go."

Rathe threw his weight against the lever. There was a moment of resistance, and then it turned, more easily than he would have expected. The shaft turned, smooth and silent, and there was a muffled exclamation as the gears turned backward.

"Stop."

Basa jerked two levers even as he spoke, and Rathe felt the windlass freeze under his hand. He straightened, catching a glimpse of the alchemists bending over the hunched body, and saw Basa, his face averted, adjusting levers and belts to hold everything in its place again.

"We'll get on this one right away," Ursine said, jerking her head toward the body, and Rathe nodded.

"I'd appreciate it," he said, and Basa turned toward him.

"Pointsman—Adjunct Point. How soon can we—when can I bring my people down here, clean this up? The blood . . . I don't want rats."

Rathe swallowed hard, saw both Sohier and Eslingen flinch at the image. "We're done," he said aloud. "So the rest of it's up to Mathiee."

"Thank you," Basa said, and shook his head. "Sweet Tyrseis, what a—the poor bastard."

"Did you know him?" Rathe asked, almost on impulse, and the sceneryman shrugged.

"Not well. The actors would know him better. Who'd want to kill a man like him?"

"Like what?" Rathe asked, but the sceneryman was already out of earshot, scrambling back up the ladder to the stage itself. Rathe sighed, and looked at Sohier. "I'll want an answer to that question. Let's go."

Gasquine was waiting on the stage, talking in an undervoice to the playwright. Aconin had changed his dark wig for one as pale as summer wine, and for once he looked genuinely worried. Rathe made a face—the last thing he wanted was to have to deal with Aconin—and beckoned to Sohier.

"You start with the actors, and any of the stagehouse staff. You know what I want, anything that might tell us why the man was killed. And I'll talk to Mathiee."

"He was the watchman," Sohier said, and nodded. "You never know what he might have seen."

Rathe nodded in agreement, and moved toward the company manager. She saw him coming, and broke off her conversation with Aconin, came toward him with a hand outstretched. "Is it—"

She broke off, as though she didn't want to put it into words, and over her shoulder Aconin made a face.

"What else could it be, Mathiee?"

"An accident." Gasquine frowned at him, but the playwright seemed not to see.

"What an ugly irony it would be if the man died for actually doing his duty. You couldn't use it in a play."

" 'Doing his duty'?" Rathe repeated, and looked at Gasquine. "I'm sorry, Mathiee, it's most likely that this wasn't an accident, so I'll need to know anything you can tell me about him."

"Tyrseis," Gasquine said, and shook her head. "He's been—he had been one of my watchmen for, oh, I suppose it's been five years now. His father was an actor, comic parts, before your time, I think, but talented."

"You gave him the job for his father's sake?" Rathe asked, and Gasquine shrugged.

"Partly, I suppose. And I know his sister, too, she's a seamstress—he lived with her and her man. So when I needed a watchman, and heard he was looking for work, it seemed to be a good match. He was willing enough."

"So you're saying he had no enemies that you know of," Rathe said, though he thought he already knew the answer.

Gasquine shook her head again. "None, and I can't imagine any.

There are men who are born to be uncles, Nico, you know the sort, big sweet men who don't want a household of their own, but live to indulge your own children. That was Artinou to the life, and he treated the actors all the same way. He was always doing them favors, carrying notes and flowers, that sort of thing."

"And being well paid for it, too," Aconin said.

Gasquine rounded on him with a frown. "And you, Master Aconite, can mind your tongue when you speak of the dead."

"I don't say he didn't mean well," Aconin said. "I believe he did. But be fair, Mathiee. He took coin for his pains, as much as any watchman did."

"Master Aconin," Rathe said. "What was it you meant about Artinou doing his duty for once?"

For the first time, the playwright looked uneasy. "Mathiee can tell you better than I can."

"There's no point in bringing that up," Gasquine said, through clenched teeth.

Rathe suppressed a sigh. He'd seen this reaction a hundred times before, the grief that wanted only to see the best in the dead, and he made his voice as gentle as he could. "It could be important, Mathiee, you know that—might explain something."

Gasquine grimaced, but nodded. "I had to speak to him yesterday. Some of the actors—not the chorus, just the actors—came to me and said things had been moved about in the dressing rooms."

"Stolen?" Rathe asked, and Gasquine shook her head.

"No, that was the odd thing. I mean, theft's a constant problem, there's always someone new to the city who doesn't know the jewels are paste—I can't count the number of times we've redeemed Anfelis's Crown from pawn, we've practically got an account with the old woman." She broke off with an apologetic smile. "And actors are careless, they leave things about that they shouldn't. But, no, nothing was stolen, just—moved around, or so the actors told me. And from what they said, it seemed it must have happened overnight. So I told Artinou to take special care to make sure the house—all of it, stage and backstage and understage and the house, too—was locked tight and no one was there who shouldn't be."

"And then he was found dead," Rathe said.

Gasquine looked stricken. "Oh, Tyrseis. I wish I hadn't said anything."

"Don't be absurd," Aconin said. "You had to say something."

"Did you know about these—disturbances?" Rathe asked, and the playwright hesitated, then shook his head in turn.

"Not I. By hearsay only. You'd have to talk to the actors about that."

"I'll do that," Rathe answered, and looked back at Gasquine. "With your permission, of course, Mathiee."

"Of course." Gasquine took a deep breath. "Oh, Nico, I so wish this hadn't happened."

And not just for the sake of the play, either, Rathe thought, though that had to be looming in her mind. The company owner seemed genuinely distressed. He murmured what he hoped was a soothing response, and glanced at the knot of actors gathered now in the pit. Sohier was talking to one of them, a tall, lanky woman whom Rathe had always seen playing the heroine's best friend, and the rest seemed to be trying to listen without actually being caught eavesdropping. Guis Forveijl was among them, carefully not meeting Rathe's eye, but also Gavi Jhirassi, and in spite of himself, Rathe's mood lifted. Jhirassi was as keen an observer as any actor, and more to the point, he could be trusted.

"Gavi," he called, and the younger man turned at once. His hair had been cropped short for *The Drowned Island*, to accommodate the young hero's massive wigs, and the short curls set off the sharp bones of his face, made him look like a Silklands carving. "Over here, if you would."

Jhirassi moved to join him, and Rathe climbed down the short stairs into the pit, moving him away from the other actors. He was aware of Forveijl's eyes following them, and did his best to ignore it, took a deep breath of air that smelled suddenly and strongly of Aubine's plants.

"What's all this about things being—disturbed—in the dressing rooms?"

Jhirassi raised his eyebrows, spread both hands in a gesture that was gracefully uncertain. "What about it? A bunch of us complained to Mathiee—you don't mean that's why poor Artinou was killed?"

"I don't know," Rathe answered. "And, frankly, Gavi, I don't even know exactly what happened, so . . ."

He let his voice trail off, and Jhirassi gave a wincing smile. "Sorry. We're all a bit—unsettled—today." He took a breath, visibly collecting his thoughts. "Sorry. What happened. Well, it wasn't much, really, but it was disturbing, thinking someone had been in the dressing rooms. It was like someone had been through everything, all our goods and clothes—"

"Looking for something, do you think?" Rathe asked.

Jhirassi gestured helplessly. "I don't think so? I don't know. There was enough for the taking, Tyrseis knows, I'd left a nice gilt chain by mistake, but it was there, just moved from one hook to another. And some clothes were taken out of the press, Guis's coat was dropped in a corner—"

"That could have been Guis," Rathe said, in spite of himself, remembering Forveijl's habits, and Jhirassi grinned.

"No, I saw him hang it up this time. The wardrobe mistress was going to fine him if he didn't take better care of it, and she did charge him a demming anyway." His smile vanished. "And there was more. All the paint pots were moved around—one was broken, Anjesine's best rouge—and she had a posy for her throat, tea herbs, and they'd been pulled apart and rearranged." He paused. "I think that was the strangest thing, someone bothering to rearrange a bunch of herbs."

Rathe nodded. "Tell me about Artinou."

"What's to tell?" Jhirassi made a face. "I'm sorry, that sounds terrible, but he was the watchman. I didn't know him very well."

"Aconin says he ran errands for people, carried notes and such."

"So do all the watchmen," Jhirassi answered. "If anything, Artinou had more sense than most—he could remember who you wanted to see, and who was being hinted away."

"A useful talent," Rathe said. *And potentially a dangerous one, if the watchman had remembered more than he should.* He took the actor through the rest of his questions without learning more than he'd already heard from Gasquine, and when he'd finished stood for a moment, hands on hips, trying to decide who to question next. Sohier was working her way through the actors; maybe he should leave them to her, he thought, and concentrate on the masters. Even as he thought that, Eslingen stepped into his line of sight.

"Excuse me, Adjunct Point?"

Rathe frowned at the formal address, and Eslingen took a step closer.

"If I could have a word?"

Rathe's frown deepened, but he nodded, stepping back out of earshot of the group still gathered in the pit.

"I think there's someone here who doesn't belong," Eslingen

said. "He's not one of the actors, or a master—I thought he was Aubine's man, but his lordship says not."

"Where?" It took all of Rathe's self-control not to turn and stare. It had been known to happen, murderers returning compulsively to the scene of their crimes, particularly when a madman was involved. . . .

"Toward the back of the pit," Eslingen answered. "On the edge of the group of actors—by the biggest tub of plants. He's an older man, brown coat, brown hair."

Rathe nodded, letting his eyes drift sideways, scanning the crowd. The edges of the pit were in shadow, the sunlight that filtered through the canvas roof not adding much to the mage-lights, but he found the man at last, leaning on the edge of the handcart that had carried Aubine's plants. And that was probably how he'd gotten in, Rathe guessed, offering to help carry pots and then staying after Aubine had paid him off. No one would have noticed him, just another laborer.

"You know him," Eslingen said, eyes narrowing, and Rathe nodded.

"Oh, yeah. All too well. That's Master Eyes himself, come to see the scandal."

"Master Eyes." From the look on Eslingen's face, he recognized the name—*and well he should, considering how many broadsheets came from the bastard's pen*, Rathe thought. Not that Eyes wrote them himself, or not all of them, but his name, and his too-astute observations, filled reams of paper. "What do we do about him?"

Rathe sighed. "He doesn't have any right to be here, and I'm sure Mathiee would be glad to see his back, if she knew he was here. So I'll do her a favor, kick him out myself—if you'll help."

"Of course."

Rathe smiled lopsidedly. "Bear in mind that he has a lot to say about actors, and the Masters of Defense, for that matter."

"I'm hardly important enough to catch Master Eyes's notice, surely," Eslingen answered. "What do you want me to do?"

It was hardly that simple, Rathe knew, but he didn't have time to warn Sohier. Eyes would be gone at the first hint of trouble, fading back into the shadows where he could lose himself, where he could stay hidden until the theatre was cleared. "Get between him and the stairs—casually, like you're looking for a place to catch a nap."

"The Masters of Defense," Eslingen said with dignity, "do not take naps during rehearsal."

Rathe grinned in spite of himself. "For a tryst, then, or whatever it is the masters do allow themselves to do. Then I'll flush him out."

Eslingen nodded. "I'm at your service, Adjunct Point."

He turned away, threading his way between the benches, and Rathe reached for his tablets, made a minor show of opening them, carving letters into the stiff wax. Not for the first time, he felt foolish, playacting in front of actors, but no one seemed to notice. Sohier was talking to another woman now, one of the masters, Rathe thought, and behind them he saw Eyes moving closer, easing toward them in hopes of catching a word or two. He ducked his head over the tablets again, not wanting to alarm the man, a part of his mind wondering if Eyes could have anything to do with these murders, or at least with Artinou's death. By his previous record, there wasn't much Eyes wouldn't do to find a scandal he could sell to the printers—but then, Rathe amended, on his previous record, Eyes was more likely to invent scandal than to create it himself. He was not notably a man of his hands, preferred to let his pen do his fighting for him. Rather like Aconin in that, Rathe thought, and glanced up at the stage. The playwright was still there, standing a little apart from the others, arms folded across his chest as though he was cold. He was looking at something in the middle distance, Rathe realized, and frowning slightly, let his eyes follow the playwright's gaze, found himself looking at the landseur Aubine, fussing over an uncovered tub of flowers. They were beautiful, brought to bloom only a few months early, the vivid blue stars of spring greeters bright even in the dimly lit theatre. He had a bank of them himself, tucked into a sheltered corner of his shared garden—they grew from corms, too, though far humbler than anything sold at market—had told himself it was for the bulb, good against fever, but the truth of it was, the bright flowers always lifted his spirits. They bloomed always in the last weeks of the Spider Moon, shoving up through snow if necessary, a full two weeks before the hardiest spring flowers showed their heads. They seemed an odd choice for the masque, there was no magistical significance that he knew of, but then, the color was certainly bright enough to show well in the theatre.

Eslingen was in position, leaning into a swordsman's stretch that brought him between Eyes and the nearest staircase, and Sohier, Rathe saw, was between him and the tunnel that led to the door. He folded his tablets, trying to look casual, and took a careful step toward the group of actors. Eyes stayed where he was, still shadowed, then, as Rathe came closer, took a slow step backward, putting another tub of plants between himself and the approaching pointsman. Rathe kept coming, hurrying now, and Eyes took another backward step, almost tripping over a bench. Rathe allowed himself a grin, and the other man turned to run, stepping up onto and over the nearest bench. Eslingen straightened to attention, and Rathe shouted, "Hold him!"

Eyes darted sideways, floundering in the narrow space, and Eslingen lunged, caught him by the collar of his coat. The broadsheet writer writhed in his grip, trying to shed it, but Eslingen had him by the shirt as well, dragged him back and around until he could catch one arm and bend it backward.

"Is this your murderer, Adjunct Point?"

The guileless voice carried clearly, and actors and masters alike turned to stare. Rathe hid a grin—*trust Philip to carry through*—and managed a sober shake of the head. "No, I don't believe so. But he doesn't have any business here that I know of."

"Master Eyes!"

The exclamation came from the actors, quickly stifled, and Rathe looked up at the stage, to see Gasquine staring down at them, something like horror filling her face. "He's not part of your company, is he, Mathiee? Or yours, Master Duca?"

Gasquine shook her head warily. "Not of my company, no . . ."

"Nor mine," Duca said, voice grim, and behind the writer's shoulder Eslingen showed teeth in a cheerful smile.

"Then maybe he is your murderer."

"Don't think I don't know who you are," Master Eyes said. His voice was clear, tinged with a southriver accent. "And I know what you are to him, so don't play games."

"The only thing Orian ever murdered was a reputation," Aconin said, from the stage. "But he has slain a few of those."

"Master Eyes," Rathe said, and felt the attention focus again on him, actors and masters alike. This must be something like what it felt like to be onstage, he thought, and wondered vaguely how they stood it. "You're not of this company—of either company. I will have to ask you to leave."

Eyes smiled with easy contempt. He was, Rathe thought remotely, surprisingly handsome, a pleasant face under brown hair just starting to show threads of grey, not at all what one would expect from his acid writing. "I'll leave if I must, Adjunct Point. But don't think I haven't seen and heard more than enough to fill a dozen broadsheets."

"I daresay you have," Rathe answered. "But bear in mind you are talking about the masque. There's a printer's ban on the details, so I'd be very careful what I said, if I were you."

Eyes laughed. "A good try, Adjunct Point, but it won't wear. Besides, everyone is much more interested in the details of these deaths. The masque itself pales in comparison—no criticism meant of Master Aconite."

It was true enough, and Rathe sighed. "Bring him, please, Lieutenant."

Eslingen nodded, increasing the pressure on Eyes's wrist until the writer gasped and took an involuntary step forward. Eslingen smiled, quite sweetly, and edged the man toward the tunnel. Rathe followed, taking a savage pleasure in the writer's discomfort. He'd earned it, Sofia knew—but of course Eyes probably counted it as one of the hazards of his profession. Leenderts was still with the watchman and Siredy, the door barred behind them, and Rathe paused, beckoning to the other pointsman.

"Len. I need to make someone known to you."

Leenderts nodded, his expression questioning, and Rathe smiled. "This is Orian Fiormi, better known to all of us as Master Eyes."

Leenderts's eyes widened almost comically, and Eyes swore under his breath. Anonymity was his stock in trade, Rathe knew, and allowed his smile to widen in turn. "Remember him," he said, and Leenderts nodded.

"Absolutely, Adjunct Point. I won't forget."

"Good." Rathe nodded to the doorkeeper. "Master Eyes was leaving."

The doorkeeper nodded, scrambling to unfasten the bar and turn the heavy lock, and Eslingen eased his grip on the writer. Eyes straightened his shoulders, shrugging his coat back into place, looked from one to the other.

"You can't stop the stories," he said. "And Mathiee might have liked to have some say in them."

"You can take that up with Mathiee," Rathe answered. "Though I doubt you would have, frankly, offered her the chance. It's so much easier to make things up out of whole cloth than to have to fit in unaccommodating things like facts. But this is a points matter, and you have no business with it."

The door was open at last, and he nodded toward it. Eyes swept him a mocking bow, and stalked away, the skirts of his coat billowing in the breeze.

"Tyrseis," Siredy said. "He'll quarter us for that."

"I hope not," Rathe answered. "Or at least maybe he'll put the blame where it belongs."

"Master Eyes is never fair," Siredy said.

That was all too true, and Rathe sighed. Eyes had seen the shrouded body carried out, had heard at least some of the actors' gossip, knew as much and probably more than anyone except the murderer about de Raçan's death . . . No, this was not going to make him friends in Dreams, and Trijn in particular was going to be livid. Keep things out of the broadsheets as long as possible, she had said, and if anyone could spot the political implications of the chorus, it would be Master Eyes. He shook himself then. That was borrowing trouble; still, the best thing to do would be to go straight to Trijn, and tell her what had happened.

He made it back to Dreams station in record time, but Trijn herself had gone out. Rathe stared down at the daybook, flipping back through the pages to hide his relief. He could leave her a note, then, and spare himself the lecture—*or, more likely, put it off until to-morrow.* Still, it was a reprieve of sorts, and he flipped back through another day's entries, wondering if he should go to the deadhouse himself. Fanier would do the job as quickly and efficiently if he wasn't there, but a part of him felt as though he should be present, somehow help shepherd the body through the alchemist's rites. And that was foolish, he knew, and turned another page. Voillemin had been to Little Chain, he saw, and frowned as he read the brief notation. *Spoke with stallholder, who had a story about flowers bought according to the Alphabet. Misadventure?*

"What do you know about this?" he asked, and the duty point—Falasca again—looked up quickly.

"Not much. He's been working on a report for a couple of days now."

"Do you know if he ever spoke to Holles?" Rathe saw the woman shrug, and said, "Leussi's leman. The one who found the body."

"Oh." Falasca shook her head. "I don't think so—but of course I could be wrong. I think, my impression is, that he thinks this wraps up the case. He said something about the matter being resolved."

"Resolved." It was an odd word, not one that went with murder, and Rathe had to take a careful breath to control his anger. "Do you know what he found?"

"No," Falasca answered. "I'm sorry."

"Is Voillemin in?" Even as he asked, Rathe knew it was a forlorn hope, and Falasca shook her head again.

"He has the night watch, sir, he won't be in until after second sunrise."

Another four hours. Rathe looked back at the daybook, at Voillemin's neat, well-schooled handwriting. If he really had found information that would allow him to—resolve—the investigation, surely he would have made his report by now; if the information wasn't good enough, surely he would have spoken to Holles. Which meant that his fears, and Holles's, were coming true: Voillemin was looking for a way to brush the case aside. He shook himself, frowning now at his own suspicions. It was just as possible that Voillemin was being conscientious, was making sure his conclusions could be justified, before he committed his opinion to a report—but if that were the case, why hadn't he talked to Holles yet? Rathe hesitated, then reached for his daybook to copy the name and direction of the stallholder who claimed to know so much. It wasn't his business to check up on Voillemin, and the regents would have a fit if they ever found out, but he couldn't not follow up on this, if only for Leussi's sake. With any luck, he'd simply confirm what Voillemin had found, and everyone could rest easier.

He crossed the Sier at the landings beside the Chain Tower, where in generations past the first watchtowers had protected the city against attack from the west. The city had spread beyond the towers now, and it had been at least a hundred years since queen or regents had ordered chain strung from jetty to jetty to foul enemy ships, but the massive links were still stacked ready, greased and rewound twice a year by the Pontoises, the company of boatmen responsible for law on the river. Today a pack of children, too young even to work as runners, were playing tag around the pile of iron, their cries carrying like riverbirds' in the cold air. The boatman was surly, sunk into a triple layer of heavy jerseys, fingers wrapped in wool beneath the leather palms, and Rathe was glad to pay him his fee, resolving to walk back to the Hopes-point Bridge before he ventured on the water again.

Voillemin's note had said that the woman was a stallholder in the Little Chain market, but a single glance at the stall, well painted and double-sized, with cressets already lit against the gathering dusk and a banner of a star and bell, was enough to make Rathe swear under his breath. Whatever else Levee Estines was, she was more than a mere stallholder, and Voillemin should have known better than to take her that lightly. The woman herself was not at the stall, but the man who tended it, busy among jars and baskets of dried herbs and flowers, pointed him willingly enough to his mistress's house. The house itself was neat and well kept, new plaster bright between the beams, and a glasshouse leaned against the southern wall where it could take the sunlight. The glass was fogged now, and in spite of everything Rathe felt a slight pang of envy. Glasshouses were expensive to build, even more expensive to heat through Astreiant's long winter; his mother had always wanted one, and in the same breath called them a waste of coin and effort. This one was small, just a lean-to, really, so that even a small woman would have to crouch to tend the plants on the lowest shelves, but he could see greenery through the clouded glass, and knew it was doing its job.

The maidservant who answered his knock seemed unsurprised to find a pointsman on their doorstep, and ushered him into what at second glance had to be a buyer's receiving room. It faced away from the glasshouse, the single window giving onto what in the summer had to be an uncommonly pretty garden, and Rathe took a step toward it anyway, admiring the shapes of the empty beds. Half a dozen corms stood ready in forcing jars, already sending up vigorous green shoots, and he wondered again exactly what Estines's trade was. Herbs and flowers, from her stall, but did she also trade in medicines, or perfumes, or even food, or just in the raw materials?

"Adjunct Point?" The voice broke off. "Oh. You're not who I expected."

Rathe turned to see a round woman frowning at him from the doorway. Her hair was caught up under a lace cap, her only concession to fashion, and as though she'd guessed his thought she shook her skirts down from where they'd been caught up for work.

"My name's Nicolas Rathe, mistress, from Point of Dreams. I understood you wanted to speak to someone from our station."

"But I spoke to someone." Her voice was wary, and Rathe made himself smile. This was one of the reasons that checking up on a fellow pointsman was difficult.

"I know. To Adjunct Point Voillemin, right?"

"Yes." Estines drew the word out into two syllables.

"I have some reason to believe that this case is connected to one of mine," Rathe lied. "So I wondered if you could spare me a few moments to talk to me as well."

"Connected?" Estines's eyes grew very round. "Oh, surely not. That would be—" She checked herself and repeated, "Surely not."

Damn Voillemin for not putting in his reports on time. Rathe said, "Oh? Why do you say that?"

Estines looked as though she wished she hadn't spoken. "I don't want to tell you your business, I know nothing of points' affairs—"

Rathe smiled again, tried for his most soothing voice. "You sent to us, said you had information on the intendant Leussi's death. What was that?"

"But I told the other man," Estines said.

"I'd like to hear it again, from you." It was one of the oldest tricks in the book, but Estines nodded slowly.

"Please, Adjunct Point, sit down," she said, and seated herself in the chair closest to the hearth. A fire had been laid there some hours ago, by the look of the embers, but Rathe seated himself opposite her, grateful for the steady warmth. Estines folded her hands together, setting them on her knees like a schoolgirl. "I sent for you because the intendant had been a customer of mine, for flowers and such—I grow flowers for half the houses in Hearts, Adjunct Point, and herbs for the midwives, too."

"I saw your stall," Rathe said, "and your garden."

Estines allowed herself a shy smile. "Thank you."

"And the intendant?" Rathe prompted, when she seemed disinclined to continue, and Estines made a face.

"As I said, a customer of mine. And he came to me two weeks before he died—or at least I think it was then he died, the other pointsman wouldn't tell me when, exactly, as if I'd sell it to the printers. But he came to me to buy flowers out of season—I have a glasshouse, and I make that a specialty of mine, I pride myself that I can have any flower all year long. At any rate, to make the story short, he came to me with a list of flowers that he wanted, and I had them all. But what struck me—you must understand, my dearest friend is a printer in University Point, she's just done an edition of the Alphabet, a licensed edition—he was reading from a list, just like one of the posies the book calls for. I'm sure he was making a posy, and—" She broke off, ducked her head, her fingers tightening on each other. "I was afraid it might somehow have harmed him."

"A posy from the Alphabet," Rathe said. "Not your friend's book?"

"Oh, no." Estines shook her head for emphasis. "Not that edition. But there are so many, and I thought . . . Of course, I don't know it was the Alphabet, but it seemed so odd, the choices, and so with the play and everything, I thought that had to be it. The other pointsman seemed to think so."

Voillemin would, Rathe thought. *No wonder he'd said "resolved" and "misadventure." This was the perfect excuse, some experiment that went wrong and could be safely brushed aside, smoothed over to the content of the regents—and I suppose it could be that. Except I think Holles would have known.* He said, "Does that mean you remember what the flowers were, mistress?"

"Oh, yes." Estines smiled again. "That was what struck me so oddly then, and later, too. They don't—I don't know if you know flowers, Adjunct Point?"

"A little."

Estines nodded. "Moonwort and trisil and trumpet flower and red star-vine, bound with lemon leaves and demnis fern."

Rathe's eyebrows rose. The flowers were individually pretty, and the trisil was strongly fragrant, but its sweetness would be buried under the still stronger scent of the lemon leaves, just as the moonwort would be lost under the showier blooms of the trumpet flower. And the demnis fern was just the wrong shade of green to match the others.

Estines nodded again, harder this time. "You see. Not a posy for looks, or for any herbal use I know. So of course I thought of the Alphabet."

And Leussi had a copy, Rathe remembered suddenly, *a copy that's locked in my own strongbox even now. Is that why Holles gave it to me?* He shook the thought away—Holles was not the sort to play games, at least in their short acquaintance—and reached for his tablets again. "You're sure of that list, mistress?"

"Completely sure," Estines answered. "It's my trade."

That was unanswerable, and Rathe quickly jotted down the names. "Had he ever bought bunches like that before?"

"Never. Usually he liked seasonal flowers, small things, posies for a gift and the like." Estines sighed. "He said once his leman didn't like flowers, so he bought them for other people. I thought that was sad, don't you?"

"Yes," Rathe said. And it was sad, though not just for Leussi's sake, meant that Holles would be unlikely to know anything about his leman's research. *But Voillemin still should have questioned him*, he thought, and folded his tablets again. "Mistress, I thank you. You've been very helpful."

"You're welcome." Estines stood stiffly, easing her back. "Adjunct Point, I wonder. I understand you can't tell me when he died, that would be improper, I was told, but I did wonder—I would hate to think my flowers had anything to do with his death."

Rathe gave her a sharp look, but saw only honest grief in her round face. "I don't know, mistress. On the face of it, it seems unlikely."

"But the Alphabet . . ." Estines let her voice trail off, and Rathe shook his head.

"I've yet to see a copy that can be said to be effective, and we— not just Dreams, but all the stations—have examined forty or fifty copies. So far, it looks like just another midwinter madness."

"Like *The Drowned Island*," Estines said, nodding. "Well, one can hope. I'm sorry to have troubled you, if it's nothing."

"No trouble at all," Rathe answered, and followed her to the door. She let him out into the sharp chill herself, the air smelling strongly of a hundred fires, and he stood for a moment, trying to catch his breath and order his thoughts. If it were any other pointsman, he wouldn't distrust the findings, would be willing to wait for the report, to see what other evidence could be mustered to support death by misadventure, but Voillemin was too eager to see this put aside. He would have to see Holles, he decided, ask about flowers, but first, he'd need to see if that posy was listed in Leussi's edition of the Alphabet, and what it was supposed to do.

7

Rathe made sure he was early to Point of Dreams, stirred up the fire in the workroom stove even as the tower clock struck nine, and reached for his tablets, unfolding them to reveal the list of flowers. Moonwort, trisil, trumpet flower, red star-vine, bound with lemon leaves and demnis fern: not a common posy, he thought again, and fumbled for the key of the lockbox. If it was listed in Leussi's copy of the Alphabet, he would have to talk to Holles, find out if Leussi had said anything about testing the formulae—though if he had, surely Holles would have mentioned it—and then . . . He shook his head unhappily. He still wouldn't have positive proof that Voillemin was failing in his job, failing the points, might only have proved that Leussi's death was after all misadventure—except for the bound ghost. That was the work of an enemy—or could it be some bizarre side effect of the flowers? It seemed unlikely, but b'Estorr might know, or would know who could tell him, if the posy was in the Alphabet. And he had been told not to pursue the matter. The best thing might be to take the whole thing to Trijn, and let her sort it out. She was the chief point, after all; Voillemin was her responsibility, and it was her responsibility to sort out what was really happening here. He made a face, wishing it was his case, that he didn't have to sneak around the edges to try to make sure the job got done, and there was a knock at the door. He looked up as the door opened, and a runner peered through the opening.

"Sorry, sir, but this just came. It looked important."

Rathe nodded, beckoned her inside. Whatever it was, it dripped with ribbon and seals, and he held out his hand. "Who brought it?"

"It was a runner from All-Guilds," the girl answered. "Stuck-up little prig."

All-Guilds. From the regents? Rathe turned the letter over, his frown deepening as he recognized the symbols on the seals. It was from the regents, all right, and he could guess what it was about. "Is she waiting for a reply?"

"No, sir." The runner shook her head. "Said she had other business. Silly cow."

"Mind your manners," Rathe said without heat. "All right, that'll be all for now."

"Yes, sir," the girl answered, and backed away, pulling the door closed again behind her.

Rathe glared at the letter, then abruptly broke the seals. The broad pen strokes filled the page, a sprawling clerk's hand ordering him to appear before the regents at half past ten, to answer for unwarranted interference in a matter he had already been forbidden to handle. He swore under his breath, wondering how Voillemin had found out—*Falasca, of course; she would still have been on duty when he arrived the night before*—and swore again, wondering which of the regents was acting as Voillemin's patronne. The clock struck half past nine then, and he shoved his keys back into his pocket, carefully refolded the letter, and headed for Trijn's workroom.

She greeted him with a preoccupied smile, but the expression faded as he shoved the regents' letter under her nose. "What's this?"

"Read it, please, Chief."

She made a face, but skimmed the brief paragraph, finally leaning back in her chair to lift an eyebrow. "And what's brought this on? Have you been meddling?"

Rathe grimaced. "Yes and no, Chief."

"I'd have preferred a simple no."

"Nothing's ever that simple," Rathe answered. He reached for the chair that stood beside her desk, seated himself at her nod. "First, Kurin Holles came to me to complain that Voillemin hadn't talked to him at all—and it was Holles who found the body, never mind anything else. I told Holles I couldn't interfere, but I'd speak to Voillemin, which I did, to tell him that he shouldn't worry about hurting Holles's feelings, he was more than willing to speak to the points."

"And?" Trijn asked.

"At the same time, I saw someone had come from Little Chain saying she had information about the death, but Voillemin had written it off—said it was just a printer trying to get details for a broadsheet." Rathe took a breath. "So I told him I thought he should speak to the woman."

"It's possible," Trijn murmured, "but he should have gone. All right. Go on."

"Then yesterday, after I dealt with another body at the Tyrseia— you did get my report on that matter?"

"I did," Trijn said. "There are too damn many of them, Rathe. I suppose we're still waiting for the alchemists' report?"

Rathe nodded.

"Then I can assume you went to Little Chain yourself to talk to this woman."

Rathe sighed. Put like that, he was at fault—he'd been warned off the case by the regents, for one thing, and for another, he had no right to interfere in another pointsman's case without gross evidence of neglect. "I did," he said, and Trijn made a face.

"Damn it, Nico, I thought better of you."

"Chief." Rathe took a careful breath. "I had cause—I had reason to think it was important. And I believe I was proved right. The woman who sent to us is a flower-seller, she sold the intendant the makings of a bouquet that she believes came from an edition of the Alphabet, and which she feared might have harmed him."

"That sounds like misadventure to me," Trijn said.

Rathe shook his head. "The ghost was bound," he reminded her, and she swore.

"So it was. Could it have been the Alphabet that bound him?"

"Chief, I don't know. But I don't think it can be written off until we find out."

"Damn the man for a fool." Trijn glared at the summons, then shoved it back across the tabletop. "And this—this is outside of enough. I'm not best pleased with you, Nico, you should have come to me, not handled it on your own, but Voillemin has overstepped himself. I'll deal with him later, but in the meantime . . ." She lifted an eyebrow. "I'm glad you brought this to me. I'd half had you written down as the sort of hero who'd try to face them down by yourself."

Rathe laughed, and knew Trijn heard the anger in it. "I'm not that much of a fool, Chief."

"Then let's be on our way." Trijn rose gracefully to her feet, reaching for a fur-trimmed cloak. "If they're in such a hurry, they can deal with us in our working clothes."

Rathe glanced down at his own coat, well aware that he'd worn it to shapelessness. Trijn, on the other hand, was almost as neat as a regent, though her wine-red skirts were brighter. He looked even more common by contrast, wondered if it was fully wise to provoke the regents even further, but Trijn seemed unaware of any potential problem. "We'll take a low-flyer," she said, and swept out of the narrow room.

They were early to All-Guilds, thanks to a wall-eyed coachman who took the bridge at a speed to make the apprentices curse him, but Trijn paid him off with a look almost of satisfaction. She led the way into the hall, moving through the chill passages with an unsettling familiarity, finally paused in the doorway of a clerks' room to beckon the woman nearest the door. The blue-robed woman, barely out of girlhood, rose with alacrity, smoothing her gown over her skirts, and bobbed a curtsy.

"Can I help you, madame?"

"Tell their mightinesses the regents that Chief Point Trijn—and Adjunct Point Rathe—are here now, and wish to see them."

The clerk's eyes widened, and for an instant Rathe thought she would protest, but Trijn raised an eyebrow. The clerk swallowed whatever she would have said, and bobbed another, deeper curtsy. "I'll tell them, madame," she said, and hurried off, her skirts billowing.

Trijn nodded with satisfaction, and Rathe's eyes narrowed. If it had been left to him, he would have looked for a doorman, not a clerk, certainly wouldn't have invaded the clerks' working space even though that seemed to be the correct procedure. "You're known here," he said aloud, and Trijn gave a weary nod.

"I suppose it would out at some point. Yes, I'm known." She forced a wry smile. "Most people have relations they would prefer not to claim. My burden is my sister. Madame Gausaron."

"The grand bourgeoise," Rathe said, and knew he sounded breathless.

"Herself."

Rathe started to say something, then closed his mouth over the words. "I'm so sorry."

Trijn choked back a laugh as the clerk reappeared, but there was no mistaking the amusement in her eyes.

"The regents will see you, madame," the clerk said with another curtsy. "And sir."

"Good," Trijn answered, and the clerk flung open the heavy doors.

"Chief Point Trijn and Adjunct Point Rathe, of Point of Dreams."

"You're very peremptory, Chief Point," Gausaron said from her place at the center of the dais, and Trijn shook her head. Even knowing they were kin, Rathe could see no similarity between them, wondered if they had perhaps had a different father.

"You have overstepped yourself, madame," Trijn said. "What do you mean by summoning one of my people without notifying me? Courtesy alone would have required it, procedure demands it. If you have fault to find with my adjunct point, I expect to be notified of it first. It is my place to correct my people, not yours."

"Adjunct Point Rathe has intervened in the matter of the Leussi death," another regent said. She was a thin woman, with deep lines bracketing the corners of her mouth, the pallor of her skin set off by the deep, true black of her high-necked gown. "As he was expressly forbidden to do. This was brought to our attention. If you cannot rectify the situation on your own, Chief Point, you must not be surprised when we are asked to intercede."

Neat, Rathe thought. *If Trijn says she didn't know I'd interfered, that she didn't know Voillemin was unhappy with it, they can accuse her of not keeping enough of an eye on her own affairs.* He bit his tongue, knowing he had to keep silent as long as possible. He was his own worst enemy here—*let Trijn handle it*, he told himself, and clasped his hands behind his back, tightening his grip until his joints ached.

"The matter was brought to my attention this morning," Trijn answered, "as it should have been, by the man whose concern it most is. The matter was brought to your attention because Voillemin is your spy in my point—and I will not tolerate that, madame, not a day longer. If you have a complaint, and I'm sure you have, you can address it to me now, as you should have done from the beginning."

Gausaron's mouth thinned. "As you well know, not only was the matter assigned to another, but Adjunct Point Rathe was explicitly ordered to keep his distance from it. And he has not done so."

"The death of a royal intendant is a grave and delicate matter," a third woman said. "We were certain you, Chief Point, would understand this."

"It cannot be handled like a southriver tavern brawl," Gausaron continued. "It must not bring embarrassment upon the family, who have suffered quite enough by this loss. Rathe's—Adjunct Point Rathe's actions threaten to bring offense to a very important family."

"And those were?" Trijn asked.

Gausaron blinked. "I beg your pardon?"

"What has Rathe done to bring offense to the family?" Trijn said. She spread her hands. "We are here at the request of the intendant's leman—"

"His kin," the thin-faced regent said. "His sister. By rights, she should have had the final say in this, it's indulgence enough that we allowed it reopened without consulting her."

That was true enough, and Rathe winced, hoping the regents didn't see. A leman's rights were limited in law; without a wife, Leussi's legal kin would be the women of his mother's family.

"There was a risk that this would all end up in the broadsheets," the third regent said. She had a bright, high voice like a singing bird's. "That would have been grave offense indeed."

"And this is what Voillemin told you," Trijn said, "that Leussi's sister was afraid of the broadsheets."

"She is a woman of probity and discretion," Gausaron said. "One can hardly blame her for her fears."

Trijn looked at Rathe. "Has this been noted in the daybook, Adjunct Point?"

Rathe shook his head. "No, Chief."

"Then I must speak with Voillemin as well." Trijn favored the regents with a bleak smile. "If such a warning is not posted, then it cannot be obeyed. You should be grateful that it was Rathe who spoke to the flower-seller, not some excitable junior."

"He should not have spoken to anyone concerned with this matter," Gausaron snapped. "No one at all."

"Adjunct Point Rathe came to me this morning to say that he had stumbled across evidence that Adjunct Point Voillemin had failed to fully follow—evidence that came to him in the course of other cases, and which, at this moment, seems to suggest misadventure rather than murder—and to ask me to take further action. Rathe is my senior adjunct, it is his right and duty to oversee the actions of the other pointswomen and -men under my authority." Trijn glared at the regents, moderated her tone with an effort. "It is my considered opinion that he has behaved properly in this matter, and my very grave concern that Adjunct Point Voillemin has not. You yourselves would dismiss any clerk caught doing what he's done."

That was a home truth, Rathe thought, seeing heads nod almost involuntarily along the line of regents.

Gausaron frowned. "Adjunct Point Rathe acted against our express orders—"

"To do his duty," Trijn countered. "And he has put the matter in my hands. Isn't that right, Adjunct Point?"

"Yes, Chief," Rathe said, his mouth suddenly dry. *I've been manipulated just as neatly as the regents. I just hope I can trust her to carry through.* But Trijn understood the issues, he told himself, understood why it might still be murder, would still be murder unless the plants had somehow also bound the dead man's ghost. She wouldn't let it go to appease a complaint that might never have happened.

Gausaron sat back in her chair, her face without expression. "Very well, Chief Point, we will accept your explanation. But if this comes before us again, we will recommend to the Surintendant of Points that he look to his stations with a more careful eye."

Trijn's gaze flickered at that, but she managed a court-deep curtsy, her skirts almost puddling on the floor. Rathe bowed, knowing better than to copy her irony, and followed her from the room.

She did not speak again until they reached the main hall, where the cold air seeped in from the main doors to turn the floors to ice. Rathe held the smaller winter-door open for her, and she swept past him into the sunlight of the open square. She stopped there, squinting against the sudden brightness, and shook her head.

"She's going to go to Fourie, and expect him to listen to that?"

"He might not have a choice," Rathe answered. Of course, with Fourie, he might advance Trijn to chief at Temple Point just to infuriate the regents: one could never predict how the surintendant might react.

"Fourie always has a choice," Trijn answered. "That's how he's gotten as far as he has." She took a breath. "I've backed you this far, Nico, and I expect you to help me now. Find me this formula, this recipe for a posy, and I'll see it gets to the proper authorities at the university. I'm well aware it may still be murder, I won't let myself be talked out of it to convenience the sister—if she even exists."

"And Voillemin?" Rathe asked.

"Leave him to me." Trijn gave a grim smile. "I will keep my eye on him, and on his handling of this matter—I'll have him reporting to me on the hour like an apprentice, if I have to. But if the regents decide they have reason to summon you again, I may not be able to protect you."

Rathe nodded. He'd been lucky to get away with this much, he knew, knew, too, that he would do it again. "I'll be careful," he said, and Trijn's eyes narrowed as though she would comment on the ambiguity.

"See that you are," she said after a moment, and lifted her hand to summon a hovering low-flyer.

They made it back to Point of Dreams in less than record time, and Rathe resettled himself in his workroom to retrieve Leussi's copy of the Alphabet of Desire. It looked like most of the others, a simple octavo volume with a formula in verse on the recto and a woodcut of the finished posy on the facing page. The woodcuts were better than most of the editions he'd seen, however, good enough that he could actually recognize most of the plants in the illustrations, and he paged slowly through it, looking for the bright spikes of the trumpet flowers. They appeared in perhaps a third of the woodcuts, he saw—in fact, the corms predominated, perhaps because they could be forced in all seasons—but finally he found the page for which he was looking. The posy was labeled "for Concord" and he made a face at the irony. If a posy intended to bring peace had somehow killed . . . *Poor Leussi*, he thought, *and poor Holles*. He reached for a scrap of paper, began copying out the formula while he thought out what he would say. He would send it to b'Estorr, he decided—well, he'd ask Trijn to send it to b'Estorr, but there was no reason he couldn't write the query himself. Trijn would give him that much leeway. He finished copying the formula, added a quick note asking b'Estorr either to analyze it himself or to recommend a magist who could, and took the sheets along to Trijn's office. She scanned them without comment, but nodded, scrawling her own name below his, and added the station's seal.

"I'll see this is sent," she said. "Now, what about the theatre murders?"

"Still waiting for Fanier's report," Rathe answered, and retreated to his workroom.

The runner arrived a little after noon, not the deadhouse runner he'd been expecting, but a skinny boy on the edge of apprenticehood, his hair cut short except for the one long love-lock that aped the consorts of the bannerdames of *The Drowned Island*. Even if he hadn't been wearing a badge identifying him as belonging to Point of Knives, the hair would have betrayed him, and Rathe eyed him without favor. No one among the points liked the idea that the inhabitants of the Court of the Thirty-two Knives might take new pride in their disreputable past.

"Well?"

"Sorry, sir, but the chief—Head Point Mirremay thought you should be informed."

The boy held out a folded scrap of paper—torn from an old broadsheet, Rathe saw, unfolding it, and he flattened it deliberately on his table before he scanned the flamboyant penmanship. Flamboyant and hard to read, he amended, squinting at letters scrawled with a pen that definitely needed mending, and looked up at the boy. "And?"

The boy seemed used to the question—as well he might be, if he had to deliver writings like this one on a daily basis, Rathe thought. He shifted his feet, hands clasped behind his back in a loose-jointed parody of a soldier's stance, and said, "Please, Adjunct Point, the— Head Point Mirremay says you might be interested in this complaint of Master Aconin's."

Rathe glanced at the note again. With that broad hint, he could make out the gist of the note, which was that Chresta Aconin had come to Point of Knives less than an hour ago with the complaint of a theft from his rooms. Someone—he couldn't make out the name— had been dispatched to document the complaint, and what she had found had sent her pelting back to Mirremay. And Mirremay had sent for him. He looked back at the boy. "Tell me about it."

The boy didn't seem to need much encouragement, but then, runners rarely did. He bounced forward on his toes, then seemed to remember where he was, clasping his hands behind his back again. "Please, Adjunct Point, they say it was a mess, the worst anyone's ever seen. Everything spoiled, and all his papers burned, and his coats cut up, and—" He stopped abruptly, as though remembering his dignity. "And the chief says she'd take it kindly if you'd lend a hand, seeing as you're already dealing with the theatres."

"Does she think they're connected?" Rathe asked, but he was already on his feet, reaching for his coat.

"He's the playwright." The boy shrugged. "And the chief says she'd swear he knows what's going on, but he says he doesn't. And he doesn't want you called in, I heard him arguing about it."

Sofia forgive me, but that would probably make me go even if I didn't already think it was important. Rathe shrugged on his jerkin, grateful for the extra layer, and slipped his truncheon into his belt. "All right, my boy, let's get on with it."

Point of Knives was exactly as he remembered it, a blocky, four-square building that had once been an armory. It had been rebuilt since then, and the neighborhood's clock perched awkwardly in an afterthought of a gable, but it still turned windowless walls to the street on three sides. The windows that faced the open market square were little more than slits along the second floor. Dark and cheerless for any pointsman who lodged there, Rathe thought, with sympathy, and noisy, with the clock gears ticking and grinding overhead night and day. *I'll lay money Mirremay lodges elsewhere.*

The doorway was thick and defensible, with old firing points hastily boarded over to keep out the chill, but it opened into a surprisingly pleasant day room smelling of herbs and only incidentally of dinner. There were a dozen mage lights spaced along the walls, supplemented in this cold weather by a hanging chandelier, and a pair of runners kicked their heels on a bench by the stove, each one at an end to make room for the dice and counters spread between them. A pointsman in a cracked jerkin was polishing his truncheon by the enormous empty fireplace, and a woman in last summer's fashionable brimless cap looked up at their approach.

"Good, you found him. Thank you for coming, Adjunct Point, the chief will be glad to see you."

"It sounded—intriguing," Rathe said, and the man in the cracked jerkin looked up quickly.

"That's one word for it—"

"If you'll come with me?" the woman interrupted smoothly, and Rathe allowed himself a quick glance over his shoulder as he followed her. The pointsman's head was down over his truncheon, and Rathe wondered what he would have said.

Mirremay's workroom was on the second floor, almost at the head of the narrow stairs. It wasn't at all as he had suspected it would be like, was, instead, a comfortable room, dominated by one of the narrow windows, and Rathe cocked his head, trying to hear the dull tick of the clock through the ceiling. Mirremay herself leaned one hip on the edge of her worktable, frowning at Aconin in the visitor's chair. She was a short, round woman, with a heart-shaped face and knowing amber eyes, and Rathe hid a frown, remembering too late what gossip said of her. Mirremay had been the name of one of the thirty-two knives, and before that of a bannerdame; in joining the points, Mirremay had been re-creating a family fiefdom here on the edges of the Court. Perhaps that was the reason that the surintendant had been so reluctant to advance Point of Knives to the status of a full station: no one wanted to make a Mirremay chief point of anything, least of all Point of Knives.

"Thanks for coming, Rathe," she said, and Rathe nodded, grateful that she'd decided to let him avoid the awkward question of her rank.

"I'm grateful you sent for me."

"Well, I'm not." That was Aconin, still lounging in the visitor's chair. A decorative pose, Rathe thought, but the playwright couldn't hide the tension in his muscles. "Honestly, Mirremay, this isn't worth his time. It's just another theft, that's all."

"And what, then, is missing?" Mirremay asked, mildly enough, but Aconin frowned.

"How can I tell that, when you won't let me look?"

Rathe lifted an eyebrow, and Mirremay smiled. "Oh, yes, that's what we have here, just another housebreaking in the Court. Except that Master Aconin can't tell me what was stolen."

"I have valuables," Aconin said. "The place was such a mess that I couldn't tell if they were there or not."

"Still, it seems odd that so many things should be happening to the people involved in this thrice-damned masque," Mirremay said. "And I say it's Dreams's problem as much as mine."

She gave Rathe a challenging look, and the other spread his hands, automatic suspicion rising in him. No chief point, and she was that in stature if not in name, gave away cases, unless they were likely to cause more trouble than they were worth. "I couldn't take it out of your hands, Mirremay, not without Trijn's approval, but I am glad you called me."

Mirremay smiled again. "Wait till you see the rooms before you say that. And, speaking of it—"

"Mirremay—" Aconin began, and the round woman held up her hand.

"Don't bother. He's coming with us."

Aconin subsided at that, straightening his wig as he rose, and Mirremay reached for her own full coat. "Let's go."

Aconin lived on the edges of the Court—even he hadn't dared to move into the rookery at the center, the decayed mansion, now broken up into a hundred or more one-room flats, where the thirty-two knives had held their macabre reign. The pointsman Rathe had seen in the day room—Sentalen, his name was—tapped at a lower door and, when it opened a crack, spoke briefly to someone hidden in the shadows. Then she vanished again, the edge of a dark blue skirt whisking back out of sight, and Sentalen turned to Mirremay.

"Same as before, Chief. No one's been in or out—she says."

Aconin rolled his eyes, but Mirremay smiled, and started up the outside stairs. It would be a nasty climb at midwinter, Rathe thought, stepping carefully, and wondered why the playwright chose to live in this neighborhood. Probably to keep his enemies at bay, he thought, and glanced over his shoulder to see Aconin hesitating at the bottom of the stairs. That was unlike him—to give him his due, Aconin never feared the results of his attacks—and in the same instant, the playwright started after them, so quickly that Rathe wondered if he'd imagined the hesitation. But it had been real, he decided, seeing the tension in Aconin's body, in the tightness of his hands on the narrow rail. Mirremay was right, this was no ordinary theft.

At the top of the stairs, Mirremay paused, looked over her shoulder, and Sentalen handed up an old-fashioned iron key. Rathe shook his head. Whoever had broken into the playwright's room had broken the locks already—kicked it in, he guessed, from the way the frame had splintered. Mirremay worked the lock, her shoulders bunching with the effort, and the door fell open under her touch. It had been the lock itself that had been holding it, and only barely, the iron striker wedged awkwardly back into place. Mirremay caught the door as it swung on twisted hinges, then stepped back to let Rathe join her on the landing.

The runner's description hadn't done it justice. Aconin's single well-lit room had been a pleasant enough place, but it would take days of effort just to make it habitable again. Clothes lay strewn across the floor, linings ripped out muddy, sleeves torn away, the press itself kicked in, so that the painted panel hung in splinters, and there were footprints visible on some of the better fabrics, as though whoever had done this had deliberately wiped his boots on the best the playwright owned. Both windows had been broken, the glass punched out into the street below, and the mirror—a large one, in an expensive frame—had been smashed against the bedpost, so that the torn bed-clothes were strewn with broken glass. Paint pots and perfume bottles, a good dozen of them, had been emptied onto the bed as well, the containers trampled into the floorboards, and the room smelled of musk and sweetgrass. A larger paint pot, or maybe an inkwell, had been thrown to smash against the far wall, leaving a fan of black across the whitewash. One chair had been overturned and broken; the other stood forlorn beside the table, where a spray of flowers stood in an untouched vase, wilting a little, as though the destruction had shocked them. Beyond the table, the door of the stove lay open, a drift of half-burned paper scattered across the hearth, and Rathe crossed to that, knelt to examine what was left of the writing. Some of it looked familiar, scenes from the Alphabet, and he glanced over his shoulder, to see Aconin framed in the doorway.

"Was it like this when you found it, or did you pull it out?"

"I pulled it out," Aconin said. Beneath the remnants of his paint, he looked very pale. "They'd overfilled it, the damper shut down, so it was just smoldering."

"Lucky," Mirremay murmured. She had come a little farther into the room, careful not to step on spilled paint or torn clothing, stood with her hands on her hips, surveying the damage with a disapproving air. She wore her skirts short, well above her ankle, and her stockings were expensively clocked.

Rathe nodded, turning the papers over. Aconin used the crabbed university script, all abbreviations, harder to follow even than Mirremay's scrawl, but from the crossed-out lines and words, and the notes scribbled in the margins, these had to be rough drafts of Aconin's work. "This was personal," he said, and set the papers carefully back where he'd found them.

"I'd've said business," Mirremay said.

Rathe glanced at her as he pushed himself to his feet, brushing the ash off his fingers, and the head point met the look guilelessly. "Burning these papers, Aconin's work, surely that's a personal thing."

"I told you," Aconin said wearily. "None of my enemies would do something like this."

"I thought better of your enemies," Rathe said, and to his surprise, Aconin managed a short laugh.

"So did I."

Rathe took a deep breath, willing himself to remember that this was a point, that he had a job to do no matter how he felt about Aconin. "Aconin. Less than a week ago, someone took a shot at you—did you think Philip wouldn't tell me, when he was there? And now this. Who have you offended this time?"

"I wish I knew." Aconin spread his painted hands, a gesture that should have dripped sincerity. "As far as I know, this was theft, at least an attempt at it. I won't know that until you let me see what's missing."

"Not that much," Mirremay said. She reached out with one pointed shoe, lifted the torn collar of a lavender coat. An enameled medallion tumbled free, not expensive, but certainly salable; she kicked the coat a little harder, exposing a scattering of gilt embroidery at the skirt. "Now, I grant you, that wasn't worth much, and it might have taken too much time to cut that gold thread free, but those buttons would fetch a few demmings, and that's just one stroke of the knife. And there's not a thief in this city who'd smash a pretty clock like that one, not with the fences paying two or three pillars for a piece like that."

She nodded to her right, where the attacker—Rathe was more than ever inclined to agree that this was no thief—had swept a single shelf clear of all its ornaments. Dishes lay broken beneath it, spoons and a dinner knife scattered, but someone had taken the time to stamp on the carriage-clock that had stood with them. Its case lay broken, the mechanism crushed, and in spite of himself, Rathe winced at the sight.

"Damn it, Aconin, this is personal. Whoever did this, whoever had it done, that's someone who wants you harmed, or worse."

"I can't think who," Aconin said flatly. He had moved into the room, was staring now at the untouched vase of flowers, and out of the corner of his eye, Rathe saw Mirremay nod thoughtfully.

"Or it's a warning, maybe. There's the altar, too."

Rathe turned to look where she'd pointed. Aconin had kept his altar in a scholar's cabinet, with a double-doored shrine at the top and a drawer for supplies above a set of shelves. Books had been emptied from the shelves, leaves torn out and crumpled; one lay forlorn, facedown, the binding snapped and scarred as though someone had stamped on it. The drawer had been pulled out and tossed aside, its contents scattered, and each of the little figures had been roughly beheaded. The candle that served as Hearth had been cut into two pieces—one more bit of proof, Rathe thought, if we'd needed it, that this wasn't an ordinary thieving—and the incense burner had been flattened. Cheap metal, Rathe thought, irrelevantly, not like the clock, and stepped closer to examine the shrine itself. There was no sign of blood, on the altar or on the floor around it, and he looked back at Mirremay.

"I think we should have a necromancer in, just in case." The surest way to curse a person was to kill something in their household space or, worse still, on the altar itself, and at this level of destruction, he wanted to be sure that more ethereal means weren't being employed against the playwright.

"Oh, for Sofia's sake," Aconin said. He pulled a flower from the vase, tossed it accurately through the broken window. "To what end?"

Mirremay nodded as though the playwright hadn't spoken. "Sentalen. Send a runner to the university."

"There's no blood," Aconin said. "Nothing's been killed."

"You're very sure of that," Rathe said.

Aconin paused, another flower dangling broken-stemmed between his fingers. It was out of season, Rathe saw, forced to bloom in some expensive glasshouse: the posy was no ordinary gift, and he wondered briefly if that was why it had been spared.

"There's no blood," Aconin said again, and dropped this flower after the other.

"Dead doesn't need blood," Mirremay said.

"Chief Point—" Aconin began, and the woman shook her head.

"Whatever troubles you've brought on yourself, Aconin, I'm not having this loose in my district. Send for a necromancer, Sentalen."

"Ask for Istre b'Estorr," Rathe interjected, and looked at Mirremay. "He's one of the best."

"Which we want," Mirremay agreed, and nodded to the pointsman still hovering in the doorway. He backed away, and Rathe looked down at the broken figures that had stood on Aconin's altar. One had been hooded Sofia, no surprise there, and another the Starsmith, but the other two were less obvious, the Winter-Son, god of wine, ecstasy, and suffering, and Jaan, the northern god of doorways and borders. *Not that odd a choice, when you consider he comes from Esling, but still.* He frowned then, a memory teasing him. Something Eslingen had said, some story about his days with Coindarel—about partisan raids along the borders, breaking into the leaders' houses to smash the altars. It had meant something very specific, a deliberate message, but he couldn't remember what. He shook his head then, seeing Aconin drop a third flower, and then a fourth, through the broken glass. He would ask Eslingen, of course, but he doubted it meant anything. It wasn't likely that Astreianter bravos would know a Leaguer code.

"Chief Point," Aconin said again. "I need to start cleaning. . . ."

His voice trailed off, contemplating the chaos, and Mirremay's voice was almost gentle. "When the necromancer's done his work. It won't get any worse, my boy."

Aconin managed the ghost of a smile, but pitched the last of the flowers through the window with extra force. The clock struck then, the neighborhood clock perched in the station's gable, and the playwright looked up, startled. "Tyrseis, I'm late—Mathiee wanted me today. Chief Point, do you need me anymore?"

Mirremay shook her head, looking almost indulgent, and the playwright wiped damp fingers on the skirt of his coat. He backed toward the door, and Rathe heard his footsteps recede down the stairs. He waited until he couldn't hear them anymore, and smiled at Mirremay.

"Now why do I not believe that?"

"He's done better on the stage," Mirremay agreed.

The clock struck twice more before Sentalen's runner reappeared, announcing that the magist was on his way, and the half hour was past before b'Estorr himself mounted the narrow stairs. He paused in the doorway, frowning at the destruction, and Rathe put aside the stack of half-burned papers. He had been sure that there would be some clue, some explanation, if not in the drafts of the Alphabet then in some broadsheet, but so far he'd seen nothing that should provoke this level of hostility. Mirremay rose gracefully to her feet, another expensive chain dangling in her hand—the fourth piece of decent jewelry she'd found untouched in the wreckage—amber eyes taking in the Starsmith's badge pinned to b'Estorr's sleeve.

"So this is your magist, Rathe?"

b'Estorr's mouth twitched at that, and Rathe nodded. "Istre b'Estorr, necromancer and scholar—Head Point Mirremay, of Point of Knives."

Mirremay looked briefly annoyed by the demotion, but b'Estorr's bow was flawless, unobjectionable, and she pulled herself up. "Then I certify your arrival, and acknowledge his presence, but I can leave the rest of it to you, Rathe. I'll want a proper report, of course."

"Of course," Rathe said.

"And I'll send a runner with lanterns." Mirremay glanced toward the windows. "It'll be dark soon, with the clouds this low."

And no one, particularly not a stranger, wanted to be caught even on the edges of the Court after dark with no lights. "Thanks," Rathe said, and b'Estorr echoed him.

"It's shaping to be an unpleasant night."

Rathe glanced at the window, seeing the clouds dropping low over the housetops, moving faster as the rising wind caught them. He could smell a cold rain in the air that swirled through the broken glass, shivered in spite of himself at the thought. As chill as the nights had been lately, rain would turn to sleet before the second sunrise, and the winter-sun's light would do little to melt the ice.

"And I intend to be home and snug before then," Mirremay said. "I meant it about the report, Rathe."

"You'll have it," Rathe said, and the head point nodded. She pushed the broken door closed again behind her, not bothering to force it closed, and b'Estorr shook his head, surveying the devastation.

"This was not kindly meant."

"No." Rathe grinned in spite of himself at the understatement.

"Who does Aconin blame for it?" b'Estorr took a few steps farther into the room, picking his way cautiously through the debris, stopped with a frown as he saw the broken clock.

"No one," Rathe said. "None of his enemies would do this, he says."

b'Estorr nodded thoughtfully. "There's truth in that."

"Yeah. I thought so." Rathe paused. "He also says he has no idea why it happened."

"There's the lie." b'Estorr stooped to finger a torn piece of cloth, a shirtsleeve or perhaps the remains of a handkerchief. "You can practically smell the fear, but it's not fear of the unknown, but of something he knows all too well."

"I heard it when he was telling me," Rathe said. "I didn't know if he was actually lying, or just not telling me everything."

b'Estorr smiled without humor. "With Aconin—it's safer to assume he's lying." He stood again, surveying the room, his pale hair almost luminous in the gathering dusk. He was silent for a long moment, and in the distance Rathe heard a clock chime the quarter hour.

"This was business," b'Estorr said at last, softly. "Hirelings' work—at least two of them, maybe more. But a personal cause at the heart of it."

"They burned his work," Rathe said. "Drafts of at least the Alphabet—"

b'Estorr gave him a startled glance, and this time it was Rathe who laughed.

"The play, I mean, not the book. Though, come to think of it, I should see if he has a copy anywhere, he must have had something to base his play on."

"Worth a look," b'Estorr agreed.

But not until we have light. Rathe shook the thought away, glanced around the room again. "But burning the papers—your average bravo wouldn't think of that. Not here in the Court."

"They could have been instructed," b'Estorr answered. "Were instructed, I would imagine, because I think your point's well taken. But I'm sure there were hirelings here, and a single, personal hate at the back of it." He paused, and a sudden smile flickered across his face. "That was what you wanted from me, yes?"

Rathe smiled back. "Part of it." He heard footsteps on the stairs again, and reached for his truncheon in spite of himself. The door swung open at the runner's touch, and the boy came awkwardly into the room, balancing a lit storm lantern and a trio of candle lamps.

"Excuse me, Adjunct Point, but the chief says, here's a light, and I borrowed the rest from the lady downstairs. She says will you be sure to put them out before you go."

"Of course," Rathe answered, seeing b'Estorr's amusement out of the corner of his eye, and took the heavy lantern, setting it on the table beside the empty vase. The runner nodded, already backing away.

"If there's anything else?"

Rathe shook his head, and the boy was gone again, clattering back down the stairs. Rathe sighed, and moved to close the door behind him.

"Well, at least there's light," b'Estorr said, and carefully lifted two of the three shutters, turning the lantern so that the wind couldn't blow out the flame. He lit the candles as well, set one on the shelf and the other, with only the slightest hesitation, on the defiled altar. Even with the blown-glass shields, the rising wind stirred the flames, making the shadows swell and vanish, and Rathe shivered again, wishing he were back at Point of Dreams. "So what was the other thing you wanted?"

"I want to be sure nothing was killed here," Rathe answered.

b'Estorr nodded, unsurprised. "I don't think so, but it's as well to be certain." He looked at the broken figures on the altar, reached for the nearest, gazing abstractedly at the beheaded Winter-Son.

"What?" Rathe asked.

"This one just seems an odd choice. He's a playwright, so why not Tyrseis? He'd be more appropriate."

"Well . . ." Rathe joined him, peered over his shoulder at the little statue. Like the others, it was decently made, not expensive, but chosen for its style. "He didn't want you here—didn't want us to call a necromancer, I mean, not you personally, but I don't know if that means anything. Of course, I don't know a single actor who doesn't include Tyrseis on their altars, but maybe it's not the same for playwrights." He shrugged. "I suppose there'd be something to surprise me on everyone's altar—including yours."

"You've seen mine," b'Estorr said absently. He laid the statue carefully beside the lantern. "Propitiating, maybe?"

"Maybe."

b'Estorr nodded, his mind clearly elsewhere, and Rathe retreated again, leaning against the table. In the hectic light, b'Estorr's hair glowed like silver gilt, and the badge of the Starsmith was dark on his cuff. He stooped to collect the rest of the headless figures, laying them carefully beside the Winter-Son, then reached into his pocket to produce a lump of chalk. Carefully, he drew a circle on the altar's flat surface, then sketched symbols around and within it, frowning lightly now in concentration. Suddenly the air in the room was perceptibly warmer, and Rathe was briefly, keenly aware of b'Estorr's ghosts, could almost—could see them, as he never had before. It had to be the ghost-tide, of course, even now that it was waning, the moon would pass out of the Maiden in the next day or so, but he'd never seen b'Estorr perform a ritual under these stars. There were three ghosts, he'd known that from the beginning: the old Fre whom b'Estorr had served in Chadron before the king had met the fate of so many Chadroni rulers, the other two figures from an older time, a king and his favorite whose deaths had been lost, forgotten until the only necromancer to be favored by a Chadroni king had touched their ghosts and uncovered the truth of their death, part of the violent cycle of succession in the putatively elective kingdom. But there were more ghosts, too, Rathe realized, not as clear, but still there, too many of them, drawn by the circle, by the ritual, like summer moths to a candle flame. The Court was full of ghosts, decades of them—centuries of them, perhaps, the Court was almost as old as Astreiant itself; of course they would come when a necromancer called, particularly at this time of year. He shook himself, made himself pick up the crumpled papers, deliberately turning his back on the other man as he began to sort through the half-burned sheets, looking for any hint of Aconin's copy of the Alphabet. There were plenty of sheets that belonged to the play, but nothing more, except for a sheet that seemed to be notes of flower combinations. *That I'll keep*, he thought, and glanced up just as b'Estorr swept his hand across the chalked circle, obliterating it. The room was suddenly chill again, and empty, the ghosts swept away with the same gesture, and Rathe shook himself back to normal.

"Was there anything?"

b'Estorr shook his head, his face bleached and tired in the uncertain lamplight. "Nothing—well, not nothing, you felt them, this is a populous neighborhood for the dead, but nothing recent, and nothing that belongs to Aconin." He stopped then, tilting his head to one side. "That may not be strictly true, I could have sworn I felt almost— a ghost of a ghost, but there was no blood behind it." He shook his head, dismissing the thought. "Someone, probably, close to him, who simply wouldn't accept death. It happens."

Rathe nodded. "But nothing killed?"

"Nothing," b'Estorr said again. He paused, absently straightening the figures on the altar. "What made you think there might be?"

Rathe paused, remembering Aconin's behavior. "I'm not sure. He was—very outspoken that he didn't want me involved, or anyone from Point of Dreams, and then that he didn't want a necromancer. And then he made damn sure he was gone before you got here."

"We don't get along," b'Estorr said, mildly, and Rathe grinned in spite of himself.

"No." He sobered quickly. "I suppose the main thing was how determined he was to downplay—all this, when I'd expect anyone to be screaming murder and crying vengeance on whoever did it. I wondered what he knew that he wasn't telling."

"It wasn't a curse," b'Estorr said positively. "A warning, I suppose?"

That was the second time someone had suggested that, and it

still didn't feel right. Rathe shook his head, less in disagreement than in puzzlement. "I suppose. But he didn't seem frightened, either, just stood there dropping flowers out the window."

"What?" b'Estorr's attention sharpened visibly.

"There was a vase of them," Rathe said. "On the table. They were wilted, and he tossed them out the window."

"All at once, or one at a time?" b'Estorr asked.

"One at a time." Rathe frowned. "All right, what am I missing?"

b'Estorr shook his head in turn, looking almost embarrassed. "I may be seeing too much in it, but—a vase of flowers, untouched in this mess? A posy he had to take apart flower by flower? It sounds like something out of the Alphabet to me."

"A spell, you mean." Rathe frowned, thinking of Leussi's Alphabet, the flowers that might have caused his death. "Istre, did you get any message from Trijn today?"

The necromancer shook his head. "Should I have? I was in classes until the runner from Knives found me."

"You will hear," Rathe said grimly. "There's another copy of the Alphabet that needs to be examined."

"There are phytomancers I'd trust with it," b'Estorr said.

Rathe made a face, looking back at the empty vase. "So that would be the counter to a posy? Taking it apart like that?"

b'Estorr nodded. "If the Alphabet exists, if you even suspect it exists and that it might work, that would be one way to counteract an arrangement, taking it apart. If, of course, you assume it works. And if it works, assuming it's not too strong a spell."

"Yeah." Rathe glanced at the sheet of paper he'd separated from the rest, folded it carefully and tucked it into his daybook. Another list of flowers to give to the phytomancers, he thought, and to check against Leussi's Alphabet. "And if anyone seems likely to make that assumption, Aconin would be the one. It didn't feel like a spell, Istre."

"It's the university's considered opinion that the Alphabet is a fraud," b'Estorr answered, with a smile that showed teeth. "For what that's worth, considering they've never seen a copy. But even if you knew that, would you take the chance?"

"Not when I was looking at this mess," Rathe answered, and nodded. "I'll have words with him, believe me. But in the meantime, I don't see much reason to stay."

"Nor do I," b'Estorr answered, and stooped to blow out the first of the lamps. Rathe collected the lantern, adjusting its shutters so that it cast a welcome beam, while the other man doused the remaining candles.

"I'll walk you to the bridge," he said aloud. "And return this with my report."

They headed back through Point of Knives toward Point of Dreams, leaving the unquiet darkness of the Court behind them, crossing the more respectable neighborhoods where most people were already at their dinners, behind shuttered windows and locked doors. Many had small lanterns burning, either at the doors or in a front window, honoring the ancestors who returned during the ghost-tide. Rathe felt something brush his calf; at any other time of the year he would have swiped at a rat or a gargoyle and cursed, but tonight, out of the corner of his eye, he caught the memory of the small rag-eared, wire-coated dog who had been his constant companion from boyhood into apprenticeship. He started to click his fingers to call it, then looked at b'Estorr, inexplicably embarrassed. b'Estorr smiled.

"It wouldn't be ghost-tide without Mud, Nico. There's nothing to be ashamed of in so constant a ghost."

Rathe laughed softly. "I've lost kin, Istre, and friends, but who do I see? My dog."

"And I've got a really difficult ancient king of Chadron, and his favorite, and I'm no kin and had nothing to do with their deaths. We don't choose our ghosts, Nico."

Rathe nodded. They had reached the edge of a market square, where cressets burned in front of a well-appointed tavern, and the smell of a tavern dinner, savory pie and hot wine, hung heavy for a moment in the cold air before the wind and the smoke drowned it again. They turned onto the wider avenue that led to the Hopes-point Bridge, and Rathe felt himself relax a little, grateful to be away from the Court of the Thirty-two Knives. Even in daylight, and even known as he was, and today brought in by Mirremay herself, it was a chancy place; the streets here, between Hopes and Dreams, were far safer, even with only the lantern to light their way.

Even as he thought that, he heard the sound of footsteps, running hard up the side street that led away from the river, looked sharply into the darkness as the cry followed them. He saw nothing, maybe the suggestion of a movement, a shadow shifting against the lesser dark where the street joined Beck's Way, but he knew what he'd heard, couldn't mistake the choked, wet sound of it, and dove into the darkness, flipping the lantern's cover as wide as it would go. b'Estorr followed, metal sliding softly against leather as he drew his long knife, and Rathe swore, seeing the crumpled shape lying against the windowless wall of the nearest building. It looked more like a pile of discarded clothes than a man, but b'Estorr dropped instantly to his knees, sliding the knife back into its sheath, and reached to probe for a wound. Rathe stood still, the lantern still held high, tilting his head to listen for any further movement. Whoever had attacked the man was long gone, he was sure of it, had been the running footsteps they had first heard, but he stood watching anyway, not wanting to be taken by surprise. The street—it wasn't much more than an alley, its central gutter rimed with ice and mud, the walls to either side broken only by a pair of carters' gates, both closed and barred against the night—was empty, nothing moving in the lantern's uncertain light, and he turned slowly, letting the wedge of light sweep behind them as well.

"Nico," b'Estorr said, and at the urgency in his voice, Rathe lowered the lantern again, spilling its light over the wounded man.

"How is he?"

"Not good, but I can't tell how bad."

Rathe knelt beside him, wincing as he saw the blood still flowing hard over b'Estorr's fingers. The wounded man looked serene enough, eyes closed, heedless of the sleet that splashed his face and hair. *Not a good sign*, Rathe thought, and set the lantern carefully on the cobbles, turning it so that the light fell strongly across the wounded man. The blood was still flowing, despite b'Estorr's hand pressed hard on the wound—too low for the heart, but high enough to kill—and he reached for his stock, unwinding the length of linen.

"Let me," he said, and b'Estorr nodded, shifting sideways so that Rathe could press the new pad into the wound. The blood slowed a little, or perhaps the man had simply bled as much as he was going to. "See if you can find a surgeon hereabouts, there must be someone. If not, I guess you'd better send for Fanier."

"They'll know at the tavern," b'Estorr answered, and pushed himself to his feet.

Rathe nodded, keeping his hand pressed tight against the wound. The bleeding was definitely slowing, he thought, and tried to tell himself it was a hopeful sign. The man's face was waxen in the lamplight, and he grimaced, knowing their efforts were likely to go for nothing, that it would be Fanier, not a doctor, who would be needed.

He looked at the assortment of garments covering the wounded man—a threadbare coat, shirt with sleeves too short, patched jerkin and breeches, castoffs, all of them, or temple handouts—and shrugged himself awkwardly out of his own coat, not taking his hand from the wound. He laid it over the stranger, knowing it was probably a futile gesture, and looked away, examining the cobbles for any signs left by the attackers. The sleet was heavier now, the ice collecting in the gaps between the stones, threatening to wash away any indication of what had happened. And there was precious little, he thought, not even a footprint in the mud of the gutter. Whoever had attacked the man was too clever to make that mistake. There was a dark stain on the wall above his head, probably where the man had fallen against it, and Rathe sighed, looked back at the man's face. There was something familiar about it, an image teasing at the edge of memory, and then from somewhere he caught a whiff of evergreen, and he knew. Grener Ogier had been his parents' friend, his mother's in particular, they were both gardeners, had worked together more than once when he was a child at the dame school. But they'd drifted apart, not unfriendly, but on different paths, led by different stars, and the city had swallowed Ogier, spat him back now possibly dying, and Rathe shivered, knowing it was more than the sleet. A talented gardener, his mother had said, she who was always so sparing of her praise, a man under whose hands the most unlikely plots flourished.

He dipped his head, swallowing tears, and saw Ogier's eyes flicker open. The pupils were huge, unfocused, probably sightless, but still he made a sound, as though he was trying to speak. Rathe leaned closer, trying to shield him from the worst of the sleet, and heard footsteps from the head of the alley. He turned, free hand reaching for his truncheon, relaxed as he saw b'Estorr, a woman in a carter's longcoat trailing at his heels. Rathe frowned, but then he saw the apothecary's badge on the cuff of her close-buttoned coat. She knelt beside him, shifting the lantern a fraction to give better light, and nodded for him to move aside, her hand sliding briefly over his as she reached for the wound. Rathe relinquished it gladly, wiping his hands on his breeches before he'd thought, swore under his breath at the thought of the laundress's bill.

The apothecary murmured something, probing, and Rathe caught a whiff of tobacco and sweetherb clinging to her hair and coat. Still, her hands were steady enough, and she moved with the ease of experience to probe the wound. The blood was still flowing, but sluggishly, and she sat back on her heels, shaking her head.

"Not even a surgeon could help him, masters, but damnation, this was a bungled job."

"What do you mean?" Rathe asked. He was shivering now, without his coat, and wrapped his arms tightly around his body, tucking his hands into his armpits.

The woman shook her head. "He can't live, but he's likely to be a while yet dying, poor bastard." She looked up at him, then her wide face suddenly, unhappily alive. "Maybe it's a clue, pointsman. Find the one soul in this city who doesn't know how to wield a knife properly, and you'll have his murderer."

Rathe bit back an angry retort, recognizing the reaction, and b'Estorr said, "Is there anything we can do?"

"You could finish the job—you'd do it for a horse or a dog." The apothecary shook her head, her hair falling forward to hide her eyes. She swept it back with an angry hand, scowled at the coat covering the body. "Keeping him warm was a kindly thought. I don't suppose you know his stars?"

b'Estorr shook his head, but Rathe said, "He was a gardener. And had the stars for it, I was told."

The necromancer gave him a startled glance. "You know him?"

"From a long time ago," Rathe answered. "He's a friend of my mother's."

"A gardener," the apothecary said. "Metenere, then, most likely." She reached into her bag, brought out a jar marked with symbols that Rathe didn't recognize.

"What are you doing?" he asked, and the woman looked up at him.

"A last chance, pointsman, to name his killer. Something his ghost can't do."

Rathe dropped to his knees beside her, heedless of the icy rime. "Will it hurt him?"

The apothecary shook her head. "He's beyond pain." She nodded to the bandage, so soaked in blood now that it was almost invisible. "Hold that."

Rathe did as he was told, wincing as he felt the feeble pulse, and the apothecary uncorked her jar, waved it under Ogier's nose. For a long moment, nothing happened, and then, suddenly, the man's eyes flickered open again, blinked and focused.

"Who—"

Rathe shifted so that Ogier could see him clearly, if he could see at all. "Who did this, Ogier? It's Nico Rathe, remember me? Do you know who did this?"

He broke off as Ogier's eyes widened, and one hand lifted, fumbling at his sleeve. "Nico."

Rathe caught the hand, ice-cold, ice damp, held it tight. "Who did this?"

It was an awkward position, one hand still on the bandage, the other holding Ogier's, and the apothecary made a soft noise, moved to take the bandage. Rathe sat back on his heels, grateful for the relief, and Ogier's head moved slowly from side to side.

"Madness," he whispered. "You remember. I was good. Too good. . . ."

"One of the best," Rathe said. "My mother said so. Who would do this? Why?"

Even as he spoke, Ogier's eyes closed, the clasp of his fingers relaxing. Rathe tightened his own grip, but the hand in his was slack, falling into death.

The apothecary shook her head, released her hold on the bandage to touch wrist and mouth, then touched the closed eyes, the gesture more ritual than useful. "Well, that was quicker than I expected. I suppose the weather helped."

"Why do you bother?" Rathe demanded, and her eyes fell.

"Did you want the poor bastard to linger?"

"And if easing his passing was the most important thing to you," Rathe snapped, "why did you raise him long enough to speak?"

"I—" The apothecary made a face. "I hate waste. I hate deaths like this. You're the pointsman, you can do something. Easing his death—that would be an office for his friends. If he had any."

Rathe sighed, the anger draining from him. "He had friends. I know he did, at least once."

"The Starsmith give him ease," the apothecary said. She found a rag in her kit, scrubbed her hands. "Will you find his killer?"

"I don't know," Rathe said. "I will try." He closed his eyes for a moment, still kneeling on the cold stones. There were too many deaths, first the landseur—no, first Leussi, and then de Raçan, and the watchman, and now Ogier, who had nothing to do with any of that, who had no enemies that he could imagine. But obviously he had had one enemy, and that was what he had to find. He pushed himself to his feet, aware for the first time that his breeches and stockings were soaked through, that his hair was dripping on his shoulders.

"I've got a cart," the apothecary said. "You can use that, if you'd like."

To deliver the body, Rathe knew she meant, either to Fanier directly or to Dreams. To Dreams, he decided, he'd had enough of the deadhouse lately to last a lifetime, and nodded. "Thank you. I'd appreciate it."

She nodded, straightening. "I'm just a couple of streets over. I won't be long."

Rathe nodded again, too tired to speak, and she turned away, the carter's coat shedding the worst of the sleet. Rathe shivered again, feeling the touch of ice on his scalp, and beside him b'Estorr shook his head.

"The poor man. What she did, it's technically forbidden, but the gods know, it'll do no harm in this case." The necromancer paused. "So you knew him, then?"

Rathe nodded. He should search the body, he knew, but for the moment it was beyond him. "He was a friend of my mother's—both my parents', in actual fact, but he was a gardener, too, like her."

He was babbling, he knew, and shook himself, made himself kneel again on the freezing stones. There was nothing in the coat pockets, and only a worn leather purse in the pocket of Ogier's breeches—not much coin, only a few seillings, but if robbery had been the intent, the thief would surely have made certain of them. There was a sprig of some dried herb, a twisted branch of short, spiky leaves, and Rathe sniffed curiously at it, but could detect no aroma. It was new to him, whatever it was, and he tucked it back into the purse, slid that into his own pocket. He checked the cuffs of the coat then, thinking of Eslingen, but Ogier hadn't shared the soldier's habit of sliding odd bits of paper into them. There was only another scrap of greenery, a flower not quite out of the bud, faded and dried. It had probably fallen there while Ogier was working, Rathe thought— but if he was working, why was he dressed so badly? Ogier had always been a tidy man, not one to spend unnecessary money on his clothes, but these garments looked more like temple handouts even than working gear. Had he fallen out of favor, lost all his employment, to leave him so shabbily dressed with winter coming on? He'd never been one to tie himself to any one house, and he'd been good enough that he'd never had to, had always had the rich, merchants and even the city-living landames, vying for his services. Maybe they'd all finally tired of the dance? Rathe shook his head, and sat back on his heels. There was no telling, though he'd make it his business to find out. "Maybe if he'd had a patronne, he'd still be alive."

"Or maybe he did find one," b'Estorr murmured, and Rathe looked sharply at him.

"What do you mean?"

b'Estorr shook his head. "Sorry, that's a Chadroni thought. A patronne protects, yes, but—" He shrugged. "They're also notoriously chancy."

There was a sound of wheels and, miraculously, the slow clop of horse's hooves, and Rathe pushed himself to his feet. The apothecary had been better than her word: not just a cart, but a small, shaggy, city-bred pony in its harness. It snorted, smelling the blood, and b'Estorr went instantly to its head, turning it upwind of the body. The apothecary nodded her thanks, and stooped to help lift the body into the cart.

"Do you want your coat? It won't do him any good."

No more would it, Rathe thought, but shook his head. He was wet through already, and there was blood already on his clothes. "No, let him keep it. But can I get your name and direction?"

The woman made a face. "Madelen de Braemer. You can find me at the Grapes."

That would be the tavern they had passed. Rathe nodded, not bothering to reach for his tablets. It was too cold, he was too wet, and besides, he was unlikely to forget the incongruously aristocratic name. "Thank you, dame."

The apothecary was already moving away, but stopped as though a thought had struck her. "And where do I send for my horse, anyway? The deadhouse?"

"No, Point of Dreams," Rathe answered. "He'll go to the deadhouse from there."

"Easier on the old boy anyway," the apothecary said, and Rathe realized she meant the pony. "I'll come by in the morning."

"I'll leave your name, if I'm not there," Rathe answered, and she turned away.

"Shall I walk with you?" b'Estorr asked softly, and Rathe gave him a grateful glance.

"I'd take it kindly." It wouldn't be that long a walk, he thought, but it would be easier with live company.

❖   ❖   ❖

By the time Rathe had written cursory reports, and sent a request to
the Temple to handle the notification of any kin of Ogier's, it was
after midnight, and he was grateful for the idle escort of a junior
pointsman, patrolling that way, to take him partway home. The
winter-sun was risen, at least, dispelling the worst of the darkness,
and the sleet had ended, a few stars showing through the breaking
clouds, but he was glad to come to his own gate. There were no lights
in the weaver's rooms as he crossed the courtyard—too late—and
none in the actors' rooms under the garrets—too early, probably—
but lamplight shone in his own windows, a welcome that was still
unexpected, and he climbed the stairs with more haste than he would
have thought possible.

Eslingen was sitting at the narrow table, the lamp set to put the
best light on a sheaf of broadsheets, chin resting on his cupped hands
as he studied the awkward printing. His hair was loose, for once,
falling forward to hide his face, but he looked up as the door opened,
shaking it back again. The lazy smile faded as he took in the condition
of the other's clothes, the dark eyes flicking from vital spot to vital
spot, and Rathe smothered a tired laugh, seeing him relax again.

"That had better not be your blood," Eslingen said.

"No." Rathe shook his head, looked down at the stains as though
he hadn't seen them before. He would owe Ardelis for the cleaning
of the station's spare coat as well as his own laundress's bill, that was
obvious. "No, it's not. I doubt I'd be standing here talking to you if
I had this much outside me."

"Maybe you're a ghost," Eslingen said. He could practically feel
the cold radiating off the other man, knew shock when he heard it,
and swung himself gracefully up from his place at the table. Watching
him, Rathe bit back another laugh, thinking it would play well onstage. Then Eslingen embraced him, pulled back to study his face,
frowning in spite of his carefully light tone.

"Not a ghost, there never was a ghost this cold. Seidos's Horse,
what were they thinking of, to let you go like this?"

"That the senior adjunct wanted to go home," Rathe answered.
"I'm not hurt, Philip."

A flicker of relief crossed the taller man's face, but he said only,
"Just chilled to the bone, it seems. Get your clothes off."

Rathe obeyed, shrugging out of the borrowed coat, and instantly

Eslingen was there to help, the gentle hand belying the rough words.

"You'll never wear those again," Eslingen said, and tossed the bloodied shirt into a corner.

"I don't know." Rathe shivered, left in his smallclothes, and Eslingen stripped the top blanket from the bed. "My laundress is very skilled—"

"With blood," Eslingen said, and wound the blanket around the other's shoulders. "What interesting people you know, Adjunct Point. Did you find this in the line of business?"

Rathe smiled in spite of himself, let himself be turned and settled on the edge of the mattress. He drew his feet up under him, worked them under the sheets—cold linen, but warming to his touch—and hunched his shoulders under the blanket. "This doesn't often happen—"

"So you tell me." Eslingen's voice was remote, his back to the bed as he fiddled with something on the stove. "So what was it this time?"

Rathe took a breath, feeling creeping back into his toes. His fingers were better already, and he worked his shoulders against the rough wool. He was desperately tired, painfully sad, but knew he wouldn't sleep now, that trying would only make him wearier in the morning, worn out with the effort. Better to stay awake, let the thoughts and memories die—share them, since he could, he thought, and cleared his throat. At the station, sure, tell all to his fellow points and let them comfort him just by knowing, but Eslingen—Eslingen was somehow different.

"There was a man killed today. Istre and I found him. In an alley between Hopes and Dreams. Only I knew him. He was a gardener— not a physick gardener like my mother, but she knew him, and I remembered him being around when I was a boy. One of the best, she always said. Could make anything bloom, anytime, knew all the right conditions, how to create them as best as possible—Metenere was better aspected in his stars than anyone she'd ever known, she said." Rathe shook his head. "He didn't die immediately. There wasn't anything we could do. . . ."

Eslingen nodded, still stirring, not surprised or shocked—*and of course he does know a lot of it,* Rathe thought. *He was a soldier, he knows about dead men, dying men and no help for them; if he doesn't know about the failure of justice, the points' failure, my failure, come down to it, well, at least he knows this much.* Eslingen turned away from the stove, then held out a stoneware cup.

"Your mother, I daresay, would concoct something infinitely more salubrious, but this can only help."

Rathe sniffed it, expecting beer, blinked at the smell of wine. He took a sip, and then a longer swallow, the liquid ropy with spices and sugar, let it burn its way down his throat, warming him.

"So it wasn't a fight, then," Eslingen said, and Rathe shook his head. "Any idea who might have done it?"

Rathe wrapped both hands around the cup, his knuckles reddening now as feeling returned. "Not a clue. It makes no sense whatsoever. I may know more in the morning, when Fanier tells me what he's found—if that's anything. I mean, there's no doubt it was murder, a bloody great wound and no knife to be found. Istre was there, I didn't think to ask him about the ghost—"

He broke off, shaking his head—one more thing to take care of in the morning—and Eslingen kicked off his shoes, settled himself on the far end of the bed, resting his back against the cold plaster of the wall. "What was he like?"

Rathe shrugged, the wine cup still hot between his hands. "A gardener, and a good one. He was unusual—he had the stars, when most men possess the stars to be groundskeepers, he had the stars to create, not just to maintain. He was in demand, I know that. Worked for a number of great houses, never stayed with one, never let one noble or another put her livery on him. It wasn't arrogance— or maybe it was, but he always demanded the freedom to work for whomever he pleased. And it was better to get him for part of a season than not at all, so . . ."

"So everyone took what they could," Eslingen said.

Rathe nodded. "And so that's where I have to start in the morning. After I talk to Istre."

"You really think you're dealing with someone jealous of their gardener's attention to a rival—plant?" Eslingen asked, and Rathe smiled in spite of himself.

"You've been working with the chorus these weeks, and you think it's unlikely?"

Eslingen shook his head, grinning, and Rathe sighed, the moment's good humor fading.

"I don't know. It makes no sense, but it's the only place to start. Only—"

"Nico, you have got to start finishing sentences."

Rathe ignored him, staring past him into the shadows that gathered in the corners of the room. The lamplight spread only so far; they sat in pleasant shadow, and the edges of the room were dark, the shutters closed against the night air and the winter-sun. A coal snapped in the stove, sparks flaring behind the grill, and he looked back at the other man. "Except that—Ogier was never really well dressed, he wasn't fashionable, it didn't make sense when you were working in the earth all the time, but he did know how to choose clothes and fabric, he did know how to be—presentable."

"Unlike certain pointsmen we could mention," Eslingen murmured.

Rathe waved the words away, intent on the memory. "But from what I could see, his clothes were old, worn—mismatched. Like Temple handouts."

Eslingen blinked, frowned. "So they were old clothes. Maybe he'd been working today."

"It's nearly winter, Philip, most gardens have been put to bed weeks since."

"Do you think he'd fallen out of favor?" Eslingen's voice was soft now, intent, and Rathe gave him a grateful look.

"I don't know. I'd lost track of him. I know who will know, however."

"Your mother?"

Rathe nodded grimly. "And I'm not looking forward to telling her her old friend is dead—is murdered."

"No." Eslingen gave him a sidelong glance, as though gauging his recovery. Whatever he saw seemed to satisfy him, and he laced his fingers together around one knee. "Apparently Chresta had some excitement today, too."

Rathe swore. Eslingen lifted an eyebrow, and the other man shook his head. "No, how were you to know? Oh, yes, he had plenty of excitement."

"He said it was a theft, he was late because of it—but surely that would be a matter for Point of Knives?"

"He said that to us. And he's still saying it." Rathe shook his head, unreasonably angry with Aconin yet again. "Mirremay—she's head point at Knives, head point, not chief point, because it's not a full station, and no one wants a member of that family being chief of anything, not in the Court—" He broke off, took a breath. "She called me in, because it was Aconin, and because of—everything. And it wasn't theft, Philip, no matter what Aconin's saying. It was total destruction, and there were plenty of goods there for the taking." He was warming, finally, and hitched himself round on the bed, holding out the cup of wine. Eslingen took it with a nod of thanks, and Rathe frowned again. "Didn't you once tell me about smashing an altar being a kind of warning in the League?"

Eslingen's face went very still. "Oh, yes, it's a kind of warning."

Rathe cocked his head at him. "What does it mean?"

"It's the last warning. It means no quarter."

8

◆ ⋯⋯⋯⋯⋯⋯⋯⋯⋯⋯⋯⋯⋯⋯⋯⋯⋯⋯⋯⋯⋯⋯⋯⋯ ◆

Eslingen leaned against the locked versatile, its sides painted now to create a mountain pass, the palatine's palace, and de Galhac's stronghold. To his untutored eyes, the rehearsal seemed to be going unusually well, even the chorus keeping its place for once, and he let himself relax, his eyes straying from the tidy lines to the wing where Aubine was arranging yet another of his massive bouquets. This one was the most spectacular he'd seen so far, at least a dozen of the red and white streaked, cup-shaped blossoms vivid against a background of smaller yellow flowers. Rathe would know all their names, of course; he himself recognized only that both grew from corms. Aubine would be happy to explain, of course, there seemed to be nothing he enjoyed more than discussing his plants, as proud of them as he would be of a promising daughter, but there was always the danger that idle conversation would lead to exactly the questions Eslingen wanted to avoid.

Onstage, Gasquine clapped her hands, bringing her scene to an abrupt end just before Forveijl's set speech. For a moment, Eslingen thought the actor was going to protest, but Gasquine smiled, shaking her head, and Forveijl seemed to relax again. He had been getting better, Eslingen admitted—maybe Aconin had had words with him, since they seemed to still be intimate. Or at least intimate enough that Aconin could still seek sanctuary with the actor, which implied that they were still lovers. Aconin's ex-lovers generally thought less kindly of him, though maybe that had changed since Aconin had come to Astreiant.

"Five minutes," Gasquine called, and nodded to the bookholder, who hastened to turn a massive minute glass in its polished stand. "Five minutes, all, and then we go through the high battle scene. Swordplay first, and then scene eight."

There was a sudden surge of voices as actors and chorus relaxed into conversation, and Eslingen looked around for the duelists. Five of them were already in sight, young de Besselin laughing with a fair girl almost his own age, while the landseur Simar idly toyed with another of his flamboyant posies. Aubine had spoken to him again about it, Eslingen thought, remembering the two men standing with their heads together at the beginning of the rehearsal, and wondered if Simar was trying to impress the other man. The horse-faced landame, Jarielle, straddled one of the benches in the pit, rolling a pair of dice between her palms, smiling at the pile of coin lying between her and one of the scenerymen. *Now, if she'd been the one to be found dead, I wouldn't be surprised*, Eslingen thought—Jarielle was a chronic gambler and a gossip to boot—but so far, at least, she'd lost enough to keep her opponents sweet. One of the remaining landseurs was watching her, soberly, Eslingen thought, until he saw the money change hands. He looked around for the remaining three, and saw Siredy and the banneret d'Yres crossing the stage toward them. They parted smiling, d'Yres climbing down into the pit to watch the dice game, and Siredy moved to join the other master, his smile fading as he saw Eslingen's expression.

"What's wrong?"

"Have you seen our missing landames?" Eslingen asked, and Siredy turned instantly to survey the pit.

"Oh, Tyrseis, we're not missing Txi and de Vannevaux, are we?"

Eslingen nodded. "I think the points would look very poorly on another death, even with the excuse of a hundred-year feud."

"Five hundred years," Siredy said, "or at least that's what Txi told me. I take your point. Out back, do you think?"

It was the logical place to go, if the women wanted to settle the quarrel privately, and Eslingen nodded. "I'll look there," he said. "You check the dressing rooms."

Siredy nodded, shot a quick look at the minute glass just as the bookholder turned it. "Three minutes," he said, and turned away.

Eslingen made his way through the tangle of machinery, found the passage that led to the courtyard, and felt his way up it, blinded by the sudden darkness. No one had bothered to put mage-lights here, since no one was supposed to be using the courtyard, and he hoped the landames hadn't gone too far. At least there were no real swords in the theatre, unless, of course, they'd brought their own. He grimaced at the thought—Rathe would call a point on them if they had, dueling swords were by definition well over the legal limit for a knife blade carried inside the city limits—and unbarred the narrow door.

To his surprise, the courtyard was empty, without even a discarded bottle or a crumpled broadsheet, and he stood for a second, staring, before he shook himself back to life. If the two weren't trying to kill each other, where were they? *Probably not working out a solution to the feud*, Eslingen thought bitterly, setting the bar back in its socket, and turned back into the theatre. There was nowhere else in the Tyrseia suitable for a duel, and to be fair, he doubted either woman would consent to anything less than a fair fight. Maybe the second tier, where the props from *The Drowned Island* were stored? It was the only other space that might remotely be considered large enough, and it had the added advantage of being off-limits to everyone but the scenerymen. *Or at least that was the theory*, Eslingen thought, and swung himself up the narrow ladder. There was nothing to keep out a determined malefactor except Gasquine's orders.

The second tier was quiet and crowded, all sound muffled by the heavy canvas drapes that covered the various set pieces and props. In the faint light that seeped in from the stage, the space seemed filled to capacity, crowded with pale shapes that only vaguely resembled the objects beneath the coverings. Like snow sculptures, Eslingen thought, dredging up a long-forgotten memory, a too-warm midwinter in Esling, snow sculptures melting on a sunny day. There was less room than he had thought, certainly not enough to fight a duel no matter how determined the participants might be. He had turned to slide back down the ladder when he heard the muffled cry.

He swung back at once, straining his eyes to see through the gloom, caught the hint of movement among the scenery stored toward the back of the tier. He took a breath and moved toward it, wishing he had his halberd, or even his bated sword, and the sound came again. It was coming from behind the tallest of the shrouded pieces, and he stepped carefully around it, trying to move silently on the hollow floor. Mage-light startled him, a lantern turned low and carefully set to throw light on a property couch—part of d'Auriens's furniture, from *The Drowned Island*, Eslingen realized, and stifled a laugh—that had been carefully freed of its wrappings, and on that couch the two landames were locked in a passionate embrace. Txi's hair was falling loose from its elaborate knot, her eyes closed in delight as de Vannevaux buried her face between the other woman's breasts. Txi's own hands were under de Vannevaux's skirts, and Eslingen took a quick step backward, embarrassed and embarrassingly aroused. He took another step, and then a third, deliberately scuffing his shoes on the hollow floor, and heard another muffled exclamation.

"Maseigne de Vannevaux?" he called. "Are you there?"

This time he was sure he heard a curse, and then a rustling, before de Vannevaux's breathless answer. "Yes. Who—what is it?"

"Lieutenant vaan Esling. You're wanted onstage, maseigne, the duel scene is about to begin." Eslingen heard more scuffling, and then de Vannevaux appeared from behind the nearest shrouded set piece. Her clothes were in order, but she shook out her skirts anyway, scowling, and Eslingen succumbed to temptation. "Have you by any chance seen Maseigne Txi? She's missing, too."

The color swept up the young woman's face, but she answered steadily enough. "I'm sure she'll be along, Lieutenant. Shall we go?"

Eslingen waved toward the ladder, let her climb down ahead of him. "Mistress Gasquine won't be happy if she finds out you've been up here."

De Vannevaux looked up at him. "I assure you, it won't happen again."

And that, Eslingen thought, *would almost be too bad*. "Just take care," he said aloud, and the woman nodded. "Now, if you please, join the others."

For a moment, he thought she would protest, but then she nodded again, jerkily, and swept across the stage, head up. One strand of hair had worked itself loose, and was trailing free of her neat cap, falling almost to her waist. Siredy, standing in the wings opposite, saw her coming, and looked past her to meet Eslingen's eyes, his eyebrows rising in silent question. Eslingen shook his head, waved for the other man to wait. Siredy's mouth tightened, and he pointed to the minute glass in silent warning. Eslingen nodded, lifting both hands in what he hoped was a placating gesture, and in the same moment, he heard a noise from the ladder. He stepped back quickly, and saw Txi climbing down. She'd done her best to tidy herself, but there was no way she could repair her elaborate hairstyle without the assistance of a maid. She'd rewound the heavy strands into a passable knot, and refastened corset and bodice—except, Eslingen saw, suppressing a grin, she'd managed to misbutton the bodice.

"Maseigne," he said softly, and she turned to glare at him.

"What do you want?"

"Your bodice," he said, and Txi blushed even more deeply than de Vannevaux had done.

"Oh, Seidos's balls." She reached for the buttons, hastily rearranging them, and Eslingen looked away quickly as the bookholder called time. Txi swore again, and darted away, taking her place hurriedly in the forming ranks.

"And what," a familiar voice asked, "was that all about?"

Eslingen turned without haste to see Aconin standing in the shadow of the nearest versatile.

"No," the playwright went on, "don't tell me. The landames have decided to settle their feud, and in the most decisive way possible."

Eslingen hesitated—the last thing he should do was betray the women to Aconin, of all people, but they'd been a monumental trouble ever since he'd met them. *Besides*, he told himself, *the story will be all over the theatre in a matter of hours. And it's too good to keep.* "What a good guess," he said. "Is it what you would have written?"

Aconin's jaw dropped. "You're joking."

"Not at all." Eslingen shook his head. "I don't know if the feud is over, but the current generation has at least found a way around it."

Aconin blinked once, a slow smile spreading over his face. "Tyrseis. No, I don't think I could write it, it would be too unlikely. But, oh, I wish I could."

"I'm sure you will," Eslingen answered, and the playwright laughed softly.

"You're probably right. But not until the landames are safely out of town."

"I never thought you'd be afraid of their reprisals," Eslingen said.

To his surprise, Aconin seemed to flinch at that. "Not exactly. But why court trouble?"

Because you've made a career of it, by all accounts. Eslingen frowned. "First a warning shot, and then no quarter," he said slowly. "You've angered somebody, Chresta. Can I help?"

Aconin hesitated, then glanced over his shoulder as though searching for eavesdroppers. Eslingen followed his gaze, but most of the actors were watching the work onstage. "I—I suppose I made a mistake, ended something badly."

Your specialty, I thought. Eslingen swallowed the words, did his best to look encouraging.

"I took something when I left," Aconin said. He made a face. "Oh, I was entitled to it, I thought—I'd been promised it, even— and I needed it, but still . . . It was a mistake."

"And the person you took it from is angry," Eslingen said. "Can you give it back?"

Aconin shook his head, looking, for the first time since Eslingen had known him, genuinely afraid. "It's too late for that. I—the person—" He broke off, flinching, and Eslingen glanced over his shoulder, but all he saw was a knot of people, Simar, Aubine, his arms full of flowers, a couple of actors, including Forveijl, Rathe's former and Aconin's apparently still current lover. "It's nothing," Aconin said, and forced a smile that held more than a little of his old mockery. "Come along, Philip, when has my life ever not been a melodrama? This is nothing new."

Out of the corner of his eye, Eslingen saw Aubine smile in rueful recognition, and Aconin turned away.

"You'd best get back to work," he called over his shoulder. "I don't think the landames will give their best without you."

Eslingen made a face—he should be onstage, that much was true—but hesitated, watching the playwright out of sight. Whatever he said, Aconin had been honestly afraid, and that was something Rathe should know. More than that, he realized, Aconin had as much as admitted that he knew who attacked him—*not that that should surprise either of us*—and Rathe needed to know that, as well. *If anybody can get the truth out of Master Aconite, it'll be Nico—and I'd like to be there when he does.*

It was mid-afternoon before Rathe was able to free himself from a tangle of reports—Fanier's on Ogier's body, confirming that the man had died from the knife wound, a pair of notes from b'Estorr, one saying he thought the dead man's clothing had indeed been Temple handouts, chosen perhaps in an attempt to throw some magistical pursuer off his trail, the second a pass-along from one of the university phytomancers, saying that the posy Leussi had apparently made up was, in fact, harmless, as unlikely to bring about discord and harm as it was to bring about its promised concord. There was a long report from Mirremay turning the attack on Aconin's rooms over to Point of Dreams, much to Trijn's vocal displeasure. And she had a right to be displeased, Rathe thought, making the turn onto the Horse Road that led through the old city walls toward the Queen's Eastern Highway. No chief point, and particularly not Mirremay, ever released a responsibility if she wasn't sure it was going to be more trouble than it was worth. Part of him wanted to be at the theatre, questioning Aconin, but his first duty was to the dead man. The most recent dead man, he amended, sighing. The folly stars seemed to be compounded by something more deadly.

Ogier had lived on the outskirts of the city, only a little south of the crossroads where the Horse Road met the Highway, and crossed the Promenade that ran back west toward the queen's residence and the nobles' houses of the Western Reach. It was typical of Ogier, Rathe thought: it would only be an hour's walk, at most, along the Promenade to reach the most distant of his clients, but it was far enough that none of them could claim to have him at their beck and call. A difficult man, he could almost hear his mother saying, but a clever plantsman, and he wished he'd had a chance to stop at her house, to ask her advice. She was as likely as anyone to know if Ogier had recently made enemies—but she lived by the Corants Basin, just east of the southern Chain Tower, across the city and on the far side of the Sier from the crossroads. *Ogier's kin first*, he thought, *but then I'll find the time to see her.*

He stopped at the neighborhood tavern, low-ceilinged and comfortable, to get the final directions to Ogier's house, found himself at last on a rutted lane bordered by tall rows of rise-hedge, still green even in the depth of winter. They were overgrown, narrowing the street even farther, filling the air with the smell of cloves as his coat brushed against them. For an instant, he was surprised that Ogier hadn't trimmed them, but then, the man was a gardener, not a groundskeeper, and the hedges were hardly his own to mend. The house itself stood at the very end of the street, an odd building barely more than one room wide, as though a series of rooms had been built one after the other, and tacked hastily together into a single building. It was neatly kept, though, the paint not new but not peeling, shutters and roof and yard all in good repair, and smoke drifted from the chimney. At least someone was home, he thought, and hoped the Temple priests had done their job.

He knocked gently at the door, and out of the corner of his eye saw a woman watching from the doorway of the house next door. She seemed to see him watching, whisked herself back out of sight as the door opened.

"Nico! Oh, sweet Sofia, I'm so glad it's you."

"Mother? What are you doing here?" Even as he asked, Rathe thought he could guess the answer. Ogier had been a friend, as well as being a guild-mate; of course the man's kin would send for her, in preference to any other, to help settle his affairs.

"Frelise sent for me," Caro Rathe said, and stepped back, beckoning him into a spare room that smelled of pipe smoke. "That's the sister. The same Temple initiate who broke the news was kind enough to come and fetch me. And of course, the crows are all flocking, trying to pick up the gossip." She touched his arm, glancing over her shoulder toward the single darkened doorway. "She's lying down, but—Nico, is it true? Grener was murdered."

"I'm afraid so," Rathe answered. He grimaced, looking around the room with its one good chair, the trestle table turned up against the wall to make more room. The only sign of indulgence was the stand of half a dozen corms, each in its own glass jar, positioned to take the light, and to be seen from the chair. "I was with him when he died, which is no comfort, I know."

"How horrible for you." She shook her head. "I'm glad you found the place. I couldn't remember if I'd ever brought you here."

"I asked at the Metenerie," Rathe said. That was the guildhall; and even they had known only the direction, not a proper address. He shook his head again, wondering if Ogier had had cause to hide, or if it was simply his well-known eccentricity.

"Sensible. I assume you'll want to talk to Frelise?"

"Yes." Rathe paused. "Is she an Ogier, too?"

Caro nodded. "There was no business in the family, and Frelise is a seamstress, so there wasn't any need for him to take another name. She kept house for him, oh, it's been years, now."

There was a rustle from the doorway, and Rathe turned, to see a tall woman leaning against the frame. She was probably older than her brother had been, a plain woman with a lined, open face, her eyes red and swollen now, the tracks of tears still visible on her cheeks.

"Caro, who—"

Her voice was little more than a whisper, and Caro moved quickly to take her hand, drawing her into the room and settling her on one of the low stools that stood against the wall. Rathe frowned, wondering why his mother didn't settle her in the chair, then realized it had been Ogier's. Too much, too soon, to remind her again that he wasn't coming back, and he moved to join them. The contrast between them was almost painful, his own mother browned and sturdy, her greying hair chopped short to fit beneath a gardener's broad-brimmed hat, Frelise pale as paper, well-kept hands—hands that handled silks, Rathe realized—knotting in her lap. Caro's hand, resting on her shoulder, looked even browner and more roughened by the contrast.

"It's the pointsman, Frelise," she said. "You knew they'd come. But there's nothing to worry about, my dear, he's my own son."

There was a warning in her voice, and Rathe nodded, keeping his voice low and soft. "I'm Nicolas Rathe, mistress, adjunct point at Point of Dreams. I was with your brother when he died. I'm so very sorry."

Frelise managed a watery smile. "Adjunct Point. Oh, that's good of them, to send someone of rank, and Caro's son, too. Tell me, did he suffer?"

Rathe dropped his head, hiding the wince. "No, mistress, not to speak of." It was a lie, but the truth was unlikely to comfort. "I have some questions I have to ask, if you think you're strong enough."

"Yes." Frelise nodded. "But—I don't understand any of it! And Elinee, and Versigine, they kept saying that he must have done something, no respectable man should be murdered, not if he wasn't doing something he oughtn't. . . ."

Her voice broke off in a gasp as she fought back tears, and Rathe glanced at his mother.

"The nearest neighbors," she said softly. "I sent them packing, but not fast enough."

"I wish it were true that folk were only murdered who deserved it," Rathe said, and Frelise looked up at him, frowning, on the verge of offense. "I'm sorry, mistress, but I've seen people killed for no reason, for being an inconvenience, for having coin when someone else didn't. It's no shame to him or you that he was killed like this, just a tragedy." He shook his head, aware that he was quoting Holles and his grief. "But we have to be sure, have to know if there was any cause, any old grudge, anything at all, that might help us find his killer."

Frelise's hands were locked together in her lap, and she fixed her eyes on them, still struggling for control. "I kept house for him, came in, oh, two or three days a week, dined with him perhaps one of them, but we didn't talk all that much. He had his life, and I have mine."

"So you don't know of any quarrel, any enemy?" Rathe asked, his heart sinking.

Frelise shook her head. "No. He was stiff-necked, stubborn, nobody'd know that better than me. But you don't kill a man for being like that."

Some people do. Rathe killed that thought, said instead, "Do you know who he'd been working for lately? They might know something."

Frelise shook her head again. "A few, I think—it was busier than you'd think, this time of year, and the corms everyone's mad for, they made for extra work." She nodded to the jars standing on the narrow table. "Those were gifts, they're supposed to be very fine. He said half the people buying them don't know what to do with them, and so some of his regulars were referring new people to him, and he couldn't say no. Not to the people, I mean, he could do that, but not to the plants. He couldn't stand to see them mistreated."

Caro nodded in agreement, and Rathe found himself nodding with her. He'd felt the same thing, more than once. He said, "Do you know the names of any of these people, the regulars or the new ones?"

"They'd be in his book," Frelise said, and looked around almost helplessly. "Caro, did you see it?"

"Not yet," Caro answered, her voice comforting, but she met her son's eyes with sudden worry. "I'm sure it's here."

"Do you happen to know any of them yourself?" Rathe asked. If the gardener's notebook was missing, that might well be a sign that it was one of his clients, or at least someone connected with their household, who had murdered the man.

"A few." Frelise frowned, loosed her fingers at last to touch her temples, as though she had the headache. "There was a vidame, Tardieu, I think. And an intendant in Point of Hearts, I can't remember, but it was a man. And the landame Camail. Donis, I can't remember."

Her voice rose in a wail, and Rathe glanced at his mother, wondering if he should withdraw.

"But there was someone else, dear," Caro said. "You mentioned someone special, I think, all kinds of extra work?"

Frelise's hand flew to her mouth. "Donis, you must think me a fool."

"Never that," Caro said. "Never that."

"It was the succession houses," Frelise said. "The landseur Aubine's houses—four of them, Grener said, the finest in the city, and all of them busy just now, producing flowers for the midwinter masque."

Ogier had worked for Aubine. Rathe closed his eyes, letting his head drop for an instant. So this was another theatre death, at least potentially, another death connected with the masque. Except that the manner was different, none of the theatricality of the other deaths, just a good, old-fashioned knife through the ribs.

"And there was another thing," Frelise said. "This I truly don't understand. When I came in this morning, before the girl came from the Temple, I found clothes in the stove. Grener's clothes, all burnt to ash. There's nothing left but the buttons." She shook her head. "I can't think why he'd burn them. It's more like him to sell them, or give them to the Metenerie."

But I can think why. Rathe kept his face expressionless with an effort. *I think I know why. He'd burned his clothes, was found wearing temple hand-outs, Istre confirmed that—he must have feared that someone would track him by magistical means, and tried to break the trail. And that's another link to the theatre deaths: they have the stamp of magistry on them as well.* "You're sure they were his?" he asked, without much hope, and Frelise nodded.

"Oh, yes, his usual daywear. Clothes are my trade, you know." Her face crumpled again. "I made that shirt myself."

Caro patted her hand gently, and the other woman smiled her thanks, drew a deep breath. "I'll look for his book, pointsman. I'm sure it must be here somewhere."

I doubt it, Rathe thought, but nodded. "I'd be grateful, mistress."

"I'll stay with you," Caro said. "If you'd like."

"Do you have someone to stay with you tonight, mistress?" Rathe asked, and Frelise nodded.

"I live with my mistress—guildmistress, I mean, above the shop, she's been very kind. And there's a journeyman who'll keep me company if I need it."

Rathe smiled, relieved, and his mother said, "I'll keep you company until you're finished, and then I'll see you home."

Frelise nodded, and Rathe touched his mother's arm, drew her aside. "And who's going to see you home, especially if you're late? The stars seem—chancy—these days, you have to admit."

Caro smiled. "I'm not a child, Nicolas. I'll take a low-flyer, even if it is an extravagance."

Rathe kissed her cheek. "Your safety's not an extravagance."

"Neither is hers," Caro said, but her tone was less sharp than the words. "Or yours. Be careful, Nico."

"I will," Rathe answered, and hoped he could keep his word.

It was, as he had guessed, a little less than an hour's walk along the Promenade from Ogier's little house to the Western Reach, a pleasant walk, except for the carriages that crowded even the wide pavement. The sprawling complex of buildings that was the queen's residence and the Reach were busier than ever, nobles visiting for the masque and the rumored naming of the heir tucked into every available room and rentable house. Rathe felt distinctly out of place, on foot, his shapeless coat hanging loose from his shoulders, and he wondered just what the passing landames thought of him, seeing the truncheon hanging at his belt.

There was no points station in the Reach, of course, but the adjunct at Point of Hearts was happy to direct him to Aubine's residence—owned, she pointed out, not rented; the man was a permanent resident. He would have to be, to have built succession houses that caught Ogier's fancy, Rathe thought, but thanked her nicely, and retraced his way through the streets until he found the house. It was smaller than its closest neighbors, but perfect, a jewel of a building, three storeys to the roof—*which means,* Rathe thought, *that this younger son isn't kept short of funds.* This house required staff and funds to maintain both, and it would cost even more to maintain the succession houses. They were invisible, tucked somewhere in the gardens behind the building, but he knew from his mother's conversation that even a small glasshouse cost a small fortune to heat, never mind the cost of building it in the first place. Four succession houses would easily consume even a landseur's income, would explain why Gasquine had sought Caiazzo's coin for the masque, content to let the landseur loan his name and flowers only.

He knocked at the door, carefully not looking to see if he'd tracked mud onto the scrubbed and swept stones of the stoop, and it was opened almost instantly by a very young girl, a child, almost, in miniature livery. Her lack of expression, however, was perfectly adult, the polite disinterest of a well-trained servant, and like a good servant, she waited for him to speak.

"Adjunct Point Rathe, to see the landseur, if he's home." *If he'll be home to me*, Rathe added silently, and the girl looked up at him.

"I—I think he's in the succession houses, pointsman—Adjunct Point, I mean. Will you wait here? And may I tell him what this is about?"

"It's about his gardener. Or possibly ex-gardener. A man named Ogier."

Her eyes widened, her voice suddenly and completely southriver. "Oh, sir, have you found Ogier? We've all been worried—the landseur's been most unhappy since he left, we all have."

"You liked him, then," Rathe said, and the girl nodded.

"Oh, yes, sir. I miss him." Her manner changed with her voice, so that she was suddenly a child again, despite the drilled manners and the livery, but then she shook herself back to her duty. "Please step in. If you'll permit, Adjunct Point."

Rathe did as he was told, grateful for his own childhood. He'd worked hard enough, his parents had needed the extra hands more than once, for harvest and planting and in high summer, when the groundsman's work was at its height, but there had always been time for play, for pleasure. He hadn't had to take on adult responsibilities until he'd become a runner, and he'd been older than this girl. She disappeared down the long hall without a backward glance, and Rathe made himself look around. He could smell the ashes of a fire somewhere close at hand, but the hall itself was almost cold, the last of the sunset filtering through the narrow window above the door. The light fell on a series of engravings, fine work, better than the average woodcut, and Rathe took a step closer. They all showed a great estate, the same estate, and its gardens, each drawn from a different angle, playing up a different feature, and he wondered if it was Aubine's ancestral home, or some as-yet-unrealized dream. There were drawings of plants as well, single plants in the various stages of their growth, hand-colored—all late-year plants, he saw, and wondered if Aubine had another set for each of the seasons. The drawing of the winter-creeper was particularly fine, the pale berries luminous against the tangle of vines, and he started when the girl cleared her throat.

"If you'll come with me, Adjunct Point. The landseur is busy in the succession houses, and asked if you'd join him there."

Rathe nodded, not at all sorry to have the chance to see them, and followed her through the house to a narrow stone-floored hall that led to a shallow courtyard. The greenhouses lay beyond, four long, glass-walled houses, smoke rising from their narrow chimneys, the rippled glass fogged by the warmth inside. They were easily the largest Rathe had ever seen, made Estines's little house look like a child's toy, and he shook his head, amazed. The girl led him to the one at the far end, opened the door and hurried him inside, careful to close the door again behind her before she spoke.

"Adjunct Point Rathe, maseigneur."

Rathe had been expecting warmth, but not the heat of summer. The reddened light poured through the glass, and for a second he could almost believe that it was a summer sun that set beyond the walls. But the winter-sun hadn't risen, no pinpoint of brilliance standing high in the sky, and he shook himself back to the present, impressed again. Aubine stood at a gardener's bench, coat and waistcoat discarded on a form, his shirtsleeves rolled back and a dozen plants standing unpotted, ready for his hand. All around him, the shelves were crowded with summer plants, most of them close to blooming, and that, Rathe realized, was part of the disorientation. The glasshouse smelled of summer, flowers and dirt and heat, and even the smoke from the stove couldn't quite destroy the illusion.

"Adjunct Point," Aubine said. "It's a surprise to see you away from the theatre." He lifted a heavy, short-bladed knife, gestured apologetically with it, scattering dirt. "Forgive me for receiving you like this, but as you know, it's a busy time for me."

"Not at all," Rathe answered. He thought for a second of saying how glad he was to have a chance to see the succession houses, but decided against it. Let the man assume he knew less than he did; if Aubine wanted to lie, this would be a chance to catch him. "I'm pleased to find you here, actually. I was afraid you might be at the theatre."

Aubine smiled, tipping a plant into a pot that stood ready for him. The girl reached instantly for a bucket that stood nearby, sloshed water over the new dirt. "Ah. Thank you, Bice. I would love to be there, but if the flowers are to be ready for the masque, well, there's still much work to be done. Bice tells me you have news of Ogier?"

"Some questions, first, if I may," Rathe said, and realized Aubine was staring at him. "Sir?"

Aubine shook himself. "Of course. Ask what you must."

"When did you last see Ogier?"

"Ah." Aubine blinked, eyes focusing on something in the invisible distance. "That would be—what, Bice, one week ago? Two?"

"Almost two weeks ago, sir," Bice answered. She reached for another pot, but Rathe saw the flicker of distress cross her face. The girl had liked Ogier, that much was obvious, and he winced at the thought of the coming sorrow.

"What happened?" he said aloud. "Did he send word, just not show up one morning?"

"Exactly that, Adjunct Point," Aubine answered. "He simply didn't arrive. I thought perhaps he was sick, but then he didn't come the next day, either, or the day after that. I have no idea where he lives, or I would have sent for him—it's probably just as well I don't, I don't think I would have been very moderate in my summons." He laughed softly, ruefully. "Master Aconin has not made my job easy, I assure you. Only someone utterly unversed in flowers would manage to feature all the most difficult to bring into bloom at the same time. But I wish Ogier had warned me. I need his help, and he knew it, knew I was counting on him. Have you found him?"

"I'm afraid so," Rathe said reluctantly, and kept his eye on the girl. "He was murdered last night, in Point of Dreams."

Bice gasped, her face suddenly as white as chalk, and she set the pot hastily on the table. Aubine took it blindly, his expression still uncomprehending.

"We had his name," Rathe said, "but we had no notion he worked for you until today. My understanding was that he never attached himself to any one household."

"No," Aubine said, "no, that's quite true. But I asked—he had worked for me before—and he graciously agreed to give me a large portion of his time so that we could get the flowers ready for the masque. I think he liked the idea of being involved in that—and of working in my houses, I know he enjoyed that." He shook himself then, as though Rathe's words had finally made sense. "But—murdered? How? And where did you say?"

"He was stabbed," Rathe said. The second question was an odd one, and he watched the landseur closely. "On the border of Hopes and Dreams, in actual fact, an alley there. He died shortly after he was found."

Aubine dropped his knife, stared at it for a long moment before stooping to pick it up. "This is terrible news. And there I was, talking about my inconveniences, when the poor man was dead. What you must think of me. I hope he didn't suffer."

Rathe slanted a glance at the girl, saw her still listening, and gave the same lie he had told Frelise. "Not much, no."

"Did he name his attacker?" Aubine went on. "Was it robbery? He could be difficult, but—why in Demis's name would anyone kill him? Why would anyone murder a gardener?"

And that's the question, isn't it? Rathe thought. There could be a dozen reasons for asking if Ogier had named his killer, not least among them the desire to see that person punished, but still, there was something about Aubine's question that raised the hackles on the back of his neck. And that was probably unfair, he told himself, but chose his words carefully. "It's early days yet, maseigneur, we're still trying to answer that. But, no, it wasn't robbery. He had his purse on him, and it was untouched." He looked down at the nearest plant, a tiny sundew, pretending to study the pattern of the gold-edged leaves, watching Aubine from under his lashes. "I can't imagine he would have had anything else of value on him, besides his purse."

"No," Aubine said, and shook his head. "I paid him what he was worth, of course, and I think I paid him only a day or so before he disappeared, but—" He broke off, met Rathe's curious stare wide-eyed. "This is simply terrible."

In spite of himself, his eyes moved, taking in the shelves of plants—thinking of the work to be done, Rathe guessed, and all the more difficult without a helper, and he wasn't surprised to see the landseur's shoulders sag. But then Aubine straightened, drawing himself up to his full height, and the moment passed.

"Had he family?"

"A sister," Rathe answered. "She did some of his housekeeping."

"Bice."

The girl straightened, face pinched and still, and Rathe hid a grimace of sympathy.

"Tell Jonneau to prepare a gift for—" Aubine looked at Rathe.

"Frelise Ogier."

"Frelise Ogier," Aubine repeated. "She mustn't suffer for her brother's death. And, please, Adjunct Point, I'd have you do all you can to discover who's responsible. I will pay any fee you require. . . ."

"I'll find out who killed him, my lord," Rathe answered, "but I don't take fees."

Aubine's eyebrows rose. "You don't? But how do you survive?"

"It is a paid post," Rathe said dryly.

"Oh, I know, but I've read . . . I've heard . . ." Aubine took a breath. "Forgive me, Adjunct Point. I hope I didn't offend."

"It's a common assumption, and mostly accurate," Rathe answered. "No offense taken." He hesitated, remembering the story Eslingen had related. "May I ask you a question?"

"Of course." Aubine's expression was controlled, and perfectly courteous.

"I've heard stories," Rathe said, "and forgive me now if I offend, that the points failed to investigate the death of your leman some years back, a death that was very probably, if not certainly, murder. Is that true?"

Aubine fixed his eyes on the plant still waiting on the table, brought the knife down in a single sharp blow, neatly severing the tangled ball of roots. He heeled one half into a trough set ready, set the other into a half-empty pot, and only then took a careful breath. "I do believe that to be true, Adjunct Point. That my leman was indeed murdered. I don't blame the points, though, please understand that." He looked up, managed a wavering smile. "The death was ordered by my grandmother, who, in practice if not in theory, would have been outside their reach, even if he was killed in Astreiant." He set the knife aside, rested both hands flat on the scarred table. "That's why it was so important to me to be part of the masque, to give to it, even if it's just the flowers, and it's one of the reasons I love, and fear, being there, at the theatre. It's so easy there, all the orders, all the proprieties of rank and station, they're all thrown aside, but when the doors close again, you daren't forget just how real they truly are. It was that way at the university, certainly, and the theatre— so much more so. It hurts, and I know I'm seeing people who are going to do themselves harm—I wonder if that isn't what happened to poor de Raçan—but they're all so eager to throw themselves into this, all so fearless. And they should fear, Adjunct Point, I know that so well."

It was more than he'd expected to hear, and Rathe nodded in sympathy, the easy words dying on his tongue. Aubine was right, and most of the actors knew it, knew how to play by the rules when they had to, and when they could discard them, Siredy had proved that, but one miscalculation, and they could end up as dead as Aubine's lost love. "Thank you," he said softly, and cleared his throat. "Maseigneur, I'm sure—I hope you understand that we'll want to talk to your people as well, at least the ones who knew Ogier."

The landseur nodded, his hands slowly brushing soil from the table into a bucket, repeating the movement even though he had to know, as Rathe knew, that it was futile. The dirt was worked into the grain of the wood, the table would never be truly free of it, but the gesture looked more like habit, repeated for comfort, like someone stroking a dog. "Of course, Adjunct Point. And if I or anyone remembers anything that might be of use, I shall assuredly let you know." He smiled then, the expression crooked. "If I remember at the theatre, should I send word by way of Lieutenant vaan Esling?"

So the gossip's got that far, Rathe thought, not knowing why he felt a chill. "No," he said, "send word to Point of Dreams. Even if I'm not there, it will reach me."

"Ah." Aubine's smile widened briefly. "I beg your pardon, Adjunct Point. If I remember anything, I will let you know."

There were lights in his windows again, and as he went up the stairs the smell of food wafted down to meet him. Not Eslingen's cooking, he guessed—the ex-soldier's kitchen skills were limited—and he wasn't surprised to see a pair of covered iron dishes stamped with the moon and twin stars that was Pires's tavern's mark. One was still covered, waiting on the hob to keep warm; the other was simmering gently on the stove itself. Eslingen was sitting at the table in shirt and waistcoat, and Rathe didn't have to look to know that the man's coat was hung neatly on its stand behind the door. A tankard of beer sat in front of him, perfuming the air, and Rathe wrinkled his nose.

"Are we celebrating something?"

Eslingen grinned. "There's a bottle of wine for you, too. In the cold safe."

"So what are we celebrating?" Rathe pulled off his jerkin, draped it carelessly on its hook, freed himself of coat and truncheon as well. Eslingen kept the little room warmer than he himself would have done, but so far the price of charcoal was good this winter. He lifted the lid on the warming pot, saw and smelled a mix of root vegetables spiced with butter and horseradish, saw, too, a fresh loaf of bread set above the safe.

"The end of a five-hundred-year feud," Eslingen answered, and Rathe blinked.

"What are you talking about?"

"My landames, remember? I told you about them."

"The ones who were fighting," Rathe answered, nodding, and reached into the safe for the wine. There was a new wedge of cheese as well, and he shook his head as he tugged open the bottle. "You'll spoil us both, Philip."

"Well, they decided to stop fighting today," Eslingen said. "Or maybe it was before then, I can't be sure."

"Try beginning at the beginning," Rathe suggested, and seated himself opposite the other man. The wine was good, the same cheap flinty wine from Verniens that he always drank, and he took another long swallow, relaxing in spite of himself.

"They were missing when Gasquine called us to rehearse the swordplay," Eslingen said obligingly. "So of course we, Siredy and I, thought they'd decided to settle the feud once and for all. But when I went looking for them, I found them in the props loft, in—shall we say—a most compromising position."

"They weren't," Rathe said, grinning himself now, and Eslingen nodded.

"Oh, but they were. I'd say the feud was settled."

"The poor women," Rathe said. "The story must be all over the theatre by now—how old are they, anyway?"

"Old enough to know how to manage an affair," Eslingen said. "Honestly, Nico, after all I've heard about their thrice-damned families and their five-hundred-year feud, I'm delighted to see them embarrassed. And before you say it, I didn't have to say anything. Maseigne Txi was foolish enough to wear her hair in an arrangement she couldn't redo without help."

In spite of himself, Rathe laughed, the day's sorrows receding even further. However they'd gotten to this point, it was good to sit here with Eslingen, good to share a drink and dinner and even this joke. "Aconin must have loved it. It's just the sort of thing he does well."

Eslingen's smile faltered, and he leaned forward, resting both elbows on the table. "Aconin . . . I had a talk with him today, Nico. I think you want to question him."

"Oh?" *Back to business*, Rathe thought, but couldn't resent it. Here in the warmth of his own room, supper waiting on the stove, Eslingen's easy presence across the table, it was almost like an ordinary profession, the comfortable chat of guild-mates, not the fraught world of the points. *I know it's serious, deadly serious, but, Sofia, it's so good to be a little free of it.*

"Sorry." Eslingen smiled regretfully. "But he knows who attacked him, I'm sure of that. You could probably get it out of him, he's scared enough he might tell you."

"What did he say?" It wasn't exactly a surprise, Rathe thought, he'd been sure of it since he saw the playwright in his ransacked room.

Eslingen closed his eyes for a second, as though that would help him remember. "He said he'd made a mistake, taken something that had been promised to him—something he needed, he said. And that was what was behind all this."

"Nothing more?" Rathe asked.

"No." Eslingen reached for the pint bucket, ladled himself another tankard of beer. "Some people came up to us—he was afraid of being overheard—and then I was needed onstage. I'm sorry."

"Don't apologize, that's more than we had before." Rathe's eyes narrowed. "Afraid of being overheard. . . . Do you think it's someone at the theatre?"

"Well, it has to be, doesn't it, considering?" Eslingen answered, and Rathe shook his head.

"That wasn't what I meant, I meant someone at the theatre today, at that moment, in fact."

Eslingen shook his head in turn. "I'm afraid that doesn't narrow it down very much. We had the whole chorus there—though not all the actors, not that I ever suspected them particularly. And the staff, and everyone."

"Was Aubine there?" Rathe asked slowly.

"Yes, fiddling with his damn flowers. The arrangements just keep getting bigger and brighter, they're going to be spectacular for the performance." Eslingen paused. "Actually, he was one of the people who came up—you can't suspect him, Nico."

"Why not?"

Eslingen spread his hands. "He's too—polite. Too calm. I just can't see it."

"Polite men have committed murder before this, Philip."

"All right, why, then?"

Rathe stopped, frustrated. "I don't know. I just . . ." He let his voice trail off, shook his head again. "I spoke to him today—Ogier worked for him, did I tell you that? Worked on the flowers for the masque, so his death is probably part of all this. But I spoke to Aubine, and . . . There's something about him, Philip, makes my hackles rise. As you said—he's too polite."

"A landseur treats you with respect, so you suspect him of murder?" Eslingen asked, grinning, and in spite of himself, Rathe smiled back.

"That's not what I meant, and you know it. No, I don't trust the man, and I couldn't tell you why. Sofia, I'd give a pillar or two to see his stars."

"Is there someone you can ask?" Eslingen asked, and Rathe shook his head, shaking himself back to reality.

"No, no one. His family aren't even Astreianter, so there won't be servants to ask, even if I thought they'd tell me. No, I'll start with Aconin, that sounds a lot more promising. But—" He hesitated, wishing he could put a finger on the cause of his uncertainty, recalled Aubine's offer to send word via the Leaguer. "Be careful, Philip."

Eslingen nodded. "I always am."

9

For once, Rathe let Eslingen leave before him, biding his time until the clock struck half past nine and he was sure the playwright would be at the Tyrseia. The square in front of the theatre was quiet, the tavern closed, though he was aware of the owner watching from an upstairs window—*probably wondering if there was going to be another body,* he thought, and smiled in spite of himself. This was probably more excitement than they'd seen since *The Drowned Island* closed and the apprentices went home. As he came around the curve of the building, he saw a familiar carriage, every available space filled with bundled plants, and sighed to realize that Aubine was there before him. In the same moment, the landseur turned, motioning for his coachman to remain where he was, and moved to intercept him.

"Adjunct Point. I hadn't hoped you would be here this morning, I thought I would have to send for you."

"I had other business here," Rathe answered, and knew he sounded wary.

"Unfortunately, I have—business—of my own for you," Aubine said, and gave a small, sad smile. "Please, over here."

Rathe followed him over to the carriage, frowning as he saw the torn leather curtain in its single window. Aubine reached through the window to open the door, and Rathe caught his breath. The floor of the carriage was covered with shards of glass, glass and water already freezing into ice, and a bouquet of summer flowers lay wilting on the seat. The warming box was cold to the touch, the coals extinguished, Rathe guessed, by the water that had spilled.

"Someone," Aubine said, "shot at my carriage this morning."

Rathe took a breath, shaking himself back to his duty. "When, maseigneur?"

Aubine looked at the coachman, who rolled his eyes almost as nervously as his horse. "I was told to bring the carriage at half past eight," he said, "and then it took half an hour or more to load the flowers. So a little after nine, then, maseigneur."

"A little after nine," Aubine said.

Rathe fingered the torn curtain. It would have been stretched taut to keep out as much of the cold as possible; the hole was small, about the size of his little finger, but the ball had clearly hit the vase with enough force to shatter it, and that would easily have been enough to wound, probably to kill. For a second, he wished Eslingen were there—he didn't have much experience with firearms himself, the average Astreianter bravo preferred knives—but pushed the thought away. Time enough to ask him later; for now, there were other matters to determine. "And where were you, maseigneur?"

"I was riding on the box." Aubine looked almost embarrassed. "There were so many flowers, you see, and all of them delicate."

"So there were more flowers in the coach?" Rathe asked, and leaned in to examine the floor and seats more closely. Sure enough, there was a tear in the far wall, where the ball had ripped through the coach itself. And it had to be a ball, he thought, couldn't have been a birdbolt or any other projectile. Anything else would have been slowed by the curtain and the glass, and he would have found it somewhere among the broken pieces. And Aubine, sitting on the box with the driver, would have been, was muffled up against the cold like anyone, no one would expect him to be riding outside, or recognize him when he was.

"Yes," Aubine said. "But we brought them inside, I didn't want them to die in the cold. They were already wilting when we got here. I only hope they'll recover—" He broke off, shaking his head, and Rathe gave him a curious look. At least Aubine realized how his obsessions must sound to outside ears.

"And where did it happen?" Rathe straightened so that he could see the other man clearly.

"Just at our gate," the coachman said. "We'd just come up to it, the boy had it open, and I heard the shot."

"The man was standing on our wall," Aubine said. "Well, not on it, not quite, but looking over it—perhaps he had a ladder on the other side? I don't know. I told Hue to drive on, and the man dropped out of sight. And we came on here."

"And why was that, maseigneur?" Rathe asked. "Surely you'd have been safer if you'd waited in your own house, with your own people."

"I—" Aubine sighed. "I'm not really sure, Adjunct Point. I suppose it would have been, at that. But I heard the shot, and I didn't think. All I wanted was to get away. Not very brave, I admit, but there have been too many deaths already."

And that, Rathe thought, *I can certainly believe. Nobody was likely to think clearly while they were being shot at, and it would be easier to keep a carriage moving than to back it through the gates.* "Did you get a good look at the man?" he asked, and Aubine shook his head.

"I'm sorry. It was a man, I'm sure of that, but he was wearing a driver's coat and a big hat, it hid his face."

"Did you see his hair?"

"No." Aubine shook his head again. "It must have been short, or pulled back."

Which could describe three-quarters of the men in Astreiant, Rathe thought, but he hadn't expected any better. "Was he heavy-built, slim—anything at all you can tell me?"

Aubine pursed his lips. "Slim, I think. I couldn't really tell his height, because of the wall, but I think—I would say he was built like Chresta, slim and light."

Like Aconin. That name would come up once too often one of these days. Rathe kept his voice steady with an effort. "Could it have been Aconin, do you think?"

Aubine blinked, startled by the idea. "No, surely not. Why would he do such a thing?"

"But could it have been?" Rathe said, and Aubine shook his head, decisively this time.

"I can't say it wasn't, but I surely can't, won't, say it was. The man was built a little like him, that's all."

There's something not right about this, Rathe thought, *he's lying somewhere.* "You know Master Aconin," he said aloud, and saw something flicker in the landseur's eyes.

"We—I counted him a friend."

"And no longer?" Rathe waited, saw Aubine's mouth tighten.

"It's a common enough occurrence, I believe, at least where Chresta is concerned. But he has been very much involved in this masque."

And if he wants to believe that, who am I to disillusion him? For the first time, Rathe felt a stab of pity for the landseur. He himself knew what it was like to lose a lover; Aconin was notorious for the brutality of his partings. "You'd best get the rest of these inside," he said, and Aubine nodded.

"Thank you, Adjunct Point. Oh, but—one more thing?"

"Yeah?"

"Is—can this be my official report to the points?" Aubine gave another of his soft smiles. "I'm reluctant to add any more to the stories about the masque."

"I don't blame you," Rathe said. Aubine was, after all, the noble sponsor; all these disasters reflected as badly on him as they did on Gasquine, perhaps worse. *And I'd hate to think what Caiazzo was making of all this. I daresay he's watching very close from Customs Point.* "I'll make your report in private. But if I need to talk to you again, may I?"

"Of course." Aubine nodded, the gesture almost a bow. "And thank you."

Gasquine was watching from the wings, resting one hip on a tall stool, her hands folded across her chest. She looked exhausted, Rathe thought, with sympathy, and no wonder. The masque was hard enough in any year, but this time . . . She looked up then, seeing him, and her eyes narrowed.

"Not more trouble."

Rathe laughed in spite of himself, shook his head. "I don't think so, just the same old ones. I need to talk to Aconin."

"Good luck to you," Gasquine said. "He's not here."

There was a distinct note of annoyance in her voice. Rathe said, "I thought he was here every day, checking up on things."

"Oh, yes, every day until today, making sure I do justice to his damned masterpiece." Gasquine sighed. "No, that's not fair, it is good, and to be even fairer, he doesn't do as much harm as your average playwright. But today, when I need him, he's nowhere to be found."

"When you need him?" Rathe asked. "I thought the script was set."

"It is," Gasquine answered. "Or at least it should be. But there's a speech one of the chorus—the landseur de Besselin—is having trouble with, and I'd like to cut it. But I don't know if that will affect the magistry of it, and Aconin isn't here to tell me. So we have to muddle on."

"So I can assume you don't have any idea where he might be," Rathe said slowly, and the woman shook her head.

"Oriane knows. He's probably holed up somewhere with a new discovery. Have you come to call a point on him?"

Rathe grinned. "No, or at least not yet. I just had some questions for him. Was he paying particular attention to anyone?"

"I have the managing of this masque, Nico," Gasquine said. "That's a cast of nearly three score, including a better-born chorus than I've ever been unlucky enough to have to deal with. Plus two mysterious deaths in the theatre, and the broadsheets bleating about a haunted theatre or a cursed play, plus Master Eyes's malice on top of it—you did me no favor there, Nico. Aconin's affairs have been, I confess, outside my notice."

"Sorry," Rathe said, lifting his hands, and Gasquine sighed.

"Not your fault, I know. But I'm starting to feel that the stars are against me."

"Mistress Gasquine?" That was one of the scenerymen, touching his hand to his forehead. "I'm sorry to trouble you, but—"

Gasquine sighed. "I'm needed?"

"Yes, mistress. Now."

Gasquine spread her hands in wordless appeal, but slid off her stool and vanished into the shadows without a backward glance. Left to himself, Rathe glanced around, looking for Eslingen among the crowd in the pit. The soldier was nowhere in sight, and he grimaced, wondering if anyone else might know Aconin's whereabouts.

"Nico?"

The voice was unwelcome—*except,* Rathe thought, *of all the people here, Guis Forveijl is the person most likely to know where I can find Chresta Aconin.* "Guis."

"I wanted to talk to you," Forveijl said. "I wouldn't bother you except it's important. It's about Chresta. And—" He gestured to the stage, the movement surprisingly ineffective for an actor, and more compelling for it. "All this."

Rathe stared at him, wondering if Aconin had finally abandoned the other man—and that, he told himself firmly, was an unworthy thought. Forveijl's face was unusually sober, troubled, and Rathe made a face, capitulating. "All right, talk to me."

Forveijl shook his head. "Please. Not here."

He tilted his head to one side, and Rathe sighed again, seeing the rehearsal momentarily at a standstill. A dozen of the chorus were trooping onto the stage, all carrying property weapons—Eslingen was among them, he saw, met Rathe's glance with a quick smile that was replaced almost instantly with the intent frown that was becoming as familiar to Rathe as any of Forveijl's gestures had been—and several of the actors, dismissed from the stage, were watching them with open curiosity. No, he could hardly blame Forveijl for wanting to keep this conversation private. "Where, then?" he asked, and Forveijl looked over his shoulder again.

"The dressing rooms, I suppose. That should be private enough."

Not from what Jhirassi had always told him, Rathe thought, but then, he had no particular desire to be closeted too closely with Forveijl. He nodded, and let the other man lead him through the wings and up a narrow staircase that ran along the theater's rear wall. The dressing rooms were there, nearly a dozen of them, communal rooms for the common actors, tiny private rooms for the leading women, and Rathe wondered idly where Eslingen dressed. Or the chorus, for that matter: they could hardly enjoy being tucked into even the largest of the rooms, forced to share with half a hundred others. To his surprise, Forveijl pushed open the door of one of the smaller rooms—but then, Rathe thought, following the other man inside, Forveijl had earned his peers' regard. Whatever Rathe thought of him, Forveijl had their respect.

The room was surprisingly warm, the air heavy with the smell of the flowers that filled a vase the size of a man's head. Silverthorn, winterspice, and the purple-splashed bells of yet another corm: someone had gotten an expensive gift, Rathe thought, blinking in the sunlight that streamed through the narrow window to reflect from the tall mirror, and wondered if it was Forveijl's. A part of him hoped it was, and another, smaller part felt a touch of jealousy. But their affair was long over, Forveijl had chosen Aconin and he himself had been lucky enough to find Eslingen, and he put it aside, frowning. The light from the mirror bounced across the far wall as Forveijl knocked against the frame, and Rathe stepped away, wincing.

"All right," he said, and closed the door behind him. "What did you have to tell me?"

"I needed to talk to you, Nico," Forveijl answered, and there was something in his voice that made Rathe shake his head in warning.

"About Aconin, so talk."

"Yes. And I will, I promise. But, Nicolas, I've missed you, and this is the first chance I've had to say so. It's a shock to have you back in my life, probably the most pleasant shock of my life, but still—"

"I'm not back in your life," Rathe said. "I'm trying to find out who killed two people just in this theatre. I'm sorry if it seems to you as though I'm doing it to torment you." He broke off, not wanting to say the words that had risen to his lips—*I wasn't even thinking you might be here*—and Forveijl took a step closer.

"You're not tormenting me, Nicolas. But, Oriane, if you wanted to, you could. You always did."

Rathe stared at him for a moment, caught by the gleam of sunlight in the other man's hair. Forveijl was gilt, warm honey skin and golden hair, where Eslingen was jet and ivory, and the actor was still very beautiful. A part of him had never forgotten that, Rathe knew, would probably never forget even after he'd lost the memory of all the petty quarrels. He took a breath, newly aware of the plants almost at his side, and shook himself, hard. "You've nothing to the purpose to say, have you?"

"Very much so, I promise." Forveijl smiled.

"About Aconin," Rathe said.

"That, too."

Rathe shook his head, stifling desire he hadn't know he still carried. Forveijl was beautiful, yes, handsome, virile, and utterly untrustworthy. He'd proved that more than once. "I'm going," he said, and realized Forveijl stood between him and the door.

"Are you sure you want to?"

No. Rathe took a careful breath, trying not to remember how Forveijl's skin had felt under his hands, how his hair had smelled of spice and the paint he wore onstage. "Get out of my way," he said, and knew he sounded less than convincing.

"I don't want to," Forveijl said softly. There was less than an arm's length between them, in the tiny room, and even as Rathe thought that, Forveijl reached out to lay first one hand and then the other on Rathe's shoulders. Rathe shivered at the touch, at the memory of other touches, and Forveijl touched his face. "I want you. I want you back in my life, shock or no shock."

And I'm still not back in your life, I have a lover. . . . Rathe couldn't bring himself to step away, refused to give in to the caress. "What would Aconin say to that?"

Forveijl laughed. "Chresta dropped me long ago, as I daresay you knew he would. We're friends now, nothing more."

"I'm sure he got the performance he wanted out of you," Rathe said, and winced at his own bitterness.

"You have to admit it worked," Forveijl said, and Rathe shook his head.

"I never saw the play."

"I know. I looked for you."

"The theatre's dark," Rathe said, clinging to solid fact. "You never could have noticed."

"I noticed." Forveijl leaned forward then, brought his mouth down hard on Rathe's. *Not like Philip's,* Rathe thought, dazed, his hands tangling in Forveijl's hair. *This is worse than folly, it's madness. I don't want to be doing this.*

Forveijl cupped his face between his hands. "You have missed me."

"Not once," Rathe answered. It was the truth, too, or had been until this hour, and he tried to pull back, but Forveijl's gentle touch held him prisoner.

"Until now," Forveijl said, and the words echoed Rathe's own thoughts so closely that he flinched away.

"Maybe," he answered, and knew the word sounded as weak as he felt.

Forveijl laughed softly, and bowed his head to kiss Rathe's throat. It was the sunlight in the mirror that was blinding, Rathe thought, not the touch, but he shut his eyes anyway. This wasn't like Forveijl, he was always too proper—a dressing room seduction was too common for him, not fine enough, elegant enough. . . . He opened his eyes to see the sunlight shattered into rainbow shards, flecks of light dancing like dust motes in the relative shadow of the rest of the room, turning and swirling to gather above the vase of flowers, as though they were drawn like bees to the heavy blooms. *The Alphabet,* Rathe thought, and felt a surge of relief—not folly, not desire, but something from without, the flowers deluding them both. Aconin had drawn them out one by one, he remembered hazily, but he didn't know, couldn't tell, where to start. And Forveijl's mouth was hot on him, it was past time to end it. He reached out blindly, fingers tingling as they touched the hovering light, shoved the flowers to the ground. The vase tumbled, spilling water and greenery, and Rathe cried out as the light seemed to turn on him, pain worse than the sting of a hundred bees lancing into his hand. It pooled there, a single heartbeat of agony, struck upward like lightning, and he dropped to his knees among the scattered flowers.

"Nico?" Forveijl's voice was distant, drowned in the angry hum of bees, of swarming sunlight. "Nico!"

Rathe looked up at him, vaguely aware of other pains, cuts on hand and knee where he'd landed hard on shards of the broken vase, but the buzzing, the pain, drove over anything he might have said. Too much, he thought, too much to bear, and at last the light slipped away, fading as he fell forward onto the splashed and scarred floor.

Eslingen glanced toward the staircase that led to the dressing rooms, frowning as he saw Forveijl slip quietly down the last few steps and disappear into the wings. At least that meant Rathe should be on his way, he thought, and automatically shook his head at a landame who had started to move half a beat too soon. She froze, not graceful but at least not out of time, and stepped off properly with the rest of them, Eslingen counting the steps aloud. The chorus finished with a flourish, and young de Besselin stepped forward, bowing, to proclaim his speech. Today he wore a lieutenant's sash slung from shoulder to hip, the massive rosette decorated with the palatine's crest picked out in gilt and dark blue paint, and Eslingen hoped it would help him remember his lines. Not that the speech was easy, a long and to Eslingen's ears earnestly dull recitation of the various claimants' connection to the palatine's line, and he wondered idly why Aconin had ever bothered with it. But of course there were parallels to the queen's situation, he thought, and wondered then if Rathe had noticed. If not, he'd definitely want to bring it to the pointsman's attention as soon as he came back down. Eslingen smiled then, recognizing his own jealousy. Not that he was jealous of Rathe, he added instantly, it was just Forveijl he didn't trust—though come to that, he doubted even Forveijl was enough of a fool to think he could win Rathe back to his side. Not from what Rathe had told him, though he had to admit that in his experience it was the people who told you loudly and in detail why they would never go back to a former lover who usually found themselves in bed with them yet again. That was not a pleasant thought at all, and he glanced over his shoulder again. There was still no sign of Rathe, and he wondered unhappily just how long it would take him to get dressed. And that was ridiculous, he told himself sharply. More likely the pointsman had slipped out while Eslingen wasn't looking, was already on his way back to Point of Dreams.

"Break!" the bookholder called.

Gasquine stepped out of the wings, nodding to de Besselin, and Eslingen wondered if the boy had finally gotten through the speech successfully. Apparently he'd done well enough to satisfy Gasquine; the manager waved to the bookholder, and then tucked her arm through the landseur's, drawing him aside.

"Ten minutes," the bookholder said, checking the expensive time-piece pinned to her bodice. "Clear the stage for a set change, please."

Eslingen shuffled back out of the way along with the rest of the cast, watched as chorus and actors dispersed to their usual spots in the pit. There was still no sign of Rathe, and after a moment's hesitation, he started up the stairs. Jhirassi met him at the top, smiling cheerfully, and Eslingen caught his shoulder before the actor could get away.

"Have you seen Nico?"

"No." Jhirassi grinned. "Have you seen Verre?"

Siredy? Eslingen blinked. "He's below. Gavi, wait."

Jhirassi paused, looked back with a lifted eyebrow.

"Which one is Forveijl's?"

Jhirassi's eyebrows rose. "I wouldn't worry, Philip, that's been over for years."

Eslingen shook his head. "It's not that." There was something wrong, he thought suddenly, Rathe should have been down by now, and the fear sharpened his voice. "Which one, Gavi?"

"Third from the far end," Jhirassi answered, pointing, and Eslingen turned away.

The door was closed, he could see that from here, but he had to flatten himself against the wall as bes'Hallen stalked past, her antique petticoats taking up most of the narrow hall, before he could tap on the unpainted panels. There was no answer, and he reached for the latch, glanced over his shoulder to see Jhirassi still watching from the top of the stairs. To hell with it, Eslingen thought, and lifted the latch. To his surprise, the door opened, spilling sunlight across the worn floorboards, and he blinked to see Rathe sprawled on the floor like a heap of discarded clothes. There were flowers beneath him, and water; he was lying in a puddle, on top of the pieces of a broken vase. *No blood,* Eslingen thought, his own breath painfully short, and knelt quickly beside the body, groping for the pulse at the neck. It was there, and strong, and he rocked back onto his heels with a gasp of relief. A strong pulse, and no visible injury—*did the bastard knock him down, knock him out, and just leave him?* Eslingen wondered, running his hands over Rathe's head and torso. There were no bruises, either, but no sign of returning consciousness—he looked, if anything, like a man lightning-struck, except that he was breathing easily, but even so, Eslingen lifted each of Rathe's hands in turn, looking for the faint burn. Maybe Forveijl had attacked him, then, he thought, but he couldn't imagine the actor winning even an unfair fight, at least not without leaving a mark.

"Tyrseis!" Jhirassi's shocked voice sounded from the doorway, and Eslingen looked up quickly.

"Fetch a doctor, please, Gavi. Quickly."

"What's wrong?" Jhirassi stood frozen, eyes suddenly huge, and Eslingen shook his head.

"I don't know. He's alive, but—send for a physician, please. He's out cold."

Jhirassi nodded, backing away, and a moment later, Eslingen heard his footsteps loud on the stairs, and the distant sound of his voice shouting for a runner. *Thank Seidos for people who can make themselves heard,* he thought, and carefully gathered Rathe into his arms, lifting him out of the spilled water. There was a scratch on the pointsman's hand where he'd fallen on a shard of glass, and another on his shin, visible through a tear in the heavy stocking, but those had obviously happened when he fell, could not have caused this collapse. Eslingen touched Rathe's cheek, feeling the first rasp of stubble, and to his relief the other man stirred slightly, opening his eyes.

"Guis—"

And was that accusation, or regret? Eslingen wondered, and stifled his own anger. "It's me, Nico. Philip. Where are you hurt?"

"Philip." That was definitely relief in Rathe's voice, and Eslingen let out breath he hadn't realized he'd been holding.

"Where are you hurt?" he said again. "What happened, Nico?"

Rathe shuddered, a wracking, convulsive movement, and Eslingen gathered him more tightly into his arms. "Talk to me, Nico. Where—?"

"Besides all over?" Rathe managed a weak grin, and it was all Eslingen could do not to squeeze him still more tightly.

"Nico, look at me. Are you hurt anywhere in particular?"

Rathe's head moved from side to side, not quite purposeful enough to be a headshake. "I—I'm not sure, I'm still . . ."

"What?"

"Tingling. The lights . . ." Rathe shook his head, more definitely this time. "I feel like I was hit by lightning."

"That's what you look like," Eslingen said grimly. *And damned unlikely, on a sunny day and no other sign of it.*

"Do I?" Rathe tried to sit up, but Eslingen held him back.

"No, don't push yourself. Tell me what happened."

"I was an idiot," Rathe answered, and Eslingen sighed.

"Possibly. It does seem to be going around. In what way were you an idiot?"

"I listened to Guis."

"It seems that would qualify," Eslingen said grimly, looking at the scattered flowers, and Rathe made a noise that might have been the start of laughter.

"Don't. I hurt."

"Where?" Eslingen asked, and Rathe grimaced.

"Everywhere."

He was looking a little less pale, Eslingen thought, though the pupils of his eyes were still too wide, too black for the amount of light streaming in the window. "What happened?" he said again, and this time the words seemed to register.

"Guis," Rathe began, then shook his head. "The flowers . . ." He stopped again, frowning, a little more color seeping back into his face, and Eslingen drew a slow sigh of relief. "Guis wanted me back—very convincing he was, too. But I don't know if it was him or the flowers, this happened when I knocked them over. Philip, it's important, you have to find out where these came from—"

Rathe's hand closed on Eslingen's arm, and the ex-soldier winced at the grip, loosened the fingers carefully. "I'll ask," he said soothingly. "Don't worry, we'll find out, I will, or someone from Dreams." *And I'll send someone else after Forveijl*, he added silently, *or the points will have another theatre murder on their hands*. He didn't doubt that the actor was long gone, and he took a careful breath, controlling his anger.

"It might have been aimed at Guis, too," Rathe said painfully, and Eslingen snorted.

"Do you really believe that?"

Rathe shook his head, but whatever else he would have said was cut off by the sound of footsteps in the hall. Eslingen looked up quickly, to see Gasquine and a stocky, moon-faced woman in a physician's robe filling the doorway. There were more people behind them, Jhirassi and Siredy among them, and he made a face, thinking of the new rumors.

"And what's the matter with this one?" the physician demanded.

The Phoebans were living up to their reputation, Eslingen thought. He said, "I don't know, exactly. I found him like this."

The woman squatted beside them, brushing flowers out of the way, tilted Rathe's face up so that his eyes met her own. "Hah. Not drunk or drugged, and not lightning, either, on a clear day, not to mention it's winter. Give me your left hand."

Rathe held it out, and she nodded as though he'd passed the first test. "Your pulse is good," she said after a moment, and reached into her case for a bodkin. Without warning, she pricked the tip of Rathe's forefinger, nodded when she saw him wince, then touched the other fingers as well. "Good, you feel."

"Yes," Rathe said, and sounded almost indignant.

"So you tell me what happened."

Eslingen saw the other man's gaze flicker, knew he was debating telling the truth. "I don't remember," Rathe said after a moment, and the woman grunted.

"Well, if you don't know what happened, all I can do is treat the symptoms. Which look damnably like you were hit by lightning."

"I feel like I was hit by lightning," Rathe said, and struggled to sit up. Eslingen released him reluctantly, sat back on his heels ready to catch the other man if he faltered.

"Not very likely," the physician said, and caught Rathe's right hand. "Do you feel this?"

Rathe winced. "Yes."

"Where else do you hurt?"

"My shoulders, both arms, my ribs—the muscles along them, not the ribs themselves." Rathe leaned forward slightly, grimacing as he tested his strength. "It's better than it was."

The physician grunted again. "And they'll be worse tomorrow." She looked at Eslingen. "If you're his leman—hells, if you're a friend—treat him to the baths tonight. He'll feel like he's been lifting barrels by morning."

Eslingen nodded, and the woman went on. "For the rest, well, there's arnica, which I would recommend for the bruising. You may or may not see it, but for my money you're bruised inside. And a tissane of moonwort, to ease things. You can get those at any herbalist. Go home, lie down, let your muscles rest, but don't sleep for a few hours. After that, it's the best thing for you." She pushed herself to her feet, frowning. "If you could remember what had happened to you, I might be able to offer more, but since you can't, all I can do is treat the symptoms that I see."

"Of course," Rathe said, and Eslingen thought he looked faintly embarrassed.

"Nico," Gasquine said, and Rathe grimaced, starting to push himself upright. Eslingen rose with him, steadying him, was pleased when the pointsman found his balance quickly. "What—where's Guis?"

"I don't know," Rathe answered, his voice grim. "But I will want to talk to him."

"Guis isn't in the theatre," one of the theater runners said, poking her head around the edge of the door, and in the same moment the crowd parted to admit Sohier, truncheon in hand. Someone was thinking, Eslingen thought, and felt almost giddy with relief.

"Nico?" Sohier asked, and Rathe waved his hand impatiently.

"I'm all right, or I will be. But I need two things from you, Sohier, quick as you can. First, find Guis Forveijl, someone here must know where to look. Second—" He glanced down at the flowers still littering the floor. "Find out where these came from. Who they were given to, and when."

Sohier nodded, her long face intent. "We'll get on it right away."

"We?" Rathe asked, and swayed unsteadily. Eslingen caught him, unobtrusively, he hoped, and felt the other man shiver again.

"Leenderts and me," Sohier answered. "And I can get Persilon as well. I didn't know what would be needed."

"Good woman," Rathe said. "But we need the answers as soon as possible."

"Understood," Sohier answered, and backed away.

"All right," Gasquine said sharply, and Eslingen suppressed a giggle, seeing half the crowd vanish as though by magic. "There's work to be done, and you'll all be disappointed to know, there's no disaster to be gawked at. Get along." She waited, hands on hips, while the last of the actors made their way back down the narrow hall, then turned to face the waiting men. "Did Guis do this?" she asked, and Eslingen was surprised by the pain in her voice.

"I—don't really know," Rathe answered. "It's possible, or it might have been meant for him as well."

"You're fairer than I'd be," Eslingen muttered, and Rathe managed a crooked smile.

"It's my job, Philip."

He was sounding weaker again, and Eslingen looked at Gasquine. "I'm taking him home, Mathiee. I just have to tell Master Duca—"

Gasquine held up a hand. "I'll speak to Duca. Take a low-flyer, Lieutenant." She held out her hand, shaking her head at Eslingen's automatic protest. "It was in my theatre, and maybe one of my people who did this. The least I can do is see him home safely. Now go."

Eslingen kept his arm around the other man as they made their way down the stairs, aware of the stares from actors and chorus as they made their way out into the plaza. He found a low-flyer quickly, for once, but as he held open the door, Rathe shook his head.

"No."

"Nico," Eslingen began, and Rathe shook his head carefully.

"I'm not going home, there's work to do. I want to go to Point of Dreams."

"The physician said . . ."

"I know, Philip, but my books, the books are at Dreams, and I need to look at them."

Eslingen eyed him uncertainly, on the verge of sending the driver to Rathe's rooms anyway, and Rathe shook his head again.

"No, I'm not babbling, truly, it's just there are things I have to know now. Before it's too late. Please, Philip, trust me on this."

Eslingen lifted his hands, and reached up to tap the driver on his knee. "Change of plans. Take us to Point of Dreams station."

Rathe was silent on the short ride, resting against the hard cushions, but as they turned the last corner before the station, he roused himself, working his shoulders as though they still pained him. "I'm sorry, Philip."

Eslingen gave him a startled look. "For what?"

Rathe shrugged, wincing. "For worrying you."

Eslingen hitched himself around carefully on the low-flyer's narrow seat. "Ah, and here I thought you meant about disobeying the physician's direct order to go to bed for the rest of the day."

Rathe shook his head again. "I'm not getting into bed in the middle of the day."

In spite of everything, Eslingen grinned. "That's not what you've said before this."

"There was never a bed available."

"You'll be fine," Eslingen said dryly. "No, I understand. If there's work to do—and besides, there's always the nasty thought that it's the surgeons, not the battle, that'll be the death of one."

Rathe smiled at that, and leaned his head back against the cushions, but Eslingen sighed, knowing it had all too often been the truth.

The low-flyer brought them into the courtyard of the Dreams station, the runners gathering to stare, and Rathe made a particular effort to descend without a helping hand. Eslingen let him, reluctantly, then paid off the driver and followed the other man inside. The duty point was a stocky, handsome woman, who eyed Rathe with a mixture of horror and relief, then looked down at her book, visibly mastering her emotions.

"Glad to see you're all right," she said roughly. "When the runner came . . ." She let her voice trail off, lifted one shoulder in a shrug. "They find the bastard?"

"Not yet," Rathe answered, "and at the moment we don't even know for sure who's responsible."

Eslingen snorted at that—it would be Forveijl, for his money—and Rathe gave him an admonishing look.

"We don't know," he repeated, and looked back at Falasca. "When Sohier gets back, send her up to my workroom, will you? And anything else I need to know about."

"Will do," Falasca said. "The chief's out, but I sent word to her, and I'll send her up when she comes. She'll want to talk to you."

"Thanks." Rathe turned to the stairs, face set as he worked his way up, not willing to concede to his aching muscles. Eslingen, following close behind, was grateful when they finally reached the workroom, and Rathe let himself collapse into the large chair at his worktable.

"I need my books, Philip," he began, and Eslingen shook his head.

"The stove first," he said, and stooped to rake up the coals. "And then tea." He found the pot, still half full of a dark, stewed brew, and added more water from the bucket that stood ready. "Now, what was it you wanted?"

"My books," Rathe said again, but he was smiling. "On the shelf there."

Eslingen crossed to the shelf that hung beside the long window. It was three-quarters full of slim, board-bound volumes, mostly octavos, but some larger, all held in place by an empty forcing jar. He lifted the first one down, and was not surprised to see a familiar title stamped on the dark blue cover. "Are these all the Alphabet?"

Rathe nodded, reaching for his lockbox. "All the licensed copies, and probably a tenth of the unlicensed ones."

"So you really do think this was the Alphabet at work?" In spite of himself, Eslingen couldn't quite keep the note of skepticism out of his voice as he set the first stack of books on the worktable.

"Yeah." Rathe had the box open, took out a red-bound octavo. "I know, I'm the one who said it wasn't likely to be real, but this—I don't have any other explanation."

"So what exactly did happen?" Eslingen asked. There was a stool in the corner, and he pulled it over so that he could sit facing Rathe. Behind him, he could hear condensation hissing on the sides of the kettle, and the crackle of the rising fire.

Rathe made an embarrassed face. "I told you, Guis wanted to reestablish our relationship—which, I might add, has been over longer than it lasted. But that wouldn't have mattered, except . . ." He shook his head. "It was the flowers, Philip, I'm sure of that. I could see the light gathering on them, I could hear it, it sounded like bees swarming, so I knew that was wrong, that I had to stop it. I knocked over the vase, and it shattered, and I felt, gods, I can't explain. It hurt worse than anything I'd ever felt—it was like being hit by lightning, just the pure jolt of it, and the light, and that's pretty much all I remember until you were holding me."

Eslingen nodded, suppressing a shudder of his own. Magistical things, magistry itself, were not meant to be handled so roughly; it was a commonplace that a magist's work disturbed was worse than a baited bull. He shook away the thought of what might have been, and said, his voice as level as he could manage, "That definitely sounds like the Alphabet." He looked at the books scattered on the table. "But which one?"

"Yeah, that's the question." Rathe managed a tired grin. He was looking better, Eslingen thought, less pale and interesting, but still not his usual self. "I would swear I'd seen that arrangement, too, or at least one very like it, something in one of these books. Which was why I had to come back here."

Eslingen nodded. The water was boiling now, and he rose to lift it off the heat, poured a cup for each of them before setting the kettle on the hob. "All right," he said, "where do we start?"

"It's a version that's come across my desk, probably in the last week or so," Rathe said, and took the proffered cup with an abstracted smile. "And it's one that Guis would also have been able to see—assuming of course it was Guis who made it."

"Which you have to admit is the most likely option," Eslingen said. The tea was stewed, thick and bitter, but warming, and he wrapped his hands around the heated pottery.

Rathe nodded. "Which should mean it's one of the more popular ones. Guis is the kind who'd buy the most popular version."

"And obviously bought in Dreams?"

"Probably," Rathe answered, "but that won't help us, at least not now. The booksellers all carry all the versions, or a good selection. We can try tracking down the stall where he bought a copy, maybe even trace the exact copy that way, but that's going to take time."

"Which you don't have," Eslingen said, and Rathe nodded again.

"Not with a working copy of the Alphabet loose in Astreiant."

There was a knock at the door, but before Rathe could say anything, the door swung open. A well-dressed woman—well-dressed pointswoman, Eslingen amended, presumably Rathe's Chief Point Trijn—stood there, scowling impartially at both of them.

"What the hell is happening at that theatre, Rathe? First I get a runner telling me my senior adjunct was attacked, next I find Falasca—Falasca, of all people—telling me you're alive and well, and then a runner shows up with a message about a bunch of flowers. For you, of course."

She tossed a strip of paper onto the desk in front of Rathe, who took it, and gave Eslingen an apologetic look. "Falasca wanted my job," he said. "We've been—sorting things out between us."

Eslingen nodded, understanding, and Trijn glared at him.

"And who in Sofia's name is this?"

"My leman." Rathe hesitated, as though he'd suddenly heard what he had said. "Philip Eslingen."

Eslingen blinked—this was not how he'd expected to hear it, though on the whole he had no objections—and he saw Rathe blush.

Oh, yes, we'll talk about this later, the soldier thought, trying not to grin, and met Trijn's stare guilelessly.

"Oh." Trijn's frown faded, and she gave Eslingen a look of almost genuine interest. "The other one who found the children. I was wondering what had happened to you."

Working for Hanselin Caiazzo, and now at the theatre. Eslingen opened his mouth to explain, and closed it again, not knowing where to begin. "I'm one of the Masters of Defense now," he said.

"Working on the masque," Trijn said. "All right. Fine." She looked back at Rathe. "What is all this about a bunch of flowers?"

"We have a problem, Chief," Rathe said. "There's a working copy of the Alphabet out there."

Trijn blinked, and closed her mouth firmly over anything else she might have said. She closed the door quietly behind her, and leaned against it, folding her arms across her chest. "Tell me."

Something—embarrassment, probably, Eslingen thought—flickered over Rathe's face, but he ran through the events concisely, not sparing his own blushes. "And so I figured the best thing was to come back here and start checking the various editions."

Eslingen frowned. "He has, of course, left out the fact that the physician told him to go home to bed."

Trijn's eyes flicked toward him. "Of course she did. You needn't try to impress me with his dedication, Eslingen, I'm quite familiar with it. And his stubbornness." She shook her head, crossed the room to perch in the embrasure of the window. "So. There's a working copy out there. Any idea which one?"

Rathe shook his head. "No. But at least we know who made the arrangement." He held up the scrap of paper. "Sohier says Tarran Estranger, who shares the dressing room, says Guis brought it in with him this morning, and the doorkeeper saw him with it, too. So it's Guis's doing."

"Are you planning to call a point on this Forveijl?" Trijn asked. "You've got bodily harm at the least. Whether he knew what the effects would be when the flowers were disarranged or not, he took responsibility when he created the arrangement."

Call it, Eslingen thought, and sighed when Rathe shook his head.

"It's not worth it. It'd be like calling a point on a child—if I know Guis, he's too scared right now to even think of trying anything like that again."

"Too scared right now," Eslingen said, and Trijn nodded.

"I agree. He may be too scared right now, but he'll feel cocky again soon enough. I know the type."

Rathe shook his head again, and this time it was Trijn who sighed. "All right. If not for battery, what about assault?"

Rathe gave a faint smile. "I don't think the point would stand. It was planned as seduction, and that's what it would have been. And the law doesn't recognize that."

"I do," Eslingen said, under his breath, and Rathe frowned at him.

"You're being very noble about this, Rathe," Trijn said.

"I'm not," Rathe said. "Look, everyone at the theatre knows what happened now. He has to face them—they're not going to replace him, and he's not going to drop the part, so he's going to have to go into the Tyrseia every day from now till the masque, with everyone knowing that even with the Alphabet to help him, he couldn't seduce his once-besotted ex-lover. That's got to be a blow to his self-regard."

I doubt you were ever besotted, Eslingen thought, but knew better than to say it aloud.

"Anyway," Rathe went on, "the main thing is the practical copy."

Trijn nodded. "Your mother was a gardener, right? So presumably you picked up some of her trade."

Rathe nodded, looking wary. "Some things, yeah."

"Can you name the flowers?" Trijn asked. "Better, can you remember how they were arranged? If you can sketch that, you and I—and Eslingen here, we might as well make use of him—can get through these books in a lot less time."

"Makes sense." Rathe rubbed his temples. "I know the flowers, they were those white corms with the purple splotches, with silverthorn and winterspice—more silverthorn than spice—but I'm not so sure about the arrangement. Let me see what I can do."

Trijn nodded. "Do what you can. In the meantime, Eslingen, you and I can at least look for those flowers in conjunction."

Eslingen reached for the stack of Alphabets, picked one at random and handed it to the chief point, then chose a second for himself. This one was bound in purple cloth, but the woodcuts were cheap, done fast by a less-than-talented artist, and as if to make up for that, the printer or her writer had added a list of all the plants in each arrangement at the corner of the print. He skimmed through the book, spotting the corms twice, and the silverthorn half a dozen times, but never together with winterspice. He started to set it aside, shaking his head, and Trijn said, "Put it here."

Eslingen did as he was told and reached for another volume. This time, the binding was plain, cheap, dark blue cloth, but the prints were beautiful, done with an unusual delicacy of line. The text was less interesting, doggerel verse followed by a prose vignette linking the flowers shown to some important event long past, but he turned these pages more slowly, caught in spite of himself by the illustrations. There were numbers in the bottom corners of some of the prints, he realized suddenly, numbers that looked like act and scene, and he frowned, looking up at Trijn.

"I thought no one was allowed to print anything about the masque until it had been played."

The chief point gave him a wary stare, and Rathe looked up from his sketching. "What do you mean?"

"This Alphabet," Eslingen answered, and held it up. "It's got act and scene numbers for every event that's in the play. Verse numbers, too, for some of it. Pretty much the whole story's in here, if you want to make the effort. Does that count?"

Trijn took the book from him, and paged quickly through. "What an interesting question," she murmured. "Probably not, it's not the play per se, but it might be interesting to try to call it—after we've dealt with this practical version."

Eslingen nodded, blushing, and Rathe sat up straight again, spinning his sketch so that the others could see. "That's the best I can do," he said, and frowned. "You know, I'd swear I'd seen it before."

"I most sincerely hope so," Trijn answered, not looked up from her own copy. "I'm already spending too much of this station's budget on these damn things."

Rathe made a noncommittal noise, his expression distant, then reached for the book he'd taken from his lockbox. He paged through that, scanning each of the prints, stopped with a noise of satisfaction. "There," he said, and held out the book. "That's it."

Eslingen took it before Trijn could stretch for it, held it where they both could see. "Seduction," he read. "Victory over an adversary. Regaining lost fortunes." That was the caption, cryptic as any broadsheet; on the page opposite, a writer of middle talent had composed thirteen couplets on the Ancient Queens.

"This reads like market cards," Trijn said.

"But it works," Rathe said. "Unlike market cards."

His voice was remote, as though he was trying to remember something, and he reached for the Alphabet again. Eslingen let him take it, watched the other man flip hurriedly through the pages, frown deepening as he got further into the text. Then he stopped, his face lightening abruptly, and he spun the book so that the others could see.

"I knew I'd seen that before. Chief, Leussi was growing this less than a full moon before he died."

"So?" Trijn demanded. "Was it one of the ones he bought from that woman in Little Chain?"

Rathe shook his head. "No. No, we talked about it, I didn't know what it was, and I asked him. He said it was a gift, but he didn't say from whom. I didn't think much of it at the time, but now—"

Eslingen nodded, staring at the plate. It didn't show an arrangement, but a single plant, rangy and rather ugly, with hairy leaves and stems that supported a surprisingly delicate blue flower. "Bluemory," the text named it, and gave instructions for planting and harvesting it safely. "What exactly does it mean, 'deadly in the right stars'?" he asked, and Rathe showed teeth in a feral grin.

"Exactly what it says, and you notice that these how-to-plant-and-harvest-it instructions actually tell you everything you need to make it a deadly poison."

"So you think that's what killed the intendant," Trijn said.

Rathe nodded. "I think it's a good bet—and I hope to all the gods that Holles can remember who gave him the plant."

"So why wasn't Holles killed?" Trijn asked.

"If his stars weren't right, it wouldn't hurt him," Rathe answered. "Look, to keep it safe you have to plant it when the moon is in trine to your natal star, and you have to avoid harvesting it when the moon's in your natal sign. It's all dependent on the gardener's signs, individual signs. The only general thing is you can't pick it when the sun and Seidos are in conjunction."

"I'll send to the university," Trijn said, "see if they know of the plant—the phytomancers might even grow it, if we're particularly lucky. But either way, it gives Fanier something more to work with." She held up her hand, forestalling anything else Rathe might have said. "And I'll ask Holles about it, too. There's no need to get you into any more trouble with the regents."

"I have no desire to get into any more trouble with the regents," Rathe answered. He shook his head. "I hope they've found Gus."

"They're taking their time about it," Trijn said. "Which edition is this?"

Rathe grimaced. "That's the thing. I don't think it's a recent one. Not one of the ones we've picked up in the markets. Holles gave it to me, after Leussi was killed."

Trijn's eyebrows rose at that, and Rathe spread his hands. Eslingen looked back at the print, wondering just how hard it would be to make use of these directions. One would need to know the intended victim's stars, but that wasn't too hard to find out, and then you'd need to know enough about gardening to bring the plant to a reasonable size—or would you? he wondered. Could something as small as a stalk or cutting kill? He pulled the book toward him, looking for the answer, but instead the last line of the description seemed to leap out at him: "the true name of Bluemory is Basilisk."

"Then we'd better find out who is printing it," Trijn said, "or who's done a new edition."

Rathe nodded, but anything he might have said was interrupted by a knock at the door. It opened before he could say anything, and Sohier stuck her head into the workroom.

"Oh, good, I'm glad I found you. Falasca said you were doing much better."

"Better enough," Rathe answered.

"We're going to have to track Forveijl down at home, assuming one of the addresses we got from his friends is correct, and I wondered if you wanted to come with us." Sohier tilted her head to one side, looking in that moment like a large and ungainly river bird.

"You don't have to, surely," Eslingen said, and Rathe shook his head.

"But I want to. What do you mean, Sohier, 'one of the addresses'?"

The pointswoman shrugged uncomfortably. "Gasquine was busy, so we asked some of the other actors—"

"Not from Gasquine, who would know?" Trijn asked, and Eslingen cleared his throat.

"Ah. I know where he lives." Both women looked at him, and he suppressed the urge to duck his head like a schoolboy. "When Aconin was shot—"

"Aconin was shot," Trijn repeated. "And when was this?"

"He wouldn't make the point," Rathe said, and Trijn allowed herself a sigh as dramatic as any actor's.

"Who shot him?"

"No idea, Chief," Rathe answered, and Eslingen cleared his throat again.

"I walked him to Forveijl's. He didn't want to go home."

"Not to the Court, no, he wouldn't," Rathe said. "Where is he living, anyway?"

"Close by the river, on Altmar Lane," Eslingen answered, and Sohier nodded.

"That checks. Next to Armondit's house."

Rathe nodded, reaching for his coat, and Eslingen stood. "I'm coming with you."

He thought for a moment that Rathe would protest, but Sohier nodded.

"I'd take it kindly, Lieutenant," Trijn said, and Rathe's frown deepened.

"It's not necessary."

"Answer me this," Trijn said. "Are you that happy at the thought of seeing Forveijl again?"

Rathe hesitated, and she nodded. "Not that I blame you. So Lieutenant Eslingen is more than welcome to join you—as long as he keeps any murderous impulses well in check."

Eslingen swept her a bow. "I am restraint itself, Chief Point."

Forveijl's lodgings looked very different in daylight, an old house kept in good repair, with a narrow band of fallow garden between it and the dirt of the street. Of course, it had to be kept up, Eslingen thought; Madame Armondit's house was too expensive for her to tolerate a slovenly neighbor. She also didn't like the points' presence, he saw, with an inward grin, and nodded to the doorkeeper watching suspiciously from his little house.

"Second floor," Sohier said. "Always assuming he's home."

That would be the question, Eslingen thought, following the others up the stairs, *and if it were me, I'd be long gone.* He glanced at Rathe, but the man's face was expressionless, shuttered against any show of emotion. Sohier knocked on the door, first with her fist, and then, when there was no answer, with her truncheon. There was still no answer, and Rathe swore under his breath.

"I didn't think he'd have the nerve to run."

"I'll get the landlady," Sohier said, and Eslingen flattened himself against the wall as she clattered back down the long stairs.

"Do you think he's gone to Aconin?" Eslingen asked, and Rathe tipped his head to one side, considering.

"He said it was over between them, though Sofia knows if he was telling the truth. But, no, I don't think so, mostly because I doubt Aconin's neighbors would want a stranger bringing his troubles into the Court." Rathe turned back to the door, pounding it with his closed fist. "If he's not here, I don't know where he'd go."

"Someone at the theatre will know," Eslingen said. Privately, he wasn't so sure—Forveijl had been solitary for an actor, seemed to keep very much to himself. "Or at whatever company he was with."

"Master Forveijl?" The voice came from the stairwell, a quavering voice, sexless with age, so that Eslingen had to look to see that it was an old man, remembered him as the landlady's man. "Are you sure you don't want next door?"

"No," Sohier answered, and from the sound of her voice, Eslingen guessed she'd answered the question before. "No, we don't want Madame Armondit's. Like I said, we need to get into Forveijl's lodgings."

"But he's an actor, not—" The old man broke off in confusion, and Rathe tilted his head again.

"Not what?" His tone was genuinely curious, and the old man bobbed his head.

"Not a criminal, or I never would have thought so, not him."

"We just want to talk to him," Sohier said. "You said you could let us in."

"But isn't he there?" The old man blinked at her, and Rathe's eyes narrowed.

"You heard him come in? When?"

"Noon, maybe?" The old man shook his head. "I've not heard him go out."

"It's urgent, master," Rathe said, and there was a note in his voice that made the hair stand up on Eslingen's neck. The old man seemed to hear it, too, and fumbled a ring of keys from under his short coat. He found the one he wanted, and fitted it into the lock, grunting as he struggled to turn it. The door swung back at last, and Rathe swore. Sohier caught the old man by the shoulders and swung him away from the opening, his mouth wobbling open in shock.

"Go across to Armondit's, get her to send a runner to Point of Dreams. Tell them we'll need someone from the deadhouse."

The old man nodded, tottering down the stairs, and Eslingen

stepped forward, bracing himself for the worst. Forveijl lay sprawled across the foot of his bed, one bed curtain pulled half off its rings to fall across the body. It was stained with blood, as were the disordered sheets and Forveijl's shirt and waistcoat—too much blood for him to be left alive, Eslingen thought, but even so Rathe went to him, feeling for a pulse at first one wrist and then the other. He checked before he touched the throat, and straightened, shaking his head.

"Dead for sure, then," Sohier said, and her voice cracked on the words.

"His throat's been cut." Rathe turned away from both of them, stood facing the shuttered window, and Eslingen winced. *Bad enough that your ex-lover attacks you, tries to seduce you, but then to find him dead like this, without a chance for either revenge or forgiveness . . .* He shook his head, and looked at Sohier.

"You'd better see to the body."

The pointswoman nodded, understanding, and bent to sort through the dead man's pockets. "Nothing much here," she announced after a moment. "But it wasn't robbery, he's got three pillars on him, plus a handful of small change."

A month's wages at least, Eslingen thought, though that depended on the contract he had negotiated with Gasquine, and out of the corner of his eye he saw Rathe turn back to them, his face set and grim.

"And we won't have to ask the alchemists how this one died," she went on, and then winced. "Sorry, Nico, I didn't think."

"It's all right." Rathe took a breath, glancing around the crowded room. It was tidy enough, Eslingen saw with mild surprise, though the man had probably had someone to clean for him. The bed curtains looked new, or at least well kept, and the door of the clothespress was open, revealing at least one other good coat. There were books everywhere, stacked in a case and on top of it and the scarred table. An open chest was stacked with the long, narrow sheets that were actor's copies of their parts, and at least a dozen broadsheets lay on top of that, spilling out across the table, the one sign of clutter. Or had someone started to search the room? Eslingen wondered.

"What we need to know is how long he's been dead," Rathe said, and Sohier nodded.

"He's cold."

Rathe nodded, expressionless. "And the old man said he'd come home at noon, or thereabouts, he thought."

"But he said he hadn't heard him leave," Sohier said. "Which means he didn't hear the murderer leave, either."

"At least not to notice," Rathe answered. "We'll have to talk to him about that. But for now—" He glanced around the room again. "First we find the Alphabet."

Sohier nodded, and together the three went through the shelved books, plays mostly, Eslingen saw, and guessed they were ones Forveijl had done well in. He knew some of the names, but not all, paused for a moment over a copy of something called *The Fair's Promise and Payment*. Aconin had put his own name down as playwright, he saw from the title page, and Rathe grimaced.

"I hope it reads better than it plays."

"Oh?" Eslingen gave it a second, curious glance, and Rathe sighed.

"That's the play Aconin wrote for him, wooed him and won him with it. I shouldn't talk, I never saw it."

Behind him, Sohier lifted her head, and then seemed to think better of anything she might have said, hunched one shoulder instead, and kept sorting through the papers. They worked their way across the room—it was a little like the looting after a fight, Eslingen thought, down to the body on the bed, except that he was careful to do as the others did, and put each piece back in its place. Sohier was first to straighten, hands on hips, but she waited until the others finished before she spoke.

"Sir, there's no copy of the Alphabet here."

"No." Rathe sighed, his eyes straying back to the dead man. "He didn't deserve this," he said softly, then shook himself. "Sohier, I want Aconin, as soon as possible."

"Aconin?" Sohier frowned. "Why him? I mean, this is hardly a lovers' quarrel—"

Rathe was shaking his head, and she broke off instantly. "Sweet Sofia, I haven't had a chance to report it, but the landseur Aubine told me this morning that someone had taken a shot at his coach as he left for the theatre."

"At Aubine?" Eslingen felt himself flush, realizing he'd spoken aloud, and Rathe looked at him.

"Broke a window on his carriage, and threatened to freeze all the plants he was carrying. Aubine was riding on the box, mind you, or it might have been him. Why do you sound surprised?"

Eslingen spread his hands, wishing he'd kept his mouth shut. "I don't know—I suppose I was wondering why anyone would want to kill him?"

"And he thinks Aconin did it?" Sohier asked.

Rathe shrugged. "He says that the man who did it was built like Aconin. But Aconin's not at the theatre, when he's been at every rehearsal since the beginning, or so Mathiee says, plus what Aubine says, plus he wrote the play using, I am certain, some copy of the Dis-damned Alphabet, and when I go to question Aconin's lover, look who ends up dead. I want him found."

"You can't think he did this," Eslingen said, and was mildly surprised by his own vehemence. "It's not like him—and besides, he's been attacked twice himself."

"Could you have done him more of an injury that evening, if you'd been the man with the pistol?" Rathe demanded.

Eslingen hesitated. "Probably—but I don't know where the man was standing, or what his line of sight was like. The light was against him, that's for certain."

"And the second time he wasn't attacked," Rathe went on. "His rooms were destroyed. You said it yourself, that's a warning, 'no quarter.' It could be he's fighting back."

"I just don't think it's like him," Eslingen said again. "Not Chresta. Oh, he'll maim you with words, all six days of the week, but use a knife . . . It's not his way."

Rathe stared at him for a long moment, his expression unreadable. "How long has it been since you've known him?" he said at last, and Eslingen swore under his breath.

"Long enough."

"People change," Rathe said, almost gently. "Besides, if you're right, he's in worse danger than poor Guis ever was."

That was true enough to close Eslingen's mouth over any accusation he might have made. Whatever else it was, this wasn't Rathe striking out blindly at the man who had stolen his former lover; that wasn't Rathe's style, any more than it was Aconin's to lash out with a knife instead of a deadly pen. And that meant he was right: for whatever reason, Aconin had to be found.

10

◆ ··· ◆

The lights were different today, the common lanterns doused, the mage-lights changed, set now into the elaborate practical housings, whose lenses and colored glass doors could turn their light to any time of day or night, and any weather. Even as Eslingen watched, a sceneryman made her final adjustment to one of the smaller globes, setting the last piece of ambered glass into its collar, and then placed a mage-fire lamp carefully in the center of the iron sphere. Instantly, she was bathed in strong sunlight, sunset light, and she stepped back, motioning to another sceneryman. He hauled on one of the ropes running up into the fly space, and the globe rose majestically, sliding into its place among a cluster of other practicals. Eslingen squinted up at them, counting at least a dozen, mostly amber or red, some left plain, one or two tinted with green and yellow, and shook his head as he looked back at the stage. The light there was almost natural now, the steady, neutral sunlight of an early summer day. The colors of the chorus's coats, which had seemed odd, too bright under the mage-lights, now looked normal, and Aubine's arrangements were vivid as a summer garden at the downstage corners of the stage.

"Impressive, isn't it?" Siredy said cheerfully. "At least this is a simple setting. Now, when I was in *Aufilia's Revenge,* we had two night scenes, and a thunderstorm. I felt as though I was spending all my time making sure I was out of range of the thunderflashes."

"You were in that?" That was Jhirassi, coming up beside them, his hair scraped back to go under a new wig. He wasn't yet in full costume, just the underpieces, breeches and stiff vest, and his eyes were made enormous with makeup.

Siredy gave him an appreciative glance, and Eslingen bit back a smile. "I was the villain's henchman—the one who never gets a line except, yes, mistress."

"But the fights were marvelous," Jhirassi said. "And I enjoyed the play."

"So did I," Siredy answered.

"Thunderflashes and all?" Eslingen asked, and both men looked at him as though they'd forgotten his presence. He smiled at them, and to his amusement, Siredy blushed.

"They made things interesting. Technically, it was a complicated piece."

"And a great deal of fun," Jhirassi added. "I'm sorry you didn't see it, Philip."

"So am I," Eslingen said. He looked at Siredy. "Thunderflashes?"

"They're sort of like the practicals," the other master answered. "Except larger, and with a mirrored back that reflects the light."

"The climactic duel takes place at the height of a raging storm," Jhirassi added. "Lit by lightning at carefully planned moments."

"Most impressive," Eslingen said.

Siredy made a face. "When the timing is right, yes. Anyway, there's a small flash charge in each pot—something chemical, I think, it stank to the central heavens—and a piece of slowmatch to set it off. Once those are lit and set, there's nothing you can do to stop them, so half the time, Bernarin and I were trying to time the fight to the flashes, instead of the other way round."

Jhirassi looked even more impressed, and Eslingen had to swallow a laugh. But still, it was impressive—he'd dealt with slowmatch before, in the field, and knew how hard it was to gauge how long it would take a length to burn. "You needed a sapper," he said aloud, and Siredy nodded.

"This was at the old Merveille," Jhirassi said. "Now the Bells. It just hasn't been the same since Madame Ombredanne died."

"For which some of us are grateful," Siredy said. "And yes, Gavi, it was impressive, but you have to admit, most of the shows were just new ways to show off her toys."

"Oh, I know," Jhirassi answered. "But they were such good toys."

Siredy lifted an eyebrow at that, but before he could say anything, the bookholder called Jhirassi's name. The actor lifted a hand in instant obedience, and took his place in the forming scene. It was the last council meeting, leading up to the climactic duel, and Siredy looked over his shoulder, automatically counting heads, before he turned back to Eslingen.

"All there," he said. "Gavi's right, it was exciting to watch. But I doubt he was ever onstage with any of the devices."

"Worse than *The Drowned Island*?" Eslingen asked idly, letting his eyes slide past the other. Yes, the duelists were all in readiness, and even in their proper costumes, antique longcoats crusted with cheap cut-glass stones and broad sashes with huge rosettes. De Besselin looked almost as pale as his shirt, and Eslingen hoped the boy could remember his lines this time.

"Much worse," Siredy said. "Madame Ombredanne believed in pyrotechnics."

Eslingen choked back a snort, remembering the lecture he'd gotten about fire backstage, and Siredy nodded.

"Exactly so. There were two small fires at the Mervcille just in the year I played there. Madame used to hire half a dozen rivermen just to stand by with buckets. I'm surprised any of us lived to tell the tale."

Eslingen laughed appreciatively, but his eyes strayed to the duelists again. Still all there, though for once the two landames weren't standing arm in arm, and he hoped nothing had happened to damp their friendship. They had defied the looks and whispers, and Aconin's acid tongue, to maintain their affair openly; it would be a shame if the family enmities won after all. "Do you want to herd them on, or shall I?" he asked, and Siredy lifted his eyebrows.

"I'll send them on, if you'll get them off again."

Eslingen nodded, knowing he'd been given the easier job, and grateful for it, and turned away, heading deeper into the backstage area so that he could cross the stage behind the massive backpiece. He had seen it from the pit for the first time just the day before, and it had taken his breath away: a mountain landscape, hills rising steeply to either side to frame the narrow valley. In the first act, and in the third, it was the Pass of Jetieve, in the second and fifth, the view from de Galhac's fortress, and in the rest, all the mountains that bordered the palatinate; the versatiles were painted to change and complete each different setting. They were almost ready for the performance, everything in place except the final blessings of the chamberlains and their magists, and Eslingen paused at the center of the backpiece, peering out through the single narrow slit in the stiff canvas. Only the amateurs used it, or so he'd been told, but he'd also seen more than one of the professionals pausing to glance through the tiny gap. The only difference was that they didn't use their hands to widen it, and risk spoiling the illusion.

Through the slit, he could see the actors standing in a semicircle around bes'Hallen, who stood stage center, draped in a floor-length veil that gleamed like gold in the warm light of the practicals. Between their bodies, posed in stiff formality, he could see the empty benches of the pit, and the dark shadows of the galleries—except, he realized, the pit wasn't entirely empty. Gasquine was sitting on one of the center benches, perhaps eight or ten rows back, her head and shoulders just visible as she watched intently. The chief scenery-man sat with her, and a tall woman in a long black gown who had to be one of the chamberlains. By rights, Eslingen thought, Aconin should be with them, but the playwright was still missing—not at the theatre, and not, according to Rathe, at his lodgings, or anywhere else he had been known to frequent. The gossips whispered that maybe he had caused the deaths, that at the least he was likely to be the person who'd put Forveijl up to trying the trick with the flowers, and quite possibly the one who killed Forveijl for it afterward, though there was a minority opinion that insisted that Rathe himself had done it. No one had said that to his face, of course, and Eslingen could guess that there were probably a few people who thought he could have done it—defending his lover—but that was easy to ignore. But Aconin wasn't responsible, he thought, and turned away from the backpiece, crossing to the far side of the stage. It was more crowded there, and he had to press himself against the brick wall to avoid a pair of scenerymen hauling what looked like a roll of canvas. Another scenepiece, he guessed, or a carpet for one of the soueraine's entrances. It wasn't like Aconin to set someone up like that—or at least it wasn't like him not to hang around to enjoy his victim's disgrace. Eslingen made a face, remembering a childhood beating for stealing fruit from a neighbor's garden. Aconin had put him up to it, and had enjoyed the outcome, the shouts and the pursuit and Eslingen's wails, almost as much as he would have enjoyed the stolen plums. He'd gotten his own back, of course, and Aconin had learned better than to try that again, but the playwright had never been able to resist that kind of manipulation. *And that*, he thought, *is why I'm so sure he isn't behind any of this. If he was, he'd still be at the theatre, too secure in his own cleverness to think of running away.* But that was almost impossible to explain to Rathe—the pointsman was right, it had been years since he'd been in contact with Aconin, but he doubted Aconin had changed fundamentally in those years.

He took his place in the wings, resting his halberd on the toe of his shoe to keep from making unwanted noise on the hollow stage, listening with half an ear to the end of the council scene. Ramani's long speech was coming up, and then the council exited, and the battle—his responsibility—would begin. He could see Siredy waiting opposite, the duelists ready behind him, lined up two by two for the fighting entrance, and took a deep breath, willing everything to go right. The chorus had worked hard, and so had the masters; Tyrseis permitting, all would go well. This was stage fright, the demon that even the professionals propitiated as much as possible, and he looked back to the pit and galleries, trying to imagine them filled with faces. The thought was dizzying—a thousand faces, more, all watching his handiwork—and he took another breath, grateful that he had no on-stage part in this particular performance. That might come, but, mercifully, not yet.

He made a face, angry at his own fears, looked over his shoulder to see the great wave still looming over his shoulder. It was too large to move, would probably stay there until some other play needed the mechanism for a similar effect, or so the scenerymen had said, and he wondered how long that would be. Probably long enough that de Raçan's death would have been long forgotten—already most of the actors and chorus talked about the dead watchman, and Forveijl, less about the landseur. But they all had to be connected, Eslingen thought, and stepped back automatically as Aubine slipped past him, murmuring an apology, a trug full of flowers hooked in the crook of his arm. All the deaths had to do with the same thing—certainly with the masque, and maybe with the succession, though exactly how that would work, he couldn't begin to see. The broadsheets, especially those fostered by Master Eyes, were having a field day, lurid tales of the haunted theatre drawing avid buyers to the stalls. The only mercy, Rathe had said sourly, was that de Raçan's death was the only one that could be construed as political, and no one had, as yet, made the connection between the members of the chorus, and the claimants to Chenedolle's throne. The other deaths covered a wide range of Astreiant's population, from guildmember to artisan to artist—no connection except for the theatre. And that was only enough for children's tales of haunting, not for anything more substantial.

Onstage, Ramani had finished her speech—Hyver was good, he thought, not for the first time, might be better than bes'Hallen someday—and stalked off, followed more slowly by the council. Above him, he heard the soft rumble of well-greased pulleys, and the light brightened, yellow-lensed practicals lowered to give the illusion of bright daylight. Across the stage, Siredy touched his leader's shoulder—Simar, the landseur with the flowers, had proved to be far more sensible than his posies would suggest—and the pairs began to work their way onto the stage, swords clashing in steady rhythm. Eslingen released breath he hadn't known he was holding as the second pair found their way past the first, took their place upstage and to the left. *So far,* he thought, *so far, so good*—except that Txi and de Vannevaux were out of step, Txi scowling at her erstwhile lover, her attacks too aggressive for pretense. Eslingen frowned, seeing the woman mouth something, saw de Vannevaux break the planned sequence with an attack, and swore under his breath. This was what they'd all been worried about, what they'd tried to drill out of the chorus, the excitement that said a fencer had to win at all costs. Txi cried out, wordless, stumbling back from another unexpected attack, and d'Yres missed a parry dodging away from her. The air was heavy suddenly, thick with tension, and the other duelists faltered, turning to see what was happening. In the pit, Gasquine rose to her feet, mouth open to call the halt, and Eslingen saw Siredy pale and staring in the far wing, as Txi swore, and wedged her blade against the stage floor, snapping the bate from the end of the blade.

"Enough!" Siredy shouted, and in the same moment Gasquine cried out for them to hold, but the women ignored both of them, de Vannevaux struggling now to hold her own against the suddenly deadly blade. And it could be deadly, Eslingen knew, even without the point, just the jagged edge could wound, maim, even kill. He saw Siredy fumbling for his own sword, set somewhere out of reach, and launched himself onto the stage, snatching the bated blade from de Besselin's slack fingers.

"Hold!" he shouted, circling for a space to intervene, but the women ignored him, de Vannevaux swearing as she made a fruitless lunge, the bated blade bending harmlessly against Txi's side. Txi's riposte was instant and effective, would have been deadly if it hadn't caught in the other woman's corset, sliding across the metal boning to tear into the flesh of her upper arm. De Vannevaux screamed, more anger than pain, and Eslingen stepped between them, blade flashing out to engage Txi's.

"Enough!" Siredy shouted again, sword in hand, and Jarielle caught de Vannevaux by the shoulders, swinging her bodily away from the other woman. And then, as suddenly as a candle blown out by wind, the tension broke, and Txi sank to her knees, sword clattering unheeded to the stage as she clapped both hands over her mouth. De Vannevaux's eyes were wide, disbelieving, and she looked from her erstwhile lover to the blood staining her shirt as though she expected one of them to vanish.

"Tyrseis, protector of this place," Gasquine said. "Would your ladyships care to explain what that was about?"

Txi burst into gulping tears, bowing until she was bent double, skirts pooled about her on the bare stage. De Vannevaux shook her head as though she were dazed.

"Madame—mistress," she began, and shook her head again. "It's—I think it's my fault, we quarreled . . ." Her voice trailed off, as though she could no longer remember what she'd done, and she sank to her knees beside Txi, reaching for the other woman. Txi jerked herself away from de Vannevaux's touch, never lifting her head, and Eslingen saw the matching tears in de Vannevaux's eyes.

"There's no harm done," Siredy said softly, kneeling in his turn beside Txi, "just nerves." The look on his face belied the soothing words.

"Oriane and her Bull," Gasquine said. "If the two of you can't control yourselves, I will personally take you over my knee and spank you as your mothers never did. I will not have this—this nonsense interfering with my play. Is that clear?"

De Vannevaux nodded, still not speaking, and Txi lifted her head, showing a face streaked with tears and paint. "Mistress, I'm so sorry. I don't know what got into me."

"It was my fault," de Vannevaux said, almost in the same moment. "Oh, Anile, can you ever forgive me?"

Txi burst into tears again, and threw herself into the other woman's lap. "I hurt you," she said, voice muffled against de Vannevaux's skirt, and de Vannevaux hugged her, heedless of the pain of her injured arm.

Gasquine stared at them for a moment longer, hands on hips, then slowly reseated herself. "This will not happen again," she said, and Eslingen stooped to help de Vannevaux to her feet. "Now. We begin again, from your exit."

Eslingen glanced at Siredy, who tipped his head toward the nearer wing. He nodded, and tightened his hold on de Vannevaux's shoulders, urging her toward the shadows. Siredy did the same with Txi, and together they brought the two women offstage, past the actors waiting to come on. Their eyes were bright and curious, and Txi buried her face in her hands again. Behind him, Eslingen could hear Simar giving a shaky count, and then the tramp of feet as the remaining duelists made their planned exit. The waiting actors made their entrance, not without backward glances, and Siredy patted Txi's shoulder gently.

"It's nerves," he said. "Stage fright. It takes people strange ways. You'll be all right."

Txi nodded jerkily, her eyes on the other woman. "But Iais—oh, I'm so sorry."

"Let me see, madame," Eslingen said, and turned de Vannevaux so that he could examine the wound. She let him move her, her eyes vacant, let him turn her arm palm out so that he could see the cut. It was little more than a long scratch up the underside of her upper arm, the bleeding already slowed, but he found a handkerchief in his pocket, folded it to a pad, and pressed it against the wound. De Vannevaux flinched, but put her own hand over it obediently enough.

"Anile," she said. "Oh, gods, will you forgive me?"

"I'm the one who needs forgiveness," Txi answered, and something moved in the shadows behind her. Aubine, Eslingen realized, and thought for an instant that the landseur held something in his left hand. Then he came forward into the light reflecting from the stage, eyes wide and appalled.

"Anile, are you all right? What a terrible thing, you should go home and rest."

His hands were empty after all, Eslingen saw.

De Vannevaux shook her head, but Txi straightened. "Aubine's right," she said. "You should have that seen to, and then, yes, you should rest. I'll never forgive myself—"

"Hush," Siredy said, and blushed, as though he'd only just realized what he'd said, but Aubine nodded in agreement.

"Quite right. There's been enough—forgive me, Iais—there's been enough raw emotion today. You need to be calm, take deep breaths. It will pass."

What will pass? Eslingen wondered. Stage fright, he supposed, if anyone was going to believe that explanation.

Txi managed a shaky nod, her costume glittering as she did as she was told.

"Iais," de Vannevaux said. "Iais, I'll go home—and, yes, to a physician, too, if we can find one that will be discreet—but only if you'll go with me."

"You can't want me," Txi said, and de Vannevaux managed a watery smile.

"I started it, Anile. I suppose I got what I deserved."

"Very wise of you both," Aubine said briskly. "Why don't you take my carriage? I'll have my man bring it round, have him take you wherever you'd like to go." He moved away, still talking, and the landames followed docilely, their attention on each other. Eslingen shook his head, watching them go.

"Seidos's Horse," he said, not quite under his breath, and Siredy shrugged.

"Passions run high at the last rehearsals, and theirs were high enough to start with. It'll be worse tomorrow."

"Tyrseis preserve us all," Eslingen answered, and surprised a smile from the other man. "Verre, you can't mean it, that this always happens. Not like this."

Siredy paused, his smile turning wry. "Well, no, not quite like this, but then, we don't usually have the quality onstage. But there's always something, these last two days. They never pass without tears and screaming."

Eslingen shook his head, not convinced, and Siredy took a step away.

"Anyway, we need to make sure the half-pikes are ready. Will you help?"

Eslingen started to nod, but a patch of something pale on the boards where Aubine had been standing caught his eye. "I'll be along in a minute," he said, and Siredy sighed.

"See that you are."

Eslingen bit back an angry answer—*and maybe Siredy is right, tempers are starting to fray, my own included*—but waited until the other man had turned away before he stooped to collect the object. It was a flower, pale and bell-shaped, its stem neatly snapped, and Eslingen stared at it for a long moment, unwelcome thoughts crowding his mind. Rathe had said that the right way to disrupt one of the

Alphabet's arrangements was to pull it apart flower by flower—to take the right flower from it, not to break it apart. Had the Alphabet been at work again—had that been the cause of the landames' sudden quarrel? He shook his head, not wanting to believe it—but Aubine had been there, he remembered, slipping across the front of the pit to fiddle with his arrangements just as the duelists made their entrance. Not Aconin, then, but Aubine; not the playwright, but the sponsor who had put his name behind it, possibly commissioned it. Ignoring Siredy's glare, he slipped across the back of the stage again, dodging actors and scenerymen, made his way to the front of the wings, looking for another patch of white. Sure enough, it was there, another broken flower, stem snapped and cast aside. He stared at it for a long moment, then craned his head to see the nearer of the two arrangements. There were no other flowers like this one in it, and its simplicity would have been lost among the showier blooms, but he was suddenly absolutely sure that it had been the keystone, the one piece that had made the arrangement active. *Which means Aubine,* he thought again, *and that still makes no sense.* Why would Aubine kill de Raçan, and the watchman—well, he might have killed the watchman for the same reason anyone would have, because the man knew what happened in the theatre after hours, and if Aubine had been testing his arrangements, the watch would have been the first to know, but there was no reason to kill Forveijl. . . . Unless he, too, had suspected something. Rathe would know, he told himself firmly, Rathe would be able to figure it out. He tucked the flowers carefully into the pocket of his coat, and started back to join Siredy. The main thing now was to get through the rest of the rehearsal as quietly, as unobtrusively, as possible, and get the flowers and his suspicions home to Rathe before Aubine noticed that anything had changed.

The day dragged to an end at last, and Eslingen was quick to leave the theatre, stretching his legs to get through the narrow streets. To his relief, Rathe was home before him, lamps and stove lit and welcoming. To his dismay, he wasn't alone. b'Estorr was there, sitting at the small table, looking as disheveled as Eslingen had ever seen him, his long hands systematically destroying a small, common flower. Eslingen smoothed away an involuntary frown as Rathe looked round at him, a harried look on his own face easing when he saw Eslingen. Eslingen managed a smile he knew was strained. He needed to talk to Rathe now, needed to show him the flowers and hear what the pointsman had to say about these—quite fantastic—events. And that was hardly something he could do in front of b'Estorr: it was one thing to risk making a fool of himself in private, but he refused to have the magist for an audience.

b'Estorr hardly seemed aware of his presence, though, not pausing in the flow of talk. "—and I've spoken to the phytomancers, all of them, including one I didn't think was a fool, but she says only that there is no such thing as a verifiable copy, a working copy, of the Alphabet, that the Alphabet is pure folly, and that we should put this aside and look for more reasonable explanations." He broke off then, looking, for the first time in Eslingen's acquaintance, chagrined. "Oh. Hello, Philip."

Eslingen nodded, knowing he looked stiff. "Istre. Haven't seen you in a while. How're things at the university?"

b'Estorr took a breath and gave a short, bitter laugh. "You can't imagine. The College of Phytomancy has ruled their business is the properties of individual plants, not plants gathered into bunches, so the Alphabet is not their province even if it did work. Ybares—the one I didn't think was a fool—says that even if it were their business, the Alphabet can't work, so she doesn't want to hear about it."

"It demonstrably does work," Eslingen said. "After what happened to Nico—"

"Oh, that didn't happen," b'Estorr said savagely. "Or if it happened, it didn't happen the way we think. Or if it happened the way we think, it wasn't the plants, and therefore it wasn't the Alphabet." He finished shredding the flower and flung the petals onto the table.

"Welcome home, Philip," Rathe said, and b'Estorr blushed, the color staining his fair skin.

"I'm sorry, Philip, I'm ranting. But it's driving me mad."

"I can see that," Eslingen said, and Rathe frowned.

"So if it's none of those things, Istre, do they say what it might have been?"

b'Estorr shook his head. "It's not their province," he repeated, unhappily brushing the mangled bloom into his hand.

"They can't mean it," Eslingen said, and b'Estorr smiled without humor.

"Of course they can. The politics of the university are easily as bad as the politics of Chadron."

"So what do we do about it?" Rathe asked.

b'Estorr sighed, visibly taking himself in hand. "I honestly don't know, Nico. I'd have thought this was enough proof for any of them, but if it isn't . . ." He took a breath. "I'll keep talking, see if I can't—persuade—at least one of them to reconsider."

"The stars don't seem to favor that," Eslingen said, in spite of himself, and b'Estorr shook his head.

"No more do they." He reached for his cloak, hanging by the door, and Rathe spoke quickly.

"No need to go—"

"I'm having dinner with Ybares," b'Estorr answered grimly, and his tone did not bode well for the other magist. "I don't want to be late."

"Good luck, then," Rathe said, and shook his head as the door closed behind the necromancer. "I think you're right, Philip, the folly stars have reached the university." Without waiting for an answer, he crouched in front of the stove, began digging through the low flat box that stood beside it.

Eslingen blinked. "What are you doing?"

"Trying to find some vegetables for dinner."

"At this time of year?"

"They keep," Rathe said mildly. "You can help, or you can comment."

"I'll comment," Eslingen said, and unwrapped himself from his cloak. He'd given up on fashion over a week ago, and tonight he'd been particularly glad of the extra layers.

"You would," Rathe answered. "So, did anything happen at the theatre today that I should know about?" He found a final long finger of parsnip, and held it up triumphantly before dropping it into a basin of water to wash away the last of the clinging sand.

"Yes," Eslingen answered, and the other man straightened, dinner forgotten.

"Tell me."

"The landames, the ones whose families are at feud?"

Rathe nodded. "The ones who've been—"

"Just so." Eslingen took a breath, let himself drop into a chair close to the stove. "Today, at rehearsal, with a chamberlain watching, no less, all of a sudden the feud is alive again. They insult each other, and Txi finally snaps the bate of her weapon and they go at it in earnest."

"Not dead—hurt?" Rathe asked, his hands very still.

Eslingen shook his head. "Not even much hurt, just a bad scratch.

And they were friends again, left together to go home and consult a physician."

"So what caused it?" Rathe came to his feet, settled automatically into the chair opposite.

"Siredy says it's nerves, stage fright making tempers short," Eslingen answered.

"I've never heard of actors doing anything like that," Rathe said.

"Ah, but they aren't actors," Eslingen answered. "At least that's the explanation that's being accepted—I think mostly because no one wants to let anything else go wrong. But—" He leaned back in his chair, fumbling with his coat, and finally produced the pair of flowers. "But afterward, I found these backstage. They were just lying there, on the floor, a yard or so, maybe, from the nearest arrangement. Each one with its—neck, I don't know—broken."

Rathe took them, frowning, turning them over in his fingers. "They weren't there before?"

Eslingen shook his head. "Too dangerous, with all the dancing and the fights. The scenerymen keep the floor clear and dry, spotless. No, these weren't there before the fight, and they were afterward."

"You think there was a posy, something from the Alphabet."

"There's more," Eslingen said, and heard Rathe sigh.

"There always is."

"When the duel scene started, I saw Aubine working with the flowers, the big bunches right downstage. And I am certain he dropped this one—I saw him with it in his hand, I'm all but certain of it, right before he offered the landames the use of his carriage to take them home."

Rathe was very still. "Getting them away before they could think how odd it was, do you suppose?"

"It's possible." Eslingen took a breath. "Nico, if it's Aubine—"

"First things first," Rathe said, and pushed himself away from the table. "I brought this home, wanted to study it, see if there was anything special about it—and it hasn't been reprinted, by the way, not this edition." He came back with the red-bound copy of the Alphabet that he had received from Holles, slid it across the table. Eslingen caught it with a groan, knowing what came next, and Rathe nodded. "I want you to see if you recognize any of the arrangements."

"I'm not a gardener," Eslingen said.

"You can read," Rathe answered. "And you have eyes—I know you're observant. Just see if you can recognize them."

Eslingen bowed his head obediently, turning the soft pages. It was very like all the other editions of the Alphabet he'd looked at in Rathe's workroom, woodcuts on one page, text on the page opposite, and he skimmed through them quickly, trying to remember the pattern he had seen. "This one," he said at last, pointing to an arrangement labeled "Confusion." "And Anger."

Rathe nodded, leaning over his shoulder now to study the pictures. "It makes sense, doesn't it? Confusion to blur the new friendship—and all of you, your thoughts, to make it seem reasonable that landames should behave like this—and Anger to trigger the feud again. But why now?"

"A test?" Eslingen suggested, leaning back to see the other man's face. "To make sure—something else—is going to work?"

"Oh, that's an ugly thought," Rathe said. "But it makes sense." He shook his head. "I said if I knew how, this time, I'd know who. And if it's the flowers, it has to be Aubine. He knows more about them than anyone. And nobody else has a connection to all the dead—including Ogier, he's the only one who is connected to both Ogier and the masque. But I've no idea why."

"Is he connected to any of the potential claimants?" Eslingen asked, and Rathe shook his head.

"In that, he's as innocent as the snow."

"Because he can?"

Rathe looked down at him, frowning. "Sorry?"

Eslingen made a face. "It was something he said once. True enough, in the original context—he was talking about providing flowers for the masque, and for all the rehearsals, too, all because he could—but it struck me odd then."

"If that's the case," Rathe said, "then he's well and truly mad. And mad he may well be, but it didn't strike me as that kind of lunacy."

"I agree," Eslingen said, and Rathe reached for the Alphabet again, his scowl deepening as he flipped through the pages. "What is it?"

"Maybe I'm the madman. I've gone through all the flowers I know I've seen at the theatre, and while a few of them are in here, they're not—not in the right combinations, or the right seasons, or anything, to give me any idea what he might be planning."

Eslingen shook his head, slowly. "They're not the flowers that will be there for the masque. He's changed them almost every day—brought in all new ones today."

His voice trailed off as he realized what he'd said, and Rathe swore under his breath. "Were they different?"

"Some were," Eslingen answered. "Maybe most were. The arrangements were certainly different."

"Of course they would be," Rathe said. "Damn the man." He shook his head. "And if it's Aubine, then he's killed everyone who's gotten in his way. Starting with Leussi."

"Leussi?" Eslingen frowned. "I know that was murder, but how does it fit in to the theatre deaths?"

"Leussi was a chamberlain," Rathe said. "He would have ruled on the masque. He had a copy of the Alphabet—an old copy, a practical copy, maybe even the same edition Aubine has. He of all people would have seen just how dangerous this might be, he was testing it out before he died. And his ghost was bound because even if he couldn't name his murderer, he might have been able to warn his fellows, or at least Holles, against the play. As it is, Aubine was careful enough—Holles has no idea where the plant came from, he hardly noticed it, couldn't even say when it arrived."

"But why?" Eslingen asked. He took the book gently from Rathe's hands, flipped back to the arrangements he'd seen earlier that day. Yes, that was them, no mistaking it, and he shook his head in confusion. "What's he going to do with this play that's so important that he'll kill to preserve it? If it has nothing to do with the succession . . ."

Rathe ignored him, his eyes fixed on something invisible, beyond the shadows. "De Raçan . . . I don't know, I've never been able to fit him in, but there's something so—well planned, well thought out—about his death that I almost wonder if it was a punishment, some private thing between them. But Ogier, Ogier's easy, he worked in the succession houses, he knew what plants were being grown, knew enough of phytomancy that he could have suspected, if not the Alphabet, then some magistry. And he was running from a magist when he died, I'm sure of that from the way he burned his clothes. Guis—Guis used an arrangement, and he could have said where he got it, which meant he had to be killed. Aconin—"

"Aconin wrote the play," Eslingen said. "So he had to have something to go on. And he's been one of Aubine's intimates. Plus, of course, he and Guis were still close. You might have thought to look to Aconin as soon as Guis was killed." He paused, remembering. "And, Nico, I never thought anything of it, but at least twice when I thought Aconin wanted to talk to me, it was Aubine who interrupted us. I just thought Chresta didn't want to be overheard."

"Sofia," Rathe breathed. "It fits, Philip, it fits all too neatly."

Eslingen nodded. "But why?" He glanced down at the book again, his eyes straying from the list of plants and their properties to the stories that accompanied them. Both Confusion and Anger were accompanied by stories about love—love denied, love scorned—and he flipped through a few more pages, looking for the most harmful arrangements, the ones designed to kill and maim. All were matched with stories of love, lost love, love rejected and turned to hate, and he looked back up at Rathe, eyes going wide. "Look at the stories. They're all about revenge—the stories aren't, actually, but that's the suggestion. The arrangements are revenge for love gone wrong."

"Revenge for his leman," Rathe said.

Eslingen closed his eyes, wishing he could reject his own idea. "His common-born leman," he corrected. "Murdered by his grandmother. And, Seidos, that could explain de Raçan, couldn't it? Everybody knew about him and Siredy, how de Raçan wanted him back just for the convenience—do you think that's why Aubine killed him, that it hit too close to home?"

Rathe hesitated, then nodded slowly. "It could be. And it might have been a nice chance to test out a new arrangement."

Eslingen shivered at the thought. "But you said the grandmother's been dead for what, seven years?"

"At least that." Rathe frowned down at the book. "Sweet Sofia, we don't have nearly enough to call a point—we've only just got enough to start asking questions—and the masque plays the day after tomorrow." He shook his head. "There isn't enough time. Not to prove this—any of this."

"Can it be postponed?" Eslingen asked, and Rathe shook his head.

"I don't know. It's never happened, not in my lifetime—but then, there's never been cause before." Rathe pushed himself upright, frowning at the vegetables still soaking in the basin, and pulled them out one by one to lay them gently on a folded cloth. "We'll have to go to Trijn."

"Do you want me to go with you?" Eslingen asked, and Rathe smiled.

"I think you'd better."

✧   ✧   ✧

Trijn lived in Point of Dreams, but in the narrow band of guildmistresses' houses, well away from the theatres. Expensive houses, Rathe thought automatically, and found himself checking the garden walls for loose bricks. He had begun his career as a pointsman in just such a neighborhood, had learned all the ways a clever thief could slip into an unwary household, make off with food, linens, spare clothes, even the family silver. The householders here seemed to know the same techniques, left nothing to chance, no loose bricks for a foothold, no windows unshuttered, lamps lit and personal watchmen drowsing in corner boxes, ready to raise the alarm. A few of them lifted their heads, watching two strangers pass along their street, and one even lifted his lantern in question and warning before he saw the truncheon at Rathe's belt.

"A nice neighborhood your chief point lives in," Eslingen whispered. "She does well in fees?"

"She comes from good family," Rathe answered, his own voice low. He didn't know much about Trijn's attitude toward fees, now that he thought of it—he hadn't been at Dreams long enough for it to become an issue—but he doubted she needed them, not if her sister was the grande bourgeoise.

"She must," Eslingen said, looking at the houses, and Rathe paused to study the carving over the nearest door. Trijn lived in the house of the two hares, according to the directions he had memorized right after coming to Point of Dreams; this house was decorated with a cheerful frieze of rats feasting on a sea of overflowing grain bags, and he moved on, shaking his head slightly. The original owner must have been born in the Rat Moon, or have Tyrseis strong in her natal horoscope, to have chosen that design.

The house of the two hares lay two doors down, a comfortable, prosperous house perhaps a little smaller than its neighbors. The twin hares lay face-to-face in the niche above the doorway, the light of the rising winter-sun adding texture to the carved fur, and when Rathe stepped forward to knock at the main door, the heavy iron striker was forged in a variation of the pattern, one hare sitting, the other standing beside it. The door opened quickly at his knock, a footman out of livery frowning at him for a moment until he saw the truncheon at Rathe's waist.

"Pointsman—?" he began, and Rathe took a quick step forward.

"Adjunct Point Rathe. I need to see the chief, urgently."

"Of course." The footman didn't blink, but threw the door open, beckoning them into the chill hall. He didn't leave them there, either, but brought them into a receiving room, where a fire burned low in a painted fireplace, bowed again, and disappeared. Rathe moved automatically toward its warmth, Eslingen at his shoulder, stood holding his hands out to the radiating embers.

"Most impressive," Eslingen said under his breath, and Rathe let himself glance around the room. It was small, but nicely kept, expensively furnished, and he wasn't surprised to see a double corm the size of a man's fist waiting in a jar by the window. He didn't recognize the species, but the care with which it was placed, set in the center of a delicate inlaid table, made him think it had to be one of the expensive ones.

"Rathe. What is it?"

He turned to see Trijn in the doorway, a lamp in one hand, her unbelted house gown half open, showing the rich wool of her heavy skirt. If he'd seen her like this, Rathe thought, instead of in the practical common wear she chose for the station, he would have known at once that she came of better than average family. One did not usually find daughters of the merchants resident entering points' service.

"I think I know who's behind the theatre murders," he said, and Trijn nodded as though she were not surprised, came into the room, setting the lamp on the mantel.

"Stir up the fire, then, and sit down. And tell me about it."

Rathe did as he was told, finding the logs ready to hand, and seated himself opposite the chief point. Eslingen came to stand at his shoulder, watchful and silent, and Trijn smothered a laugh.

"Sorry. I'd never understood the black dog comments before."

Rathe kept his face expressionless, knowing that Eslingen's eyebrows would be up, and leaned forward, resting his elbows on his knees. "It's Aubine, Chief," he said, and Trijn sobered instantly. "It has to be."

Quickly, he outlined what Eslingen had seen, and Aubine's connections to the dead men, but even before he had finished, Trijn was shaking her head.

"It's thin, Rathe. Very thin. Aubine sponsored the masque, for Sofia's sake."

"To use it," Rathe answered. "To get revenge for the leman his grandmother had murdered."

In this house, he didn't like to say common, but Trijn nodded slowly. "I remember the matter," she said. "It was never referred to the points, but there were always rumors, whispers that it was more than they claimed. But the soueraine took the boy away with her, and there was nothing we could do." She shook her head, shaking memory away. "All right, assuming you're right—and I think I believe you, Rathe—what's the point of it all? What are these—arrangements—supposed to do?"

"I don't know," Rathe answered. "The grandmother's dead, long dead, and if he was blaming the sister, surely there were easier ways to attack her. Ones that required less elaborate planning, anyway."

"They're on good terms." Trijn shook her head. "Or so it's seemed, anyway."

"The only thing I can think of—" Rathe stopped abruptly, not wanting to voice his sudden fear, as though saying it would somehow make it more likely to be true. "The only thing I can think of is revenge on the law, the law that let his leman die and offered no justice. The law in the person of the queen."

"Sofia's tits," Trijn said. She drew a shaken breath. "I hope you're wrong, Rathe."

"Can you take the chance he's not?" Eslingen asked, and the points looked at him as though they'd forgotten he was there.

Trijn scowled. "No. But what in hell's name do you expect me to do about it? I'll say it again, there's not nearly enough to call a point on the man, not for a single one of these deaths, and we'd be laughed out of court if we tried."

"Postpone the masque," Rathe said.

Trijn laughed aloud, an angry, frustrated sound. "And how likely do you think that is? If I can't call a point, what chance do I have of persuading the necessary authorities—and that's the regents and the chamberlains, Rathe, who aren't particularly fond of you—that this is necessary?" She shook her head. "The masque has to be done in conjunction with the solstice, for the queen's health and the health of the realm. The stars have to be right for the magistry to work."

"And if Aubine wants to kill the queen," Rathe said, "what better occasion than the one time and place he knows she must be? There must be precedent. It must be possible."

"But not without cause," Trijn said again. "To postpone—to

change anything about the masque—we'd need the approval of the regents, and the chamberlains, to see if it can be done without destroying it. And I cannot see how we can convince them without more proof."

She was right, that was the problem, and Rathe shook his head. "Is there anyone else who has authority?"

"The queen herself, of course," Trijn said, "but that doesn't get us anywhere. Astreiant—" She stopped, anger turning to something more speculative, and Rathe leaned forward again.

"Would she listen?"

Trijn nodded, slowly. "She might. It's worth a try, at any rate."

"Will she listen to you?" Eslingen asked, and Trijn gave him a glittering smile.

"I—the metropolitan knows me. She'll give me an audience, she owes me that much."

And I don't think I want to know why, Rathe thought. He said, "And if she doesn't agree—or if she can't?"

Trijn took a breath. "I was hoping you'd have some suggestions, Rathe."

"Bar Aubine from the Tyrseia," Rathe said. "Remove all the flowers—"

"If you can move them without triggering their effects," Eslingen said. "Remember the last time you tried that."

Rathe winced at the memory, but nodded in agreement. "All right, maybe moving the flowers wouldn't be a good idea. But we can make sure he doesn't—for example—offer Her Majesty any posies as a token of his esteem."

"I think I can persuade Astreiant of that much, at least," Trijn agreed. "But keeping Aubine away from his own play—Sofia, if you're wrong, Rathe, or even if you're right and we can't prove it, we'll lose everything. I'll lose my station, and you, Rathe, will never call another point. Is it worth that much to you?"

Rathe paused. Trijn was right again, if he couldn't prove his case, provide at least as much evidence as he would need to call a point and to win a conviction in the courts, Aubine would see him banished from the one profession he had ever wanted to follow. *And suppose I'm wrong? Suppose I've misjudged everything, cast my figure and come up with a reading as false as a broadsheet astrologer's?* But there had been four deaths already, five if Leussi's was indeed part of the sequence, five deaths unresolved, justice ignored, and a sixth—

or possibly more—in the offing. More important even than the already dead was the chance to prevent another murder, and that was worth even this risk. "Yes," he said slowly. "I'll take the chance."

Out of the corner of his eye, he saw Eslingen nod, silent support, and Trijn took a deep breath. "Then I'm with you, Rathe." She rose to her feet, the heavy silk of her robe falling into place with a soft slur of sound. "Wear your good coat, if you have one. We'll attend the metropolitan tomorrow morning."

11

◆ ·· ◆

$\mathcal{T}$rijn was as good as her word, arriving at Point of Dreams with a low-flyer in hand. Rathe followed her across the station's courtyard, newly aware that his best coat was several degrees below what anyone else would consider suitable for visiting the Metropolitan of Astreiant. Trijn looked as fine as ever, a dark, hooded cloak drawn close over a bottle-green suit, her hair tucked under a stylish cap that still managed to cover her ears, and he wondered if perhaps he should have borrowed something from Eslingen. Not that it would have been that much of an improvement, he thought, settling himself on the cushions opposite the chief point. Eslingen was a good two inches taller, and thicker in the chest; his coats would hang on Rathe like an empty sack. But at least it would have been obvious that he'd made the effort.

"Don't worry," Trijn said, as if she'd read the thought, and lowered the window just long enough to signal the driver. "Astreiant knows you don't take fees. It wouldn't do for you to look too presentable."

Rathe managed a smile and leaned back against the cushion as the low-flyer jolted out of the station yard. In the cold light of morning, his conclusions seemed even less likely than before, and he wondered if he was making the worst mistake of his life. But nothing else explained all the deaths, he thought. Aubine's presence, Aubine's involvement in the dead men's lives, was the single common thread—

that and the Alphabet, he amended silently. Everywhere he looked, the Alphabet of Desire seemed to lurk, the lavish illustrations hiding deadly possibilities.

"How much do you think Aconin knows about this?" Trijn demanded suddenly, and Rathe blinked.

"I don't know."

"Enough to run away, in any event," Trijn said. "Assuming he isn't dead, too."

"There's a happy thought." Rathe rubbed his chin, glad he'd taken the time to be shaved this morning. He had done the barber a favor two summers past, in the matter of a stolen clock that had ended up in Point of Hopes; the man had been glad to open early for him, and had given him breakfast as well. "Philip said he was afraid of something—of Aubine, I'd guess—so I'm hoping he's just gone to ground. If we could find him, Chief, he might be able to confirm what's happening."

"If he was likely to do that," Trijn said, "he'd've come to us with his problems."

"Not Aconin," Rathe said. "But if he thinks the point will be called on him, he'll talk quickly enough."

Trijn lifted an eyebrow at that, but Rathe looked mulishly away. It wouldn't be that simple, of course, it never was, but once Aconin was found, he was confident a bargain could be made. If Aconin was still alive. He shoved that thought away, too—so far, Aubine hadn't troubled to hide his bodies—and glanced out the low-flyer's narrow window. To his surprise, they were already in City Point—Trijn always seemed to find the drivers with Seidos strong in their stars— but they turned past the metropolitan's official residence and turned onto the broad road that led into the Western Reach. So the metropolitan had agreed to see them at her town house, he thought, and felt his own eyebrows rise. Trijn was indeed well connected, if she could persuade the metropolitan to see them there.

The metropolitan's residence was a large and pleasant house, flanked by lower outbuildings and enclosed by a stone wall with a wrought-iron gate. As the low-flyer drew up to the narrow gatehouse, Trijn leaned forward, lowering the window again, and the first flakes of the winter's snow swirled in on the cold air. They were expected, however, and the liveried gatekeeper bowed, waving them through as her assistants hauled back the heavy gate. Another woman in livery, red coat bound with ochre piping, a silver badge showing Astree and her scales on a scarlet ribbon at her neck, was waiting for them at the main door, and showed them into a long, narrow library, its shutters barely cracked even in the pale winter light. Astreiant herself was waiting there, but as they entered, she rose from behind her worktable, blowing out her lamp, and gestured for their escort to throw open two sets of shutters. The cool light streamed in—snow-light, Rathe thought, watching the flakes scattering down out of the milky sky, the first threads of it blowing like dust across the narrow paved terrace that lay outside the windows—and he was grateful for the fires that blazed in the twin stoves.

"Chief Point," Astreiant said, and waved dismissal to the servant. "And Adjunct Point Rathe. It's a pleasure to see you again."

Is it my imagination, Rathe thought, *or did she lay the faintest of stresses on the word "you"?* He managed a wary bow, and Astreiant gestured toward a pair of stools drawn close to the nearer stove.

"Please, sit down, and let's talk." She seated herself in a tall chair as she spoke, stretching her feet toward the stove in unconscious habit. She was a tall woman, well built, with grey-blue eyes that slanted down ever so slightly at the outer corners. There were lines on her face as well, and Rathe guessed she and he were probably much of an age, but the lines were good lines, echoing a ready smile.

"You read my report, then," Trijn said.

Astreiant inclined her head, copper curls dancing. Her hair was almost red, Rathe realized with some amusement, but no one would dare tell the metropolitan she was out of fashion. "To be sure," she said. "And tell me, Dema, what you expect me to do about it?"

"Postpone the masque," Trijn said promptly.

"It can't be done." Astreiant lifted a hand to forestall any further protest. "I mean that literally. It cannot be done. The stars are most propitious at midwinter, and this year more so than usual, to postpone—to change the date at all—would be as bad as not performing it. And you know what the masque means to the realm, and to Her Majesty."

"Even though it's proved detrimental to the health of at least four other people?" Trijn asked, and Astreiant frowned.

"You haven't proved that yet."

"The deaths are real enough," Rathe said, in spite of himself.

Astreiant ducked her head in apology. "I misspoke. The deaths are real, and I do not discount them, Adjunct Point, I promise you that. But I don't see the connection to the masque."

"De Raçan and the theatre's watchman died in the theatre," Rathe said. "Guis Forveijl was actually in the masque—one of the actors, your grace. Leussi was a chamberlain who would have ruled on the masque, had he lived. And Grener Ogier worked for the man who is providing the flowers for the masque, knew what was being grown, and what it might be used for."

"That's five," Astreiant said.

"I'm less certain about Leussi," Trijn said. "But growing more so all the time."

Astreiant shook her head. "Heira forgive me, I took comfort in the watchman's death. I thought sure that meant this couldn't have anything to do with the succession." She took a breath. "Take me through this again, Adjunct Point, in your own words. Why are you so sure this is all a connected plot?"

Rathe took a breath in turn, trying to order his thoughts. "The first death was the intendant's, Leussi's. I am all but sure he was killed by a plant grown specially for the purpose, and listed in the Alphabet of Desire. I believe he was killed because he also owned a copy of this edition of the Alphabet, the working Alphabet, and could have seen what Aubine's play could do. The second death was the landseur de Raçan." He hesitated, knowing this was the weakest link in his chain, but made himself go on. "I believe the reason for his death is less important than the manner of it. He was found drowned, Your Grace, in the middle of a dry stage, with nothing around that could have held the water that drowned him. And the alchemists say he died where we found him. The body was not moved."

"But you have some idea of the reason?" Astreiant asked.

Rathe took another breath. "I believe that he was killed because he was a useless man, and because he had behaved badly to a common lover of his, and possibly because Aubine"—Astreiant stirred, and Rathe said hastily, "The murderer, then, no name—wanted to test his arrangements."

"Aubine's leman," Astreiant murmured, and shook her head. "Thin, Rathe. Very thin. Go on."

"The watchman knew everything that happened in the theatre, knew that things, particularly posies, the actors' gifts, had been rearranged," Rathe went on. "Possibly he even saw Aubine at the theatre after hours, could testify to what he was doing there. The gardener worked for Aubine—"

"I knew him," Astreiant said. Her eyes strayed to the long window, the dormant garden beyond the terrace. "My head gardener thought the world of him. How did he die?"

"Stabbed to death," Trijn said.

"I believe he knew something," Rathe said. "He didn't want to be found, Your Grace, he'd burned his own clothes and begged for Temple castoffs."

Astreiant nodded. "So he couldn't be traced. Like the children this past summer."

"And like anyone who doesn't want to be found using magistical means," Rathe agreed.

"And the actor?"

"Also stabbed." Rathe suppressed a pang, sorrow and vague guilt combined. With any luck, he would resolve this, and Forveijl would not become one of his ghosts. "He had put together an arrangement from the Alphabet of Desire, and while it had accomplished part of what he intended, it had also betrayed that there was a working copy of the Alphabet in existence, possibly in the theatre. I believe he was stabbed to keep us from finding out where he'd gotten it."

"What does Aconin say about all this?" Astreiant demanded. "It's his play, he must know something."

"Aconin," Trijn said, "has disappeared."

Astreiant grimaced.

"He was friends with Aubine," Rathe said. "Maybe more than friends. And he's been afraid of something for most of the rehearsal period. Someone took a shot at him, and someone trashed his rooms, destroyed his household altar."

Astreiant's eyes narrowed, and Rathe remembered that she had spent a season on the northern borders as a young woman. "Aconin is a Leaguer, is he not?"

"Yes, Your Grace," Trijn said.

"No quarter." Astreiant shook her head. "Sofia, I wish you could find the man."

"So do I," Rathe said, and Astreiant grinned in spite of herself.

"I daresay." She sobered quickly, looking at Trijn. "So I say again, Dema, what do you want me to do?"

"Postpone the masque," Trijn said again, and Astreiant waved the words away. "Failing that—must Her Majesty attend?"

"What reason do you have to think that anything is aimed at the queen?" Astreiant demanded, and Trijn leaned forward on her stool. "There is the old story about Aubine's leman, murdered and the killer—Aubine's grandmother, at least indirectly—never brought to justice. Who is the symbol of justice in this realm?"

Astreiant shook her head. "Thin," she said again.

Trijn spread her hands. "Then assume there is some other target, unknown—the sister, perhaps, or someone else. But can you risk allowing Her Majesty to walk unknowing into the middle of what we believe is intended to be a killing ground?"

Astreiant took a deep breath, covered her mouth with one hand. Behind her, the snow was strengthening, clinging to the grass and low bushes of the garden. "I cannot postpone the masque," she said, finally. "I said it before, and I meant it. Nor can I ask Her Majesty not to attend—that would violate the mystery, destroy the potency. And yet . . . I do believe this is a real threat, Dema."

"Will you grant me the authority to confine the landseur Aubine, then?" Trijn asked, and Rathe gave her a startled glance. That was more support than he'd really expected, and he was grateful for it.

Astreiant hesitated, her eyes distant, and then, regretfully, she shook her head. "I can't. First, I don't have the authority—he may be resident here, but he's a native of Ledey. My writ runs only to the city."

"But—" Trijn stopped as the other woman held up her hand.

"Hear me out, will you? Second, times are chancy, with Her Majesty being prepared finally to name a successor. To imprison a noble now, without cause, would make me and, through me, Her Majesty look capricious and power-hungry, now when we can least afford it."

And that, Rathe thought, is the first true confirmation that Astreiant will be queen in her turn. Trijn shook her head. "And what do you expect me to do, Your Grace, when you tie my hands?"

"I don't know," Astreiant said. "Bring me evidence, solid evidence that would stand in the courts—that you, Adjunct Point, would consider enough to call a point on—and I'll do whatever you need. But without that, it's my hands that are tied."

Rathe let his head drop, knowing Astreiant was right, and the metropolitan went on, spreading her hands.

"And if there is anything else you want, anything else you need, in Astree's name, ask."

Trijn laughed. "The prince-marshal and his men to guard the theatre these next two days?"

Astreiant blinked, and nodded. "If it will help you, he's yours."

"It couldn't hurt," Trijn said.

Rathe nodded, more slowly. He was known to Coindarel, and more importantly, Coindarel knew and liked Eslingen. It might be possible to use him to keep Aubine from bringing in any more of his deadly arrangements—if he didn't have everything in place already, of course, Rathe added, with an inward grimace. That might be the best first step, to search the Tyrseia, and see if he could identify any of the arrangements from his copy of the Alphabet.

"I daresay it would amuse him, too." Astreiant rose slowly to her feet, ending the interview, and the others copied her. "Very well, Chief Point, I shall draft the order this morning. Coindarel and his men will be at your—or Mistress Gasquine's—disposal by three o'clock this afternoon."

Rathe bowed, grateful for this much support, and Trijn made a courtier's curtsy. Astreiant lifted her hand.

"But remember, if you find anything, anything at all, that would allow me to act—send to me, at whatever hour. I will be ready."

"Thank you, Your Grace," Trijn said. "I pray Sofia we find something."

They rode in silence back to Point of Dreams, listening to the shouts of the street sweepers. This time, the driver took his time, let his horse pick its own pace across the icy bridge, and by the time they dismounted at the station's main gate, the fine snow was already drifting in the corners of the buildings. Rathe waited, his back to the wind, as Trijn paid off the driver, and together they made their way across the courtyard and into the warmth of the main room. It was crowded with the aftermath of what looked like a quarrel between carters, and Trijn rolled her eyes.

"Everything under control?" she asked, in a voice that presumed an affirmative answer, and started up the stairs without waiting for agreement. "Rathe, I need you."

"Yes, Chief." Rathe followed, not sorry to avoid the arguments below. Leenderts seemed to have it well in hand, anyway, and the carters seemed more concerned with cash values than with pride or status, which would make it easier to resolve.

Trijn paused at the top of the stairs, looked back at the busy room. "Will Coindarel be a help or a hindrance?"

"You asked for him," Rathe answered, surprised, and Trijn gave a crooked smile.

"I didn't expect to get him."

"A help," Rathe said.

Trijn nodded. "I'll expect you to deal with him as need be."

"I can do that," Rathe said. *Or rather, Eslingen could.*

"What about your magist friend," Trijn asked. "Can we press him into service, too?"

Rathe grimaced. "He's a necromancer, Chief. And the phytomancers have been singularly reluctant to involve themselves with the Alphabet."

"Any chance of him prodding them a bit? Or finding someone else who can help? A magist's eye couldn't hurt."

"I'll send to him," Rathe said. "It can't hurt to ask." He shook himself. "If you'll excuse me, Chief, there's some work I need to do."

Trijn lifted an eyebrow. "There's something we can do?"

"I thought I'd look through my copy of the Alphabet, see if I can identify any of the arrangements at the theatre," Rathe answered.

"Not until they've left for the day," Trijn said sharply. "We don't want him to know he's suspect—that's about the only advantage we do have."

Rathe nodded, and turned into his workroom. The stove had gone out, this time, and he shouted for a runner, settled himself at his table while the girl brought kindling and made up the fire. He scribbled the note to b'Estorr as she worked, hardly knowing what to ask, except his help—but the magist understood as well as anyone what was happening, he told himself. He would find someone to help, if he couldn't do it himself. The girl took the folded paper cheerfully, returned a few minutes later with the word that she'd sent one of the others to carry it to the university. She brought a pot of tea as well, sweet and smoky, thick with the candied rind of summer fruits, and Rathe sipped at it gratefully as he paged through the Alphabet. The trouble was, he thought, there was too much there, too many possibilities. It seemed as though every other story dealt with lost love, and the arrangements that matched them were all equally dangerous, in the right measure. And the one thing that was missing was the way to undo an arrangement without disrupting it—his own experience had been painful enough; he hated to think of what would happen if they tried to destroy Aubine's arrangements without first rendering them harmless. There had to have been a dozen of them, onstage and in the theatre itself, when he was last at the Tyrseia.

There had to be a way to undo the arrangements, some way safely to neutralize their power, even without knowing the key flower. The

Alphabet, of course, didn't indicate which one that might be in any arrangement, and simply disrupting an arrangement was far too dangerous, as he had learned to his pain. No one would create this dangerous magistry without providing a better safeguard, at least for herself—proving once again, Rathe thought grimly, that Aconin had to know more than he had been telling. Surely someone at the university would know, he thought, and hoped b'Estorr would hurry with his answer. But that was going to take time, time to find the scholar, time to explain what was needed, time to find a phytomancer willing to analyze the Alphabet, time even to return to Point of Dreams . . . There was a knock at the door, and he looked up sharply.

"Come in."

"Pardon, Adjunct Point." It was one of the younger runners, bundled in a cut-down carter's coat wrapped tight over coat and knitted jerkin. "This is from the magist, the one you sent to."

Rathe took the folded paper, its edges a little damp from the snow, frowning as he recognized b'Estorr's elegant hand. It was only a few lines, and he swore under his breath as he took in the sense of them. b'Estorr was still searching for a phytomancer who was willing to take the Alphabet seriously enough to help them; *if I haven't found one by second sunrise*, he finished, *I'll come myself and do what little I can.*

Rathe took a deep breath and forced calm as the runner give him a wary glance. He dismissed the boy with a smile and a demming, and made himself look again at the open book. That was not the answer he had wanted, nothing like it—this was magists' business, not something for the points—and then he shoved the thought away. There was nothing else he could do, except what he'd promised Trijn. He shook his head, turning another page, and caught his breath. It had been there all along, tucked in the plant dictionary, a simple plant, even familiar, something he'd seen now and then in the ditches at the edge of the city. The Alphabet labeled it "the Universal Panacaea," but he knew it as hedgebroom, and salvarie. *And I know where to get it, too*, he thought, and shoved himself back from his table.

"Chief!"

Trijn looked up from her own work, wariness and hope warring in her expression. "Well? Has b'Estorr come?"

"No, not yet, he's still trying to find someone who's willing to help. He'll be here at second sunrise, if he doesn't find one. In any case, I may have an answer," Rathe said. "But I have to find it, have to pick up something—there's a plant, Chief, you may know it, hedge-broom—"

Trijn nodded, but he rushed on anyway, turning the book to show the illustration, wanting to be sure.

"Tall, rangy, pale blue autumn-blooming flowers."

"I know it," Trijn said. "Go on."

"The Alphabet calls it the Panacea, it should neutralize any mag-istical arrangement—"

"But who in Metenere's name saves hedgebroom?" Trijn de-manded. "It's a weed. Gods, Rathe, the last of it bloomed two months ago."

"Aubine will have it," Rathe said with sudden certainty. "Anyone who knows the Alphabet this intimately will grow it, just in case of accident."

"That hardly helps us," Trijn said.

Rathe nodded. "I wasn't proposing to ask him for it—or the uni-versity, either, I doubt they'd grow it. I know someone else who may have it."

Trijn paused, staring, then nodded. "Go. I'll deal with b'Estorr, if—when he comes."

It wasn't a long walk to the Corants Basin, but the snow was in his face the whole way, a fine, stinging mist that caught in his hair and scarf in spite of the cap pulled low on his ears. The top of the Chain Tower was dark against the snowy sky, the banner at its peak pulled straight out by the wind. His mother's house was closed tight, but lamplight showed in the gaps between the shutters, and when he knocked, he heard the faint sound of music. It stopped instantly, and a moment later a young woman opened the door. Not an apprentice, he thought automatically, and wondered if it was her he had heard singing.

"I need to see Caro Rathe," he said, and the girl's eyes widened with recognition.

"You must be her son. Come in."

"Thank you." Rathe followed her down the long hall toward the stillroom that stood opposite the kitchen, surprised as always that his mother's friends saw any resemblance between them. It wasn't phys-ical, couldn't be—they were very different, bar a few tricks of voice and gesture—but somehow his mother's friends seemed to know he was her child.

The stillroom was warm, a hearty fire roaring in the stove, and the scent of lavender warred with the homelier smells of a slow-cooking dinner on the kitchen fire. His mother looked up from her place at the long workbench, surprise and pleasure turning to wariness as she studied his face.

"What is it, Nico?"

Rathe shook his head. "Nothing amiss, or at least not with us, anyone we know. But I need your help."

Caro nodded, wiping her hands on her apron, and set aside the heavy brass mortar. "Name it."

"Did you dry and keep hedgebroom this year?" Rathe held his breath for the answer, saw Caro blink in surprise, and relaxed only when she nodded.

"Some, yes. Why?"

"May I take it?" Rathe was scanning the bunches that hung from the ceiling as he spoke, and Caro frowned.

"Yes, I suppose—but why? I keep it for Dame Ramary, you know."

"Sorry." Rathe shook his head, getting his own impatience under control with an effort. "It's the theatre murders, I think I know who's doing it, and why." He reached into his pocket, brought out the red-bound Alphabet, and opened it to the right page. "I am right, this is hedgebroom, isn't it?"

Caro accepted the book, nodding slowly as she read through the text. "Yes, that's hedgebroom, all right, salvarie they call it out west and by the coast. I've never heard of it as a panacea, though."

"Magistical, not medicinal," Rathe said.

"Obviously. But I haven't known any magists to use it, either."

"Sorry," Rathe said again, and took a breath. "I'm—we're not able to do the things we should do, to stop the man, and I'm trying to find other ways."

"Does this have anything to do with Grener's death?" Caro asked, and Rathe nodded.

"I think so. Well, I'm certain, but I don't have the evidence to call a point. Yet."

"Poor Grener," Caro said, and rose from her stool, walking along the long beams where the dried plants hung in bundles. "Here's what I have," she said at last. "Is it enough?"

The bundle she lifted from the hook looked meager enough, barely a dozen stalks bound with a loop of string. The stems were brittle, their rich green faded almost to the pallor of straw, and only a few of the flowers remained. They, too, had faded, were no longer the startling blue that caught the eye at the end of summer. *But at least they are there,* Rathe thought. *Assuming, that is, that it's the flowers that are important.*

"Which is the active part?" he asked, and Caro smiled, this time with approval.

"It's all active, actually, at least for what I do. You boil the stems and leaves to make a decoction, or you can use the leaves in a tea. The flowers can go in the tea as well—they have a sharper taste—or you can use them alone. Dame Ramary tops her small-cakes with them, the savory ones, serves them for her eyes."

"That's something," Rathe said, and hoped the same would hold true for its magistical power. He glanced around, looking for some easy way to carry the bundle, and his mother stepped forward, plucked a single stalk from among the tangle. She tucked it into the front of his coat, a poor man's posy, and stepped back.

"If it's good against this murderer's work, I want you wearing it."

"Thank you," Rathe said, knowing the words were inadequate, and Caro looked away, stooped to rummage blindly in the bins below the shelves that held her tools.

"Here," she said at last, and held out a linen bag. "And be careful."

Rathe took it, tucking the bundle of plants carefully inside, and slipped the ties over his belt. "I will," he said, and hoped he could keep the promise.

Eslingen took a careful breath, watching the last of the chorus—his trainees—make their way off the stage. They still weren't perfect, and he'd be ashamed to lead them in a proper drill, but at least they wouldn't disgrace themselves on the day. Even as he thought that, one of the landseurs tripped, dropping his half-pike with a clatter and nearly bringing down the man following him, and Eslingen couldn't restrain a groan.

"Don't worry," Siredy said softly. "It'll be all right tomorrow."

Eslingen gave him a glance, and the other man managed a smile.

"Better to get that over with today, right?"

"If you say so." Eslingen winced as another landseur stumbled over his own toes.

"Trust me," Siredy said. "Let them get the worst over with now, and they'll be fine tomorrow."

"I hope so," Eslingen answered. That was the last scene for which the masters had responsibility, and he allowed himself a sigh of relief as the actors playing Ramani's henchmen made their entrance. Just the aftermath of the battle to get through, and the final scene, the restoration of the palatine, and then the massed chorus performing the final valediction. At least he didn't have anything to do with that, he thought, and looked away as Aubine moved past them, a trug filled with flowers and greenery tucked over his arm. Eslingen had been doing his best to stay away from the landseur, and he was careful not to meet his eye this time, trying not to shiver at the thought of what the flowers in the trug might be capable of doing. So far, everything had been excruciatingly normal, Aubine busy in the corners, adding and subtracting stalks, culling blooms that had passed their prime, and more than once Eslingen had wondered if Rathe had gotten it right after all. Surely no one plotting something this outrageous could be so calm—and yet it was the only answer that fit.

Siredy touched his arm, and he jumped, met Siredy's amused smile with a grimace.

"Let's go out front," the other master said. "You haven't had a chance to see how it'll play."

Eslingen followed the other man back behind the backpiece and out the actors' entrance into the hall, where the theatre's doorman sat in solitary silence, a jug of ale at his side. Siredy rolled his eyes at that, and Eslingen nodded, making a face at the sour smell of beer rolling off the man. Drinking off his tips, most likely, he thought, all the bribes he'd earned for carrying messages and gifts—and telling tales to the broadsheets, probably—and he suppressed the unworthy urge to kick over the jug as he passed. Only one more night, anyway, one more night to watch and keep the stagehouse safe, and after that, the man could do as he pleased.

Siredy brought them out not into the pit, but into the two-seilling seats in the first gallery, not the best seats—those were in the royal box, directly above—but certainly better than anything Eslingen had even been able to afford. He had not seen the stage fully dressed, and caught his breath at the sight, impressed in spite of himself. To either side, the versatiles displayed the walls of de Galhac's palace, with the mountains sloping away to a narrow valley in the distance. The actors stood well downstage, clothes gleaming in the light of the practicals, all their attention focused on the two ragged messengers who had brought the news of the palatine's victory. De Galhac was overthrown, despite her armies and her magic, and the palatine stood in her palace, the rightful monarch restored. Eslingen shook his head in wonder, not really hearing the words—he'd heard them too many times already to be more than vaguely conscious of their rhythms— wondering instead how the play would look without the masque's trappings overlaid on it. After all, de Galhac might have lost, but she was definitely the center of the play, the best part, or bes'Hallen would never have consented to play it; the second best part was Ramani, and the palatine was a poor third, not a villain, but not nearly as compelling as the other two. But it was the formal shape of the play that mattered, at least for the purposes of the masque: the rightful ruler was restored, and that was enough.

The practicals' light glittered on the palatine's crown, and she bent to accept a sheaf of snow-white flowers from the highest ranking of the chorus. That was another magistical gesture, Eslingen knew, symbolic submission to the royal will and authority, and he leaned forward against the railing as the palatine finished her final speech. The chorus glided onstage behind her, the professional musicians hidden offstage already beginning the anthem, and he shook his head, amazed in spite of himself at the spectacle unfolding in front of him. This was the moment for which the chorus had been waiting, for which they had spent hundreds of crowns of their own money, and the rich fabrics caught the light, real gold and silver and gems outshining the paste jewels that decorated the actors' costumes. By comparison, the two huge flower arrangements, one at each side of the forestage, looked almost drab, their colors drained by the glitter. The other arrangements looked normal, though, Eslingen thought, craning his head to see them all—great bunches of them hanging from the side boxes, another pair of massive arrangements set on the floor in front of the stage itself—and he wondered for an instant if he was seeing some manifestation of Aubine's magistry. Then the light changed, subtly, and the moment was past. The chorus began its part of the song, voices swelling in an ancient litany. It was older than the masque itself, had been sung for the monarch at midwinter since time immemorial, and Siredy leaned back, sighing.

"It'll play," he said, and Eslingen wondered if the other master was trying to convince himself.

"What happens once the masque is done? To the play, I mean."

Siredy reached across to tap one of the carved acorns that decorated the side of the box. "Tyrseis willing, we all take a week's holiday, and then Mathiee announces a new version of *The Alphabet of Desire*—opening around the twenty-fifth of Serpens, probably, that'll give us about three weeks to pull all the extraneous stuff out of it and make any changes. Assuming that Aconin deigns to put in an appearance, that is." He paused, gave the other man a curious look. "You don't think Aconin killed all these people, do you?"

Eslingen shook his head. "I don't."

"Then where is he?"

Hiding, if he knows what's good for him. Eslingen said, "I wish I knew. He could answer a few questions, I think, if he were here."

Siredy gave him another sideways glance. "I hear the points are looking for him."

I wouldn't know. Eslingen killed the lie, knowing it wouldn't be believed, said instead, "Even if I knew, I couldn't tell you. You know that, Verre."

Siredy grinned. "True enough. I can't help asking, though." Onstage, the chorus was coming to an end, and he straightened, sighing. "Come on. Mathiee's bound to have some last notes for us, and then I'm for home."

They came back to the stage through the all but empty pit, passing a trio of chamberlains huddled in final conference, and threaded their way through the sudden crowd backstage, found themselves at last beside the left-hand wave. Duca was there, too, scowling to hide his own nervousness, and he beckoned them close.

"I saw you in the boxes. How'd it look?"

"Good," Eslingen said, and Siredy nodded in agreement. "It'll play, Master Duca."

"It had better," Duca answered.

Gasquine had detached herself at last from the chamberlains, and made her way onto the stage, the bookholder calling for attention. The hum of conversation quieted, even the chorus falling silent almost at once, and Gasquine took her place center stage, lifting her hands.

"My ladies, my lords, all my fellows." She paused, and then smiled suddenly, like the true sun rising. "What is there to say? We're ready—go home, get a good night's sleep, and be back here tomorrow at the stroke of nine."

Eslingen blinked, startled, and Siredy grinned. "Well, that's a good sign. Come on, Philip, I'm for the baths. Why don't you join me?"

It was tempting, and Eslingen wished that the masque was all he had to worry about. "Sorry," he said, "I'm promised elsewhere."

Siredy nodded without offense. "Your pointsman, I'm sure. Another time, then."

"Another time," Eslingen echoed, and let himself be drawn into the stream of people leaving the theatre.

To his surprise, the square in front of the Tyrseia was less crowded than usual—or rather, he amended, the crowds were restricted to the far side of the area, by the tavern, and a bonfire burned in the center of the square, the snowflakes hissing as they landed in the flames. There were figures around the fire, familiar shapes, men with pikes and muskets and the queen's white sash bright in the firelight, and he stopped abruptly, shaking his head. It looked like Coindarel's badge, his regiment, or what was left of it, but the last he'd heard, they'd been quartered in the Western Reach, near the queen's palace. What were they doing here, set out as what looked like a perimeter guard around the theatre?

"Philip!"

Eslingen turned at the sound of the familiar voice, his mood lightening in spite of everything, and Rathe hurried to join him, picking his way carefully over the snow-slicked cobbles. "What's Coindarel doing here?" he asked, and Rathe took his arm, drawing him deeper into the shadows.

"A favor to Astreiant. Trijn asked if we could have them, if they would guard the theatre."

"Not a bad idea. Though she might have asked for a magist or three."

Rathe made a face. "We tried that. We haven't got one yet."

"Damn." The wind was cold, driving the snow under the edges of his cloak, and Eslingen shivered. "So what now?"

"Yeah." Rathe made a face. He was wrapped in a heavy cloak as well, more, Eslingen suspected, to hide the truncheon than to cut the wind. "Well, now we wait, make sure everyone's left, and then— then we try spiking Aubine's guns." He grinned suddenly. "I think that's the proper phrase."

"Depends on what you have in mind."

"I'll tell you inside," Rathe answered, his eyes shifting, and Eslingen turned to confront a familiar figure.

"Lieutenant Eslingen."

The words were cool, and Eslingen braced himself for insult or worse: Connat Bathias was the real thing, a true twelve-quarter noble, and not likely to suffer his usurpation of a title.

"Pardon me, vaan Esling. I understand your family has claimed you now."

Eslingen frowned, suspicious, but the tone and the expression on the other man's face was pleasant enough, and he decided to take them at face value. "I'm dealing with nobles, Captain. Better they think I'm one of them, when I don't have the regiment to back me."

Bathias nodded, soberly still, but without hostility, and looked back at Rathe. "The doorkeeper says they've all gone, Adjunct Point."

Rathe nodded. "And the landseur Aubine?"

"Gone with them, I would assume," Bathias answered, and Eslingen turned, hearing the sound of a carriage pulling away from the theatre.

"There's his coach."

"Right." Rathe took a deep breath. "Let's go, then."

The actors' door was closed, a soldier leaning at his ease against the painted wood. He straightened to something like attention at their approach, and Eslingen's eyes narrowed. Six months ago, he would have had the right to give the man the lecture he deserved; as it was, he frowned, said nothing, and had the satisfaction of seeing the man pull himself to rights.

"You're sure everyone's gone?" Rathe asked, and the soldier nodded.

"The doorkeeper said so, and then the sergeant and I took a quick look around. No one there."

"Good enough," Rathe said, and pulled open the door. Eslingen hesitated—the theatre was a warren of passages, had too many odd corners for a "quick look" to be sufficient—then shrugged away his doubts, and followed Rathe into the broad tunnel. It was dark, but the simple mage-lights were still lit over the stage, casting enough light to let them pick their way into the main body of the theatre. It was very quiet, the air utterly still, and cold now as the building emptied, and Eslingen could just hear the faint hiss of the snow on the canvas roof far overhead.

"So what are we going to do?" he asked after a moment, and realized he had spoken in a near-whisper.

Rathe untangled himself from his cloak, and held out a crumpled linen bag. "I found something in the Alphabet, a panacea—it's a plant, hedgebroom, I've also heard it called—that can neutralize any and all of these arrangements." He smiled then, wryly. "At least, it's supposed to. I thought we could begin by slipping a few stalks into each of these big arrangements."

"Spiking the guns," Eslingen said with new understanding. "Nico, a spiked gun explodes if you try to use it—"

"Let's hope the analogy isn't that accurate, then," Rathe answered. He looked around, eyes widening as he took in the changed scenery. "Where do we start?"

"I suppose the big ones at the front of the stage," Eslingen said after a moment. "I'm sure they were the ones that operated against the landames."

"Right, then," Rathe said, looking around for the short steps that had stood in the pit, and Eslingen shook his head.

"Not there, not with the performance so close. We'll have to go through the stagehouse."

Rathe nodded, and Eslingen led the way through the actors' door, its carvings so closely matched to the wall around it that it was almost impossible to see. It was dark backstage as well, just the trio of mage-lights glowing on the stage itself, and Eslingen paused for a moment, letting his eyes adjust.

"This way," he said after a moment, and stepped into the light.

The blow caught him by surprise, a soundless explosion, as though he'd walked headlong into an invisible wall. He swore, startled, and his breath caught in his throat, as though the air itself had gone suddenly thick. Too thick to breathe, he thought, fingers going to his stock, and he stumbled to his knees, fighting for air. He choked, his mouth suddenly full of water, the bitter water of the Sier itself, and he looked up, searching for Rathe, but saw only the carved shape of *The Drowned Island*'s wave, looming overhead. He spat, but his mouth filled again in an instant, sight failing now, as though the water was rising inside his body, an impossible tide covering his eyes. This had to be how de Raçan had died, he realized, realized, too, that there had to be flowers somewhere, and reached for them, willing to chance the lightning if only he could breathe again. His fingers scrabbled across bare boards, found nothing, and he wrenched his stock loose, lungs frozen, aching. If he breathed, he knew they would fill with water, and he would hold his breath as long as he could, fight somehow toward the surface of this impossible river, but he could feel the property ice below the stage, changing its nature and rising to cover him, trapping him in *The Drowned Island*'s frozen Sier. In the distance, he could hear Rathe calling his name, but he had no breath to answer, no strength left for anything at all.

And then, miraculously, the pressure eased, and he spat out the last mouthful of river water, drew a whooping breath, coughed, and breathed again, his head hanging between his shoulders.

"Gods, Philip." Rathe was beside him, kneeling on the bare, dry stage, and as Eslingen moved, Rathe wrapped an arm around his shoulders, one hand tightening on his arm. "Are you all right? Can you breathe?"

"Yes." Eslingen coughed again, the taste of the Sier still filling his mouth, and Rathe thumped him on the back. "Seidos's Horse. Was it—?"

He broke off, not quite knowing what his question was—*was it the Alphabet, was it your plant that stopped it*—and Rathe nodded. He was very pale, Eslingen saw, and he shifted to grip the other man's hand.

"I'm all right," he said, and Rathe nodded again.

"I think we know how de Raçan died," he said, and his voice was less steady than his words.

Eslingen shivered, the memory too raw, and in spite of himself looked up again at the looming wave. "I saw that," he said, "but I was—drowning—first. The wave just made it easier to believe. Like the ice."

"Ice?" Rathe asked, and Eslingen nodded to the boards that covered the wave troughs.

"Under the stage. For the final scene. I was trying—to swim to the surface, I suppose, but the ice came over me, and held me down."

"Sofia," Rathe breathed, the word a prayer.

"But it didn't touch you?" Eslingen pushed himself up, sat back on his heels, working his shoulders.. His ribs would be sore in the morning, he thought, inconsequentially, but it was better than the alternative.

"No." Rathe released his hands, visibly shook himself back to business. "I'm not completely sure why—I could feel it, like a current, like the river, but it wasn't dragging me under. Maybe it was this." He touched the breast of his coat, where a single ragged flower hung limply from a buttonhole.

"The panacea," Eslingen said, and Rathe nodded.

"Plus you were first onto the stage. You crossed between the arrangements, they may have been meant to catch the first one through."

Eslingen looked where the other man was pointing, saw two small vases tucked at the bases of the nearest versatiles. They were almost pretty, pink cornflowers and pale yellow sweethearts wound about with a strand of the heavy vine that grew wild along the riverbank, and he shook his head, unable to believe that such a small thing could have nearly drowned him. But they had, he knew, seeing the stalks of hedgebroom tucked haphazardly among the flowers. Only the panacea had stopped them.

"I've been told more than once my stars are bad for water," he said thoughtfully.

"And I grew up swimming in the Sier," Rathe said. "If my stars would drown me, I'd've been dead long ago. It could make a difference."

Eslingen nodded. "Those weren't here when I left," he said.

"I don't doubt it," Rathe answered, and pushed himself to his feet, a haunted look on his face. He held out his hand, and Eslingen let himself be drawn upright, wincing again at the ache in his ribs. He felt bloated, as though he'd swallowed gallons of river water, hoped the feeling would pass soon.

"Philip, we have a problem." Rathe held up the linen bag, turned it upside down so that a few strands of fiber fell to the stage floor, a leaf and part of a stem and a few petals from a flower. Automatically, Eslingen stooped to collect them, tucked them into his pocket. "It took everything I had, everything my mother had saved, just to stop this one trap. I don't have anything left to spike the other arrangements."

Eslingen blinked, trying to focus. "What if we take these two apart, now that they're neutralized, save the panacea and use it in the big arrangements?"

Rathe shook his head. "There's not enough. I don't know if it's because it's dried, not fresh like the flowers, but it took half a dozen stalks in each arrangement to make it safe. It'll take more to neutralize those big arrangements, and Dis only knows what else he'll have waiting for us."

Eslingen looked down at the twin vases, the pale delicate flowers wound with vines and spiked with the furry stems of the panacea. "So what do we do?" he asked, and Rathe met his eyes squarely.

"Hedgebroom's long past, it dies over the winter, and we won't find any in the ditches, or anywhere else, for that matter. But Aubine will have it. If he's playing with these powers, he will grow it, and in quantity."

"You can't think he'll just give it to you," Eslingen said, appalled.

"Not likely." Rathe managed a faint, unhappy grin. "But he's got four succession houses. He can't be in all of them at once."

Eslingen blinked again, wondering if the near drowning had affected his hearing. Surely Rathe couldn't be suggesting that they rob the landseur's house—succession houses, he corrected himself. Not with Aubine presumably at home, along with all his household. . . . "It's not going to work," he said, and Rathe scowled.

"I'm open to better ideas, believe me."

"I wish I had one." Eslingen looked down at the flowers again, and shivered as though the icy waters had soaked him to the skin. In a way they had, he thought; he could still feel their touch beneath his skin, in his lungs and guts, and he shuddered again, thinking of de Raçan. "Poor bastard. A nasty way to die."

"Are you with me?" Rathe demanded, and Eslingen nodded.

"Oh, yes, I'm with you. But let's see if we can't find a more practical way to steal a landseur's plants."

"Maybe if one of us provides a diversion," Rathe said without much hope.

Eslingen shrugged. "We'll see when we get there."

12

◆ ·· ◆

Aubine's house stood still and silent, only a few servants'
lights showing between the shutters, and Rathe drew a careful breath,
hoping that was a good sign. Most of the other houses on the avenue
were shuttered as well, against the snow and against the long night.
The winter-sun had not yet risen, and the street was very dark, just
a few lamps burning at doorkeepers' boxes, casting more shadows
than light. He touched Eslingen's shoulder, drawing him farther into
the shadow of the house opposite, out of sight of the nearest box.
With any luck, he thought, the watchman would be tucked up in the
warmest corner, his feet firmly planted on his box of coals. Midwinter
Eve was no time for thievery, bad luck in the professionals' eyes, and
even Astreiant's most desperate poor could find shelter at the temples
and hospitals. As they passed close to a shuttered window, feet slur-
ring in the snow that was beginning to drift against the foundation,
he heard faint music, a cittern inexpertly played.

They skirted the last box successfully, and drew together in the
shadow of the stable wall to study their approach. Their breath left
clouds in the cold air, and Eslingen rubbed his gloved hands together,
hunching his shoulders under his cloak. Still chilled from the drowning spell, Rathe thought, and hoped the effect would pass off soon.

"Over the wall, do you think?" Eslingen asked softly, his voice
muffled further by the thin snowfall, and Rathe tipped his head back
to study the structure. Ordinarily, it wouldn't be impossible to climb;

the stones had been well fitted, but there were cracks and projections that would take feet and hands, and the spikes at the top would merely require extra care. Tonight, however, with the snow, it would be much more difficult, take more time and risk discovery, and he shook his head slowly.

"I don't know that we can. Tell me, how would you storm the place?"

"With a company at my back, for one thing," Eslingen answered, and Rathe saw his teeth gleam as he smiled. "Seidos, I'm not sure. Distract the guard, for one thing, and get you over the wall to open the gate."

Rathe glanced back at the wall. If he didn't have to worry about the watchman, he could probably do it, and he nodded. "All right. What did you have in mind for a distraction?"

"What about a drunken noble who can't find his way to his lodging?" Eslingen answered. "I'll let him set me on the right road, and then slip back and join you."

"Thin," Rathe said, and realized he was quoting Astreiant. He made a face, looking again at the relative positions of the gate and the watchman's box. It might be possible—just possible—for Eslingen to pass along the wall itself without attracting attention, and if he had the door open by then . . . "But I guess it'll have to do," he said aloud, and Eslingen nodded, stooping to collect a handful of snow.

"No time like the present," he said, and flung the snowball at the box. It hit with a soft thump, not enough to wake the neighbors, but certainly enough to jar the doorkeeper, and Eslingen stepped out into the middle of the street. There was no response from the box, and Rathe frowned. Sleeping off too much drink? That was more likely tomorrow night, when the household presents were traditionally given. He saw Eslingen bend again, brushing snow aside to come up with a pebble. The soldier shied it accurately at the box, and it hit with a clatter that made Rathe look reflexively over his shoulder at the nearest house, but still nothing moved in the box.

Eslingen looked back at him, gave an exaggerated shrug, and stepped up to the doorway, leaning inside for a moment before he backed away.

"Nico!"

Eslingen's voice was low, wouldn't carry more than a yard beyond where Rathe stood, but the pointsman winced anyway. Eslingen beckoned urgently, and Rathe moved to join him, scowling.

"What—?"

"Look." Eslingen took a step backward, and Rathe peered through the open doorway. The watchman was curled into the warmest corner, all right, wrapped in a heavy blanket that smelled faintly and pleasantly of horses, his feet propped up on the warming box that was making its presence felt in the confined space, but he was sound asleep, head down on his chest. Eslingen tapped sharply on the door frame, enough to wake the soundest sleeper, and Rathe ducked back out of sight, cursing under his breath. The watchman didn't move.

"So what's wrong with him?" Eslingen asked.

Rathe shook his head. Sleep like this wasn't natural, not in a watchman, chosen as they were for nocturnal stars to be the sort of folk who lay wakeful all night, and he stepped into the box before he could change his mind, letting his coat fall back so that his truncheon showed at his belt.

"Here, now," he said, and grabbed the watchman's shoulder, shaking him lightly. The watchman's head rolled back, releasing a sort of snore, but his eyes stayed firmly shut. The blanket slipped down from his shoulder, and Rathe caught his breath, seeing the posy pinned to the watchman's coat. "Gods. Philip, look at this."

The light dimmed as Eslingen leaned closer, and he heard the other man whisper a curse. "Aubine's work."

Rathe nodded, and eased the watchman back into his corner, careful to draw the blanket up around him again. The hot coals and the man's own body heat would keep the box warm enough that he shouldn't freeze, sheltered as he was from the wind and the snow.

"I suppose he wanted to be free to work, without the danger of witnesses," he said aloud, and turned to go. Eslingen stepped out of his way, fell in at his shoulder as Rathe turned to the main gate.

"You're not just going to pick the lock, right here on the open street."

"Why not?" Rathe managed a grin, reaching into his purse for the set of picks he carried with him. "Look, if anyone's watching, which I doubt, they saw us go to the box, speak to the doorkeeper, and come out with the key." He slipped the first pick into the ancient lock, nodded with satisfaction as the wards slid home under his probing. "And here we are."

Eslingen shook his head, grinning. "And you an honest points-man, too."

Rathe returned the smile briefly, closing the gate again behind them. When he had been to the succession houses before, he had been taken through the main house—not really a practical option just now, he thought, but the glasshouses stood separate from the main building, in a courtyard of their own. With any luck, the alley between the stables and the house would lead there, but that road passed one of the few lit and unshuttered windows. *No hope for it*, he thought, and pointed to the passage.

"This way."

He saw Eslingen's eyebrows rise, but the other man followed him obediently enough, scuffing his feet to blur their tracks. The snow of the courtyard looked almost untouched, Rathe saw, and wondered what the household was doing. As they came closer to the window, Eslingen caught his shoulder, pulling him back until he could whisper in Rathe's ear.

"Duck down low, and hope for the best?"

Rathe shook his head, frowning. There was no sound from the stable, none of the usual murmur of voices that went with the flickering lamplight, click of dice or the slap of cards—not even the stamp and shifting of the horses, he realized, and took a quick step forward, peering in the window. The glass was bubbled, and the stove's warmth had fogged the pane, but he wiped a corner clear, ignoring Eslingen's hiss of protest.

It was the tackroom, he realized at once, the walls festooned with harness and brasses, all in various stages of repair. Four grooms sat slumped around the rough-hewn table, lamp burning brightly in its center, cards and a handful of demmings scattered around it. A fifth groom was frankly asleep in the far corner, rolled into a horse's traveling rug, and Rathe straightened, clearing a wider patch of glass. A small vase of flowers, pink bells and sallewort, stood on a shelf between the cans of oil and harness grease.

"They're all asleep, too," he murmured, and Eslingen leaned over his shoulder, shaking his head in disbelief.

"Why? What's the point?"

"So no one can bear witness, I suppose," Rathe said grimly.

"Or so they can't be blamed," Eslingen said, and Rathe looked at him.

"You think well of him."

It wasn't a question, and Eslingen made an embarrassed face. "I don't condone the murders, believe me. But—yes, I liked him, Nico. And he's always been good to his people." He paused, seemed to read Rathe's next question in his face. "And it won't stop me from helping you call the point on him, don't worry about that."

"I wasn't," Rathe answered, but he was relieved all the same. He turned, glancing at the higher, unshuttered windows of the main house. "I suppose he's done the same to the rest of the household."

"I'd bet on it," Eslingen answered, and reached up to chin himself on the windowsill, scattering snow in fluffy clumps. He shook his head as he landed. "I couldn't quite see."

"Give me a hand," Rathe said, and Eslingen obediently braced himself, offering bent knee and cupped hands. Rathe chose the knee, and stepped up, clinging to the sill. This window was frosted, too, and he rubbed a little of the ice away, peering through the gap. The hall was dark, but in the faint light of the fading fire, he could see a woman curled in the settle, a child—Bice, he remembered, the girl who had first escorted him through the house—snuggled in her lap. They looked like any sleeping family, mother and child, except that there was a huge arrangement of flowers, at least three times the size of the one in the stables, looming like a pale shadow on the sideboard. He dropped back to the snowy cobbles, and knew he was shivering with more than cold.

"Yeah, they're all asleep there, too, or at least what I can see of them." He saw the same unease he felt reflected in Eslingen's face, and went on more roughly, "Let's go. At least we know no one's going to bother us."

"Unless Aubine's home," Eslingen answered, and Rathe grimaced.

"Let's hope not." *But if he isn't, where is he?* he wondered, and then shoved the thought aside. Time enough for that after they'd gathered enough hedgebroom to neutralize the theatre arrangements.

The glasshouses almost filled the courtyard, unlit now, but steaming gently from the warmth within. There was no snow on the roofs, but the eaves dripped softly, their puddles hardening to ice as they flowed away from the glass walls. Rathe slipped on one and swore, catching himself against Eslingen's shoulder, and both men stepped more carefully after that, watching the ground as well as the overshadowing buildings.

"Seidos's Horse," Eslingen said under his breath, and shook his head. "Four of them?"

"I thought you knew," Rathe said.

"I suppose I'd heard, but I thought . . ." The ex-soldier shook his head again. "I suppose I thought they were smaller, or something. Not like this."

"One for each season," Rathe said, and narrowed his eyes, remembering. The glasshouse where he'd spoken to Aubine had been filled with summer plants; logically, the autumn house should be the one to its left. He reached for his picks, worked the lock with ease, and opened the door into the unexpected warmth of an autumn evening. He heard Eslingen swear again, softly, and shut the door behind them, sealing out the cold wind. There should be lamps ready to hand, Rathe knew, and found them almost at once, tucked neatly beneath the nearest bench, flint and tinder ready to hand. It was just where his mother would have left them, just where any gardener would have put them, and he shook his head. How could anyone who had made these houses and the nurturing of so many plants and species his lifework have murdered five people? The one didn't follow, he knew, and he shoved the thought aside, concentrated on lighting the candles in the narrow lanterns. They were both sturdy, practical things, each with a metal hood and a glass door to shed the light, incongruous with the good candles they held, and he smiled in spite of himself. Only someone as rich as Aubine would use wax instead of tallow. He shook that thought away, too, and handed one lantern to Eslingen.

"You know what we're looking for," he said, and forced himself to speak in a normal voice. "You take the right-hand aisle."

"Right," Eslingen said, and lifted his lantern.

Rathe nodded, and turned away, lifting his own lantern to throw more light on the narrow aisle between the benches. Aubine was true to his seasonal theme, he thought. The central bench was lower than the others, and the long trays were filled with the tall flowers of the harvest, daymare and connis and horsetail and collyflag, their stems confined by a lattice of string. Surely the hedgebroom would be there, he thought, but to be sure he searched the left-hand bench as well. It was crowded with smaller plants, creepers and dwarfed shrubs studded with berries, and he caught the sweet smell of honeyvine as his coat brushed against a spill of leaves. *So many*, he thought. *How will we ever find hedgebroom among all this?*

And then he saw it, the first stand of it, tucked into a heavy stone pot as big as a washerwoman's cauldron, the stems poking free of the string, flowers bright even in the wavering candlelight. There were more pots of it, too, a haphazard selection of clay and stone and even a wooden half barrel, as though Aubine had pressed every available container into service to make sure he had enough of the panacea. *And very wise, too,* Rathe thought, *and I'm in the peculiar position of being grateful to him for his foresight.* He glanced around, found a clear space on the opposite bench, and set the lantern there, reaching for his knife to begin the harvest.

"Philip—"

"Nico! Over here!"

There was a note in Eslingen's voice that stopped the pointsman in his tracks, and he resheathed his knife, moving to join the other man. His voice had come from the back of the house, and he rounded the last pot of hedgebroom to see Eslingen standing well clear of one of the long tables Aubine preferred for his workbench. A body was laid out there, arms folded across its chest—Aconin's body, Rathe realized, and in the same instant saw the playwright's chest move. So, not dead, but deep asleep, more deeply even than the watchman or the household servants. There were flowers at his head and feet, two plain, alabaster vases filled with greenery and a single weeping branch from a familiar tree. Both were heavily in bloom, studded with flowers only a little smaller than a man's palm, each streaked with pink and red.

"Love's-a-bleeding," Eslingen said, and gave a shaky laugh. "Even I know that one."

Rathe nodded. Each of the flowers looked vaguely like a tear-streaked face; in the shifting candlelight, it was as though a hundred mourners wept for Aconin. "Lad's-love, we call it," he said. A snatch of an old song ran through his head, incongruous—*lad's love is full of folly, sorry tears, and no tomorrow; maid's love is true and gay, full of laughter all the day*—and he shook it away.

"He's not dead," Eslingen said, and his voice was suddenly hard and cold. "I say we leave him—we'll know where to find him when it's over."

Rathe hesitated—it was a tempting thought—then shook his head. "We can't. Think, Philip—you yourself said Aconin knows more than he's telling, he's our best evidence against Aubine. Gods, he's our only evidence, as it stands, he's the only person who can say it was Aubine who bespelled him."

"If he can," Eslingen said.

Rathe sighed. That was true, there was always the chance that Aconin had been taken by surprise, had no idea who had attacked him and left him here. . . . "No," he said aloud. "He has to know more than that. He wouldn't have been attacked if he didn't."

Eslingen nodded. "All right. But how do we break this?" He waved a cautious hand toward the flowers in their twin vases.

Rathe hesitated. At the theatre, all he had done was shove the stems of hedgebroom blindly into the arrangement, stabbing them haphazardly into the greenery until the pressure, the sense of the river's waiting presence, had eased, and Eslingen had drawn a whooping breath. *Too close*, he thought, and forced his attention back to the matter at hand. "We have to use the panacea," he said. "Well, we could try taking it apart, flower by flower, but I don't know where to start."

"And that could be crucial," Eslingen said.

"Yeah." Rathe reached for his knife again. "Let's try the hedgebroom."

Eslingen followed him with only a single glance over his shoulder to where the playwright lay in solitary splendor. He had left his lantern, Rathe saw, and as he stooped to cut the hedgebroom, he saw the light flicker on the motionless body. *Metenere send I'm right*, he thought, and sawed through the first tough stem. He cut half a dozen, and then cut them in half, so that he and Eslingen each had six stems, each with at least a few flowers blooming on them.

"All right," he said, sliding his knife back into its sheath. "Let's do it."

"Do what, exactly?" Eslingen asked, and followed the other man back to the bench where Aconin lay.

Rathe paused, studying the plants in their containers. The branches were turned so that they faced Aconin, as though that directed their power toward him and him alone. There were gaps in the foliage, too, places where another flower could easily be forced into the water, and he pointed toward the nearest. His fingers tingled as he came within a hand's breadth of the arrangement, a nasty reminder of the other flowers in Forveijl's dressing room, and he was careful to move his hand away before he spoke.

"What we need to do is place at least one stem of the hedgebroom into each of these arrangements—there's a gap there, see it? But we'll do it at the same time, and with stalks that are as similar as possible."

Eslingen nodded, and rummaged in the little bundle of greenery, pulling out a stalk tipped with half a dozen flowers. "Will this do?"

Rathe glanced at his own sheaf of plants, found one that matched. "Yeah." He moved toward the vase at Aconin's head, and without being told, Eslingen mirrored the movement.

"There?" he asked, pointing to the gap, and Rathe nodded.

"Yeah. On the count of three." He took a breath. "One. Two. Three."

Their hands moved together, angling the stems of hedgebroom toward the gap in the arrangement, and Rathe flinched as he felt the arrangement's power tingling in his fingers. It wasn't as sharp as it had been in Forveijl's dressing room, but it was definitely present, an unnatural warmth and tingling, as though he were slowly dipping his hand into hot wax. From the look on Eslingen's face, he felt the same thing, and Rathe wished he could spare the other man an encouraging smile. The stem touched the water, and he felt a spark, like static on a winter day, and the hedgebroom slid into place with sudden ease. He looked up, knowing his eyes were wide, and saw Eslingen looking at him with the same wary certainty.

"We've done it," Eslingen said, and Rathe leaned back again, reaching for the bundle of hedgebroom.

"If one is enough."

"It's enough," Eslingen said, sounding suddenly assured, and before Rathe could protest, Aconin's head rolled to one side, eyelids flickering.

"Easy," Eslingen said, and leaned close over the table. "Easy, Chresta."

The playwright shifted again, like a man waking from a nightmare, and his eyes fluttered fully open. "I couldn't possibly write this," he said, and Eslingen lifted an eyebrow.

"Are you all right?"

Aconin closed his eyes again, hard, as though they pained him, raised hands to massage his temples. "Where in Tyrseis's name—"

He broke off, visibly recognizing his surroundings, and Eslingen snorted. "He'll live."

"You're in the landseur Aubine's autumn glasshouse," Rathe said. "Bespelled by his flowers."

"Now I know this is real," Aconin said faintly, and got his elbows under him, pushing himself upright. He moved as though his entire body ached, and Rathe stifled a twinge of sympathy. Eslingen grunted and caught the playwright's wrist, tugging him into a sitting position. Aconin winced again and turned, letting his legs dangle over the edge of the bench. "You wouldn't feature in my dreams, Adjunct Point."

"For which I'm grateful." Rathe took a breath. "You've lied to me enough, Aconin. You can tell me now what Aubine's planning. And why he's left you alive."

"Sweet Tyrseis." Aconin shook his head, and then looked as though he wished he hadn't. "Oh, gods, I hurt."

"Answers," Rathe said, and somehow Aconin dredged up a shaky laugh.

"Well, you must know some of it, or you wouldn't be here."

"We know Aubine is planning something at the masque," Eslingen said brusquely. "Probably to kill whoever it is he blames for the death of his leman, using these Dis-damned flowers."

"We know you knew about at least some of it," Rathe said, and stopped abruptly, remembering something Eslingen had said. "You had a working copy of the Alphabet, you must have, or Guis couldn't have used it against me. Stolen from Aubine?"

Aconin managed another nod. "He promised it to me—it was for the play, he suggested it to me, when I said I was working on a play about de Galhac. He was right, too, it was brilliant. . . ." His voice trailed off, and Rathe restrained the urge to shake the story out of him. If Aconin had spoken earlier, at least three people might still be alive.

"He promised me the copy," Aconin said again. "But then when the play was written and accepted, he told me I'd have to wait until the run was over, that he didn't trust me not to take it to the broadsheets. So I took it."

"But he still had enough information to make all this," Eslingen objected, waving his hand toward the arrangements, and Aconin's eyes fell.

"He had two copies."

"And he's had plenty of time to practice," Rathe said. "So why hasn't he killed you, Aconin? He's killed everyone else who got in his way."

"I think I'm left to take the blame for the last murder," Aconin said. "Or maybe all of them." He shook his head. "I crossed him, betrayed him, by his own lights, and he doesn't take kindly to that."

"How long have you known about this?" Rathe asked through clenched teeth, and Aconin looked away, refusing to meet his eyes.

"Not long enough to stop it, I swear to you. Not so that you could do anything about it."

Liar. Rathe said, "I should call a point on you, for abetting these murders."

Aconin looked up. "And if I had said anything, I'd be dead myself a week since."

Rathe stared at him for a long moment, mastering his anger with an effort. There was some truth to what the playwright said—but not enough, not when so many people had died. "We'll leave that for later," he said at last. "For now—tell me this, and tell me the truth, for once. Does Aubine mean to kill the queen?"

Aconin nodded slowly. "Yes." As though a dam had broken, the words tumbled out. "It's the arrangements, of course, you figured that much out, but it's also the play, little alterations his friends will make in the lines, nothing that wouldn't pass for a stumble, a simple mistake, but, oh, gods, deadly, deadly in the right stars and with these plants to focus the power. You must believe me, I didn't know, I had no idea what he would do—"

"His friends?" Rathe interrupted, and Aconin drew a shuddering breath, got himself under control with an effort that wracked his slender frame.

"Yes. It's not just him, though the arrangements, the idea, it's all his. He's found others who've lost their loves, maybe not the same way he has, but for the same reasons, the differences of station driving them apart, and he's promised them their chance at revenge, if only they'll help him take his. A conspiracy of lovers, all of them hurt, hurt badly—that's why de Raçan died, you know, for treating Siredy so badly."

"Siredy's not part of this, surely," Eslingen said.

Aconin shook his head. "Call it a—generous impulse."

"More likely he wanted to be sure the flowers would work," Rathe said. "Can you name the conspirators, Aconin?"

"Some of them." Aconin took a breath, and slid off the table, wobbling for a moment before Eslingen caught his arm. "There's an intendant, Hesloi d'Ibre, I know for sure, her mother made her abandon her son by a common man, so she could have a granddaughter better born, and the Regent Bautry, she loved a woman too far above herself. And Gisle Dilandy, she's the one who'll speak the lines."

Eslingen swore again, but Rathe nodded. He recognized those names, had always thought d'Ibre and Bautry to be honest women, had admired Dilandy's acting. "Who else?" he demanded, and Aconin shook his head again.

"Those are the only ones I know for sure. But there's a list, in the house. Aubine made it, made them sign it, to keep them loyal."

Rathe sighed, grateful for the small favor. "Right, then," he said. "First we cut as much hedgebroom as the three of us can carry— yes, you, too, Aconin, you're coming with us—and then we find that list."

"And then?" Eslingen asked.

Rathe took a breath. "And then we go back to the theatre. Thank Astree and the metropolitan that Coindarel is guarding the Tyrseia tonight."

It took them the better part of three hours to harvest the hedge-broom and to fashion small protective posies for each of them, Rathe listening with growing impatience to the distant chime of the clock. They found covered baskets to carry their harvest, and then Rathe turned his attention to the door leading into the house.

"I'm worried about Aubine," he said, reaching for his picks again. "Where the hell is he, anyway?"

"Probably with the others," Aconin said, and Rathe straightened, glaring.

"What haven't you told us?"

Aconin passed his free hand over his eyes. "I'm sorry, Rathe, I— keep forgetting what I've said. I think, I'm almost certain, the con-spirators were dining together tonight. To be sure no one betrays the others at the last moment."

Eslingen laughed softly. "Then they'd better spend the night to-gether."

"I have no idea," Aconin answered. He was pale even in the light from the winter-sun, rising now above the roofs of the houses beyond the wall, and Rathe sighed.

"Let's hope he's right," he said, and applied himself to the lock.

It didn't take long to find the list. The house was dark and silent, the air thick with the smell of the flowers and the power they har-nessed, and they moved through it as though through an invisible fog. It felt a bit like the ghost-tide, Rathe thought as they moved past another sleeping footman, except reversed, as though they were the ghosts moving secretly through the world of the living. Aubine's study was impressively tidy, and the lockbox stood on a side cabinet, its presence and function equally blatant. It took Rathe two tries to work the lock, but at last it gave way, and he rifled quickly through the papers. As Aconin had said, the bond was there, a pledge signed by half a dozen women and men to support Aubine in his plan, and Rathe folded it carefully, tucking it into his pocket. Aubine had been wise enough not to specify just what the plan was, but coupled with everything else, and with Aconin's evidence, it should be—barely— enough to call a point. *Or at least I hope it is,* he thought, and shepherded the others out of the house, locking the doors again behind them. It might not do much good, particularly if Aubine decided to check either his succession houses or the papers, but it might delay him for a few hours more.

There were no low-flyers to be found, of course, and it took another hour to walk from the Western Reach to the Tyrseia, shoes squeaking in the snow. It was almost over the tops of their shoes already, and Rathe knew the street sweepers would be cursing in their beds, thinking of the work ahead of them the next morning. Coindarel's encampment, however, looked almost indecently comfortable. The bonfire still blazed in the center of the square, soldiers off watch huddling around it, hands wrapped around tankards that had probably come from the tavern opposite. Or maybe not, Rathe amended, seeing the sergeants on watch for stragglers. Coindarel seemed to be taking this seriously after all.

They were challenged as soon as they entered the square, but a quick word from Eslingen squelched the soldier's automatic refusal, and they were brought at once to the tent Coindarel had had set up for his own headquarters. It was warm and lamplit, the snow no more than a memory, and Rathe set his basket down gratefully.

Coindarel himself was seated at a folding table beside the fire-basket, and waved them closer to the glowing embers. "So, Adjunct Point. And Lieutenant vaan Esling, of course. Have you had success tonight? Your chief sent word, your magists are delayed."

"Wonderful," Eslingen said, not quite under his breath.

"Success of a sort," Rathe answered. He would have preferred a magist's help, but there was no time to wait for them. "First, this is Chresta Aconin—"

"The broadsheet writer," Coindarel said, his eyebrows rising. "And this year's playwright."

Rathe nodded. "And a person we've been looking for these last four days. I would take it very kindly indeed, Prince-marshal, if you'd keep him in custody—for his own safety," he added quickly, seeing Aconin ready to protest, "and as a witness."

"You don't have a choice, Chresta," Eslingen said, and the playwright subsided, shaking his head.

"I can keep him safe," Coindarel answered, and smiled thinly. "He'll lodge with me tonight, will that satisfy you?"

"Thank you, Prince-marshal." Rathe took a deep breath. This was the hard part, the biggest risk he'd ever taken to his career—but there was no other choice, he told himself firmly. They couldn't take the chance that Aubine or one of his people might take mundane means to finish their revenge. "And there's another thing I need from you."

He reached into his pocket and pulled out the list. Coindarel took it from him, smoothing it out onto the tabletop, his frown deepening as he read.

"These are the people who have conspired with the landseur Aubine to kill Her Majesty," Rathe said. "They must be kept from entering the theatre tomorrow morning, stopped and held for the points."

"Do you really think you can call a point on one of the regents?" Coindarel asked, his voice almost amused. "Or on Aubine, for that matter?"

"The proof is there," Rathe answered, with more confidence than he entirely felt. "And the queen's life is at stake."

"Treason is not a matter for the points," Coindarel said, sounding shocked.

"Then whose is it?" Rathe demanded. "Prince-marshal, I am serious about this. Someone has to act. These people have to be stopped."

The prince-marshal hesitated, the light from the firebasket reflecting up on his thin, hard-boned face. "And I can hardly see you sending a horde of pointsmen to do it."

"Don't I wish I could," Rathe said fervently, and Coindarel's grim face relaxed into a smile.

"Leveller to the core." He looked down at the list. "Very well. No one on this list will enter the theatre, tomorrow or tonight. And I'll keep your stray playwright safe as well—I'm sure he can answer any questions that might arise. Will that suffice, Adjunct Point?"

Rathe nodded. "And if you could order your men to stay out of the theatre, for their own sake—"

"I wouldn't order them in there on a bet," Coindarel answered. "You can have it all to yourself."

"Thank you," Rathe said with real gratitude. That left only the arrangements, and he looked at Eslingen. "Shall we?"

In the shifting light, it was hard to tell, but he thought Eslingen swallowed hard. "Let's get on with it."

If anything, it was even quieter in the theatre the second time they entered, and colder, the wind finding its way through the tiniest gaps in the canvas roof. There were tiny drifts of snow on the edge of the gallery, where a window fit imperfectly, and Eslingen paused, scanning the pit and the galleries above it.

"You don't suppose it's too cold for the plants," he said, and Rathe shook his head.

"I wish it were. But Aubine will have taken precautions."

"Damn the man," Eslingen said, and hefted the baskets. "I liked him, Nico."

"So did I," Rathe said. "It—happens, Philip."

"The man had cause."

"But not for murder," Rathe answered. "Not for all these murders."

Eslingen nodded slowly. "No, I know, you're right." He touched the flowers at his buttonhole. "Let's hope these work as well here as they did at the house."

They made their way back onto the stage, past the arrangements still studded with the dried stalks of hedgebroom. At least the fresh plant seemed to be more potent, Rathe thought, and knew he should be grateful for that small favor. The air on the stage itself was heavy, more like midsummer than midwinter—and warmer, too, he realized, and guessed Aubine was making sure that his flowers would survive the night. But it was more than mere warmth, too; there was a sense of expectation, the heaviness of a summer storm, the lightning dormant in the thickening clouds. He shook the image away, impatient, but saw the same wariness in Eslingen's eyes.

"He's ready for us," the soldier said, and Rathe shook his head, refusing to give in to the ridiculous sense of foreboding.

"Or he's just ready for the play. Come on, it's going to take us at least an hour to spike all of the vases."

Eslingen nodded, forcing his voice to keep its normal tone. "Where do we start?"

Rathe looked around. There were too many flowers, he thought, too many little arrangements, as well as the big ones that dominated the forestage; he'd underestimated things, it would take most of the night to be sure they had them all. Maybe he should have waited for the magists after all. "Let's start with the big ones," he said, shoving away the thought, and hefted the heavy basket. *I just hope there's enough hedgebroom to go around.*

He could feel the power in the arrangement as he came closer, and stopped just out of arm's reach, skin tingling. It was like Forveijl's arrangement, like the arrangements that had held Aconin captive, but heavier, stronger, the power leashed in it, heavy as an impending storm. It would take more than one stalk of hedgebroom to neutralize this, he knew instinctively, and bent to open his basket, looking for the largest, best-grown stalks.

"No!"

Rathe turned, cursing, to see Aubine emerging from between the last two versatiles, a pistol leveled in his hand.

"Step away from it, Adjunct Point," Aubine said, almost sadly. "I won't permit any interference now."

"Or ever," Rathe answered. He kept himself from looking at the other arrangement, saw Eslingen easing back out of Aubine's line of sight, to vanish behind the first versatile. "How many men have you killed for this?"

Aubine flinched. "Too many. But I've suffered enough, and too long, with no redress. Stand away from the flowers."

Rathe did as he was told, lifting his hands to show them empty. He thought he saw something move in the shadows between the versatiles, hoped it was Eslingen and not some trick of the mage-light. "Maseigneur. What good does this do your leman?"

Aubine winced again, but shook his head. "It's too late to stop this. I've gone so far, I cannot—I will not—end it now. Not without vengeance."

"Vengeance isn't justice," Rathe protested, and Aubine managed something like a bitter smile.

"Justice was denied me twenty years ago and more. I'll settle for this."

"No—"

As Rathe spoke, Eslingen lunged from the wings, reaching for the landseur's pistol. Aubine staggered sideways, the pistol discharging. Rathe ducked, and Eslingen flung himself forward, falling against Aubine in a clumsy attempt to bring him down. *Not shot,* Rathe thought, *Dis Aidones, not shot,* and then he saw Eslingen shake his head hard, black flecks scattering his cheek and the white linen of his stock. The pistol had discharged practically in his ear, Rathe realized, left him half stunned, and even as he moved to help, Aubine had thrown the pistol aside and seized Eslingen by the throat, a knife appearing in his other hand as if by magic. Rathe froze, too frightened even to curse, saw Eslingen struggle to get his feet under him, and stop dead as he realized what had happened.

"He's your leman, isn't he?" Aubine asked.

Rathe took a careful breath. "That's not—"

Aubine lifted the knife. "Isn't he? And it's very much to the matter, Adjunct Point."

"You know he is," Rathe answered, and Aubine's hand relaxed a fraction.

"You've made the same mistake I did," Aubine said sadly. "A terrible, glorious mistake, and it cannot last. His family will kill you when they find out, and there will be no justice."

Rathe blinked. Aubine believed in Lieutenant vaan Esling, believed that he was from an old and noble Leaguer family—*oh, Dis, Philip, Duca's plan's worked too well this time.* "So you'll kill me first?" he asked.

"Your death is inevitable," Aubine answered, still with the note of sorrow in his voice. "It was inevitable from the moment you swore lemanry with someone above your station."

"Maseigneur." Eslingen's voice was strained, high and loud like a deaf man's. "Maseigneur, you're making a mistake. I'm no noble. I'm a motherless bastard from Esling, Gerrat Duca renamed me for the masque and the benefit of the Masters."

Aubine shook his head. "Very noble, Lieutenant. I'm afraid I don't believe you." Even at a distance, Rathe could see his arm tighten on Eslingen's throat, saw the ex-soldier wince, bracing himself against the new strain. "But tell me, Lieutenant—would you die for him? A common pointsman?"

"I'd rather live for him," Eslingen said.

"I'll fight you for him," Rathe said, in the same instant, and Aubine shook his head again.

"No. Come here, Adjunct Point, away from the flowers."

"No." Rathe took a quick step sideways, putting himself in front of the arrangement of flowers. "Let him go, Aubine."

"Come here," Aubine said, his teeth clenched, "or I will kill him where he stands. And his blood will be on your hands, pointsman."

"Touch him, and I'll destroy this arrangement," Rathe said. "I can have it over, broken, before you can stop me."

"No!" Aubine's eyes widened, but he steadied himself instantly. "No, I don't think so. That would mean your death, pointsman, as well you know. You've seen what happens when the plants are disturbed before their time."

Rathe swallowed. Oh, he knew, all right, could still feel the residual soreness in his ribs and arms—and this arrangement was easily twice as large as the one Forveijl had made. It was easy to believe that Aubine was telling the truth, that this could kill.

"If you kill him," he said steadily, "I'll have no reason to live." He took another step backward, hand outstretched to the plants. He could feel their presence, could almost hear the angry humming, like bees disturbed in their hive. "I will do it if I must, Aubine. Let him go."

"I will kill him," Aubine said again, and from somewhere Rathe dredged up a laugh.

"And then we'll all die." He reached for the nearest flower, his fingers pierced by a thousand needles, and in the same instant Aubine shoved Eslingen away, drawing his sword. Eslingen stumbled to his knees, still half dazed by the pistol shot, and Rathe reached for his own knife. It was too short, too light; he caught the first blow on the hilt, but Aubine slid away as he tried to come to grips. He couldn't match the landseur at swordplay—hadn't the weapon for it, if nothing else, had to bring him to close quarters, where a street fighter's skill could help him—and he danced away from the landseur's thrusts, trying to force the man to close. Aubine was good, he realized, very good indeed, was forcing him upstage, away from the flowers. Aubine lunged again, drawing a thread of blood from the peak of his shoulder, and Rathe swore, backpedaling furiously. It wasn't much of a wound, just a scratch, but it hurt, could slow him down—

"Nico! Back!"

It was Eslingen's voice, from the wings, high and urgent, and Rathe flung himself backward without thought, almost falling. There was a rush of air, a shadow blurring the air, and then a crash rocked the stage beneath his feet as the wave panel crashed down behind him, crushing Aubine beneath its massive weight. He made no sound—hadn't even seen it, Rathe guessed, and shuddered violently, seeing the body crushed beneath the carved panel. There was blood already, but not so much of it as one might expect; he stooped, wincing, and saw that Aubine's chest was caved in, his eyes already glazed in death. Just like the sceneryman, he thought, and wasn't sure if he would laugh or vomit.

"Nico?" Eslingen came out from between the versatiles, his face very pale. "Dis, Nico, are you—"

"I'm fine." Rathe swallowed hard, and stepped carefully around the end of the carved wave. "Did you do that?"

Eslingen nodded. "There wasn't anything else, all the swords are locked up—and they're bated, anyway. Oh, gods, Nico, are you all right?"

"Are you?" Rathe answered, and was seized in a tight embrace.

"Stunned," Eslingen said in his ear—still too loudly, Rathe thought, and stifled a giggle in the other man's shoulder. "And half deaf for a day or two, I shouldn't wonder. But—I'm alive. And so are you."

Rathe took a deep breath, gently detached himself from the other man's arms. "So we are. But there's work still to be done."

"The Dis-damned flowers," Eslingen said, and Rathe nodded.

"And the body. And the rest of the conspirators, and anything else Trijn can think of."

"Tyrseis," Eslingen said. "The chamberlains will want to purify the stage, won't they?"

"Probably." Rathe fumbled in his pocket, failed to find a handkerchief, and Eslingen held one out, a smile barely touching his dark eyes. Rathe took it, wadded it roughly into a bandage, and pressed it to the cut on his shoulder. It wasn't much, he could tell that, but enough to be painful. Another laundress's bill, too, he thought, coat and shirt both, not to mention mending, and he wondered if Point of Dreams would stand the cost. Eslingen rubbed at his neck, scalded red and flecked with black from the too-close discharge, and Rathe frowned. "Are you sure you're all right?"

"Like you, sore. But it'll heal." He looked around. "And where the hell are Coindarel's men? I'd expect them to come running."

"Obeying orders, I hope," Rathe answered.

Eslingen nodded, and they made their way back out through the actors' tunnel into the firelit courtyard. Coindarel's tent was still brightly lit, and the prince-marshal looked up from his chessboard with a frown. Aconin, Rathe saw, looked relieved, sitting opposite: from the position of his pieces, the playwright had been losing handily.

"Done already, Adjunct Point? Or is there more trouble?"

"No and no," Rathe answered. "Or not exactly." He held up a hand, forestalling Coindarel's indignant question. "Prince-marshal, I need you to send for Trijn—I'll write what's needed, you can read it if you'd like. But Aubine is dead, and we need help to make the theatre safe again."

"Dead?" Aconin said, eyes wide, and Coindarel ignored him.

"Dead how?"

Rathe took a breath, trying not to remember too closely. "He attacked us—he was in the theatre, guarding the plants, I suppose, and when we started to spike the arrangements, he tried to stop us. One of the wave effects fell and crushed him."

"I dropped it on him," Eslingen corrected. "In self-defense."

Coindarel's eyes flickered as he took in the marks of the fight, Rathe's torn coat and bloodied shirt and the burn on Eslingen's neck and chin, and he smiled faintly. "That explains the faint, strange noises reported to me not a quarter hour past. I very nearly sent a troop in to investigate."

"Thank you, sir," Eslingen said.

Rathe said, "He's dead on the stage, Prince-marshal, which makes it a matter for the chamberlains, or so I'd think. And we still need to neutralize all the arrangements."

Coindarel waved vaguely at the traveling desk that stood opposite the firebasket, the gesture far more languid than the look in his eyes. "Write all you will, Adjunct Point, I'll see the notes delivered."

"Thanks." Rathe seated himself at the desk, a wave of dizziness washing over him. Reaction, he knew, and shook it angrily away. There would be time for that later, he told himself, and reached for a sheet of the fine paper stacked in a traveler's box. It seemed a shame to use all of it for such a short message, and he tore it in half, writing small and neat to get everything in. Just a note to Trijn, he thought; she could see to the rest of it.

"Lieutenant," Coindarel said. "You'll find the makings for punch on that table. You always had a talent for it."

"Yes, sir," Eslingen said again, and Rathe heard the clank of bottles and glass, but didn't look up until the note was finished. It was longer than he'd intended, filled most of the half sheet, and he only hoped it would be clear enough for Trijn to understand what was needed.

"I'll take that," Coindarel said, and twitched the paper away before Rathe could change his mind. "Sergeant!"

"Drink this," Eslingen said, and slid a steaming cup under the other man's nose. Rathe took it gratefully, smelling sweet wine and spices. There was brandy in it, too, and he took a deeper swallow, glad of the inner fire.

"I'll be drunk if I have much more," he said, and blushed to realize he'd spoken aloud.

"No harm if you are," Eslingen answered. "Let the rest of Dreams take care of things."

"We'll have to show them how to neutralize the arrangements," Rathe protested, and Eslingen shook his head.

"We can tell them that—I can tell them that, if it comes to it. Drink up. You need it."

The inward shivers were easing, and Rathe nodded, took another, more careful swallow of the punch, edging his chair closer to Coindarel's fire. The prince-marshal was nowhere in sight, he realized, and guessed he was making sure that the theatre was still secure.

Trijn arrived within the half hour, just as the clock struck three, a tousled Sohier at her side. Most of Dreams's personnel was there, Rathe realized, as he followed one of Coindarel's soldiers out into the courtyard, the day watch dragged early from their beds as well as the night watch.

"The prince-marshal tells me we'll need the chamberlains," Trijn said abruptly. "And their magists to cleanse the stage. b'Estorr's finally coming, too, with phytomancers in tow, I understand."

Rathe suppressed a shudder, thinking of the more mundane cleaning that would be required first, and nodded. "Yes, Chief."

"Are you all right?" Trijn shook her head. "Never mind. Tell me what happened."

Rathe took a careful breath, all too aware of the other points huddling close to hear, and did his best to order his thoughts. "After I found the panacea, Chief, I brought what I had to the theatre, but it—wasn't enough to neutralize all the arrangements. It was dried, you see, and we needed fresh."

"We being yourself and Lieutenant vaan Esling?" Trijn asked.

Rathe nodded, suddenly aware that Sohier was scribbling his

words into her tablets. "Yeah. I knew Aubine would have the panacea, had to be growing it, with everything he was doing with the plants, so we went to his succession houses."

"Intending to steal it?" Trijn gave a thin-lipped smile.

"Intending to get it however I could," Rathe answered. He had known there would be an official record, an explanation that could be shown to the regents and anyone else who feared the points' influence, but he'd hoped it could wait until after the masque. He shook himself, frowning, chose his words with care. "I would have asked the landseur's permission, but when we reached his house, we found all his household asleep, bespelled with flowers." He went through the rest of the story in equally careful detail, emphasizing Aconin's testimony and the list they had found in Aubine's study, glossing over the details of the fight to keep as much blame as possible from Eslingen. "And the landseur is dead," he finished at last, "and his arrangements still have to be neutralized before Her Majesty arrives at the theatre."

"You say that neutralizing them just means adding springs of hedgebroom to each one?" Falasca demanded.

Rathe nodded, too tired to wonder when she'd arrived. "But carefully. You—well, when you get close to one, you'll feel it. There should be a gap, though, among the flowers, where you can add a stem or two."

Trijn nodded. "We'll take care of that," she said.

"The hedgebroom is in baskets," Rathe said. "We left them on the stage. There should be enough. . . ."

His voice trailed off, and Trijn nodded again. "We'll take care of it," she said, her voice unexpectedly gentle. "Us and b'Estorr's people, and I've sent to the chamberlains, told them we need their magists as well as them. The flowers will be neutralized. And I'll send to the other stations, make sure they call points on Aubine's co-conspirators."

"Thank you." Rathe shook himself. "The flowers, I can show you how—"

"No," Trijn said. "Rathe—I'm sorry, Nico, but I'm calling the point on you, for Aubine's death."

"You can't do that," Eslingen protested. "Seidos's Horse, if he hadn't stopped him, I hate to think what would have happened tomorrow."

"A man lies dead, and by his own admission, through Rathe's actions," Trijn said. "I have to call the point."

"I killed him," Eslingen said. "I was the one who worked the lever—I dropped the damned wave on him. If you call a point on him, you have to call one on me."

"Rathe's actions were the first cause of the landseur's death," Trijn said. "You acted on his orders and to defend him."

"He was defending himself," Eslingen said, and Rathe touched his arm.

"It's all right, Philip. This—" His mouth twisted into a wry smile. "This is necessary, right, Chief? To keep the regents off your back."

Trijn had the grace to blush, but she met his gaze squarely. "That's right, Rathe. And I'd rather keep my place and have a chance to protect heroes like you than lose it when it might be prevented."

"But—" Eslingen began, shaking his head, and Rathe's grip tightened.

"Philip. It won't mean anything. The law is clear. This is just a formality."

"A formality that keeps her in office," Eslingen said, "and puts you in a cell."

"Let it go," Rathe said. "Please."

Eslingen drew a ragged breath. "All right. But, Chief Point, if you're going to call the point on him, you should take me in, too. It was my hand that struck him down."

"If you insist, I will," Trijn answered. "But if you're free, you can see that he gets all the amenities while he's in the cells—good meals, wine, clean clothes."

"Don't you feed your prisoners, Chief Point?" Eslingen asked.

"Not as well as you'd like," Trijn answered, and Eslingen sighed, defeated, glanced sideways at Rathe.

"Are you sure about this, Nico?"

There was a lot that could go wrong, Rathe thought, remembering other cases that had seemed equally clear until a clever advocat had her say, but he made himself nod. Trijn would see him right, he trusted her that far, and her influence seemed to be considerable. "Yeah. Let's go."

"Will you permit that?" Eslingen demanded, and Trijn gave him an ironic glance.

"I'll even let you escort him, Lieutenant. You see how I trust you."

Eslingen swept an equally ironic bow, and turned away. Rathe hesitated.

"You're sure you can handle the flowers, Chief?"

"There are magists on the way if we can't," Trijn answered. "And the sooner you're gone, the sooner we can begin."

Rathe nodded, defeated, let Eslingen turn him away. Beyond the theatre, the streets were dark and empty, the snow not yet trampled and rutted by the day's traffic. It was very quiet, the usual sounds deadened by the snow, and Eslingen shook his head, rubbing at his ear again.

"If she trusts you so much, couldn't we spend the night in our own bed, turn you in in the morning?"

Rathe hesitated, sorely tempted—the cells at Dreams were penitential—but shook his head. "No, I promised."

Eslingen nodded, looking suddenly exhausted, and Rathe touched his shoulder in sympathy. They were almost at the station now, turned the corner to see the station's lights blazing in the unshuttered windows. Trijn hadn't left many people on duty, Rathe knew, and he pitied the day watch, called to early duty. Then a thought struck him, and in spite of everything he smiled.

"What?" Eslingen asked, and held the gate for them both.

Rathe shook his head, unable to lose the smile. "I just realized, this will be the first midwinter in—oh, it must be fifteen years or more that I'm not working."

Eslingen's eyebrows rose. "Don't make a habit of it," he said, and they stepped together into the station's welcome warmth.

13

Epilogue

$\mathcal{T}$he day of the masque passed, and the routine of Dreams station returned to normal, except for the fact that its senior adjunct was kicking his heels in the station's best cell, and the best was still, as Rathe had described it, penitential. But it was clean, the small stove kept it warm enough, and Eslingen had left the evening before only to fetch dinner from Laneten's, and in the morning brought breakfast from the markets. But he couldn't stay; Duca expected all his masters present that day to help clean, sort out, and restore the weapons to their proper places at the salle. By the afternoon of this second day, the enforced inactivity was fretting Rathe almost more than anything else, or so he told himself, resolutely putting aside fears that the point for Aubine's death might be upheld. But he realized, even without Trijn's pointing it out, that he was better off taking his chances with the judiciary and the intendancy than seeing it fall to the regents. Bad enough he had been involved in the landseur's death, far worse would be the fact that he had been right—about Leussi's death, about Aubine's involvement.

He set aside the broadsheet he had been reading—Eslingen had brought him a sheaf of them along with breakfast that morning, all extolling Astreiant, now officially named the queen's successor—and looked at his report on the events, ready to hand it over when it was required, and when he was reinstated. There was nothing more to add, and he pushed it aside as well, got restlessly to his feet. He could move about the station itself, under escort, but he was reluctant to pull anyone from their actual duties and besides, he found it galling that he should need to. He prowled the length of the chamber. He couldn't expect Eslingen back again until evening, and b'Estorr was stuck at the university, reading the riot act to the phytomancers who had viewed the Alphabet as, in b'Estorr's own words, so many market games.

So he was surprised at the rap on the door, and to see Sohier stick her head in. "Sorry to bother you, Nico, but—it's the advocat Holles to see you."

Rathe hid a grin—she was acting as though he were in his usual workroom, blithely disregarding anything so inconsequential as a point for murder—and then she had stepped aside for the advocat.

Holles waited till the door was closed behind him before he said quietly, "I feel terrible about this, Rathe."

Rathe looked at him. "Advocat?"

Holles gestured around the small room. "After all you did—and not just for me—you shouldn't be in here."

It was funny, Rathe thought, that he was the one comforting and reassuring his friends—not Eslingen, he had given that up, and just listened to his leman's rants about the unfairness—about a couple of days spent in Dreams's best cell. He gestured for the advocat to take the chair, and sat down himself on the edge of the cot.

"It's better if we observe all the formalities," he said with a wry smile. "You wouldn't throw me to the regents, would you, sir?"

"Sweet Sofia, no!" Holles said, horrified, then slowly smiled in turn as he realized what Rathe had done. "Bourtrou always spoke well of you. I can see why he liked you. You're a good man, Rathe," he said quietly.

Rathe shrugged. "And a lucky one, if truth be told."

Holles nodded. "I still don't understand, though—why Bourtrou?" It was the question, torn from the heart, that Holles had managed not to ask until this point, but he deserved an answer, although it would cause him more pain. Rathe stared down at the floor for a moment, then took a breath. He had put it all together for Trijn. Holles deserved no less.

"Leussi was one of the chamberlains this year. Which meant he would have passed judgment on the play for the masque. The version of the Alphabet he had—the one you gave me—was authentic. It was the same edition Aubine was working from. But Leussi never suspected any ill of Aubine, probably suspected Aconin instead, summoned Aubine to warn him about the dangers of the play he was sponsoring. Aubine listened, was probably politely appalled—and then brought him as a gift, as thanks, the bluemory. Which was fatal under those stars to someone with Leussi's stars. Quickly fatal, Istre tells me. That gave him the time he needed to bind the ghost." It sounded harsh, was harsh, stated so simply, but Rathe didn't know any way to cushion the words. Holles at least had known his leman had been murdered; now he knew why. A bitter comfort, but then, most knowledge was.

The advocat was staring at a shaft of sunlight that was creeping across the floor from the high, narrow window. "It seems so unreal," he murmured. "It makes no sense—for Aubine to have deprived me—and others—of loved ones, lemen, because of his own loss."

"I know." Unbidden, the memory of Eslingen on the stage of the Tyrseia, Aubine's knife at his throat, rose in his mind, and he shook it away physically. "He was beyond rational thought. I don't think he meant, don't think he thought about the pain it would cause you. He only knew that Leussi was dangerous to his plan. Leussi died because he was an honorable man, a learned man, and too damned good at his job."

Holles looked up at Rathe, his eyes bleak, but a small smile on his lips. "Not a bad eulogy, Rathe. I would hope to earn as much."

"Not for a number of years yet, I hope, sir."

"No." Holles stood up. "I am in your debt. Aside from this"—he gestured with expansive contempt around the cell—"there is the matter of your having been called before the regents. I put you in an impossible situation with your superior and them, Rathe, and I'm sorry."

"But you were right about Voillemin, sir, and I might have chosen not to believe it if you hadn't come to me."

"What happened to that one?" Holles wouldn't even say the name.

"Voillemin?" Holles nodded, and Rathe's eyes glinted with humor. "Oh, he's been demoted from adjunct point—even the regents had to admit he had only gotten so far on his mother's guild-standing. He's a common duty point now, and will be for a while, I would say."

"Still here?"

Now Rathe grinned openly. "No, sir. It was felt he had been protected and privileged for too long. He's been sent to Fair's Point."

It was not lost on Holles: Fair's Point was the newest, most junior of the official districts. Voillemin was now the most junior of adjuncts in the entire city. Holles nodded slowly, his face grave, but his eyes betraying a grim satisfaction.

"The surintendent has a remarkable sense of justice."

Rathe nodded. "He does that. If it had been up to me, I might not have been able to resist sending him someplace grittier, more southriver. Like Knives, say."

Holles laughed out loud. "The good citizens of Knives surely don't deserve that visited upon them."

"No, but seeing him dealing with the descendants of the bannerdames in the Court might have been worth it. But Fourie has, I think, a soft spot in his heart for the district."

"If he does, it's the first soft spot I've heard of Fourie possessing," Holles said dryly, and got to his feet. "I am in your debt, Rathe, and I won't forget it."

"Then I'd better hope I don't have any cases that come before you. You're an honorable man, Advocat. Let's not talk of debts between us. You helped me when you gave me the intendent's copy of the Alphabet. We're quit."

"Not until you're out of here, justly," Holles said, his voice quiet, but implacable, and for the first time since he had acquiesced in Trijn's actions, Rathe felt confident that justice would, in fact, fall to him.

Eslingen paused at the Owl and Lamb's kitchen door to settle the cover more securely on the basket. Two days Rathe had spent in Point of Dreams's best cell, and no matter what Rathe said, it wasn't justice. And he still wanted to say as much to Trijn, would do it as soon as Rathe was released—except, of course, that would only make things worse.

"Lieutenant vaan Esling?"

He looked up, to see a runner in Dreams's livery poking a folded slip of paper at him, and he juggled the dinner basket awkwardly as he unfolded the note. It was from Trijn, her spiky hand unmistakable, bidding him attend a formal hearing at Point of Dreams at one o'clock that day. He frowned, and in the same moment heard the nearest tower clock strike one.

"She's left it a bit late," he said, and the runner looked up at him, uncomprehending.

"Please, Lieutenant, you need to hurry."

"And whose fault is that?" Eslingen asked, but stretched his legs, so that they reached the station only half past the hour. To his surprise, there were two unmarked coaches in the yard, their horses stamping and blowing at the unfamiliar quarters, and a third that bore the crest of the queen's judiciary. The unmarked carriages had to belong to someone of importance, from the quality of the horses, but he wasn't prepared for the sight that waited for him inside. The usual furniture had been hastily moved to the walls of the large main room, the duty point's table commandeered to form a makeshift bench, and Astreiant herself sat behind it, robed in red like any member of the judiciary. There were at least four other advocats as well, all in black and scarlet, and Eslingen recognized one of them as Kurin Holles. The woman with the impeccably painted hands had to be Rathe's patronne Foucquet, he guessed, but the others were strangers to him, as was the woman in the regent's respectable black, a silver badge around her neck. Her lips were pursed as though she had eaten something sour, but Astreiant was careful to include her in the proceedings. b'Estorr was there, as well, in dark grey university robes, with the Starsmith's badge vivid on one sleeve. Rathe stood to one side, hands clasped politely behind his back—very much at his ease, Eslingen saw with relief, and close to the stove, too. Trijn stood with him, dressed in her best green wool, and seeing her, Eslingen wished he'd had sufficient warning to put on his own good coat. He set his basket down as discreetly as he could, and the movement drew Rathe's eye, so that they smiled at each other across the crowded room.

"—seems to be fully resolved," Astreiant was saying. She touched the faceless doll that stood on the table before her, the visible symbol of the queen's authority, a gesture that looked more tender than was strictly necessary. "The advocats Foucquet and Holles have spoken on behalf of the accused, and the Soueraine de Ledey herself has declined to pursue the point. We have also heard testimony from both the points and from—other parties currently under restraint— that the landseur Aubine had taken actions that were intended to bring harm to Her Majesty the queen. This testimony has been accepted by this court, and by the Soueraine de Ledey. Therefore, I find Adjunct Point Nicolas Rathe blameless in this death, and release him to the company of his fellows, to enjoy all rights and privileges of a free man of this city, and an adjunct point under Her Majesty's seal." She paused, smiled suddenly. "I am also authorized, as Her Majesty's representative, to offer this small gift in some recompense for the inconveniences he has suffered."

She nodded to a liveried page, who came forward with a bulging purse. Rathe accepted it, a strained expression on his face, and Eslingen had to suppress a chuckle. Rathe prided himself on never taking fees, but he could hardly refuse this—and it was hardly a fee, Eslingen told himself sternly. Compensating a man for time he'd been unjustly imprisoned could hardly be considered a fee.

Astreiant rose to her feet, and the rest of the people crowding the room made their obeisance. Eslingen bowed with them, hoping to catch Rathe's eye again as he straightened, and the page struck her staff on the stone floor.

"The session is hereby ended."

The formality dissolved into excited conversation, and Eslingen shouldered his way through the crowd, nearly tripping over someone's lapdog. The woman—one of the advocats—scooped it up, glaring, and Trijn grinned at him.

"Well, Lieutenant, I'm glad the girl found you."

"So am I." Eslingen looked around, unable to suppress his surprise. "That's it? You didn't need my testimony?"

"You're Rathe's leman," Trijn answered. "They knew what you would say."

That made a certain amount of sense, and Eslingen nodded, looked at Rathe. "What now?"

"Adjunct Point?"

The voice was at once strange and familiar, and Eslingen turned to see a tall woman in the stone-grey of northern mourning. She looked vaguely familiar, too, and then he saw the badge at her collar, and recognized Aubine's sister.

"Maseigne," Rathe said warily. "I'm sorry . . ." His voice trailed off, and Eslingen could guess what he was thinking. How did one offer sympathy for killing someone's traitor brother, particularly when that brother had been more than willing to kill them?

The woman smiled faintly, as though she, too, had read the thought. "I wanted to say . . . You, and Lieutenant vaan Esling, you gave him a kinder end than he deserved. My, our, grandmother was a proud and hateful woman, and for no other reason than that she could be, it was her right—her obligation and her blood duty to be harsh on her kin and heirs, to make sure they were fit for what she would leave them. Our mother was not, so it was up to us. I tried to shield him, and when she was dead I tried to give him the life he wanted—it wouldn't have hurt anyone, certainly not our name. But it was too late then." She shook her head. "I wish I'd never let him go to the university, but he wanted it so. . . ."

Her voice trailed off, and Rathe shook his head. "He made his choices, maseigne. I'm sorry if I sound harsh, but he made his own way."

Ledey nodded, but she hardly looked convinced. "All my grandmother did was in the service of our name. My brother's ended that, very effectively."

"Surely not ended," Rathe said.

"No?" Ledey gave a bitter smile. "This is more than scandal, Adjunct Point, this is treason and murder and attempted murder. My family will continue. But I think the name of Aubine needs to be buried with my brother."

It was her right, of course, as head of the family, but Eslingen shivered, hearing an echo of the grandmother's iron will in the soueraine's implacable voice. He bowed automatically as she turned away.

"She's right."

Eslingen and Rathe turned to b'Estorr. "It's a pride that needs burying—in his way, your landseur was every bit as prideful as his wretched grandmother," the necromancer said.

"You didn't know him," Eslingen protested softly, and b'Estorr shook his head.

"No. But forgive me if I feel less than charitable toward someone who did his best to kill two friends of mine."

"You just didn't want to be bothered by our ghosts," Rathe said, and b'Estorr smiled.

"Not after this ghost-tide, no, thank you."

"Istre—" Rathe sounded unusually hesitant, and both Eslingen and b'Estorr looked at him. "Come up to my workroom, please, both of you."

"Won't we be missed?"

"In this throng?" Rathe asked, nodding toward the crowd of pointswomen and men, advocats, intendents, and regents. Obediently, they followed him up the stairs to his workroom, chill from having been uninhabited for almost three days. When he closed the door, he looked at b'Estorr.

"I think you mentioned once before that if the university had a working copy of the Alphabet, no one would be able to find it?"

"I was mostly joking, but you have no idea what the cataloging is like in the older parts of the library," b'Estorr replied, almost warily.

Rathe nodded as though satisfied. He picked up from the small table three books. "I want you to lose these as best you can. Aubine's copy, the one Aconin stole, and Leussi's."

b'Estorr looked at the three simple, cloth-bound volumes, a thoughtful expression on his face. "You could simply burn them."

Rathe shook his head. "If, Metenere forbid, we should ever need their knowledge again, you'll know where they are, you're the only person I can trust with them, Istre, who has the wit and training to deal with them. Take them, and lose them in the library, so no one can use them like this again."

"Done," b'Estorr said simply. He took the three books, tucked the small volumes away under his coat. "And, Nico?"

"Yeah?"

"I also told you that this—" He nodded toward him and Eslingen. "Did not feel like folly. Thanks for proving me right. My reputation would have suffered terribly," he said with a quick grin, and was gone.

Eslingen let out a breath he hadn't known he'd been holding. "I never know if I want to kill him or not." But he was smiling.

"Think of the ghost."

"Good point." He looked at Rathe. "What now?" he asked again.

"Home," Rathe said. He looked tired—*the cell couldn't be that comfortable*, Eslingen thought, *in spite of all the care we took*.

"The baths?" he suggested, and Rathe grinned.

"Yeah, that, too. But later."

"Can we go?" Eslingen asked as they made their way back down the stairs, looking around the still packed room, at the press still crowding to speak to Astreiant.

"I doubt we'll be missed," Rathe said, but looked at Trijn.

She spread her hands. "Be off with you. I don't have any need of you—take a few days for yourself, Rathe, but I'll expect you back at the new week."

"Thank you," Rathe said, and turned for the door.

Eslingen followed him, pausing only to collect the basket, and together they made their way across the rutted courtyard. Outside, the streets were mostly clear of snow, and the sky had the seashell haze of clouds that promised warmer days. Rathe looked up with satisfaction, breathing deep, his breath frosting the chill air. They made their way back to Rathe's lodgings in companionable silence, crossed the frozen remains of the garden—no sign of hedgebroom anywhere, Eslingen thought—and climbed the stairs to Rathe's single room. He had kept the fire going, not wanting anything of value to freeze, and Rathe gave a contented sigh as he crossed the threshold.

"It's good to be home," he began, and stopped abruptly, looking around the single large room. "Philip. Where are your things?"

Eslingen paused, blinking, set the basket on the table, and stooped to stir the embers back to life. "Oh. I rented a room of my own, didn't want to keep sponging off you."

"Philip—" Rathe's eyes were worried, and Eslingen abandoned the pretense, contrite.

"I rented the two rooms next door—you know, the little ones that no one wanted. The landlady said that we could knock out the old connecting door, come the spring." He paused. "If you want to, of course."

Rathe stood for a moment, then, very slowly, smiled. "Considering everyone already thinks we're lemen, I suppose we might as well."

Not quite an invitation, Eslingen thought, but the simple acceptance was more than good enough for now. "Don't let the gossips push you into anything you don't want," he began, and Rathe rolled his eyes.

"Idiot."

Eslingen smiled, satisfied. He reached for the basket, brought out the bottle of wine he'd bought in the hope that Rathe would be released today. "Good. I don't have a bed of my own. Let's drink. It's not every day you're let out of jail."

"Did you see the masque?" Rathe asked, and Eslingen laughed, almost spilling the cup he was filling.

"No. I never did."

"All that work, and you didn't go back?"

Eslingen shook his head. "I was too tired, and my head hurt and—frankly, Nico, I couldn't stand the sight of another bunch of flowers, no matter how harmless they were. But Siredy says it went off very well."

"Siredy?" Rathe asked.

"I ran into him yesterday morning," Eslingen answered. "He and Gavi have been seeing something of each other, you know."

"No, I didn't know." Rathe accepted a cup, relaxing, and Eslingen lifted his own in a toast.

"The health of the realm at the turn of the year."

"And a quieter year to come," Rathe answered. The room was warming nicely now, the fire roaring, and he settled himself easily in his usual chair. Eslingen stretched a hand to the stove, hoping the wish would come true. "Will you stay with the Masters?"

Eslingen paused, shrugged. "Why not? They want to keep me on. And it can't be this—exciting—all the time."